Hell hath no Passion

Ashuan Lust 3

Janna Ruth

First published in New Zealand in 2024

Copyright © 2024 by Janna Ruth

www.janna-ruth.com

ISBN-13: 978-1-0670001-6-5

also available in ebook: 978-1-0670001-5-8

ASHUAN LUST BOOK 3

HELL HATH NO PASSION

JANNA RUTH

A note about sensitive topics

While there is a lot of magic and fantastical creatures in this series, the teenagers at the heart of the story are just that: teenagers. As such, they deal with a number of very real issues alongside their magical ones.

If you don't like spoilers and you're cool with everything, skip this note and start the book. If you want to be prepared, read on. I'm writing this because reading should be fun, not bear nasty surprises.

While this series started out as a YA fantasy, all the main characters are now eighteen or older, and over the legal drinking age in Germany. As this trilogy is about the Archdemon of Lust, sex will be a topic, particularly in this book, where Melaney unleashes her sin on the characters.

Saying that, if you're uncomfortable with allusions to sex happening just off the page and/or light allusions to sexual abuse, you might want to skip Parts 3 and 5. You will miss important relationship developments and a pretty big plot development, but there are scenes in there that—despite my best intentions to keep it from going too dark—might be triggering. No rape happens on or off page, but there is a lot of sexual coercion. There will also be positive sexual experiences, and it is very clear which are which.

Apart from those two parts, which lean heavily into the sin of lust, there is a traumatic injury in Part 1 and another in Part 2, which includes a car accident and the loss of a parent in the past. In Part 2 there's also a scene with self-harm.

Part 5 is the big finale. It doesn't just include a slew of passionate encounters but a lot of fighting, with quite a bit of blood (less than you see on TV, but you know how the imagination can often run wild). Obviously fighting demons is dangerous. Characters get hurt and some might get killed. In fact, some *will* get killed. This is the finale of *Ashuan Lust*, after all.

Lastly, this series deals a lot with demons, Hell, and the seven deadly sins. Demons have no morals to speak of and will engage in incestuous relationships. If any of this makes you uncomfortable, then this is not the book for you. Skip ahead to *Ashuan Envy*, which has none of that stuff.

Lots of warnings for this one, but while the characters live in a dangerous world, it's also a beautiful one. For every dark place there is light and humour, and—of course—magic. Lots and lots of magic.

Enjoy!

Love, Janna

Part 1
Regret & Forgiveness

Caspar

Bright light flooded the darkness of his world. Caspar's eyes filled with tears at the sudden intensity. In the back of his mind, he told himself it probably wasn't that bright, not like daylight on one of the many surface worlds. But after the days, maybe weeks—certainly not months—he'd spent in total darkness, even the smallest source of light was enough to blind.

"Your sentence is up," a voice called from outside the walls.

Caspar knew instinctively what had been impenetrable before was now easily traversable. All he had to do was get up and jump out, leaving the darkness behind. The demon outside wouldn't stick around to wait for him, especially if they knew who their prisoner was.

But Caspar didn't get up. He didn't feel the rush of anger that filled him so often. He just sat there, wishing for the darkness to return.

The light was cruel. Not because it came so suddenly and was far too bright for his eyes after all this time, but because it didn't allow him to retreat. Instead, it laid everything bare, forcing him back into a world without her.

Jeyne.

For five hundred years, Caspar had managed to push her to the back of his mind. He'd blocked every memory and every feeling he'd ever had. One visit to the Web of Memories had brought it all back with the force of an avalanche.

Down here in the darkness, there'd been nothing else to distract him from his feelings. He'd allowed himself to relive it all, to recall every fleeting moment they'd shared. He'd wallowed in his pain, allowed himself to stay in it, with no one to witness his weakness, no one to use it against him. But now his sentence was over. He'd have to return to the world and he'd have to bottle it all up again if he wanted to survive.

The problem was... Caspar wasn't sure if he wanted to do that anymore.

His eyes had stopped burning and adjusted. With a heavy sigh, he pushed himself to his feet. There was no point in feeling all that he felt. Jeyne was long gone. So long gone, her soul would have been reincarnated by now. Somewhere in the multitude of worlds she'd get another chance at life. Hopefully, this time, she'd been born to better parents. And hopefully, this time, she wouldn't fall in love with a demon.

Caspar knew better than to seek her out. Her soul would have been washed clean with no memory of him left. And judging by what had happened last time, it would be better if he stayed far away.

Satisfied that he'd regained his sanity, Caspar left the Dark Cells behind and jumped straight into the Residence of Lust, where his room awaited him.

As soon as the sparse furniture appeared, he bit down a curse. The layer of dust indicated he'd been locked away for at least two months. Two months wasn't much in demon terms, but in human terms...

Caspar shook his head. He couldn't think in human terms. He didn't give a damn about what humans could have done in two months.

He'd almost convinced himself when he heard voices outside his room.

"Samantha assured me it would work."

Melchior. His hated half-human half-brother. Had he used these two months of Caspar's absence to make himself the new Archdemon of Lust or had something else brought him here after such a long absence?

"As soon as we're done here, she'll summon you and bring you back to Ashuan," Melchior continued.

"I can't wait." The female voice that answered belonged to Menuha, Caspar's twin sister. She'd been banished from Ashuan by mistake when Melchior and his little group of humans had banished Caspar. Now they were going to bring her back.

Caspar shrugged. He had no desire to return to Ashuan. Sure, it was annoying to find himself banished from a world, but if it were possible, he'd never visit a human world again.

Melchior and Menuha moved on, neither bothering to check Caspar's rooms. The thought left him with an annoying little pang. So, what if his twin sister hadn't sensed his presence? She was clearly distracted by the prospect of seeing her beloved humans again. Caspar had assumed it was she who'd finally managed to get him released, but clearly, she was preoccupied.

That suited him just fine. This way he'd have a little more time for himself.

For Jeyne.

A few hours later, Caspar had cleaned up and collected reports from his Blood Riders. Standing over a strategic model of the Southern Provinces, he moved his markers, trying to recreate the campaigns in his absence.

The door opened. Caspar recognised his older brother Balthasar from the confident tread of his shoes even before he'd opened his mouth.

"You're settled back in. Good. We've got work to do."

"*You* got me out?" He'd been expecting Menuha or his mother. Or even Volac, who'd been down a general.

"Well, who else would care about your sorry ass?"

Caspar raised an eyebrow. "You care?"

Balthasar must have come straight from the Small Council. He was still wearing his black robes. "Well, 'care' isn't exactly what I was after. I need your help."

"You? Need my help?" Contrary to what Balthasar thought, Caspar wasn't stupid. He knew his brother was up to something. "For what?"

"Melchior, of course. Or have you given up?"

Caspar lost interest. The only important information was that nothing had changed while he'd been away. Melchior hadn't made his move. Of course he hadn't. "He's hiding in Ashuan. I'm tied to Hescaryn. Unless you have a plan to get him to Hescaryn, I don't see how I can be of help to you." He didn't mention Melchior had been here only hours ago.

Balthasar rolled his eyes. "Thanks, Caspar. I know all that, and of course I have a plan on how we can lure him here."

"How?" The question was more because it was expected of him than because he really wanted to know.

"There's a birthday party tomorrow," Balthasar said, with a sly grin. "And you know how exciting birthdays can be in Ashuan."

Caspar frowned again. Had he actually only been away for two weeks? No, it couldn't be. "Aren't you a bit late for his nineteenth?"

"Not his," Balthasar snapped, "Samantha's. Do you really have to pretend to be dumber than you are?"

"What do I care about a human witch's birthday?"

"You care because she's his weakness. He loves her. Or at least he's convinced himself he's in love. Whatever. Fact is, he'd come here for her. To you."

Love. Caspar would've gone to the end of all worlds and beyond for Jeyne. It hadn't helped. "And how would I get my hands on Samantha?"

"I'll bring her to you with one of your transport runes, if you still have enough brain cells left to make me one. Samantha disappears from her birthday party, your signature is in the air, and three seconds later Melchior shows up here."

Caspar snorted softly.

Exasperated, Balthasar clenched his fists. "By the gods, you're slow today. Did the Dark Cells imbue you with sloth?" He rolled his eyes and turned away. "I expect the rune in the morning." He waved vaguely around the room. "And perhaps prepare yourself. Samantha is full of surprises."

"I can handle a human girl."

"She is the reincarnation of Gwydion, the god of magic—*and* Dianthos, the god of flowers." Balthasar took a scroll from his robe and threw it at Caspar. "I found this in Chay's notes."

Caspar snatched the scroll from the air and unrolled it. Reincarnations mattered so little when everything was washed clean in the Land of the Dead. Gwydion may have been a formidable human, a genius of magic who'd served the goddess Freya until raised to divinity himself, but the human soul he'd left behind had carried none of his greatness. Caspar bet most of his reincarnations had never even touched magic.

"It's an impressive line of reincarnations," Balthasar droned on in that particular voice of his, trying to make a point Caspar couldn't see. "Her soul has two ancestral lines."

"It happens," Caspar muttered, trying to identify one of the many names. "Two souls can become one or one can split."

"And how do you know this?" Balthasar asked.

Caspar's gaze remained glued to the scroll. According to Chay's notes, Dianthos' line had ended with Mireille Durand, an Ashuan girl who'd died at the age of seventeen, shot while on the run with her supposed lover, one Henri du Ammel, *exactly* 526 years ago. "Twins. One soul separated."

"Fascinating. Pity all the positive qualities of your soul went to Menuha."

Caspar didn't respond. His gaze was fixed on the end of Gwydion's line. Another teenage girl. Again, 526 years ago. Executed for consorting with demons. *Jeyne Wynter.*

"Try not to underestimate Samantha. With that line of ancestors, she'll probably surpass you in a few years. In magic, of course. In intelligence, she's already way ahead." Balthasar sighed. "Caspar? If there's any activity in that tiny brain of yours, you could shrug or grunt or something."

Caspar couldn't do either. The name before his eyes burned a hole in his stomach. Not a child in a faraway world, impossible to find, but right in front of him. And he was supposed to lure her to him. To Hell.

He wet his lips and took a shaky breath. "What am I supposed to do with her while we wait for Melchior?"

Melchior, who was head over heels in love with her. With *his* Jeyne.

"Whatever you want," said Balthasar, unaware of how tightly Caspar's fingers gripped the scroll. "Let off some steam. Tear her apart. I don't care. Are you with me or not?"

Tear Jeyne apart? End her short life prematurely again? The scroll ached under his grip.

"Caspar!" Balthasar snapped.

The harsh tone helped Caspar tear his gaze from the scroll. *From her name.* "I'm in. Yes. Bring her to me."

Balthasar snorted. "Now, was that so hard?" With another eye-roll, he left, his robes blowing in the wind behind him.

Caspar clutched the scroll again, his gaze fixed on Jeyne's name. It didn't matter that Samantha had two divine ancestors and a number of impressive witches and mages in her soul history. All that mattered was that she was Jeyne.

His Jeyne.

Samantha

With a month to go before her written exams and her parents separating, the last thing on Samantha's mind was her birthday. Instead of the usual birthday table, all she'd found that morning had been a hastily signed card and some money. The only real present had been a book from Meg, ordered from her wish list. There hadn't even been the usual quick get-together and congratulations. Her mother was in Cologne, setting up her new flat, planning to return later today, and her father had already left for work. Once again, Meg was the one left to bring up the rear, and her sister had never been big on celebrating her.

As far as birthdays went, this one ranked right at the bottom.

At school, Samantha sorted her books in her locker for the day. Her gaze fell on the yearbook proof and she sighed. That was something else she had to take care of. But not today.

She closed the locker door and found Cian leaning behind it, a box of chocolates in his hand. "Happy birthday."

Just like that, her day looked a little brighter. "Thank you."

As she hugged him, she could see Matt and Lucille approaching. Her lips tingled at the memory of the featherweight kiss Matt had planted on them a week ago, and she pulled away.

Cian noticed her stare and looked over his shoulder. "Oh well. See you later, birthday girl."

"See you," Samantha replied automatically, then remembered there was no Chemistry today. Before she could ask Cian what he'd meant, the others arrived.

Lucille went straight for a hug. "Happy birthday!"

"Yeah, all that," Matt said in a strangely blasé voice and with an even stranger hand wave. Then he simply walked away.

Confused, Samantha watched him head down the corridor. "Is he alright?"

"Yes, why wouldn't he be?" Now Lucille sounded strange too.

"Yeah, all that?" Samantha repeated irritated. "Is he upset because he saw me hugging Cian?"

Lucille linked her arm with hers. "Nah, I don't think so. He probably just doesn't care much about birthdays. You know, being half-demon and all. It's no big deal."

That made sense, although it still hurt. She'd thought Matt would have been exposed to enough human birthdays by now to know they were some kind of deal. "Oh well, it's only my nineteenth. Nothing important."

"Exactly."

Now, that was *really* out of character for Lucille, no matter how positive she sounded. Lucille loved parties and never missed an opportunity to celebrate. Between her airheaded chatter and Matt's don't-care attitude, Samantha thought she knew what was going on.

"You've got another surprise party planned, haven't you?"

Startled, Lucille stared at her. Then she wet her lips. "You didn't hear it from me."

Samantha chuckled. "Don't worry. I'll act surprised."

Samantha dreaded going home. They may have defeated the soul parasites that had eaten away her parents' marriage, but it had still fallen apart. Now that her mother and Meg were moving to Cologne while she was staying with her father, her family had been effectively halved.

Moving to Cologne was out of the question for her. She had a life and responsibilities here. Besides, big cities always lacked magic, and

Samantha couldn't imagine living in a place that wasn't brimming with it.

When she arrived home, there was a moving van outside the house. Movers were going in and out of her home carrying boxes of stuff, as well as the furniture from Meg's room and a few other select pieces. Samantha slipped inside between two movers and found her mother directing people in the living room.

Her eyes lit up when she spotted Samantha. "Ah, if it isn't my little birthday girl." She opened her arms for a hug.

Samantha ignored the invitation. "You booked the movers for today?"

"It was the only available date this month," Juliane said with an apologetic smile. "I know it's not what you wanted, but Meg told me you were celebrating somewhere else anyway."

"You mean my *surprise* party?"

Juliane's mouth made a small 'O'. "Did I just spoil the surprise?"

Something bitter tried to worm its way out, but Samantha swallowed it. "No, I figured it out myself." As much as she appreciated the effort her friends had put in, she felt a little too fragile for surprises. What she needed today wasn't feigned indifference to be surprised later. What she needed was positive attention and distraction.

"Of course you did." Juliane laughed softly, then took a step forward to cup her face. "You're my smart one."

"*Excuse* me?" Meg cleared her throat behind them. She was coming down the stairs, dropping cuddly toys into a moving box. "What am I? The dumb one?"

Juliane groaned a little, then laughed again. "You, my dear, are my feisty one."

Meg snorted and rolled her eyes. "I'm all packed for now. So, if you two are finished, I'll have to kidnap Sam."

"Are we finished?" Samantha asked, not quite sure what to make of her own voice. Was it confrontational or meek? What kind of question was that even?

Her mother's gaze softened. "We could never be finished. I'm your mum, even if we live in different cities. And I'm sorry this has come at one of the worst times. You should be concentrating on your final exams and not on this bullshit." She shrugged. "There, I said it. And I'm also sorry for ruining your birthday like this. I know it's not what you wanted."

"It's just my nineteenth. Nothing special."

"Every birthday of yours is special to me. I just had a lot to do this year. As soon as Meg and I are settled in, you'll come and visit us, and we'll go for a big dinner in Cologne. Something really nice. None of those boring small-town options."

Samantha liked the so-called boring options. They tasted like home. "Sure." It probably wouldn't hurt her to try something new once in a while.

"Are you done now?" Meg nagged. "This is sort of my party, too."

"Sort of?" Samantha asked, fearing the worst. Meg's circle of friends was much bigger than hers.

"Don't worry, I'll have a separate farewell party tomorrow, but it's still kind of a goodbye. Now, can we please go?"

Samantha looked at her mother and Juliane smiled. When she opened her arms this time, Samantha came willingly.

"Happy birthday, darling."

Halfway to Blackstone House, Meg insisted on blindfolding her. "Remember, it's a surprise party. Matt will flip out if his surprise is spoiled."

"*Matt* will flip out?" Her heart did a little flip of its own. Matt cared.

Meg rolled her eyes. "He's so annoying. Almost as bad as Fabian. I think the only reason that one hasn't been on my case is because he's busy with Lia."

"But Matt has been?"

Meg stopped trying to get the blindfold on for long enough to throw her a look before giving in. "I don't know why, but for some reason the hottest guy in school is obsessed with you. Now shut up and let him surprise you." With that she pulled the scarf over Samantha's eyes and knotted it at the back of her head.

As Samantha blindly followed Meg, she wondered what surprises Matt had planned. She still didn't know how she truly felt about him, but if the bubbling heat in her stomach was any indication, the thought of him was exciting.

"Careful, step," Meg said. Samantha could feel a winter breeze.

"Is that you, Neve?" Samantha asked, amused.

"Neve is hiding," the little snow witch whispered.

Samantha grinned. "Neve is hiding very well. I can't see you at all."

Someone groaned, probably Fabian. She could feel the others around her as someone came closer. "I'll take it from here."

Her heart skipped a beat as she recognised Matt's voice. Meg's hand fell away, replaced by another pair of hands on her shoulders. A puff of hot air brushed against her ear. "Just keep going."

She was glad he hadn't asked her to speak because she wasn't sure she could've. But walking worked. With bated breath, she let Matt lead her through what she thought was the living room. To her surprise, he kept going, out the back, and outside again. "Where are you taking me?"

"You'll see." Again with that low voice close to her ear. Samantha had to remind herself that all her friends were probably standing around to avoid turning into a puddle. This blindfold thing was dangerous.

"Ready?"

She almost answered "No," but managed a gentle nod instead.

Matt's fingers disappeared from her shoulders to loosen the knot. As the wool fell away, Samantha found herself standing in Jan's garden. But it wasn't the garden she'd seen when they'd renovated the place. The garden then had been almost non-existent, a bare wasteland of dry bushes covered in snow. This garden was green. And not the pale green of early bloomers, but a deep, lush green. There was a meadow decked with fairy lights at her feet, but around it the vegetation was almost forest-like, with winding paths leading through the thicket. At least half the bushes and trees were in bloom.

"I don't understand," Samantha said. Every time she tried to look away, she found some new, exciting plant. It reminded her of something, but it wasn't until she saw the little stone pool with its silver liquid that she understood what she was looking at. A miniature version of the gardens they'd visited in Hell. "Where are we?" she asked with growing trepidation.

Matt laughed softly. "We're still in Jan's garden. Or rather *your* garden. I asked Adrianes for help."

"This is for me?"

"It's your birthday present," Matt said, amusedly. He bit his lip. "Do you like it?"

"Do I like it?" Now she was laughing. "It's magical!" In every sense of the word.

She turned and wrapped her arms around Matt, still laughing. "Thank you! This is... I think this is the best birthday present I've ever had."

His face lit up like the winter sun and Samantha swore he grew two centimetres at the compliment. She laughed again, then noticed the rest of her friends waiting expectantly inside.

When Lucille caught her eye, she grinned. "Surprise!"

Matt let go of her as the others came out to congratulate her. A garden party in the middle of March. Now *that* was a surprise party to her taste.

Jan

Jan had been grumbling a lot in the run-up to this surprise party. He'd barely finished renovating the necessary parts of the house and was a little overwhelmed by all the action. But now, as all these people gathered in the living room or on the magically heated patio, he felt something like pride fill his chest.

He'd done it. After all the trials and tribulations of dropping out of school, losing his job, and being kicked out of his home, he felt he was finally on the right track. He was about to start his paramedic training and he had his own house. At *twenty*.

That deserved a celebration. Though the choice of guests was a little off.

Rachel had brought Hugo along, much to Neve's delight—and Hugo's distress—while Lu and Fabian had brought their respective partners. Matt was currently surrounded by his demon friends: the bubbly Menuha, who couldn't stop grinning at being back in Ashuan, the tense Chay, and a younger demon—probably older than Jan's parents—with his leathery wings on full display. He was Balthasar's son, Adrianes, and Hell's head gardener. Jan had become strangely acquainted with him as he and Matt had worked together to transform the dead patch of land behind the house into a garden worthy of a conservatory. Fortunately, the nearest neighbour was far enough away to avoid attracting attention.

On the other side were his sister, who'd brought her boyfriend Robert, and Meg, who was talking about her first few days in Cologne. Jan grabbed some punch and made his way over.

Meg took a glass from him without even looking and continued with starry eyes, "There are so many people. It's unbelievable. Nobody knows you. Nobody's going to tell your mum they saw you hanging out with this person or that person or ask if you remember some incredibly embarrassing childhood moment. Best of all, people come from all over the world. One week and I already feel like I've outgrown Greenvalley. How did I ever manage to live here?"

Jan put an arm around her shoulders and grinned. "With me, of course."

As if by accident, Meg twisted out of his embrace and grabbed a handful of snacks. While Robert was telling Meg how much he liked this close-knit community with its own little rules, the doorbell rang.

Jan got up before Neve decided to show herself and opened the door. Outside, Cian stood with his hand raised, Alan and Shayna behind him.

"Um, can I help you?" Jan asked, confused. He understood Cian, although the boy must be crazy to try to get close to Samantha with Matt and his demon relatives around. But Alan and Shayna? Surely that was a mistake.

"We're here for the party," Cian said with an easy smile, lifting up a pack of beers he was carrying.

"What kind of dump is this?" Alan asked, craning his neck to look up at the facade.

"Mine," Jan snapped.

Just then, Lu hurried over. "I invited them. Come on in!" She pushed Jan aside to make room. "The birthday girl is in the garden."

Cian gave her a friendly nod and headed straight outside. Shayna looked equally excited, while Alan wrinkled his nose in disgust at the sight of Adrianes. "Is this a costume party?"

"Why on earth did you invite the Elite Clique?" Jan hissed when they were all gone.

"Just the three of them," Lu apologised. "Actually, just Cian, because he and Sam... well, you know, they're friends. Anyway, Alan and Shayna heard me and Shayna asked if they could come. I couldn't possibly say no."

Jan groaned. "Next time that's exactly what you're going to say."

The last thing he needed was a fight in his brand-new house. Even if it was a dump.

Matt

Matt's surprise had been a complete success. One look in Samantha's sparkling eyes and he'd known he'd done the right thing for once. It wasn't just that her Emblem of Power was a bunch of flowers. He remembered how much she'd missed her childhood garden when they'd found the emblem. And the way she'd looked at Hescaryn's gardens. If she hadn't been ill and their town in desperate need of the cure, she would have probably begged him to stay there for a week. Now she had her own little hellish garden, green even in winter. And he hadn't even shown her the swing in the back yet.

Of course, not everything had gone so smoothly. For some reason, half of the Elite Clique had turned up, and now Matt was forced to watch Samantha chatting with Cian on the terrace while he stood at the buffet with Chay and Adrianes.

"If you want to study at Fader," Chay said, "you should apply soon before all the places are filled. Interglobal Studies is a competitive course, but if I write you a recommendation, they should offer you a place."

Adrianes grinned. "Oh yes, when the Great Chay recommends a student, they'll light up the cave."

Matt chuckled at the thought of any humans caring about cave lighting—and Chay's reputation. "Do they know you there?"

He was still deciding what to do after school. The University of Greenvalley was an option, but none of the courses there interested him much. As fascinating as school had been, there was not a single subject he could see himself pursuing for a couple of decades. The big

University of Fader had the opposite problem. There were far too many courses to choose from.

Chay shrugged. "I've taught a few classes now and then."

"He's massively understating his notoriety," Adrianes claimed. "I've heard Balthasar say he's something of a folk hero in Fader."

The notion made Chay snort. "That depends on who you ask."

Adrianes grinned and shook his head, as if he didn't believe Chay, while Matt almost burst with curiosity. He was well aware Chay had visited many worlds and saved almost as many. Fader was a city on the world of Lukrya and home to the Interglobal Parliament. It was the centre of all connected worlds, a crossroads as well as a meeting place.

It wasn't Chay's hometown, though Lukrya was the world the half-demon had been born in, but it was where he spent most of his time. Many years ago, Chay had studied at the great university. These days, he worked mostly with the parliament as a valued advisor.

Still grinning, Adrianes turned to Matt. "Anyway, if you're going to Fader, please, please, please send me copies of your botanical notes. I'd like to learn more about the flora of other worlds. Like this one." Adrianes had brought as many plants back from Greenvalley's flora as he had from Hescaryn to Greenvalley.

"Of course. General Botany is a mandatory course, but if I end up doing a specialised one, I'll send you everything I find. Honestly, when I look at the choice of classes, I would almost say choosing a subject is easier." There were dozens of paths through Interglobal Studies.

Chay laughed out loud. "Yes, that's what we call the Fader Effect. It's the biggest university in all the worlds. Over two thousand faculties and over a million students—more than there are even demons in Hescaryn."

"Wow." Matt couldn't even imagine that many demons in one place.

Just then, the sudden movement of several guests alerted them to Balthasar's appearance in the middle of the living room. He looked disoriented for a moment before his gaze found Matt.

Meanwhile, Alan was staring at him with eyes as big as saucers. "What the hell?"

Lucille quickly stepped in and started clapping. "A big hand for Balthasar!"

With a glance at his brother, Matt clapped enthusiastically, and the others followed, albeit much more reluctantly. Balthasar looked a little confused but shook it off, as he did most things.

"That was the beginning of our little magic show," Lucille continued. "Philipp, can you pass me the top hat?"

For some reason, Philipp had one at hand. "Of course, my enchanting Lucille."

Lucille smiled at him before she began to pull coloured handkerchiefs from it. The applause after the demonstration was much more sincere, although Matt didn't understand why.

"Excuse me. I need to find the relief area." Adrianes ducked away just before Balthasar reached their small gathering. The older demon didn't even spare him a look.

"What are you doing here?" Matt bit out. He was still angry after Balthasar's last visit to Greenvalley. It had almost cost him his humanity.

Balthasar smiled, as if he didn't remember anything. "I'm here to attend Samantha's birthday party, of course."

"I don't think she'll appreciate it. You know, after you got her parents to split up. A *week* ago," Matt added sharply.

"As if they weren't splitting up anyway." Losing interest in the subject, Balthasar looked outside. "Hell plants?"

"They're harmless."

"I know." Balthasar rolled his eyes. "I just wondered why they're here."

Matt pressed his lips together, refusing to explain his actions to the elder.

Balthasar studied him carefully, then sighed. "Let me guess, the little witch loves her nature? And you're still head over heels for her." He nodded at Chay. "I hope you know what you're doing."

"Generally," Chay replied tersely.

Confused, Matt looked back and forth between them. "What do you know about Chay's plans?"

"Doesn't matter." Balthasar waved him off. "So, what ridiculous games are you playing at this party?"

Somehow Matt had come to terms with Balthasar's presence. He'd watched him closely at first, but Balthasar had congratulated Samantha, then made polite conversation with the other guests. And after a few hours, Matt had decided he wasn't here to stir things up. Except for his annoying presence, that was.

For the moment, Menuha was keeping him distracted, leaving Matt to his own entertainment. Time had passed and darkness had fallen. Most of the party had moved outside, where fairy lights illuminated the meadow which had been transformed into a dance floor. There were three couples dancing at the moment. Matt was about to make it four.

He walked over to Samantha where she was standing with Hugo and Rachel, laughing at something the ghost had said. But before Matt could ask her to dance, Cian swooped in out of nowhere and asked for her hand.

Instead of backing down, Matt went ahead and took Samantha's hand from Cian's. "I'm afraid Samantha was waiting for a dance with me. You've had plenty of time."

Cian glared at him while Rachel and Hugo quickly backed away. "Who says she wants to dance with you?"

"Um... guys?" Samantha asked.

Matt pulled her towards him with such force she gasped. "She wants to."

Cian's face darkened. "Does she? Then why was she willing to dance with me until you showed up?"

He tried to grab Samantha's hand, but Matt twirled her elegantly out of the way and straight into Balthasar's hands.

"I'll take it from here," Balthasar said, easily extricating Samantha from Matt's grip and leading her to the dance floor. With a grin, he told her, "Boys."

Matt was seething with jealousy, but he knew better than to start a fight. Silently, he wondered if this was Balthasar's new plan: to seduce Samantha away from him.

"Who's that?" Cian asked, anger in his voice.

"My brother," Matt snapped. The mean streak in him won out when he remembered Cian knew all about the magical world from Samantha. "Demonic side."

As expected, Cian swallowed hard and immediately lost all interest in making a scene. If only Matt could silence Balthasar as easily.

Samantha

How on earth had she ended up dancing with Balthasar? One minute Samantha had been talking to Rachel and Hugo, the latter complaining about the atrocity of modern music. The next, Cian and Matt had been fighting over her. And then Balthasar, of all people, had saved her from the embarrassment.

He was a surprisingly good dancer. It wasn't something she'd expected from a demon, but then again, he had a millennium of life experience. He could have picked up any skill he'd wanted out of sheer boredom. If only she could find out *why* he was dancing with her. Or why he was at her party in the first place.

As she slowly accepted her fate, Balthasar's hand slid down her back. Deeper and deeper it went until Samantha realised he wasn't going to stop.

"Don't you dare!" She tried to slap his hand away, but it landed in her back pocket, squeezing her ass. "I said stop."

Balthasar grinned. "Shouldn't I at least test what's so special about you? Seeing how you have two boys fighting over you?"

"They're not fighting." Hopefully they weren't. Samantha tried to catch a glimpse of them, but Balthasar blocked the view with his shoulder. "What do you want?"

His hand had left her pocket and was now resting on the small of her back. "Just having a bit of fun."

Just then, Fabian spotted them. "Hey!" He strode towards them. "Leave Sam in peace!"

To Samantha's great surprise, Balthasar immediately backed away, though he was still grinning. "Looks like I'm no longer welcome here."

Fabian scowled at him. "You never were."

Instead of taking offence, Balthasar simply walked away. Fabian turned to her with a worried look. "Are you alright?"

"Yeah, no worries," Samantha said distractedly. At the other end of the meadow, Matt was confronting his brother. She shook her head in a vain attempt to clear it. "I need some air." The winding paths looked extremely welcoming at the moment. "I'll be back in a minute."

"Okay. I'll make sure he doesn't bother you again."

Samantha smiled at him. Choosing one of the paths, she lost herself in the thicket. Some of the plants Matt had planted glowed in the dark, giving off a faint light to guide her. He'd really put a lot of thought into the garden—or maybe Adrianes had.

Either way, the garden was beautiful. Samantha noticed a few empty raised beds, just begging to be filled with witch herbs or vegetables. But what she loved most about the garden was how secretive it was. Each winding path led to a different little nook. One time it was a fountain. Another time she found a charming little drinking bowl for birds. But neither could have prepared her for the sight of the next hiding place.

Under the large oak tree at the back of the garden hung a romantic wooden swing. Solar lights were flickering around it, imitating a circle of candles. Samantha couldn't resist and sat down.

Something jabbed in her pocket.

Irritated, Samantha got up and slid her fingers into the same pocket as Balthasar had. With a growing sense of trepidation, she pulled out a small wrapped present. She tried to feel the contents, but if she had to guess, it was a bundle of small sticks tied together.

Was it some kind of demon joke she didn't understand? There was only one way to find out, although Samantha was tempted to just burn it instead. In the end, it was the feeling of tightly wound magic inside of it that gave her curiosity the upper hand.

What kind of magical web was concentrated in such a small object? It didn't feel hostile, yet Samantha unwrapped it as if she were holding a live grenade.

It *was* a pair of sticks, bound together in a crude form. Magic flew through the knots, brimming in the wood. As she held it, it began to heat up.

Hastily, Samantha did the only thing she could think of. She broke the branches apart. Immediately the magic unfolded. The moment she realised what it was for, it had already grabbed her and whisked her away.

Samantha stumbled forward, only to be met by a sudden, intense heat. A red, bubbling mass appeared before her, hissing and gulping. Lava!

She jumped back with a shriek and crashed into a wall. Her fingers clawed at the stone, trying to find a way out, but there was nothing. She was in some kind of cave—Hell, no doubt—with a pool of lava just two metres in front of her.

Her heart was pounding. With every breath she took, she tasted the unmistakable rotten stench of sulphur. Sweat was already running down her face, whether from the heat or the fear, Samantha didn't know.

Trying her best to keep the panic at bay, Samantha took a quick look around the cave. The first thing she noticed was there was no way out. The second was she was not alone.

"Caspar."

The white-blonde demon leant against the far wall, seemingly unaffected by the lava pool bubbling between them. "You kept me waiting."

Samantha remembered the magic that had brought her here. A transportation spell, though she didn't know how it had been coiled in the twigs. What she did know was she needed to move quickly if she was to survive long enough to find a way out. Her fingers began to weave a simple but effective shield.

"You don't look like her," Caspar said.

"Like who?" Talking might buy her some time.

As soon as the web was finished, a greenish film covered her from head to toe. A darting flame shot up from the lava pool, making Samantha jump. "What are you planning to do to me?" she asked, hating how weak she sounded.

"Nothing."

Nothing? For a moment Samantha was confused, but then the plan unravelled in her mind, just as the spell had. "I'm the bait, right? For Matt? You want me to call him here so you can push him into the lava."

"Melchior can stay where the swamp flies go to die."

Caspar pushed away from the wall and slowly walked around the pool. Samantha tried to back up, but the cave ended a few metres to her side, the lava flowing underground. She was completely trapped, the only way forward blocked by Caspar.

"Are you scared?" the demon drawled.

"Why? Should I not be?" Samantha asked sarcastically. She knew Caspar. He was a brutal, ruthless monster. The only reason she was still alive was because Matt wasn't here yet.

Caspar kept approaching. "I could throw you in the lava lake. Or rip your skin off. Balthasar suggested I tear you apart."

Samantha whimpered in fear, feeling like she was about to faint. The heat was unbearable, but the fear was worse. She wouldn't put anything past him if it would hurt Matt. She should never have opened Balthasar's 'gift'.

"I'm not defenceless," she warned him. "I can..."

Her breath caught in her throat as Caspar stopped in front of her. He raised a hand, but instead of blasting energy at her, he stuck out a finger and drew something into her shield.

He shouldn't have been able to touch it. Not like that, not that easily. But Caspar's finger went through her shield as if it was softened butter, and the magic around his drawing fell to the ground like a curtain dissolving.

Samantha tried to take a step back, but there was only stone at her back.

Caspar's hand shot out and grabbed her by the throat. "It would be so easy."

His grip was firm, but Samantha noticed he wasn't squeezing. Matt wasn't here, so Caspar wasn't going to kill her. Yet.

"What are you waiting for?" Samantha whispered, despite her conclusion.

"Jeyne."

She'd expected many answers. Matt—or *Melchior*—would have been her first guess, but not a woman's name. "Jeyne?"

A muscle twitched in Caspar's cheek. "Wynter. She was on your list."

"Jeyne Wynter." Samantha wet her lips. She recognised the name now. More than that, she knew exactly which list Caspar was talking about. She'd read it herself in Chay's book about the Emblems of Power. "You knew her?" she guessed. "She died over five hundred years ago."

"I'm 576."

Samantha swallowed hard. "So, you were..."

"Fifty when she died. Jeyne was seventeen."

Suddenly he *did* squeeze. Samantha's fingers clawed at his hand in vain.

"You're her reincarnation."

Stars danced in front of her eyes. Now would be a really good time for Matt to show up.

Fabian

The party was a complete success, and for a few precious hours, Fabian was able to forget about the looming doom of his final exams. Balthasar had threatened to ruin everything, but he'd been surprisingly tame and had left half an hour ago. Now nothing was stopping them from enjoying a dance or three.

Fabian had never been much of a dancer, but with Ophelia he never wanted to leave the dance floor. Her arms were around his neck and she was pressing so close to him they were almost one. And if that wasn't enough, kissing was officially one of the dance moves.

He was just about to ask her to take their slow dance somewhere more private when someone bumped into them and separated them. Before Fabian could react, Alan had grabbed Ophelia and was dancing away with her.

"What the—?"

Ophelia's spot didn't remain empty for long as Shayna slipped into her position.

"What's going on?" Fabian had no idea why the Elite Clique was here. Apart from Cian, none of them were friends with Samantha or any of them.

Shayna batted her eyelashes at him. "Oh, you know. Alan's got the hots for your girlfriend."

"What?" Fabian's mind raced, fuelled by anger. Leave it to Alan to ruin everything good he had. It wasn't enough that he'd bullied him years ago, now he had to steal his girlfriend? Right out from under his arms?

"She has sex appeal," Shayna said reluctantly. "Never thought you could pull someone like that."

Annoyed, Fabian tried to break free and rush over to Alan, but Shayna put a hand on his chest. "Relax, Bendtfeld! That girl only has eyes for you." She winked at him.

Fabian glanced at the odd couple and noticed Ophelia's murderous eyes. If she'd brought her sacrificial dagger, Alan would have had a few new holes in him by now. Not that Alan noticed anything wrong. He was looking incredibly proud of himself.

Shayna leaned over and whispered in his ear. "Just enjoy the show!"

"What show?" Fabian grumbled. Usually when the Elite Clique enjoyed a show, it ended with one of his friends getting hurt.

"Your little girlfriend will be back in no time." Shayna patted his chest. She took his arm and wrapped it around her back. "In the meantime, dance with me."

Fabian did as he was told, though he gave Shayna only a fraction of his attention. The rest was firmly placed on Alan and Ophelia. The latter was now positively seething, resisting every move Alan made to lead her.

"You're not bad, Bendtfeld," Shayna said.

He sighed and looked at her. "I'm practising."

"For prom?" Shayna smiled at him like he was a cute pet. "I assume you're taking your sexy girlfriend."

"Who else would I take?" He shrugged, then turned the conversation. "I assume you're consoling Alan after he was rejected by Lia."

Shayna burst out laughing. It wasn't the mean laugh Fabian was used to, but an open, fresh sound that made his own lips twitch. "I don't think he'll be crying for long. But no, Alan's going with Cheryl. They decided that years ago. The King and the Queen, you know?" She rolled her eyes. "I'll probably go with Cian, unless there's a miracle and Samantha falls in love with him after all."

"I highly doubt that." That strange relationship still grated on Fabian's nerves. He couldn't believe Samantha would ever get involved with a boy from the Elite Clique. Sure, they'd had Chemistry for almost two years now, and apparently he was a different person without his friends, but Fabian preferred people who remained one person, no matter who was around to see it.

"I doubt it, too," Shayna admitted. "So, yes, I will console Cian. Unless you want to ask me."

Fabian almost tripped over his feet. Had Shayna Richards just asked him to take her to prom?

She laughed again, amused at what must have been his stupid face. "Relax, Bendtfeld. I'm not trying to steal you away." She bit her lip seductively and batted her eyes again. "Unless... you want me to."

Fabian snorted and took a step back. "Everything's just a big old joke to you, isn't it?"

Shayna's eyes sparkled. "I'm having loads of fun." She chuckled. "You guys are so serious all the time. Oh, it's starting."

With a broad grin, Shayna turned away, watching Ophelia and Alan.

Fabian realised he hadn't really been paying attention for the last few minutes. The two had stopped dancing and Ophelia was pushing Alan away.

"Aren't you going to join in?" Shayna asked amused.

"Lia can hold her own." In the end it was just Alan. No demon or crazy cultist, just stupid, entitled Alan.

"Hm, a man who isn't intimidated by strong women."

Fabian looked at her, annoyed. It really was all a game to her.

Shayna chuckled, but then the sound of skin on skin made them both gasp. Ophelia had slapped Alan, causing the self-proclaimed king of the school to stumble back in indignation. For some reason, Shayna was cackling with glee.

"I thought Alan was your friend."

"Oh, he is. But he needs a bit of a smack from time to time. Takes himself too seriously otherwise, you know?" She winked at him again.

Meanwhile, Ophelia came running over and put her arm around Fabian's. "He's mine, you stupid cow."

"Oh, please, go ahead!" With another wink, Shayna began to walk backwards. "Until next time, Bendtfeld." She gave him a cute wave then blew him a kiss.

"What's with her?" Ophelia asked immediately.

Flustered, Fabian turned to her. "Nothing, absolutely nothing."

Shayna had always confused him. Some days he didn't even know why she bothered with the Elite Clique. Apart from Cian and Alan, she didn't really seem to like any of the others.

Ophelia was still fuming, looking incredibly hot as she did so.

"Are you alright?" Fabian asked, worried about Alan's unwanted attention.

"Of course I am." She snorted. "That Alan suggested we could have a quickie." After another snort, the anger slipped from her skin. She cuddled up to Fabian and grinned mischievously. "You're the only one I'd do that with."

Blindsided, Fabian coughed. He instantly felt the heat rising in his ears. "Well, I wouldn't say no."

Ophelia giggled and placed a hand on his neck. On her tiptoes, she reached up to kiss him gently. "I wouldn't say no, either."

Fabian felt a sudden urge to leave the party. "Do you want to call it a night?"

"Far from it." She took his hand and pulled him towards the door. "The house is big enough. Come on."

Flustered, Fabian checked to see if anyone was watching them, but no one was seemingly paying them much attention. A cheeky smile played across his lips as he followed Ophelia inside.

Jan

"I missed you last week," Jan whispered in Meg's ear as they slow danced on the terrace.

His girlfriend had been in Cologne with her mother to look at some apartments and nearby schools. He still hadn't come to terms with the fact she was moving away. It was only a few hours away by train, but it would mean they'd see each other a lot less.

Meg had her arms around him. She opened her mouth once without speaking, then sighed and let her hands fall. "Can we talk somewhere else?"

"Sure." With so many people gathered outside, no one would notice if they were gone for an hour or two.

Meg took his hand and led him inside, but instead of taking him to his bedroom, she pulled him into the kitchen.

"The kitchen?" he asked, amused. "We've never tried that before." In Jan's mind he already saw himself lifting her onto the counter.

"I wanted to talk to you."

The image burst like a soap bubble. "Okay, sure. About what?"

"You need to know this isn't easy for me."

"Meg, you can talk to me about anything." They'd been together for a year and a half. He already knew everything about her. They'd been through good times and some really shitty times. This was just another challenge they'd face together. Unless... "No. No, no, *no*, Meg." Tears formed in her eyes and his stomach sunk like lead. "Please don't tell me you want to break up."

"I do," she cried. A few tears rolled down her cheek, but she quickly wiped them away. Meg hated crying in front of people.

Jan didn't understand where this was coming from. They were *good*! "Why? Meg, I love you. It doesn't matter how far away you live. We can make it work."

She winced. "See, that's the thing. I... I don't think I love you the same way."

Surely, she hadn't just said that. Surely, he must've misheard.

"I *like* you," Meg said, as if that made it any better, "but as you said, we live in different cities now."

"There are trains and cars."

"I know that," Meg said, not appreciating his contribution. "Even with those, we'd only see each other once a month or every two months."

Jan swallowed hard. "There's Zoom, there's FaceTime, there's literally a hundred apps that allow you to video call."

"I don't want to video call. I've had enough of those to last a lifetime." She shook her head, all traces of tears gone now. "What I want is a boyfriend I can visit whenever I want, with whom I can just have a spontaneous date, go for a coffee in the city, catch a movie..."

"Then why did you leave with your mum?" Jan asked, still stunned. "You could have stayed in Greenvalley." It had never been a question for Samantha.

Meg snorted. "I didn't want to stay, and I like Cologne. It's so different and vibrant. It's so much bigger than Greenvalley. Like me. And I like being there with my mum, too. It's actually quite fun. We spend a lot more time together and we go out for dinner. She treats me differently there. Like an adult."

"You're choosing your *mum* over me?" Talk about a low blow.

"No," Meg said, with a small pout, "I'm choosing my future life there."

"A life without me."

She gave him a one-sided shrug. "I'm just not interested in a long-distance relationship."

Bile rose in Jan's mouth with every word. It was as if the last eighteen months had meant nothing to her. "You don't even want to try?"

"I already know it's not for me. I want to flirt and have fun."

How fortunate this move must've been for her, Jan thought bitterly. "And we already decided that I've become too boring." When Meg didn't answer and lowered her eyes, he snorted. "Wow." And here he'd said the big L-word. "Amazing. Well, in that case, don't let me stop you." His voice grew harder with each word. "Have fun in your new life! All the fun."

Meg rolled her eyes. "You don't have to be mean!"

"Me? Be mean?" Jan couldn't believe it. Here he was, ready to fight for their relationship, and she hadn't just thrown it away, she'd trampled on it for good measure. "Just go, Meg! Just piss off and leave me alone. Go party somewhere else."

She gasped in indignation. "It's my sister's birthday."

"And it's my house," Jan shot back.

Meg stalked to the door. Once there, she half turned to him. "You know, you really got boring fast."

"Piss off!"

The door slammed behind her. It was as if the violence of the act had transferred directly to Jan, and he kicked a kitchen cupboard in response. As the wood splintered, so did his anger, and the heartbreak behind it seeped through the jagged edges.

Jan doubled over as a flood of thoughts overwhelmed him. Meg had left him. He was too boring. *Him*, Greenvalley's troublemaker. Had she really preferred it when he hadn't had a home, when he'd frozen his ass off in the back of the Magic Circle, when he'd lost his job, when he'd dropped out of school? Or had she missed the good old days when he'd taken drugs with his so-called friends on the docks, the danger of a fight brewing just below the surface?

He thought he'd worked so hard on himself. For a few precious days, he'd even been proud of himself. And for what? What had he worked so hard for?

The bile rose in his mouth again and Jan knew he had to wash it out, and everything else with it. He grabbed a bottle of vodka and stormed out of the kitchen.

Matt

As soon as Balthasar left, the party had returned to its former cheerful state. There was much dancing and laughing, and the food was delicious. Menuha was delighted to talk to Cian, who'd recognised her from last year's Walpurgis Night party at Lucille's. It was the perfect time for Matt to slip away, find Samantha, and show her the swing he'd bought for her.

He still remembered the short sweet kiss they'd shared after she'd saved him from himself—and the soul parasites. He hadn't tried for more at the time, but now they'd had some time to process what had happened, he was ready for some good old-fashioned romance. There was a spark between them and it seemed like Samantha could no longer deny it either.

His plan was interrupted when Lucille came out of the house carrying a cake with burning candles and singing Happy Birthday. Everyone turned and rushed in, only to realise one very important person was missing.

Instantly, Matt's heart sank. He hadn't seen Samantha since Balthasar had danced with her, but she'd been fine. He hadn't hurt her and had left soon after. Unless he *hadn't*.

"Has anyone seen Sam?" Lucille asked, looking worriedly at the burning candles.

"I thought she was inside," Robert suggested. "I'll go and have a look!" And off he went.

Matt strode over to Lucille and lowered his voice. "Did you see Balthasar again?"

Lucille's eyes widened in shock. "Balthasar?"

Before he could explain his fear, Menuha and Cian joined them. "Has something happened?" Menuha asked, blowing out the candles before all the wax dripped onto the cake.

"Did your crazy brother do something to her?" Cian huffed, as if the next thing to come out of his mouth would be how he'd hunt down Balthasar if that was the case. A ridiculous notion.

Matt snorted at him. "Stay out of this and deal with your own shit."

"Samantha *is* my own shit." Cian shook his head, annoyed at himself. "I mean, I care about her wellbeing. A lot."

Meanwhile, Philipp took the cake from Lucille's hands. "I'll take this back inside and have another look. You search out here." He gave Lucille a quick kiss and carried the cake into the house.

"Thanks." Lucille frowned in concentration. "I'll try a spell."

It took an enormous amount of effort for Matt to keep his feet still and wait for Lucille to mumble her spell. As she worked her magic, he was hyper-aware of everyone around him. Fabian and Ophelia were missing. So were Jan and Meg. Both couples had probably taken the party elsewhere.

Robert and Philipp searched inside, while Rachel sent Hugo and Neve into the air. Across the meadow, Alan and Shayna were clearly watching them. Whereas Shayna tried to hide her curiosity, Alan had no such qualms. The only one not paying attention was Anne, who was texting on her phone.

Matt's gaze drifted to Chay, cautious, too afraid of what he might see on his face, but Chay had his arms crossed and was staring at the ground in contemplation, while Adrianes looked worried.

"I've got something," Lucille announced, quickly crossing the meadow and entering the garden, following a red glowing arrow point.

"Don't," Chay called after him, but Matt was too eager to find Samantha to pay any attention. Whatever ominous warning Chay had for him could wait.

The arrow led him, Lucille, Cian, and Menuha deeper into the garden. Matt knew where they were going before the magic took them, and for a moment his heart eased. Samantha had just retired to the swing he'd built for her. It didn't matter that he'd wanted to be the one to show it to her. All he wanted was for her to be safe.

But as they hurried around the bushes, the swing was empty. Lucille came to a halt as the arrowhead quivered in the air. "She should be here."

"Try again," Cian urged, "this is obviously a dead end."

"Wait a moment." Menuha crouched down and picked something out of the grass. She came up again with two wound twigs in her hand. "A transport rune."

Matt's stomach plummeted to the depths of Hell. "Caspar."

Before anyone could stop him, he snatched up the transport rune and followed its magic to Hescaryn.

Samantha

Caspar let go of Samantha long before she lost consciousness. Still, she gasped and clawed at her throat, the panic coursing through her veins. Frantically, she looked around the cave, but there was no exit as far as she could see. She was still alone with Caspar.

"What are the chances you're her reincarnation?" Caspar said in a hoarse, raw voice completely unlike him. "Out of all the trillions of humans on all the worlds? She wasn't even from Ashuan."

Samantha didn't know anything about Jeyne Wynter other than her name and that she was the last of Dianthos' line. "Where was she from?" Her own voice was barely more than a raspy whisper.

"Meriand." The name was unfamiliar. "You don't need to look it up. Nobody lives in Meriand anymore."

Samantha froze. "No one?"

"I killed them all."

An undignified whimper escaped her lips and she squeezed her eyes shut, trying to control the fearful shudder that had taken hold of her body. The last thing she'd needed was a reminder of how cruel and brutal Caspar had been. Jeyne had obviously hurt him deeply and he'd taken his revenge by killing everyone. What if he wanted to kill her reincarnation next?

But Caspar didn't seem to be in a hurry to kill her. Instead, he walked away, staring into the lava lake, as if the heat didn't bother him at all. If it burnt him, his healing powers were faster.

"It was one of those worlds that's terribly afraid of demons for no real reason." A ghastly grin spread across his face. "I gave them a reason."

"And Jeyne?"

"They killed her."

Tears filled Samantha's eyes as she saw her own life flash before her. "Who did?"

Caspar turned around. "The humans, of course. Your kind is so righteous and judgmental they'd murder their own for nothing but appearances. They condemned her to death. Do you want to know why?"

Samantha shook her head, her thoughts both racing and completely unintelligible.

"They said she struck a deal with a demon."

Her heart pounded in her chest. Could it be Jeyne and Caspar had been on the same side? Had she been a stupid girl, summoning a demon only to have him kill everyone she'd ever known?

"Were they right?" she whispered.

"Were they *right*?" Caspar roared. He strode quickly back to her, causing Samantha to press her body against the stone behind her. "You think they were right? She was *innocent!*" he shouted so loudly his spittle hit her cheeks. "She didn't hurt anyone. She didn't betray anyone's secret. She didn't switch sides. She just fell in love with someone she shouldn't have."

Love? A terrible truth unfolded in front of Samantha's eyes. Jeyne had loved this monster of a man. And Caspar... Suddenly everything made sense. He wasn't angry, he was in *agony*. Five hundred years ago, he'd lost someone he'd cared about, and even after he'd killed everyone who'd hurt her and then some, it hadn't erased the pain.

"I'm sorry," she said before she could stop herself.

"I don't need your pity!" Caspar spat. "You humans are disgusting. You think just because you're so many you get to decide who's good and who's evil."

Samantha swallowed hard and found her own anger rising. "And when have you ever given us reason to decide otherwise? Are you telling me demons aren't all evil?" Usually, she hated generalisations, and Menuha had shown her there were exceptions, but the whole lot of them—their whole society? "You take what you want."

Caspar snorted. "Like you do."

"And you kill anyone who looks at you the wrong way." Though she tried to hold them back, images of Daniel's bloodied body in the snow flooded her mind. That was what demons did.

"And you kill *everyone* you don't like." Caspar's voice rose. "You don't stop at one person who looked at you the wrong way, you kill anyone who looks like them. You wage wars to take what isn't yours, while glorifying your attacks with righteousness so you can sleep better at night."

While his words struck a nerve, Samantha couldn't help herself. She'd never waged a war and she'd never justified one. Hell, she'd never even killed another human being and wasn't planning to. Because she wasn't a demon. She wasn't like them.

There were bad people in the world, probably more than she'd like to admit, but there were also a lot of good people. In fact, the majority were as good as they came. Not always right or flawless, but with good intentions. Just like the people of Meriand had been.

"So, *all* those people in Meriand killed your Jeyne?"

"They didn't lift a single finger to stop the ones who did." Caspar growled. "Because you're all cowards. You lie and betray and make up reasons to destroy what you're afraid of. You murder and slaughter, quaking in your boots with fear, calling it justice or prevention or protection of your precious freedom, while you gather more and more chains around you."

"We're not all like that," Samantha whispered.

"We're not *either*!" Caspar shouted in her face.

Something snapped inside Samantha, as if all her feelings had burst through the dam of self-preservation and flooded her with fear and anger and something else. "But *you* are!" she shouted back, tears streaming down her cheeks. "You are cruel and brutal, capricious and bloodthirsty. You are everything they ever feared!"

Reason slammed back into her. What was she doing, provoking Caspar? Calling him out? If he was everything she thought he was, he wouldn't wait for Matt to take the bait. He'd tear her apart and smear her blood all over these walls.

For a moment, Caspar seemed stunned, as if no one had ever dared shout back at him. Certainly not a fragile human girl. Then his face distorted, but instead of anger, his eyes filled with despair. And then *he* was crying. "You killed her. You killed Jeyne. I hate you!"

Samantha was so shocked by what she saw she forgot to be afraid. "I'm sorry about Jeyne," she whispered again.

This time he didn't roar at her. He just took a moment to collect himself. Then he wiped his cheeks with a rough motion and blew his nose. "It's not your fault."

That sounded very different from a few moments ago. "I thought it was all humanity's fault."

"Don't be ridiculous." He tried to snarl, but his voice was far too soft for that. "I know not all humans are horrible. Jeyne wasn't." Unwillingly, he regarded her. "And you're not half bad either."

Samantha caught her budding chuckle in her throat. This was no laughing matter. Though she knew his pain now, he was as volatile as ever, whether it was the sin he was born with or five hundred years of mourning when there was no place for it in his world. And yet she was no longer afraid of him.

He tried so hard to be the perfect monster, to be everything people thought a demon was. But he couldn't hide the emotions underneath. Not anymore.

"You're not who I thought you were," Samantha admitted. "You loved Jeyne as much as she loved you, didn't you?"

"More than anything." Caspar swallowed hard. "I never thought I'd find myself facing her again."

And there it was, the truth Samantha had been trying to avoid. "I'm not Jeyne."

Caspar took a step closer. His eyes roamed over her body, as if trying to find all the similarities between them and coming up short. In her heart, Samantha knew she looked nothing like Jeyne. They weren't the same person, no matter what the reincarnation said.

"You carry her soul," Caspar whispered. He laid a hand on her cheek, gently now.

"Caspar!" Matt's voice whipped through the cave.

Instantly, Caspar whirled around, then jumped out of the way.

Samantha's breath caught in her throat as she saw black magic flying straight at her. She tried to turn away, but she'd already lost the precious second and the energy shot across her face. Pain erupted around her eyes as she fell to her knees and screamed.

Lucille

Lucille huffed in frustration. Everything had gone so well. The party had been a complete success. Matt had worked his magic with the garden, the food she'd ordered had been delicious, and Samantha had actually looked like she'd enjoyed herself after weeks of sorrow. And then Matt's brothers had come and ruined everything.

She should have known that Balthasar wouldn't just leave when he was told to. That demon always had an agenda. And, just like with the soul parasites, he'd targeted Samantha instead of Matt.

"Who's Caspar?" Cian asked.

Menuha had followed Matt, leaving Lucille alone with Cian. She sighed as she turned back to the house. "Matt's other brother. They hate each other's guts."

"Another demon, I suppose," Cian said, his mouth an angry line. "And this demon has Samantha now?"

"Looks like it." Lucille hoped Matt had followed them in time. Caspar knew no restraint, and she knew it'd amuse him to kill Samantha, if only to hurt his brother.

"So, what's the plan? How do we get her back?" Cian asked eagerly. "Can you summon her or do you have a spell so we can follow her? Find out where they're hiding her? Or maybe some kind of blessing?"

Right now, Lucille wanted a spell that would make him shut up. Then she had an idea. "There's something you can do for us."

"Anything."

He looked at her so seriously Lucille believed it. But she knew Samantha and what she'd been through. Her friend might not be in love with Cian, but she didn't want him to get hurt, which meant Lucille had to find a way to divert his energy. "There's something you can do for me. *Her.* We may have to move quickly, so can you get Alan and Shayna to leave? Like, make sure they go home or to another party. And if you see Robert, take him, too." Before Cian had a chance to agree, she added: "I'll keep you informed, I promise!"

It looked like he was going to protest, but after taking a deep breath, he nodded sharply instead. "Very well. Consider it done."

Lucille let out a sigh of relief as Cian hurried away. "Alright. Now, Sam..."

Just then, she heard the sound of heavy breathing behind her and spun around. "Matt?"

He'd only been gone for ten minutes at most. Now his face was white and his breath was catching in his throat. He was carrying Samantha in his arms, but she'd lost consciousness and her face... Lucille gulped. Her face was terribly burned and smeared with blood.

"I need Jan."

"You need..." Lucille swallowed again. "Let's hurry!"

She wove an illusion around them in case Cian hadn't managed to lure his friends away yet, and ran back to the house, Matt at her heels. Her thoughts were running wild in her head. How badly was Samantha hurt? What had Caspar done to her? Would Jan be able to work his magic?

They'd almost reached the house when they ran into Philipp and Rachel.

"Is it true what Cian said?" Rachel asked, but after a glance at Matt's arms, she waved her hand and pulled Philipp out of the way. "Never mind. Should I call an ambulance?"

"I need Jan!" Matt said through clenched teeth. "Only magic can save her now."

"Matt..." Lucille put a hand on his arm, but he drove on, having no patience for her. In an instant he'd disappeared into the house, leaving Lucille to share a look with Rachel. "I don't know."

Philipp pulled her into his arms. "She'll be fine."

"Only if we can find Jan," Rachel murmured, and followed Matt.

Lucille shuddered, then pulled away from Philipp's comfort. "It's looking bad. Really, really bad."

"But Jan has healing powers, doesn't he?" Philipp asked, unwilling to let go of her hand as they followed the others inside.

"Yes, but if it's a particularly bad injury there's only so much he can do." Lucille tried to tell herself there was still hope. Matt's mind didn't work properly when it came to Samantha, so there was a good chance the injury wasn't as bad as it looked. It was a feeble hope to hold on to, despite the images of Samantha's burnt face flashing through her mind.

Inside, they bumped into Fabian, who was tucking his shirt into his trousers as if he'd just gotten dressed. "What happened?"

"Caspar got to Samantha. She's badly hurt. Have you seen Jan?"

Fabian's face went white. "Sam... No, I haven't seen anyone." Before Lucille could ask him, he ran off in the opposite direction. "I'll find him."

Lucille continued into what turned out to be Jan's bedroom. Matt had lain Samantha down on the bed and was kneeling beside her, holding her hand. "Please wake up. I'm sorry. I'm so, so sorry. I wasn't thinking. I..."

"What happened?" Lucille asked, putting a hand on his shoulder. In the light of the room, Samantha's face looked even worse. There was no chance it was just a minor injury, but she was breathing, ragged as it was.

Matt's face was contorted with pain as he looked up at her, but before he could explain, Anne entered the room with a bowl of water and a towel. "You're Jan's sister. You..." Matt swallowed.

Anne looked frightened and Lucille realised too late she'd forgotten about Anne. "I don't have any healing powers, if that's what you're asking. But my mum always said to clean the wounds." She put her bowl on the bedside table and knelt on Samantha's other side. Then she moistened the towel, but hovered over Samantha's face, unable to bring herself to do it. "You called an ambulance, didn't you?"

Lucille took a shuddering breath. They were *supposed* to call an ambulance, weren't they? And then what? Jan would be denied access to Samantha while non-magical personnel failed to save her?

"Hanna," Matt whispered, his eyes closed, "Goddess of life. If you're really my ancestor, do something."

Lucille had never seen Matt pray before.

"To all the damn gods, don't let Samantha suffer for my wrath. It's not her fault. It's mine. I'm the one who should be punished. Not her."

Meekly, Anne began to dab at the blood on Samantha's face.

Lucille couldn't bear to watch any longer. "Jan will be here any minute." She knew how to find him now and could've kicked herself for not thinking of it sooner. "Just hang on, Sam."

Fabian

Samantha was hurt. Badly hurt.

Fabian rubbed his face, trying to control the panic that swept over him. What had happened while he and Ophelia had been making out in the study? He hadn't heard any fighting or screaming, just the sudden bustle in the hallway. Lucille had said something about Caspar getting his hands on Samantha, but that was impossible, wasn't it? After all, they'd banished him. Or rather, Samantha had banished him. Which meant he'd absolutely get his revenge on her as soon as he could.

He groaned. They'd become too complacent. Somehow the constant threat of Matt's brothers had become just another part of their daily life in this monster-infested town. Not that Fabian had ever forgotten about it, but there had been other pressing matters—final exams, his mother's mental health problems, and Ophelia—that had made it easy to ignore it.

If only Matt had taken care of it when Fabian had instructed him to. A small voice of reason told Fabian Matt had tried, but surviving was all he'd been able to do. It wasn't enough. Not when Samantha got caught in the crossfire. Always in Matt's crossfire.

Fabian swallowed the unhelpful anger before he accidentally flooded Jan's house. With their luck, Neve would just turn the water to ice, and he'd split his head open on the stairs.

Just then, Fabian noticed the door to the cellar was only half closed. He was about to check it when Lucille caught up with him. A red arrow shot down the stairs in front of her. "He's down there," she declared, wheezing.

"What is he...?" It didn't matter. Fabian burst through the door and followed the arrow, Lucille at his heels.

The red glowing magic zoomed around a shelf and disappeared. Even before Fabian and Lucille had crossed the room, they could hear Jan's voice. "And she said, I was a boar... No boring. Me. Boring."

Was it Fabian's imagination or was Jan slurring his words?

"I don't think you're boring," another voice replied. Robert. What was Robert doing down there in Neve's basement? "I think you're pretty cool."

"Yes, very cool. When my snow witch starts, there'll be snow in the living room."

Fabian shared a look with Lucille and a terrible fear came over him. "Jan?"

They found the two boys sitting behind the last shelves, an almost empty bottle of vodka between them, though it looked like only Jan had been drinking from it. Robert looked up at them full of hope. "Meg broke up with him."

"She wants to flirt now," Jan said in a sing-song voice.

Robert turned to him. "Has she met anyone?"

"Just her mum."

"Meg wants to flirt with her mother?"

"Oh, come on!" Lucille exclaimed, having no patience for Robert's cluelessness. Then she walked over to Jan and took the bottle out of his hands. "How much did you drink?"

Jan just looked at her and burped. "Not enough."

Fabian grunted in frustration. "Come on, Jan. Sam needs you. Now." He grabbed Jan's wrists and pulled him to his feet. It only worked because Jan staggered up by himself, but then he almost collapsed in his arms, and Fabian stumbled against the shelf.

"I don't think he's in the mood to celebrate," Robert said wisely. "Heartbreaks are bad. I had a girl break up with me once because she didn't like my hair."

"Shut up, Robert," Lucille muttered.

But Jan perked up. "What about your hair?"

Fabian began to drag Jan towards the stairs with a little help from Lucille.

Robert followed cheerfully. "She suddenly liked blond guys."

"I like your hair," Jan confessed, making Fabian groan.

This wasn't good. If Jan was well and truly drunk, there was no way he could cure Samantha. If anything, he'd just make things worse.

Meanwhile Robert was still babbling. "Thank you. Anne likes it too. She says it's very soft." Apparently *he* didn't have to be drunk to babble nonsense.

"Robert," Lucille said, "I mean this in the nicest way possible: shut up and go. The party's over." Then, after a moment, she added, "Anne's already left."

"Without me?" Robert looked surprised.

"That's teenage girls for you," Jan drawled. "They just up and leave. Like leaves on a tree."

Robert followed more quietly now and thankfully excused himself as soon as they'd managed to lure Jan upstairs.

Fabian didn't know if he could have held it in any longer. He looked at Lucille. "It won't work. Not when he's in this state."

"Look, I know it's another state," Jan interjected, "but it's not a country state or a steak. Or a stake." He stared into the distance, lost in thought.

"Don't you have a sobering spell?" Fabian asked, exasperated. He managed to drag Jan to the couch, but that was as far as he would go.

Lucille shook her head. "Not in my notes. And I don't remember coming across one in my grandmother's diary. What about cold water?"

Without hesitation, Fabian splashed Jan's face with cold water from his hands. Jan groaned and raised his arms, then stumbled off the couch. "Urgh, go away!" he moaned.

A scream came from his bedroom and Fabian's head jerked up. He shared a glance with Lucille before they both ran back towards it. Barely able to keep himself from crashing into the door frame, he skidded to a halt. "What happened?"

Too many people were standing around the bed where Samantha lay. Anne was on her left, holding a bloody towel, while Matt had jumped on the bed to hold Samantha. Ophelia stood near the door, looking terribly lost, while Menuha and Chay looked on with unreadable expressions.

"I can't see," Samantha whimpered, her face hidden by Matt's body. "I... Matt? It hurts! Why can't I see?"

Matt's shoulders knotted. "I'm so sorry, Sam. Jan's on his way and everything will be fine."

"Jan's not coming," Fabian forced himself to say. "He's dead drunk, incapable of healing anything."

Matt turned with a horrified look in his eyes, and for the first time Fabian saw Samantha's ruined face. The upper part of her face was charred and reddened, tears of blood falling from her ruined eyes.

"Sam," Fabian whimpered. Suddenly his legs could no longer support him and he fell to his knees. In an instant, Ophelia was at his side, throwing her arms around him and crying into his shoulder.

"What do we do now?" Lucille asked. "Jan can't help her. Shall we take her to the hospital?"

"They wouldn't be able to save her eyes," Chay said, terribly calm. Then he sighed. "You'll have to ask Caspar."

Even Menuha turned to him in surprise. "Caspar doesn't heal humans. He can hardly bring himself to heal me."

Fabian shook his head in disbelief. "Caspar would kill her." He pointed at Samantha, who was writhing in Matt's arms, moaning in pain. "He did this."

Matt struggled to look away from Samantha. When he did, he nodded to Menuha. "Go and ask him. Please."

"Matt," the demon warned, "you know him. Fabian's right, it's too risky."

"Tell him..." Matt wet his lips. "Tell him he owes me. He owes me a favour. Trust me."

Fabian had no idea what this favour business was about, but he felt something twisted, like a surge of hope. Could it be? Could Caspar be persuaded to heal Samantha after hurting her in the first place?

"Try him," Chay added. A heartbeat later, Menuha was gone. "Matt, this is not your fault."

But Matt's face was one of pure agony. "It is. Caspar didn't do this. I did."

Caspar

After Melchior's sudden appearance and his badly aimed shot, Caspar had returned home to study his runes. His stay in Meriand had been marked by abuse and shame and then terrible heartbreak, but it had also left him with a great understanding of magic. Alecto had introduced him to the runes, and over the centuries, Caspar had continued his studies. To what end, he couldn't even say. Maybe he hadn't been able to shake the stupid, obedient boy he'd been as completely as he'd thought. Or maybe because they'd proven to be quite useful now and then.

Maybe even today.

Balthasar appeared in his study. "Is he dead?"

"No." Caspar had never even tried to touch Melchior. He hadn't returned the shot, but had let him go with Samantha in his arms. With his *Jeyne*.

"Excuse me?" Balthasar raised an eyebrow. "I practically handed him to you. How could you not manage to kill him?"

Caspar shrugged nonchalantly. "Samantha got in the way. She got hurt."

"So?" Balthasar asked, confused.

"He took her back to Ashuan." It might have been better if he'd stayed, but Caspar wasn't sure yet if he trusted himself enough to do what needed to be done. She wasn't Jeyne, not really.

"And you just let him go?" Balthasar asked, his voice sharp with disbelief. "You really are too stupid to live, aren't you?"

Before Caspar could slam him into the wall for his audacity, Menuha appeared, an uncharacteristic ferocity in her eyes. "Caspar!"

He'd known it would come to this. Part of him had even hoped it would. "Let me guess. Melchior needs my help?"

"Samantha needs a healer," Menuha confirmed. "Their healer is drunk... and inexperienced." She took a deep breath, completely ignoring Balthasar's presence. "Melchior said you owed him."

It was as good an excuse as any. Caspar took another moment to study the runes in his collection, ready for use. "Very well."

Beside him, Balthasar wrung his hands in an unmistakable gesture. "I swear, if he brings her here, I'll kill her with my own hands."

His brother rarely got his own hands dirty, but Caspar had already decided he couldn't do it in Hell. He would need the extra magic of Greenvalley. "I guess I'll have to go up then."

"Volac kicked you in the head one too many times," Balthasar snapped. "You've been banished from Ashuan. How exactly are you planning to get there?"

Menuha looked at him with worried eyes and bit her lip, still not sure if she could trust him.

Caspar didn't know either, but he'd try it for Jeyne. Even if it wasn't truly her. He picked up one of the more complex runes, the one he'd created the moment he'd been banished. It couldn't undo his banishment, not completely or permanently, but it would be enough for what needed to be done.

"With rune magic, of course."

Matt

Matt was still struggling to make sense of what had happened in Hescaryn. He'd followed Caspar's trail of rune magic into a lava cave and found him hovering over Samantha. And then... He stared at his hand, wishing he could just cut it off.

Samantha had lost consciousness again, her breathing too shallow and irregular for comfort.

"My mum always says shock is the most dangerous part of any trauma," Anne said in a soft voice, her hands in her lap. "You could get her to the hospital quickly, couldn't you?"

Matt swallowed. Put Samantha's fate in the hands of human healers. He'd seen their work. They couldn't cure this.

A hand fell on his shoulder. "Matt," Lucille said quietly. "It might be better."

"Caspar will do it," Matt said. "He owes me."

It couldn't be his own life, but it was Samantha's life that had to be saved. It was worth whatever Caspar would throw at him. His fate didn't matter. Not to him.

"I'm no good for her." The truth of the words almost strangled him. "I bring her nothing but pain." If she survived this, he'd stay away from her. Anything to keep her safe.

"That's not true," Lucille said, but her voice caught in her throat and she gulped. But then she closed her eyes. "Are you sure Caspar will help her?"

"He has to." Of course, there was no reason for Caspar to keep his promise. After all, there was no love lost between them. "Lucille, please."

Lucille's eyelids fluttered. When she looked at him again, her eyes were steely. "We banished him for a reason."

"Is Jan sober?"

She shook her head.

"Then Samantha *needs* him."

"I see," Lucille said a little curtly. "Danger aside, we don't have time for a summoning circle. Besides, this is Samantha's area of expertise."

Before Matt could snap at her, Ophelia raised her voice. "What about taking Samantha to him? To Hell?"

"It's Hell?" Philipp pointed out, horrified.

But Matt nodded. "You're right. I'll take her to him." Determined, he slid his arms under Samantha.

"Matt, wait." Chay's voice was annoyingly calm. He'd never really seemed to like Samantha in the first place.

"She's dying!" Matt snapped at him. "There's no time to—"

Just then, Menuha returned, a complex rune in her hand. "He agreed to it." There were several gasps of surprise in the room. Menuha offered the rune to Matt. "This will get him here despite the ban. But it only allows him a very small radius. You should use it right next to her bed."

"Does that mean Caspar can only jump into this room?" Lucille asked. When Menuha nodded, she sighed with relief. "This will work. We can all stay here and protect her."

"Or you could all leave."

While Lucille had been formulating her plan, Matt had simply broken the rune, allowing Caspar to appear. There he was now with his perpetual scowl, as if he was planning to skewer them all alive and then—maybe—pay his debt and heal Samantha.

"You have to help her," Matt begged. He didn't care how much they hated each other or what it would cost him. If Caspar demanded a life for a life, he'd gladly give his. "You said you owed me."

Caspar snorted. "I don't need you to keep repeating that. I already told Menuha I'd do it." He swept his gaze around the room, taking stock of everyone. "If you want me to save your little human, you have to leave. All of you." His gaze fell on Anne, who'd been staring at him in horror. "All but her."

"Her?" Matt asked, confused. "What's this about?"

"The clock is ticking," Caspar said in a lacklustre voice, clearly not caring whether he succeeded today or not.

Matt looked at Samantha, at the terrible burns from his hands. Her breathing was so shallow he almost thought they'd lost her while they'd been arguing. How much longer did she have?

It didn't matter. Matt wasn't willing to risk Samantha's life. Slowly he rose to his feet, but then she whimpered and his ass was down again. He could feel Caspar's eyes burning in his back as he took her hand and whispered in her ear. "It's going to be alright now, Sam. You'll feel better soon, I promise."

A part of him wanted to threaten Caspar if he thought about going back on his promise, but he managed to restrain himself. It would only irritate his brother more. Instead, he put a hand on Lucille's back and gently pushed her in front of him. Most of the others had already left. Only Menuha and Fabian remained—and Anne, of course, her eyes growing wider with each person who left.

Menuha noticed her. "Caspar, let the girl go. If you need someone to help you, I can do it."

"I said everyone but her," Caspar growled. He still hadn't touched Samantha. "I'm not going to kill the girl."

"Come on," Matt urged Menuha, afraid they were wasting precious time. "Let him do what he came for."

Fabian glared at Caspar, seemingly unwilling to leave. Matt nudged him too, causing his friend to take a deep but shaky breath. "If he acts suspicious in any way, Anne, scream as loud as you can. We're right downstairs." Then he turned abruptly to Matt and said darkly, "I hope you know what you're doing."

"Caspar," Menuha was still pleading with her twin.

"I don't want you here," Caspar snapped. "Now go, before there's nothing left for me to do."

Menuha swallowed, obviously shocked, but finally she relented. "Of course. Adrianes is here. Balthasar's offspring."

"The gardener?" Caspar asked, mildly interested.

"The same."

Caspar came towards the group, pushing Menuha out of the room with the sheer bulk of his body. "Very well. Send him here. He may as well gather healing herbs for me." Then he shut the door in their faces.

"He's never..." Menuha whispered, still in shock. "He's never shut me out before."

Matt knew that wasn't the truth, but he'd promised to keep the secret. And if that secret saved Samantha from his terrible miscalculation, he'd do whatever it took to keep it. "Let's get Adrianes."

Rachel

While the rest of her friends had crowded into the room with Samantha, Rachel had taken it upon herself to be a little more proactive. She'd found a bucket of water and persuaded Neve to put some ice in it. Then, ignoring Jan's protests, she dipped his head in and out of the bowl as Hugo watched.

"Such a shame to drink yourself into oblivion like that," Hugo complained. "Of course it's all going to end in blood and tears."

"Hugo, please. The last thing anyone needs is a lecture." *From a ghost,* she added mentally, not wanting to hurt his feelings.

Meanwhile, Neve was flying in circles around them. "Jonathan tried drinking. He didn't like it. But then he did it again."

"Yes, that's usually how it goes," Rachel said sourly. When her mother had come home drunk, she'd never bothered to sober her up. Usually she gave drunk people a wide berth, but this was Jan, and he'd apparently had his heart broken. Besides, Samantha needed him.

Jan had gone from incoherent babbling to inconsolable crying and apologies. "What if I moved to Cologne?" he wailed. "I'd follow her to the ends of the earth."

"No, you wouldn't." As stable as his relationship with Meg had appeared, Rachel hadn't exactly started planning their wedding yet.

"I'm a terrible boyfriend."

She submerged him again. "Right now, you're a terrible friend." Not that Jan could've known what other tragedies would strike that night.

Just then she heard footsteps in the corridor. One by one, her friends entered the living room. Their faces told Rachel that the situation was dire, but that Samantha was still alive. Matt looked on the verge of a nervous breakdown, rubbing his face incessantly, while Fabian was quietly seething. Probably because Matt's brothers had wreaked havoc once again.

"He's never cut me out before," Menuha complained, making Rachel wonder who they were talking about. "There's something wrong with him."

"Call me when there's something right with Caspar," Fabian snapped. "We need to get back upstairs." But before he could do so, Ophelia put her hands on his chest and talked him down.

"What's going on?" Rachel asked Lucille as she dropped onto the couch like a sack of potatoes.

"Matt called in a favour with Caspar, and now Caspar is upstairs healing Samantha."

Not a word of it made sense. "Caspar is upstairs?"

"He can only enter Jan's room, nowhere else," Lucille said quickly. "Something about rune magic."

"Huh." Rachel elbowed Jan. "Did you hear that? Caspar can visit while you're sleeping now."

Lucille frowned slightly. "I think it's a one-off."

"I was trying to sober him up."

Jan, however, had trouble processing what she'd said and mumbled something about not wanting to date Caspar.

"But I guess that's not a priority anymore?"

Lucille sighed. "I don't like it, but I suppose"—she looked at Chay pointedly—"he'd be a bit more proactive if another healer was needed."

In Rachel's opinion, Chay had the same guarded look on his face as always. As if he knew the future and couldn't do anything to change it, no matter how terrible it was. "There's nothing wrong with him," he reassured Menuha, before admitting, "nothing that wasn't wrong with him in the first place."

Rachel noticed Matt looking away and found the reaction interesting. Had Chay told him about the future he'd seen for Caspar to give him an advantage over his brother?

Suddenly, Matt also became aware they had a seer in the room. "Please tell me it wasn't a mistake to leave her alone with him."

Chay shook his head. "It wasn't a mistake."

"Did you just say that because I asked you to or because it's actually true?" Matt pushed unnecessarily. As if there was any point in Chay lying when the future was unfolding at this very moment.

"What's going to be is going to be," Chay said quietly. "Everything was set in motion a long time ago and nothing either of us could do would change the outcome. There are no mistakes, only one thing leading to another."

Matt groaned in frustration. "I can't just wait here and twiddle my thumbs!"

"If you want Samantha to open her eyes again, that's exactly what you're going to do."

It was as direct a warning as Chay was probably capable of, and this time Matt listened and dropped to the floor, burying his face in his hands. Chay had trained him well.

Unfortunately, the same couldn't be said for Fabian, who'd started to pace. "I just don't get it. She was with Caspar, then she got hurt and you brought her here, and now Caspar is here to heal her. It doesn't make any sense. What was the point of him kidnapping Samantha in the first place?"

For once, Rachel thought he was right. It seemed a bit out of character for Caspar not only to let someone live, but also to go out of his way to heal them. Especially considering how painful healing was for the healer. "How long were they together?"

"I don't know," Matt whispered. "Ten minutes? Half an hour?"

"What was he doing with her for that long?"

Matt's shoulders knotted and it took him a moment to look up. "He had her against a wall in a lava lake cave. I don't know what happened. I just saw red and shot at him, but the energy hit her."

"You did this?" Rachel's eyes widened.

Matt winced in pain. "It's all my fault, yes."

"You didn't kidnap her," Lucille said determined. "Caspar did. Or rather Balthasar did. This was Balthasar's plan."

"Probably?" Matt shrugged, as if he didn't care who'd started the whole thing. "Wouldn't be the first time they teamed up to take me out."

"Yeah, but somehow it's always Sam who gets hurt!" Fabian flung at him. As usual, he was deaf to reason when it came to his best friend.

Matt took the accusation in stride and nodded sharply. "I know."

"This has to stop."

"I know."

"Do something!" Tears of anger and despair rolled down Fabian's cheeks. He wiped them away furiously as Ophelia rubbed his back.

Rachel exchanged glances with Lucille, who looked equally exhausted. With a sigh, Rachel resumed her sobering efforts. This was going to be a long night.

Caspar

For a moment, Caspar listened at the door. When he was sure they'd all gone, he turned around, causing the little girl at the bedside to whimper like the coward she was. Caspar paid no attention to her, instead taking in the damage to Samantha's face.

Melchior had really outdone himself. This shot had been meant to kill.

The stupid girl was crying softly now, annoying the daylight out of him. He growled at her. "Don't make me regret letting you stay. Take the pillow away and then change the water and towel."

The girl swallowed hard, tried to control her tears, and ended up with hiccups. But she did as she was told. She gently removed the pillow from under Samantha's head and set it aside. Then she picked up the water bowl, shaking so hard half its contents spilt onto the floor.

Caspar opened the door for her and let it slam behind her. He was alone with Samantha now. With Jeyne.

Carefully he approached the bed, listening to her laboured breathing. He probably should've been hurrying a little more, but as usual his mind was building a barrier around the healing powers. Or rather, his willingness to use them.

"Jeyne," he said loudly, forcing himself to tear down the walls. Just this once. Just for her.

He sat down on her bed and held his hands over her eyes, letting his magic show him the damage. In the golden glow of healing he found cauterised nerve ends, damaged eyeballs, and badly burnt skin.

His hands moved down her body until they came to rest on her chest. Her heartbeat was erratic, faltering, and her lungs were struggling to fill with enough air. She was one collapsed lung away from a heart attack.

With a deep breath, Caspar sank his magic into her chest, strengthening her heart and relieving the pressure on her lungs. Slowly, Samantha began to breathe more easily. Something like a smile appeared on Caspar's face. It had hardly hurt at all.

Someone knocked at the door. "What?" Caspar demanded.

Instead of getting a reply, the door was opened by Adrianes. The girl followed with a fresh bowl of water. The second-class demon kept his distance as he eyed Caspar. "What do you need?"

"An armful of balendel leaves, some sylverweed, and niadrin bulbs." The injuries were extensive enough he could use all the help he could get.

Adrianes nodded. "I'll see what we have in our Lucin nursery." It would take him several days to return to the actual gardens of Hescaryn.

As he left, the meek little girl stood against the wall, bowl in hand, staring.

Caspar groaned. He had to do something. "You're back." She didn't move. "The water."

"R-right." Again, she sloshed some of the water on the floor before she managed to put it on the bedside table. Then she stood there like a prey animal ready to bolt.

"I can heal her eyes," Caspar said, ignoring the fear in every muscle of her face, "but it'll cost me. The burns will have to wait. As soon as Adrianes is back, you'll help me make a balendel bandage to ease her pain."

She whispered so softly he had to assume she'd agreed.

"Your brother's a healer, right?" They had the same dark brown hair and large brown eyes. "So you know what to do."

Her face contorted. "Not really."

He'd overestimated her. "Healing someone is painful. It'll be painful and exhausting for me. I might lose control. So, if you think I'm about to faint, you'll have to push me away from her. Understood?"

The girl gave the slightest of nods.

"*Before* I lose consciousness." It was a risk to put his hands into someone as meek as this, but at least he didn't have to worry about her deciding to kill him instead.

Caspar turned to Samantha again to see how she was doing. Her lips moved and she moaned, on the verge of waking again. Before that happened, he took another rune from his bag and placed it in Samantha's hands. She immediately fell into a deep sleep.

"What is that?"

It took Caspar a moment to realise the girl had spoken. That was good. Curiosity was slowly warming her up. He'd need it. "Just giving her body a chance to rest while we rebuild it. Keeps her from waking up, freaking out, and screaming her head off."

"So, like an anaesthetic?"

"If you want to call it that." In truth, Caspar had no idea what she was talking about, but he assumed it had something to do with human medicine in this world. The non-magical kind.

Just then Adrianes returned, arms full of fleshy leaves and a bag of herbs. "I couldn't get you niadrin, but vazaleen blossoms should do the trick."

"Put them over there and go. We've got work to do."

Adrianes was quick about it, as eager to leave as Caspar was to see his back. He'd seen enough of Balthasar already. He didn't need to deal with his offspring as well.

"Alright, girl. These big fleshy leaves are balendel. I want you to cut off the stems and soften them in water. That should take about ten minutes. In the meantime, you're going to crush the sylverweed into a coarse paste." Again, she just sat there with her big brown eyes. "What?"

"I don't have a knife or a mortar."

"Then get some!" he snapped, sending her running.

Annoyed, Caspar turned back to Samantha. "Useless. Most humans are useless." But this time she didn't argue back, didn't tell him how useless *he* was.

The girl returned while he mentally prepared himself for the pain he was about to experience. No rune could save him from the effects of healing, or if it could, his old master had never bothered to show him.

"Don't forget to watch me." Then he plunged into Samantha's injury.

Left to natural healing, the girl would never see again. The energy had burnt the surface of her eyes and taken out the nerves. The skin around them had melted hideously. Caspar's own eyes began to burn as if they were on fire. Not needing to see, he squeezed them shut, even though it did little to stop the pain.

As he began to mend the flesh around her eyes, he couldn't help but grunt. His hands trembled, though they did little more than hover over Samantha's face. The magic was in his mind. It connected him to her, to everything that was broken and needed fixing.

Cells moved back into place, restoring themselves under his guidance. Then he turned to her eyes and his knees almost buckled. So much destruction. The pain only increased as he repaired the burnt nerves and his muscles began to ache. Not just aching, but tearing. His whole face felt on fire. A fire that burnt and burnt, even though there was nothing left to burn.

Then, suddenly, the connection was broken. Caspar staggered backwards into the wall behind him, barely able to stand. He noticed the girl had moved around the bed to push him away from Samantha. She'd actually been protecting him.

"The blossoms," he croaked.

She ran to the bedside table, grabbed the blossoms and handed them to him. Caspar stuffed half of them into his mouth and chewed relentlessly. The taste was absolutely disgusting, but it restored him enough to try again.

"Was I too late?" the girl asked, concern written all over her face.

"No, maybe a little early. I can endure more." But not very much. "Melchior did a thorough job. I can't do this alone." Not if he wanted to restore Samantha's sight. "Give me your hand."

She looked at him as if he'd suggested she cut it off first. His patience was wearing thin, but then she pulled herself together and held out her hand.

Caspar took it as gently as he could and drew on her palm with his right. A simple circle with a line that split into three like a tree. "Hanna's rune." As soon as the last line was in place, the rune glowed golden. "It will help you see what I do." And more importantly, do what he was doing. To a lesser extent.

He led her back to Samantha and placed the glowing hand on her temple. "Close your eyes. Do you see the golden threads?"

Healing was more than just visual enhancement and the ability to stimulate cell growth. When he closed his eyes, he didn't see cells and individual nerves, but a complex web with holes in it. A glaring hole where the connection between the eyes and the brain had been severed.

"Do you see this?" he asked the girl again. When she nodded, he continued, "And do you see the hole in it?"

"N-no... yes!" She opened her eyes in shock. "That's—"

"Don't care. Eyes shut," Caspar snapped. "I want you to concentrate on the sides of the hole and imagine you're holding them together, like mending a dress."

The magic moved in response to her efforts, making the gap a little smaller to bridge. Caspar jumped back in and got to work. The pain was as bad as before, but his magic flew more easily, aided by the blossoms and the girl's assistance.

They worked together for almost an hour before Caspar was convinced he'd repaired Samantha's sight and the worst of her burns. He felt bone tired when he finally let go and sank to the ground to catch his breath.

"It's whole again!" the girl exclaimed. While he'd struggled in pain, she'd had the easy part.

"Yes, yes. Now apply the paste and cover the burns on her skin with the leaves." As she worked, creating a natural bandage, Caspar pulled himself up and began to repair the more superficial wounds. It was still painful, but not nearly as bad as the eyes.

Finally, he pulled away and stared at his achievement. Samantha's face was covered by leaves, but he could feel the skin underneath rejuvenating in response to the magic.

"Not bad for a novice," he murmured.

"Novice?"

Caspar nodded at the girl. "I mean you. You carry Hanna's blessing. Why do you think I asked you to stay?"

"Who's Hanna?"

He blinked. "Don't you know the goddess of life? She's worshipped on countless worlds."

"Not on this one," the girl replied. "At least I've never heard of her." Then she swallowed. "There are other worlds?"

"Of course there are. Where do you think I come from?"

"I thought..." Her voice caught in her throat and her eyes began to shimmer. "You're the school shooter. And you're Matt's older brother. I thought you were an old student. From out of town, maybe."

Caspar narrowed his eyes. What was this girl talking about? "School shooter?"

The tears that had only threatened to fall ran down her cheeks now. "You were firing in the school. My best friend Meg almost died because of you."

He vaguely remembered groups of screaming people in long corridors. At least now he knew why she was so afraid of him. "I see. I only wanted to kill Melchior. Matt."

The girl whimpered pathetically.

"It had nothing to do with you."

"You're a killer."

"So? Matt's a killer too." The girl's eyes widened. "So is Samantha and your brother and all their other little friends." His voice took on a mean tone. "Oh wait, that only counts if you kill a human, right? If you kill a demon or a vampire, it's not murder."

"Demons?" the girl squeaked. "There are vampires?"

Slowly the realisation hit Caspar. "You know absolutely nothing, do you? Your brother fights side by side with mine against the monsters in your town and you never even noticed?"

"I knew Jan could heal. The monsters..." She swallowed. "Dad always said he made them up. And Jan... he never told me."

Caspar snorted. "Unbelievable. No wonder you have no idea of your potential."

"My potential?" She wiped her eyes, curiosity overtaking fear.

"You were chosen by Hanna. To be her priestess. It's a great honour."

"What does that mean?"

Caspar sighed. He wasn't inclined to help this human girl on her way to becoming a priestess. But she'd helped him with the healing, so it was only fair to set her on the right path. "A student of Hanna strives to preserve life in all its forms. Her priests maintain the balance of nature. Some can talk to animals, others to plants, and they tend to the rivers of magic, ensuring their unhindered flow." Even in Hescaryn, Hanna's priests were usually left alone.

"I can't do any of that."

"Of course not. You haven't taken the time to learn it. If I were you, I'd find a temple and start devoting myself to it."

And that was as much as he was going to offer her. After all, he was only here for one reason.

His gaze fell on Samantha's resting body. He'd known her as the little girl his brother lusted after—no, not just lusted after. Caspar knew what was between them was genuine love. Melchior loved this witch as much as he'd once loved Jeyne. Perhaps more, for he was half human. And if he didn't come between them, they might actually have a chance. No one in Ashuan cared that Melchior carried demon blood, and from what Menuha had told him, Samantha had forgiven him for letting her down before.

They could share years of happiness that Caspar and Jeyne had never had. *If* he left her alone. If he didn't claim her for himself.

For despite what she said, and despite what she looked like, there was so much of Jeyne in her. Her intelligence and her curiosity. Her bravery in the face of adversity, and her pride in the face of defeat.

He'd waited five hundred years to see her again. He'd be a fool to give her up. Especially if it meant giving her up to Melchior.

Caspar looked at the human witch who carried the soul of his beloved and swore to himself that he'd fight for her. To the death, if necessary.

Jan

Once more Jan emerged from the icy hell he found himself in. He spluttered and gasped, his face burning from the heat of the air. Someone tried to push him back under, but he managed to grab the bucket and lock his arms.

Water dripped from his soaked hair onto his nose and he blinked, trying to ease the pain in his eyes. As far as he could tell, even his clothes were wet.

"Feeling any better?" his tormentor asked.

"Better?" His face was burning, he was shivering, and his head felt like the house had collapsed on him. But he recognised the voice. For some reason, it was Rachel trying to waterboard him here in his living room. "Are you trying to kill me?"

There were more people. A lot of them, now that he had a moment to look around. Lucille was sitting beside him, looking tired. "You were dead drunk."

Jan vaguely remembered drinking. And something about Robert. And Meg. There it was, the cause of his misery. Meg had broken up with him just like that. Because she'd never really been in love.

Grumpy now, he muttered, "So what? A normal friend would let me sleep it off, not try to drown me in ice water."

"Neve made ice water," the little snow witch announced proudly.

"And Neve did a great job," Rachel said, glaring at him as if daring him to disagree.

Lucille rubbed her face and took a deep breath before speaking. "We had to do it. We desperately needed a healer, and with you drunk, we had to summon Caspar instead."

"Caspar?" He vaguely remembered something about Caspar being locked in his room, but he couldn't make sense of it.

"Samantha's been injured," Rachel explained tersely. "Caspar and Anne are looking after her upstairs."

Jan felt as if she'd put his head under water again. "Anne—as in my little sister—upstairs with Caspar—as in kill-happy demon general?"

"I think he needs another turn," Lucille suggested.

But Jan didn't give up his position, too busy putting the pieces together. "And you're sitting here?"

"Not by choice."

"What the hell?" Jan jumped to his feet and ran for the stairs. They'd left Anne with a demon. And not just any demon but the most brutal and insane demon they knew. There was probably a good reason for this, but nothing could justify the danger they'd put Anne in.

Just as he reached the door to his room, Matt appeared in front of him with a panicked expression on his face. "Don't. Caspar said—"

"I don't give a shit what Caspar said," Jan shouted, then flung the door wide open.

There he was, the demon so out of control his friends had to banish him from Ashuan, and his little sister, all wide-eyed and innocent. Someone was lying in the bed between them, her face covered with strange fleshy leaves. Jan recognised her only by the black curls and the context. Samantha.

He glared at Caspar, who just stood there, chewing as he watched Jan with utter disinterest. Then he hurried to Anne's side and quickly checked every inch of her body.

"Jan. I'm fine. He didn't hurt me."

While that seemed to be true, it did little to ease Jan's worries. He glanced at Caspar again, only to find the demon locked in a staring contest with Matt. Unlike usual, Matt looked cautious, almost submissive.

"I fixed your mistake," Caspar said with a sneer. "She'll be okay."

"Thanks," Matt replied stiffly. He wrinkled his nose as if he were about to swallow something bitter. "I owe you one."

Caspar snorted. "I don't want any favours from you."

Matt nodded, giving in immediately. "I'll withdraw." When Caspar raised his eyebrows in confusion, Matt explained. "You and Balthasar can fight it out for the position. I won't stand in your way."

Caspar narrowed his eyes. "You got in my way the day you were conceived."

"Please." Matt looked absolutely miserable. "I don't want to fight you. Not if it means Samantha gets caught in the middle of this conflict."

"If Samantha gets caught in the middle, it'll be because you dragged her there." Caspar spat out a clump of purple blossoms. "There's only one way you can protect her."

Matt snorted. "Is there?"

"You just have to stop loving her."

The suggestion made Matt take a shaky breath. "Like that's so easy."

Caspar sneered at him and retorted angrily, "Then you'll just have to live with the consequences!" And without further ado, he vanished into thin air.

Anne breathed a sigh of relief. Meanwhile, Matt looked at Samantha, his shoulders clenching as if he were about to cry.

Jan took a step towards him. "Ignore that psycho's crazy talk. He doesn't even know what love is. I'm sorry I wasn't there to heal her in his place." He patted Matt on the shoulder, then took Anne with him to give them some space.

Even though he was told Caspar was still banished from Ashuan and couldn't return, Jan wouldn't let her go home alone. The demon may have been remotely helpful today, but that didn't mean he wouldn't show up tomorrow to shoot at anything that moved. And now he knew Anne's face.

"You're staying here," he told Anne, and made a bed for her on the couch. Samantha was still in his bed, recovering from her healing with Matt by her side, which was fine with Jan after he learnt his room was the perimeter for Caspar's visit to Ashuan. He'd probably start renovating the room next door and turn his into a guest room, just to be on the safe side.

To his surprise, Anne didn't argue with him, but climbed into the makeshift bed. "I want a bedtime story."

"Excuse me?"

For some reason, Anne glared at him. "A lot happened today and very little of it made sense. The school shooter was here."

Jan had a sinking feeling she was about to open a can of worms. "Did he hurt you? Threaten to hurt you?"

"No, he was... quite peaceful. He let me help him heal because he has the same power as you," she said reproachfully. "And he told me things."

"What things?"

"Like that I carry Hanna's blessing within me. She's a goddess. The goddess of life. Because there are gods and goddesses I've never heard of. From other *worlds*. Worlds full of *demons*. And *vampires*. And I don't know what." She was glaring now, delivering each word like a fist punch. "Why did you never tell me?"

He felt grumpy enough to blame it on how little anyone had ever believed him. But Anne wasn't the one to blame. His father was. And to some extent, his mother. Anne, however, had stood by him as best she could. She may have been the little Miss Perfect he could never live up to, but she'd always looked up to him regardless.

Instead of letting his pride dictate the answer, he offered honesty. "Because you're my little sister and I could never forgive myself for putting you in danger." But he had put her in danger. If he hadn't gotten drunk, he would have been there to heal Samantha and then Anne wouldn't have had to spend two hours alone with Caspar. "I'm sorry about today."

Anne's gaze softened. "Meg told me what happened."

"She did?"

"I'm actually quite angry with her."

"Don't be. She's your best friend."

"But you're my brother."

While Jan appreciated the sentiment, he didn't want to be responsible for ruining their lifelong friendship. "I can take care of myself."

"You're okay with this?" she asked doubtfully. "Meg said you took it badly."

"Of course I took it badly. It was completely out of the blue, but she's probably right. And this way I'll save a lot of money on trips to Cologne. Silver lining and all."

"Jan..."

He stroked her hair and forced a smile. "Don't worry about me. It wasn't that serious." It was for him. "I hope she finds it easier to keep in touch with you or I *will* drive down there and kick her butt."

Anne rolled her eyes at him, then pulled up the covers and turned over. She was asleep before he'd even gotten up.

Jan stood and surveyed the living room. His friends had helped tidy up before they'd left, leaving him with only a bit of dishwashing to do and mountains of food in the fridge. Another silver lining. Maybe if he could find enough of them this day would somehow be okay.

He shook his head and immediately regretted it as his hangover reared its ugly head. Since he still hadn't worked out where he was going to sleep tonight, he did the next best thing and went outside. The fairy lights were still on, illuminating his impossible garden. A week ago, it had been nothing but barren branches and overgrown brambles.

Something white shot past his cheek and splashed against the tree, falling apart on impact. Snow, Jan registered groggily.

"Jan looks sad," Neve said curiously, already forming another snowball out of nothing.

He sighed. "Please, Neve. I just need a moment to myself."

Neve cocked her head. "Neve has to make Jan smile."

"I—"

"Meg is gone, but Jan still has Neve. Neve can make much better snowballs than Meg."

"I'm not interested in a snowball fight right now." He regretted his words when Neve let the snow fall to the ground.

"What makes Jan smile?"

Jan tried to smile at her to get her off his back, but whatever was happening on his face felt painful and wrong.

Neve sighed. To his relief, she soon flew away, leaving him alone in the garden. Jan turned away from the house and walked along the paths until he came to Matt's swing. While the garden and everything in it had been meant for Samantha, it was only right that Jan, as the homeowner, should enjoy it as well.

He sat down and thought about sleeping out here, but he knew it was far too cold. Still, the soft swing in the fresh air brought him some peace.

At least until Neve returned. "Found Jan," she announced with great relief, and sat on the swing next to him, almost climbing onto his lap. She showed him what she'd brought—one of her many lolly bags. She pushed the bag towards him. "Does Jan want a lolly? Lollies make happy."

This time he really smiled. How could he not, bombarded with such cuteness and honesty. Taking a deep breath, he put his hand in the bag and pulled out a lemon hard candy. "Thank you, Neve. You're the best friend a guy could ask for."

Her wide smile far surpassed his, and she snuggled into his side before popping a sweet into her own mouth. "Neve loves Jan."

And even though Meg didn't, Jan felt a little more at ease now.

Samantha

When Samantha's senses returned, she saw nothing but darkness. She could tell she was lying on her back in a bed under a blanket and that someone was holding her hand. Her face tingled and she waited for the pain to return, but there was none. Still, she panicked as she remembered the agony and fear.

Unintentionally, she squeezed the hand for support.

"Sam?"

She recognised his voice at once. "Matt?"

"I'm here." A second hand wrapped around hers, encasing it.

He was at her side, but she still couldn't see him. The black magic had shot across her face. All she remembered was searing pain, followed by agony. She swallowed hard as the dots connected. "My eyes..." She couldn't say it, didn't dare to acknowledge it.

"You still have a bandage on. Let me see if it's time to take it off."

As he let go of her, Samantha immediately felt untethered. She dug her fingers into the blanket beneath her, holding on for dear life, as if the world was about to tip over and throw her off its surface. Then she felt fingers on her lower cheeks, gently working their way between her skin and some shield-like barrier on top of it.

"Let me know if it hurts," Matt said a little too softly, a far cry from his usual cocky self. Something was wrong. Samantha could sense it.

Whatever he was doing didn't hurt, but it didn't seem to be leading anywhere either. "I'm afraid I'm going to ruin it," Matt finally confessed. "If it's not rea—"

"Just take it off." Her voice came out much harsher than she meant to, her voice laced with panic. "I need to know."

"I've got you."

When it came off, it was with a sudden pop, like a shell cracking. And then there was light, sudden bright light, almost as painful as her memories.

"Bright," she cried, then gritted her teeth and squeezed her eyes shut.

"Sorry." There was a click and the light dimmed considerably. Only now did Samantha realise that it had only been the lamp on the bedside table. "Better?"

Slowly, Samantha let go of the tension and took a deep breath. Then she opened her eyes. They were still tender, but they didn't hurt. Slowly, shapes came into focus as they adjusted to the darkness of the room.

Samantha didn't recognise the room. It wasn't hers and it wasn't Matt's, but it was definitely an Ashuan bedroom, so she assumed she was still in her world. She faintly remembered being in Hell and facing Caspar. Then him standing right in front of her, using his...

"What happened?" Her voice was much softer now that things were slowly returning to normal.

Matt sat on the side of her bed and snorted derisively. "What do you think happened? I nearly killed you and Caspar saved your life."

"Shouldn't it be the other way round?"

It didn't make sense that way. Matt wouldn't try to kill her, and Caspar... She inhaled sharply as the memories of the lava cave came back to her. Caspar had a connection to her previous incarnation. He'd shown a completely different side to the one he usually displayed to the world. A surprisingly heartbroken one. If what he'd told her was true, then her life was completely safe in his hands.

Which made things with Matt inherently more difficult.

"I wish it were," Matt said, in abject misery. He took her hand again and raised it to his lips, as if he needed the extra contact to reassure himself she was still alive. "I'm sorry, Sam. I just rushed in and... My anger was stronger than any reason."

"Were you angry with him or were you afraid for me?" she asked quietly, turning slightly to face him.

"At that moment it was the same." He pulled a face. "I'm sorry I ruined your birthday in the worst possible way."

"Maybe birthdays just aren't our thing," she joked quietly.

It was a ridiculous idea. She'd had a perfectly normal birthday last year. And nothing bad had happened at Fabian and Rachel's joint party in November. Still, she understood his reluctance. Almost getting killed made it second-to-last on her list of worst birthday parties.

Matt snorted in disgust. "Yeah, they don't seem to be happy occasions."

His self-loathing was getting to her. Gritting her teeth, Samantha sat up to face him. "Matt." He looked at her, the very picture of misery. "It was an accident."

"I lost control. Again," he added, so quietly she almost thought she'd imagined it.

Samantha's heart clenched, as it always did when he reminded her of the worst birthday party by a long shot. But it was an old pain, one she'd overcome and survived. She looked at the boy in front of her. It was hard to believe that what had happened to Daniel had only been a little over a year ago. The Matt from back then had been callous and haughty, too stubborn to even try to take responsibility. This one was piling it on, almost crumbling under the weight, for reasons far beyond his control.

"It's not the same," she found herself saying. "It's not your fault."

Matt shuddered as some of the weight lifted. Only a bit, and not even the biggest, but it was enough for him to let her in. As the tears began to roll, she pulled him to her chest and held him there, gently rubbing his back as he let go of all the anguish he'd endured since that fateful shot.

"It's alright," Samantha whispered into his hair. "I'm okay."

"You are?"

"I am."

Part 2

Spiders & Poison

Rachel

The Greenvalley Forest was an eerie grey-blue instead of its usual vibrant green. Not a single bird was singing, and no insects were munching on the leaves. Trees and bushes were covered in glistening grey veils.

Spiderwebs, Rachel thought, as she followed the others deeper into the darkness.

Suddenly there was a loud clicking noise behind her. Rachel spun around and found herself face to face with a giant spider, easily as big as her room at home. Its barrel-shaped, blood-red, shiny body rested on eight jointed legs covered with barbed bristles. A pair of antennae protruding from between eight iridescent compound eyes probed the air, as if sniffing for scent. Two powerful venomous claws protruded from beneath the armoured black head, from which sizzling yellowish venom dripped onto the ground.

Rachel recoiled in horror as her friends attacked the spider. Then things moved quickly. Matt shot energy at the big legs, but it bounced off, Samantha was thrown to the ground, and Lucille was stabbed in the stomach. Rachel picked up a crossbow from the ground and was aiming it at the spider when Jan jumped in front of it.

"Don't you dare!" he hissed, then grew eight legs and eight compound eyes until he looked like a grotesque baby spider.

Meanwhile Lucile screamed in agony, and the spider clicked its claws, all eight eyes focused on Rachel.

Her own scream mingled with Lucille's, then drowned it out, until it was the only sound in her empty room.

"Did you have a nightmare, Miss Rachel?" Hugo's silvery form floated in front of Rachel's eyes as she slowly realised it had only been a dream.

Rachel wiped the sweat from her face and turned her face up to check the dreamweb above her bed. It was glowing softly, but there were no silver beads falling from the feathers. "If it was a nightmare, the dreamweb would have caught it. Or at least weakened it."

Hugo paled even more than usual. "What else could it be?"

The answer made Rachel shudder. "A vision."

Her door opened and her father's head appeared. "Hey, Bug, everything okay? We heard you scream."

We. Her father wasn't supposed to be here, but just as Hugo had said, her parents had found each other again. A fact Rachel still didn't know how to feel about. On the one hand, her parents could do whatever they wanted. On the other, she felt cheated. All the drama, the neglect, the pain... Even Nico's death could have been avoided if they'd stayed together in the first place.

"Just a nightmare," Rachel suggested, borrowing from Hugo, who had become invisible the moment her father had appeared. "You can go back to whatever it is you two are doing."

"Rachel." Her father looked suitably guilty.

She crossed her arms over her chest and braced herself. "Why now? What changed?"

He raised an eyebrow. "We've changed." His posture loosened and he took a step into her room. "Look, Bug. I know it's not fair. It wasn't planned."

"Neither was I."

His face froze for a moment and he held his breath. When he let it out again, pain flashed across his face. "Rachel, you and your brother may not have been planned, but you were always wanted."

She rubbed her face, well aware she was using this argument to distract herself from the horrifying vision. It was too late to care, she told herself. She was an adult now, and had learnt to roll with the punches. "Is this more than just a nostalgic fling?"

Her father looked down at the floor and inhaled sharply before answering. "It's a little too early to tell at this point. I'd like to think it's more, but I'd say we're both being careful not to fall too far too fast at this point. I know it doesn't help you, but you should know we're both being careful."

"Don't want another unplanned pregnancy."

"That's not what I... Can we talk about this when it's not one o'clock in the morning? Maybe all three of us?"

And maybe when her heart wasn't racing from the horrible images in her mind and the fear that accompanied them. "Sure, that's probably a good idea. And for the record, I'm fine with it. I'm just... surprised."

"Fair enough." He nodded at the dreamweb. "I hope that thing works better for you for the rest of the night."

"That would be nice."

"You want to talk about it?"

Rachel shook her head. She would definitely talk about it, but not with him. "I'm fine. Sleep well."

"Good night, Bug." With a final smile, her father left, closing the door behind him.

As soon as he was gone, Hugo reappeared. "Are you all right, Miss Rachel?"

"No," she replied with a huff. "But I'm not the one you need to worry about."

She told the others about the vision as soon as they all came together in their German class. Mr Zobel had them working on their group presentation on post-war poetry, which allowed them to talk without drawing attention in class.

"Yeah, but don't you think we would've noticed if a giant spider had taken up residence in the Greenvalley Forest?" Fabian asked doubtfully.

Matt made a face. "Does it have to be a spider?"

"Would you prefer a giant worm instead?" Lucille joked, making Matt shudder and everyone else laugh.

Always the one to tackle a problem head on, Samantha asked, "Rachel, are you able to determine *when* a vision comes true?"

"It's not as specific as I'd like, but I've got a feeling it's pretty imminent."

Fabian groaned. "Looks like we'll have to skip the study group this afternoon and go monster hunting instead."

Samantha rolled her eyes and elbowed him. "As if you cared that much about study group."

"It's a bit like being caught between a rock and a hard place, I have to admit."

Again, they all chuckled. Mr Zobel looked over, and Samantha immediately made some notes on their poster.

In the silence that followed, Rachel recalled all the details of her vision and her amusement faded. She nudged Lucille gently. "I think it'd be better if you sat this one out."

"What? Why?"

"Can't *I* sit this one out?" Matt whined, earning himself a kick in the shin from Samantha. "Ouch." The look he gave her in return was nothing short of smouldering.

Rachel noticed some colour creeping into Samantha's cheeks and shook her head. There were more important things she had to deal with. "I mean it, Lucille. The spider got you badly in my vision. I didn't see you get up after it stabbed you in the stomach."

Lucille tried to smile but her pale face betrayed her. Nervously, she ran her fingers through her hair. "But you woke up soon after, didn't you?" When Rachel nodded, she seemed to gain confidence. "There you go. If you'd stayed with the vision, I'd have jumped right back up. Besides, Jan turned into a baby spider and that's not going to happen, so let's not take it all at face value."

"I don't know," Samantha said softly. "If Rachel saw it, I'd be careful. Look, we'll probably be fine with just the five of us. Why don't you enjoy the afternoon and relax a bit?"

"You could study for finals," Fabian suggested jokingly, not winning any brownie points with Lucille.

Matt nodded solemnly. "If Rachel saw it in her vision, I'd take her seriously. With spiders involved, three times more." He shuddered again.

"I hate to interrupt what I'm sure is a fascinating discussion about arachnoids, but you have five minutes until your presentation." Mr Zobel had suddenly appeared behind them and looked at them disapprovingly.

Immediately, the five of them returned to their work and Samantha began to speed write on their poster.

Lucille

Lucille would much rather have joined her friends on the spider hunt than study alone in the sunny parlour. With exams starting in two weeks, she should've welcomed the opportunity, but as the afternoon wore on her concentration wavered, and she found herself checking her phone more than making notes.

Any hope for a productive study session was completely dashed when Linda entered the room with Albert and a woman Lucille didn't recognise. The group barely seemed to register her presence as Linda showed them around.

"I want this turned into a jungle set."

Lucille raised her head and frowned at her stepmother. Had she really just said the word "jungle"?

"You know, one of those indoor playgrounds," Linda clarified. "Pascal wants to have his party in one of those, but with all those germs flying around, I don't want him going there. So, we'll build a temporary one here. I expect top quality, of course."

"Of course." The woman nodded. "If you send me the room specs, I'll have the designer on it this afternoon."

Linda laughed. "Wonderful. Albert will send you whatever you need. He'll take you to the kitchen so you can have a look. I want the catering done from there, so it's all fresh."

"If you'll follow me." Albert led the woman outside.

The door had barely closed behind them when Lucille took a deep breath. "May I ask why you're turning our parlour into an indoor playground?"

"It's only temporary, my dear. We'll donate it all after the party."

"Party? What kind of party?"

Linda smiled and came closer, her fingers wiping an imaginary speck of dust from the back of a chair. "Your brother's birthday is in six weeks' time. He's never really celebrated before, so I want to make sure it's the perfect children's party."

Something twisted in Lucille. She and Linda were getting on much better these days, but that didn't erase the years of hurt between them.

"The perfect children's party? I thought that meant high tea with a white lace dress that couldn't get dirty."

Admonished, Linda pouted as she was reminded of the first party she'd thrown for Lucille, four months after she'd come into her life. "I thought you'd like to spend the day like a proper lady."

"I was seven! And all my guests were grown-up friends of yours. You didn't even notice I retired to the house after a while." She'd spent most of that birthday crying in her room, missing her grandma and her real mum—and her dad, who'd been away for the day. "The following year I got money for my bank account. 'Investment is worth more than a frivolous party'," she said, imitating the words that had been imprinted into her memory.

Linda had the grace to look aghast. "I knew nothing about children. Your father always left everything to me when it came to you."

"A tragic mistake."

Lucille had to remind herself that her father had been the real problem here. But Linda hadn't exactly made an effort. Nothing like this, that much was certain.

Linda's fingers tightened around the back of the chair. "Lucille, I know I haven't been the best mother. You deserved better, but I was younger, inexperienced. I want you to know that I've learnt a lot since then."

Lucille grimaced, unable to push the hurt back where it had come from. "Well, isn't that great? You can be the best mother to Pascal now."

"Is that so wrong? I want to do better."

"No, it's perfect," Lucille said bitterly. She grabbed her study cards and stuffed them into her bag. "After all, you got to choose him. Me, on the other hand... You had to work with what you got. Oh, and while Pascal's birthday is in six weeks, mine's in three."

Her head held high, Lucille stalked out of the room, ignoring Linda's horrified face. If she had to choose between giant spiders and childhood disappointment, the spiders would come first. Besides, she really felt like stabbing something.

She made it to the other side of the town just as the others had gathered behind the Magic Circle. Samantha was checking her bag of potions while Rachel shouldered a crossbow. Matt had his sword at the ready and Jan was stretching, as if he was planning to use karate moves on the spider.

Fabian was the first to notice her, his eyes widening in shock. "Lucille. What are you doing here?"

"I know, I know—you said I shouldn't come—but I'll be careful and stay in the back. You can lead from the front."

As expected, he cringed at the suggestion.

"I'm not sure about this." Samantha looked at her with worry. "What changed your mind?"

"Linda." Lucille rolled her eyes. "Please. I need to hit something."

"Good luck with that from the back," Jan joked.

Lucille snorted in amusement. "Hitting it with a spell counts, too." She noticed Rachel biting her lip and Matt frowning. "Relax, guys. I promise not to do anything rash."

It was a tall order, but fortunately her friends didn't put up much of a fight and got going instead. Lucille followed as promised.

Up front, Jan bumped into Matt as they entered the forest. "Are you sure you'll be able to handle looking at that spider?"

"Spiders aren't insects," Fabian argued from behind them.

Matt still shuddered. "But they crawl the same way."

When Jan raised an eyebrow at him, his shoulders relaxed.

"It'll be fine. One shot of energy and the spider's done for, anyway."

Lucille still remembered their encounter with the wyrm in the mines. Matt had frozen at the sight of it, just like he'd frozen in the zoo. If anyone needed to worry about getting accidentally stung, it was him.

They'd been walking under the trees for twenty minutes when Samantha suddenly halted. "I feel something."

"Could you be a little more specific?" Jan joked.

Samantha's eyes widened. "It's magic. Someone's been weaving webs all over the place."

Lucille tried to catch sight of one of the webs Rachel had described in her dream, but she couldn't see anything. The only thing that had changed was the fading sun.

"Someone or something?" Fabian pointed to the left and Lucille did a double take.

When Rachel had said giant spider, she hadn't thought it would be *that* big. The spider rose up on its legs from a depression near them, and it kept rising until Lucille could have walked underneath it without touching its abdomen. The legs alone were a nightmare, with their hardened bristles and barbs. The huge compound eyes and clicking claws ripped a scream from her throat.

She wasn't the only one affected by the sight. Matt had started breathing sharply. "That's impossible."

"What is?" Jan hissed, a hint of nervousness in his voice.

"That's an adult Carrax Arachna. They nest in the deepest parts of the Dûr Lôrac. Ashuan's air and light should be toxic to it."

Now that he'd said it, Lucille noticed how unnaturally dark the hollow was. As if the sunlight had been filtered through heavy webs.

Jan chuckled. "Why don't you tell that to the spider? Maybe it'll accept that it should be dead and fall over."

Lucille grimaced, not feeling amused in the slightest at the sight of the spider. Especially not when it made an impossibly high-pitched sound and began to wave its front legs in the air, as if challenging them to a fight.

"It's seen us," Samantha whispered.

Next to her, Rachel turned. "Run!"

But before they could take another step, the spider catapulted itself into the air and landed in the middle of them, almost crushing Fabian.

The water mage rolled to the side then came to a halt against a tree, puffing and huffing.

Lucille screamed as the spider waved a hairy leg in front of her face, just before Jan grabbed her arm and pushed her back. "Stay back," he hissed, stepping in front of her.

Panicked, she stumbled back, and for a moment she regretted coming out here. What had she been thinking?

She turned around, ready to run, when she suddenly hit something sticky. Disgust rolled off her body in waves as she realised she'd walked straight into one of those magical spider webs. Lucille couldn't see them, but the adhesive was strong enough to keep her leg suspended in mid-air. Was this how she was going to die? Caught in a web like an overgrown fly?

Behind her, Samantha screamed as she fell over a root and was trampled by the spider. Matt was at her side in an instant, but the spider only needed to lift one leg to slam him into a tree. Groaning, Matt slid down the bark, not far from Lucille.

Then Fabian was at her side, spraying her face with water to free her from the web. It gave just enough for Lucille to rip her head and one shoulder free. Fabian grabbed her hand and pulled until she was loose, and they tumbled to the ground.

Lucille gasped as she hit the ground. "Thanks." But when she tried to get up, she found her limbs were still covered in spiderwebs and she was unable to move. And now they were clinging to Fabian, too.

Another scream caught in her throat as the spider crawled past them. Jan kicked it in the stomach, but he could've just as easily kicked a tree for all it did. The arachnid didn't care about anything but its victim in front of it.

"Matt, move!" Lucille cried.

The monster kept moving until it was right on top of Matt, and still Matt just stared, his eyes wide. Its antennae moved over Matt's face almost lovingly as it lowered its heavy bottom. A previously hidden stinger emerged from its rear, aimed at Matt's chest. But just before it stung him, the spider reared up, screeching.

A crossbow bolt protruded from one of its eyes, sent there by Rachel, who stood behind the tree, her arms shaking as she reset.

Shaken from his stupor, Matt fired black energy straight at the spider's abdomen. Instead of splitting it open, the magic was lost in the hairy leather.

Samantha skidded to a halt beside Lucille and Fabian and began weaving at record speed. "The spider webs are magic. That's what makes them so strong and invisible. Hold still while I untangle the threads."

"Could you hold the lecture and hurry?" Fabian hissed, his gaze racing to the spider that had left Matt alone and was now coming for them.

Its venomous claws dripped as it crawled across the forest floor. Where the venom hit moss, it shrivelled instantly. Lucille swallowed hard. She knew she needed to cast a spell, but her mind was blank. She couldn't even remember the name of her fireball.

Just before the spider reached them, Matt appeared at their side and sliced through its legs with his sword. Or at least he tried, because the sword got stuck into the first leg it touched. Wide-eyed, Matt put his foot against it and pulled.

"Watch out!" Samantha cried as Fabian shot water into the spider's eyes.

Matt rolled to the side, but a leg caught his arm and ripped it open with its barb. He gasped in pain, then scrambled to his feet as the spider tried to lower itself onto him again.

The water pushed the spider away long enough for Samantha to unravel the web, but it didn't hurt it any more than Matt's energy had. So far, only the eyes had proved to be a weakness.

Samantha pulled Lucille up and grabbed her shoulders. "You have to go. Remember Rachel's vision."

"We all have to go," Lucille shouted back.

Just then, they heard Jan yell. Their heads whipped around in time to see him grab hold of one of the legs, despite the barbs, and pull himself up. Though his hand was bleeding, he managed to land on top of the spider, his feet sinking into its fur.

"Is this his spider moment?" Fabian asked doubtfully.

"Probably." Lucille took a moment to centre herself. The fog in her mind had lifted with the cobwebs and she mentally catalogued her spells and what she knew about the spider. A fireball would probably singe a few hairs, but not penetrate the skin. Her usual tour de force, her black magic arrows, would probably be as ineffective as Matt's natural magic.

The eyes, she thought. The eyes were the key. What had Matt said?

Jan kicked the spider's head with little effect. "Rachel, throw me the—"

The spider bucked suddenly and Jan was thrown off its back, straight into Matt's arms. They both went down in a heap and the spider hurried to get its body on top of them. The terrifying stinger came out again. A crossbow bolt sank into the fur, missing the eyes by an arm's length.

The eyes, Lucille thought. They were the spider's weakness. Not just because they were soft where everything else was hard leather, but because the spider was used to the dark. *Ashuan's light should be toxic to it.*

"Erit Lux!"

Blinding light flooded the forest and the spider screeched nauseatingly high. Lucille blinked against her own spell, trying to make out the monster as it tried to cover its eyes with its legs.

It was working. It was—

"Lucille, no!" Rachel cried, but it was too late.

Instead of fleeing, the spider jumped again. This time it landed on top of Lucille, sinking its venomous claws into her stomach. Instantly, fire raced through her body, consuming her soul as she fell headfirst into darkness.

Fabian

In the end, it was Samantha who'd sent the spider fleeing by destroying one of the light-blocking webs above its lair. But by then it had been too late. Lucille had been stung and wouldn't respond to any of their attempts to rouse her. Jan had nearly exhausted himself trying to heal her, but while he'd managed to stop the bleeding and heal some of the internal damage, he hadn't been able to counter the venom.

Now Lucille was in a coma in hospital and they had to go back to school as if nothing had happened. What should've been a distraction failed when two classes were cancelled due to staffing problems. With rain pouring down outside, half the year group had gathered in the cafeteria to study for finals or just goof off.

The four of them sat at a table with their books in front of them, but not even Samantha did much more than stare at her study cards without even moving the stack. Meanwhile, Fabian was staring at one of the empty chairs around the table that should've been Lucille's.

"I don't know why she was even there," he said, when the silence hanging over their heads had become unbearable. "She was supposed to stay home."

Samantha raised her eyebrows at him, looking as if she hadn't slept an hour last night. "You know Lucille."

"She wouldn't listen to me," Rachel whispered. Her face looked ashen, as if she blamed herself for Lucille's fate.

Fabian rubbed his face. "First Sam, now Lucille. Why are we even bothering with these exams? We'll all be dead by the end of the year, anyway." As his anger rose, so did he. "Fuck school. I'm going home." Jan had the right idea.

Samantha's hand shot out and grabbed his wrist. "And what are you going to do there?"

"Scour books, kill the spider..." He shrugged helplessly. "Just whatever makes sense."

"Very little," Samantha said with a weary sigh. "I went through the books last night. It didn't help."

Matt glared at the table, his mouth a thin line of anger. "My sword should have been more effective." He looked at Samantha, only then noticing that Fabian had stood up. "What are you doing?"

"Nothing," Fabian spat, falling back into his chair as Samantha let go.

Matt dismissed him immediately. "It's the sword that broke the world, right? But it couldn't even cut through a hairy spider's leg."

"Maybe you didn't use enough force, paralysed as you were," Fabian shot back, attracting everyone's attention.

"I wasn't paralysed," Matt growled.

"Guys!" Rachel looked at them in horror, then nodded towards the other tables.

Fabian rolled his eyes and relaxed his shoulder muscles. He wasn't angry with Matt. Not really. His water hadn't had any effect on the spider, either. Still, he'd bet his right hand that Matt's brothers had something to do with a spider from Hell nesting in their forest.

"I can at least answer that," Samantha said, distracting Matt.

"Why my sword was so useless?" he asked, surprised.

Samantha nodded. "I can't count how many times I've read the parts about our emblems. The Sword of Amain has the *potential* to cut through anything, even divine magic, but not in this state."

"And what state is that?"

Fabian leaned forward, sharing Matt's curiosity. "I thought it was sharp."

"It *is* sharp, just..." Samantha took a deep breath, sorting her thoughts before presenting them. "The sword and the other emblems are connected. It says in the book that the others have to be awakened before their power can charge the sword. The more emblems that are awakened, the more powerful it'll be. We probably only need one or two to cut through the spider's leg."

Confused, Fabian leaned back again. "To wake Lucille, I have to wake my feather first?"

"Awaken," Rachel corrected quietly.

Matt folded his arms and snorted. "I guess you better hurry up and *awaken* them then."

Rachel sighed. "Like that would help Lucille."

"It would help a little. If it's the poison that's got her in a coma, I need someone to cut off the poison glands," Samantha pointed out.

Fabian almost rolled his eyes again, but decided it wouldn't serve any of them. "How do we do that?"

"We need to use them more and... somehow become one with them."

Fabian snorted. "Should I grow wings now?" The thought was ridiculous. As cool as flying was, he'd never sprout wings like a bird.

Samantha looked so tired as she replied, "I don't know. There are no step-by-step instructions on how to awaken the emblems. I mean, *becoming one* surely means embodying the different aspects of power, but my emblem is the power of change. What should I change? Myself? The world?" She fell silent.

Meanwhile, Matt searched Rachel's and Fabian's faces. "Devotion. Hope." He snorted. "Maybe we just have to hope Lucille gets better."

"Don't you think I'm already doing that?" Fabian shot back.

"Guys!" This time it was Samantha who shouted loudly enough to make several heads turn in their direction. She quickly lowered her voice. "Fighting won't get us anywhere."

Just then Cheryl, Ani, and Jennifer walked past. Cheryl glanced at them and snorted. "Look at them. Losing their minds without their ant queen."

Fabian was on his feet in an instant. "Say that again!" he shouted at Cheryl as Matt jumped up to hold him down.

In response, the sprinklers above their heads turned on, dousing the entire cafeteria. Cheryl and her friends squealed, and the whole hall emptied as students grabbed their belongings and ran for cover in the foyer.

Matt let go of Fabian, his arm slowly sinking as he looked at him with sympathy, while Fabian just stood there in the artificial rain, feeling it seep into his clothes. If hope alone was the key, Lucille would have been awake by now.

Jan

Jan returned home from orientation to find Anne and Matt waiting outside his house. He'd spent the whole day freaking out about his schedule and the amount of work that lay ahead of him, while still trying to sneak off to see how Lu was doing, and had been looking forward to some quiet at home. Especially as his chest had been hurting all day, as if he'd suffered a particularly bad asthma attack.

"What's on fire?"

"Lucille," Matt replied promptly. "Well, she's not on fire, I hope, but Sam needs the venom glands to try and cure her, so I'm going to go and kill the spider."

"Alone?"

Matt spread his hands. "I'm here, not in the woods, right?"

Anne giggled, but the amusement quickly faded when she noticed how serious they both looked. "Is everything okay?"

"No." Jan walked past them to open his door. "I'm coming, but I'm going to need food, so get yourselves com—"

"Jan is back!" Neve flew towards him and jumped into his arms without warning. He barely caught her and she responded by nuzzling her head against his chest.

"Ow... not there."

"Does Jan have a boo-boo?" Before he could stop her, Neve was blowing ice on his chest.

He quickly put her down. "That's too cold. Don't worry, Neve. I'm fine."

Matt followed him inside, barely glancing at the snow witch. "You hurt yourself?"

"A big fat spider sat on me, remember?" It'd happened after the spider had reared up and thrown him into Matt. For a moment they'd both been trapped under the spider and Jan had thought he was going to meet his maker, when Lu's light had saved them.

Matt shuddered and had no more questions.

It was a testament to how starved Jan was that he only noticed how strange Anne's presence was now. He turned around immediately. "What are you doing here? You're not invited to the spider hunt." Her spending time with Caspar had been bad enough.

Anne pretended to sulk for a moment. "Don't worry. You can keep your giant spiders to yourself. I just... I thought we could talk more about Hanna."

"Now?" Jan had a growing suspicion that Anne was a bit lonely now that Meg had left and had nothing better to do than visit her brother after school. But then he remembered something else. "Go and talk to Matt about her while I get something to eat. He's supposed to be her reincarnation."

Anne spun around with a heavy frown. "*You're* the reincarnation of the goddess of life?"

"And the god of youth. Or rather their human counterparts." Matt looked at Jan in confusion. "What's this about?"

"Your brother." The word came with a lot of bile and Jan shuddered.

Immediately, Matt's eyebrows shot up. "Caspar? Did he do something to you?"

Anne sighed, seemingly unaware of how close she'd come to a painful end. "He wasn't hostile or anything. He healed Samantha and asked me to help. And when we were done, he told me he saw Hanna's blessing in me. So, what's this about reincarnation?"

"Oh dear."

Jan left it to Matt to explain, as he had more experience with the concept, and went into the kitchen to make himself a bowl of ramen. It was quick, easy, and—above all—cheap. Perfect for his limited income.

When he returned to the living room, Matt was still talking about Hanna. "She was like a warrior princess, very skilled with a sword, and betrayed her father when he allied himself with the Muron mages."

"That's the bad guys," Jan quipped between slurps. He hadn't bothered to read Chay's book, but he'd gotten an abridged version from Samantha. The truth was, the whole reincarnation thing still weirded him out. What did it matter who his predecessors had been eons ago?

Meanwhile, Anne was lapping it all up. "And she stole the sword for Kairos."

"She did. And then they defeated Draken together, which is why they became gods after their deaths."

"Draken?" Anne asked, her eyes wide with wonder. "That was the evil mage who tried to take all magic for himself, right?"

Jan cleared his throat. "I'm almost done eating if you want to wrap it up."

Matt nodded at him. "Right, if you want the whole story, ask Samantha. She's safeguarding the book and knows a lot more about the war that broke the world. As for Hanna, she's one of the more popular goddesses. She gives life, so a lot of healers or pregnant women pray to her. In some regions, she's also worshipped as a fertility goddess. Even Hell has a Hanna temple, which is strangely ironic when you think about it. Their priests are very particular when it comes to worshipping life."

"Let me guess, a lot of survival of the fittest down there?" Jan asked, lifting the bowl to slurp down the liquid.

"Pretty much. They honour those who cling to life. But if you happen to get yourself killed..." Matt shrugged with a pained grimace. "Just means you weren't blessed by Hanna."

Anne swallowed hard. "Blessed by Hanna. That's what your brother said. He also said I had all this untapped potential, but I don't know what that means. What does it entail to be a priestess of Hanna?"

"Honestly, I don't know. A lot of them are healers, which"—he nodded at Jan as he wiped a few droplets from his face—"seems to run in the family. But they also look after the plants and animals. I suppose it's a very life-affirming religion. I've never been a follower."

Jan chose this moment to clap his hands, snapping them out of their discussion. "Which is great, because we are now going to unaffirm the life of this spider."

Anne wrinkled her nose in disgust. "Unaffirm is not a word." She dropped it quickly, though, and her eyes lit up. "Can I come?"

"No."

She pouted immediately. "Fine, spiders aren't really my thing anyway. But next time—"

"No."

Jan noticed Matt was hiding a chuckle behind his hand. "You may laugh, but my sister isn't like yours."

"Which one?" he shot back with a sly smile, reminding Jan that while they'd only met Menuha, Matt had many more sisters who didn't care about the human world.

He rubbed his chest, still feeling a bit tight, and nodded towards the door. "Let's get this over with. You can stay and play with Neve if you want," he said, but Anne shook her head, much to Neve's dismay.

"Sorry, Neve, I have to go home and do my homework. I have two essays due tomorrow and I haven't even started the first."

"Neve doesn't like essays," the snow witch said with a straight face. "Neve prefers short stories."

Anne grinned at her. "You and me both. Maybe you can help with my homework when we have another short story unit."

Jan's response was a mere snort. The only short stories Neve had ever heard were those by Jonathan Blackstone. He doubted the little snow witch would be any good at the kind of analyses Anne had to do.

"Great plan. Now let's go and evict that overgrown spider."

Although the sun was low in the sky, Jan's eyes were itching. That's what he got for working in a hospital now. He'd probably caught a case of pinkeye or something stupid like that.

Matt had drawn his sword and was stalking through the forest as if the spider was hiding behind a puny birch tree.

"Relax, man. The Arachna is far away." Jan strolled behind him, not feeling the same urgency as yesterday.

Matt scoffed at him. "You sure about that?"

"If it was close, it would have attacked us by now."

"That's helpful."

Jan rolled his eyes, still finding Matt's vigilance absurd. "That thing can jump several metres. As far as we know, it's also an excellent climber and will drop on us from the trees."

It was almost comical the way Matt suddenly looked up.

"I'm kidding!" Jan snorted as Matt glared at him. "Hey, you asked me to distract the spider while you cut off its venomous claws. I deserve a bit of fun first."

"It'll be fine."

"That's what Lu said."

Another glare shot in his direction. "In case you weren't paying attention, I'm doing this for her."

"No, you're doing it for Samantha who's doing it for Lu. I know you." Jan grinned at him, earning another glare. "Fine, be like that. But since we still have some ground to cover, how do you think the spider got here in the first place?"

"Someone obviously brought it here."

"Your brothers, I suppose." Why had he even asked?

Matt spat on the forest floor. "This stinks of Caspar. If anyone keeps dangerous pets, it's him."

"As opposed to the guy who would've loved a hellhound?"

"Hellhounds are a hundred times better than a Carrax Arachna." Judging by his tone, Matt was deadly serious, as if both of them hadn't tried to kill them equally. "But Caspar's definitely a spider guy. I think he has several arachnids in his precious little guard."

Jan snorted. "Charming guy. Too bad they didn't keep him in isolation longer."

"I wish. Then again..."

"Yeah, yeah, he healed Samantha." Jan shook his head. "That doesn't change the fact he's a psycho, you know?"

Matt scoffed at him. "You're barking up the wrong tree. That's why he and the spider are such a good match. They're both disgusting, repulsive—"

"Hey, the spider's not that bad."

Matt narrowed his eyes. "Is that supposed to be a joke?"

Jan rubbed his chest, trying to ease the discomfort. "Of course it was a joke." It hadn't come across as one because everything annoyed him. The pain in his chest, Matt's hyper-vigilance, the forest, the too-bright sun. "Why do we have to do this in daylight?"

"You want to hunt a Carrax Arachna in the dark? Do you value your life at all?" Matt shuddered, but then his eyes narrowed. "What's wrong with you?"

"Nothing," Jan bit back.

"I'm serious. You're acting weird. And what the hell's wrong with your eyes?"

Jan rubbed them in response, trying to shield them from the sunlight. "It's too bright."

"It's a cloudy day and the sun is already behind the mountain." Matt's frown deepened. "The spider did something to you, didn't it? When you fell on me yesterday—"

"Leave the spider out of it!" Jan snapped back. Realising how ridiculous he sounded, he cleared his throat. "We're close now. There are the webs."

Matt turned his head. "I can't see anything."

To Jan, the webs were undeniable. Whole trees were covered in them. The deeper they went, the more the webs shielded them from the light. Soon, the blissful darkness soothed Jan's irritated eyes.

They continued on until they suddenly heard a familiar clicking sound. Excitement coursed through Jan's veins and he turned his head to the side, hoping to see the spider. Instead, they found Balthasar leaning against a tree, playing with a small toy that mimicked the pleasant clicking sound.

Matt had drawn his sword and pointed it at Balthasar. "You?"

"Who were you expecting?" Balthasar asked, amused.

"Caspar, of course. How did you get your hands on a Carrax Arachna? You hardly ever go to the Dûr Lôrac."

Balthasar grinned as he put his toy away. "Naturally, I borrowed it from Caspar. I offered him the chance to come since the spider's weaving a small extension of Hescaryn, but he's become disappointingly lazy."

"Sure. He's too lazy to come here himself so he's lending you his Arachna." Matt didn't sound like he believed any of it.

"His *pregnant* Arachna." Balthasar chuckled softly. "Shouldn't you be carrying her brood by now? You know, preparing for a few hundred Arachna babies? I've made sure to give her your scent as a worthy candidate."

As Matt gasped and turned pale, Jan frowned. "Are you planning to make him a spider daddy?"

"Don't worry, Melchior. The process doesn't require any sexual effort on your part. It is possible, however, that you won't survive the hatching process. In fact, I hope you don't."

Balthasar opened his little toy again and made a series of clicking noises that echoed in Jan's chest. He knew the spider was coming even before he heard the scuffling sounds in the undergrowth.

"Just stay still," Balthasar advised as the spider appeared behind him. "It'll be over quickly."

"Never!" Matt spat, almost doubling over. "I'd rather rip out every single leg with my bare hands before I let it touch me."

Jan growled. "Don't you dare."

Instead of backing down, Matt raised his sword and roared. Then he lunged at the spider.

In an instant, Jan was on his back, slamming him to the ground. Matt tried to throw him off, but Jan punched him in the face. As Matt's eyes widened, Jan put his hands on his neck and squeezed.

"Oh, dear," Balthasar mused unaffectedly. "Looks like the Arachna has already chosen another mate. I have to admit, though, this version has its charms."

Matt managed to break free of his grip, but he still looked stunned. Like easy *prey*. Jan didn't wait for him to recover and started throwing punches. Instead of fighting back, Matt just tried to defend himself, blocking Jan's punches left and right while trying to roll out from under him.

"Go on, he's threatening your brood," Jan heard in his ear, and panic filled him. Nothing was allowed to threaten the brood. Fortunately, the spider was now approaching, its soothing clicks promising safety.

Matt grabbed Jan's arms and rolled them both over just as the spider sunk its venomous claws into the ground beside them. He raised his arm as he always did before shooting energy, and Jan quickly grabbed it. The black magic hit the tree Balthasar was leaning against instead, causing the older demon to retreat and disappear.

In that brief moment when Jan was distracted, Matt kicked him off and grabbed his sword. Once again, he aimed at the spider.

"Oh no you don't." Jan jumped up and put himself between the spider and Matt, spreading his arms.

"What the hell, Jan?"

"I won't let you hurt her!"

Behind him, the spider lifted a leg and gently stroked his cheek. At first, he shivered in pure bliss, but then reality crashed down on him and he felt a wave of nausea sweep over his body.

Matt leapt forward, grabbed his arm, and pulled him through the abstract space—away from his beloved.

Rachel

While Matt had promised to get the venom glands from the spider, Rachel, Samantha, Fabian, and Ophelia visited Lucille in hospital. The doctors had managed to stabilise her, but she was still in a coma, kept alive by a variety of machines.

Rachel sat by her bedside and held her hand. "Why did I have to be right about this?" She'd experienced many visions over the years, but this one took her right back to when Nico had died. She'd been terribly right then, too.

"She's not dead," Samantha offered, but her voice was far from certain.

"She's not waking up either," Fabian pointed out, causing Ophelia to stroke his arm in comfort.

Samantha groaned in frustration. "It must be the poison. According to the books, the poison of the Carrax Arachna is one of the strongest in all the worlds."

"But you'll find an antidote. Jan and Matt will get you a sample and then you'll work your magic and show up tomorrow with the antidote," Fabian said in a surprisingly cheerful voice.

"Is that your way of trying to awaken the Emblem of Hope?" Samantha asked doubtfully.

Rachel almost snorted. "You have to succeed."

This couldn't be the end of Lucille. As reckless as it had been to ignore a vision, Rachel had a feeling it wouldn't have made any difference. The visions came true, no matter how hard you fought them.

"I know," Samantha replied and Rachel immediately regretted the pressure she'd put on her when she saw the pained look on her face.

The last time she'd demanded a cure from Samantha... Rachel closed her eyes as images of blood soaking into purple flowers filled her mind.

The door opened and Linda de Cerque entered with a cup of coffee. She'd been the parent who'd come last night—apparently Lucille's father was on a business trip halfway around the world. It didn't look like Linda had left the hospital since then, her clothes slightly rumpled from sitting in the chair Rachel was currently occupying.

"Did she wake up?" Linda asked, a painful note of hope in her voice.

The four shook their heads and made room. Linda slipped into her designated seat after Rachel had vacated it and stroked Lucille's hand. "She needs to wake up, you know? The artificial coma was necessary, but they've brought her out of it, and Lucille should... She should wake up."

"I'm sure she will," Samantha said softly. "Her body just needs a little more time."

"I know she will," Linda replied absentmindedly, her focus entirely on Lucille.

Feeling as if they'd interrupted an intimate moment, the four of them left the room, then stood in the hallway, unsure whether to go or stay. Fabian hugged Ophelia as if his life depended on it, while Samantha opened her mouth several times to speak, but never said a word.

Meanwhile, Rachel replayed the scene in her mind. Lucille should have woken up, but she hadn't. She was in the deepest sleep Rachel had ever seen. Sleeping. Waking. *Dreaming.*

"I have an idea."

All three of them looked at her with tantalising hope. "You do?" Samantha asked.

"What you said at school about awakening our emblems. Maybe there is a way to use mine to help Lucille." Rachel bit her lip, unsure if she should continue. There was no indication her idea had any merit. "I'll visit Lucille in the dreamworld."

Ophelia raised an eyebrow. "To do what?"

"To tell her to wake up."

Rachel bypassed her parents and slipped into her bedroom. It was only five in the afternoon but she was practised enough to fall asleep on command. It was as if the dreamworld was pulling her there. This time, though, she had to be careful and make sure she was using her dreamweb to help her navigate what was sure to be a nightmare.

"I think you are taking an unnecessary risk," Hugo said in his genteel nasal voice. She'd discussed her plan with him, but hadn't found his approval.

"It's no different from any other time. Lucille may be asleep permanently at the moment, but she is asleep."

Hugo frowned and shook his head. "A coma is no normal sleep. You are planning to venture into her subconscious."

"Which can't be that different from the dreamworld. After all, what are dreams if not our subconscious thoughts?"

"Are you sure about that?" The frown got heavier and heavier.

Annoyed he would doubt her, Rachel lay on her bed. "I didn't ask your permission." She looked up at the dreamweb, swaying in the light breeze from her window, the knotted web swirling in and out of patterns.

"I..." Hugo seemed to grow for a moment, then deflated again. "Be careful, Miss Rachel."

She smiled, her consciousness already slipping away. "I will be."

The mesmerising pattern above helped her to fall asleep almost instantly, and soon she arrived in her meadow of dreams. As usual, walking among the dreams filled her with a confidence she often lacked in real life.

It wasn't difficult to find Lucille's dreams. Her friends were always close, and while most of them were awake, Lucille's flower was firmly closed—and completely covered in cobwebs.

"No surprise there," Rachel muttered.

Tentatively, she stretched out her fingers. Perhaps if she simply removed the webs, the flower would open and Lucille would wake up. But when her fingers touched the webs, they slipped right through. Whatever was holding the flower closed was inside the dream, not outside.

"It's different, you know?"

She smiled as she heard the familiar voice and didn't even have to look to see Nico. "I know."

"It's more intense, more real. The dreamworld is just an image of the turmoil inside us. It protects you from going too deep."

Rachel's resolve didn't waver. He wasn't warning her, just preparing her. "But I have to go deep. I have to face whatever's holding her captive down there."

"Good luck."

"You're not coming?" She'd hoped to have him with her when she ventured into Lucille's subconscious.

But Nico made a face. "It's no place for dreams." Then he faded like the dream he was.

Rachel took a deep breath, not that she needed to breathe in the dreamworld. It was only a familiar gesture that made her feel safer. Once more, she brought her fingers up to the covered flower, reached out to the dream behind it, and let it pull her inside.

When the sensation of crossing the boundary had faded, she found herself in a harsh, hostile area. Grey rocks were rising all around her, with only the flimsiest of vegetation clinging to the crevices. An icy wind blew and the sound of crashing waves filled the dream before her.

Rachel was standing beside a solitary tree. It was devoid of leaves, its bark old and crumbling. She gazed towards the horizon and found nothing but fog. "What a desolate place."

Lucille was all glitz and glamour, high drama and style. This was nothing like her.

"Lucille!" Her cry shot out into the landscape and returned to her with a faint echo, despite the lack of an echo chamber. It made the dream feel hollow, abandoned. "Where are you?"

Slowly, Rachel ventured into the dream, following the only path. It wasn't long before she came to a cliff. Below her, powerful waves crashed against the rock face, sending white billows high into the air.

Rachel wasn't usually squeamish about heights, but just looking at the ocean made her body feel light and fragile. At any moment the wind could pick her up and throw her into the rolling water.

"Don't tell me that's what they meant when they said you had to dive deep." Sometimes she hated how literal the dreamworld was.

She looked around, trying to find another way, but her surroundings were swallowed by the incoming fog. The only way forward was down.

The wind tugged at her impatiently, as if wondering what was taking her so long.

"This isn't real," Rachel told herself. "It's just a dream. I'm safe."

She just had to believe it hard enough, which was difficult with the wind pulling at her and the salt spray in her face. But the fog was getting closer, and she wasn't keen to find out what it would do if she let it swallow her up. With another useless deep breath, Rachel stepped off the ledge and *fell.*

Jan

One moment Jan and Matt were in the forest, facing the spider, the next they were falling into a field of snow, toppling a snowman. Cold spread beneath Jan and he blinked up at two ice-blue eyes. Neve.

"Jan has a door."

They were in his living room, though at the moment it looked more like Winter Wonderland—or Winter Nightmare Land after he and Matt had ruined it.

"What the hell was that?" Matt shouted at him. He was already staggering to his feet, brushing the snow off his clothes.

Jan felt irrational anger surge through him, but the snow helped keep it in check. Unfortunately, it did little to ease the discomfort in his chest. "What do you mean?"

"Your sudden passion for giant spiders." Matt calmed a little, worry replacing the conflicting emotions that had gripped him earlier. He still bore the bruises from Jan's punches, but the guilt didn't last as they were already starting to fade. "She got to you, didn't she? You're carrying her brood."

"That's ridiculous," Jan barked, then rubbed his chest again.

His chest.

He forced his fingers to unclench and pat his chest gently. His heart skipped a beat when he found a bump just above his ribs. It was shaped like a chicken egg, maybe a little smaller—or maybe not.

Nausea hit him as Matt's words—and Balthasar's from earlier—finally registered. He felt like he'd fallen headfirst into a nightmare. "I don't want any spiders to hatch out of me." He hated how whiny his voice sounded.

"Spiders don't belong in the house," Neve said wisely. "Jonathan always said a house should be clean."

Jan didn't pay much attention to her. "We have to get them out."

The room swayed as his mind circled around the idea of something living in his chest. Something with way too many legs, especially if they really were talking about hundreds of baby spiders.

"Maybe there's a way to cut the brood out or—"

Before he'd even thought about it, Jan was charging at Matt, driven by an immeasurable wrath. The half-demon was *not* going to hurt them.

Matt stepped aside, causing Jan to tumble into a second snow structure, much to Neve's dismay. The cold shocked Jan out of it and he scrambled to the nearest wall, trying to get as far away from Matt as possible.

"Looks like you're not a fan of killing the spider anymore," Matt said, his gaze full of horror.

Anger rose again but Jan forced it down. "Yes, yes, I am." With the wall at his back, he crawled further away. "It's not me. It's..." His breath caught in his throat as he realised where the anger was coming from. *"Them."*

"Neve doesn't like spiders." The snow witch half hid behind Matt's legs. She looked at Jan as if *he* were the monster.

"Them?" Matt asked, looking almost as pale as Neve.

"Her children," Jan hissed. A moment later he wondered why he was hissing.

Matt's gaze followed him as he moved along the wall. "Are they talking to you?"

Jan shook his head. There were no words in his mind. He couldn't even sense a presence. Just... anger. "No, but every time you talk about hurting their mother or them, I can't think straight." He stopped, horrified. "I tried to kill you." Just now and back in the forest.

"I noticed," Matt said in a terse but surprisingly calm voice. His gaze never left Jan, like a hunter zeroing in on his prey.

"I'm sorry," Jan said, but it felt performative, as if he knew he'd do it again if the situation demanded it.

Matt's face softened. "*I'm* sorry. Balthasar clearly intended for me to be the host. Unfortunately, he got you instead."

"We could kill him." The thought filled Jan with unprecedented eagerness. "I'm sure the spider wouldn't mind."

"But it won't stop the babies from hatching."

Jan made a face. He didn't want to be the hatching ground for a hundred baby spiders. Just the thought of thousands of legs crawling out of his chest filled him with nausea.

"Don't worry. I won't let you down." Matt approached slowly, putting Jan's nerves on edge. "We're staying here for now. Can't let you run off with the spider and elope."

"Thanks for the nightmare image." As horrible as the thought was, it was better than his own imagination.

Matt took another step. "We'll find a way. I promise."

Jan craned his neck back, as if that would keep his feelings at bay.

As Matt got even closer, he broke. In one swift movement, he shot past him and out of the room. "Just throwing up!" he shouted, before hurling himself into the downstairs bathroom.

After emptying his stomach into the toilet bowl and taking a long, hot shower, Jan looked into the steamy mirror. It was all a bad dream, he told himself. There was no way, a nest of spiders was growing in his chest.

Rachel's vision came back to him and he winced. She'd seen him turn into a spider in her dreams, and now he was destined to father a bunch.

Feeling another wave of nausea coming on, Jan clenched his fingers around the sink and took one deep breath after another. When he'd pushed the nausea aside, he wiped his forearm across the mirror and forced himself to look at his reflection.

The first thing he noticed was how red his eyes were. He'd always had a bit of hay fever, and it was certainly the season for it, but it had never been anything like this. His eyes couldn't stop watering, either, and they itched terribly.

There was a knock at the door. "Are you alright?"

Matt, the spider killer.

Jan's fingers gripped the sink again as he forced the words back into the angry turmoil they'd come from. Matt was on his side. He was his friend.

"I'll be out in a minute."

His gaze returned to the mirror, and this time they went deeper—to his chest. A red swelling rose just above his heart, definitely the size of an egg.

Jan let go of the sink with one hand and lifted it to the protrusion. Maybe he could heal himself? Treat it like a tumour.

He flinched as his fingers touched the egg, gingerly tracing it under his skin. It gave a little, as if it were a sac rather than a hardened egg. The thought of him pushing baby spiders back and forth made the bile rise in his throat.

Before he lost it again, Jan forced himself to dive in with his senses. The golden shimmer appeared, revealing a black growth with tendrils that reached deep into his skin. It was attached to him by countless hooks. And it was alive. Horribly, terrifyingly alive.

Jan rushed back to the toilet and vomited again, spewing until nothing came out but bile, then still gagged a few more times before he managed to regain control of his body. The egg in his chest didn't move, but it felt more alive by the second.

Tears streamed down his cheeks, whether from panic or the intensity of the artificial light, he couldn't tell. He pushed himself up and back in front of the mirror, but when he tried to touch the swelling, he couldn't bring himself to do it.

His breathing got harder and harder, his chest hurt and his eyes wouldn't stop itching. He was losing it. Quickly.

In a panic, Jan lunged at the light switch and slammed it down. Immediately, darkness enveloped him. And it was glorious. He could still see as much as before, but his eyes no longer hurt. Even his chest had eased.

Jan sank to the floor and hung his head between his legs. "Damn it, Rachel."

Samantha

After visiting Lucille in hospital and dropping Rachel at home, Samantha followed Fabian and Ophelia to the Magic Circle. They were still helping out as best as they could, but Caroline insisted they should use the time to study instead. Samantha hadn't been sure if Fabian's mum could handle being back, but for the last half hour in the shop, she'd seemed like her old self, catching up with every customer she hadn't seen for a while.

Ophelia took the afternoon shift at the café, leaving Samantha and Fabian to read monster books at a small table near the window. At first, they'd been researching the antidote, but then Matt had called and told them about Jan's predicament.

"'The brood of the Arachna matures in seven weeks'," Samantha read, then looked up at Fabian with relief. "That'll buy us some time at least." When Fabian raised his eyebrows in doubt, she lowered her eyes to read on before she got too carried away. "'After seven weeks, the swelling occupies the entire chest.' Ouch. 'Over the course of several hours, the swelling ruptures, releasing about fifty to seventy spiders, of which only two or three will reach adulthood'."

"Jan will love that," Fabian said, looking as disgusted as Samantha felt. "Is there any way to stop it?"

Samantha sighed and scanned the page for any useful information. The more she read, the less hope she had. "Not really. It says here: 'Soon after implantation, the sac tissue becomes tightly attached to the host's chest, and the lungs and arteries are tapped. After hatching, scar tissue remains to prevent haemorrhaging'."

"So, the host survives?"

"Looks like it." The silver lining faded as soon as she read the next paragraph. "At least until the baby spiders decide to eat them after hatching."

Fabian threw back his head and groaned. "This isn't fair. Jan is turning into spider food and Lucille is in a coma. How are we supposed to—?"

"Lucille is in a coma?"

They both spun around to find Philipp staring at them. He must have entered the shop and been sent their way by Caroline.

"Um, she..." Fabian started but couldn't finish the sentence.

Samantha took a deep breath before hurrying to get the words out, "Lucille was badly injured. She's fine now... I mean, they repaired the damage, but she's still in a coma to help her body heal."

"Which is the opposite of fine," Fabian muttered.

"Hope, Fabian, hope," Samantha hissed in annoyance. If ever an emblem was mismatched, it was his.

"Hey!" Philipp barked, snapping them out of their quarrel. "What happened?"

Samantha shifted uncomfortably in her chair. "We were attacked by a giant spider. Lucille wasn't supposed to be there—Rachel had a vision —but she's always been stubborn." She swallowed.

Lucille had said something about fighting with Linda. They'd never found out about what, but if the last two years had taught Samantha anything, it was that their relationship was fraught with tension and childhood trauma.

"She was poisoned by the spider and lost consciousness immediately. I'm sorry."

Philipp stared at her, a muscle in his face twitching. "Monsters are your strength, though, right? You can think of an antidote or a spell or something?"

Samantha shrugged helplessly. Matt hadn't managed to secure the poison for her, and now he was busy babysitting Jan, who'd discovered his passion for giant spiders. Without a chance to look at the poison, there was little Samantha could do.

"You can't give up!" Philipp huffed in disbelief. "Lucille said you were chosen or something, so act like it."

"Oh, shut up. Like you know anything about magic." Ophelia had come over and put her arms around Fabian protectively. "They're chosen to fight a great evil, not become miracle workers."

Fabian put a hand on her arm and leant into it, drawing some strength. "Thanks, Lia."

Philipp snorted. "I'm not surprised you don't care if someone's life is in danger. You'd probably sacrifice it yourself."

Ophelia gasped in outrage. "I care about Lucille."

"Hey, Lia didn't choose to sacrifice you," Fabian shot back.

"No, she chose you, but apparently you're into that." Philipp shook his head, dismissed them both, and turned to Samantha. "I'm assuming she's in hospital, since no one felt the need to inform me."

"Intensive care," Samantha replied quietly as guilt filled her. She hadn't even thought about Philipp before he'd burst into the shop.

He nodded sharply. "You have to find a solution to this." Then he turned on his heel and strode out, ignoring Fabian and Ophelia's twin glares.

"What an idiot," Fabian said as the chime above the door sounded a second time.

Samantha sighed. "He just found out his girlfriend is in a coma. *Our* friend." Philipp was right. They had to do something. She stood. "We've got to get the poison ourselves."

"Right now? Just the two of us?" Fabian asked, his eyes wide.

"Three," Ophelia reminded him, pointedly. "I'll come with you."

"Fine with me," Samantha said, "but I'm just going to get more books. There's no point facing the Arachna without more research. We have to find out how to kill it."

Fabian breathed a sigh of relief. He had really expected her to storm off into the forest in some desperate attempt to succeed where Matt had failed.

Samantha rolled her eyes and went to do some more research.

Three hours, twelve books, and four coffees later, they'd moved to Elda's library. The Magic Circle was closed now, and Elda didn't mind the late-night visit, even providing them with snacks and drinks. Samantha and her grandmother scanned book after book, while Fabian tried to study Biology, yawning frequently, and Ophelia had fallen asleep on his shoulder.

Samantha was about to give up when she spotted something. "Here!"

Fabian started so much he woke Ophelia. "You scared me."

"Did you find something?" Elda asked.

Excited, Samantha nodded. "I did." Everyone was all ears. "What we need is a basilisk. Basilisks and arachnids are mortal enemies."

"A basilisk," Fabian repeated. "And how are we going to get one? Buy one on eBay maybe?"

"How should I know?" Samantha shot back in a whiny voice. She rubbed her face wearily, knowing full well he was right. It had been a long day after a very long night.

Elda reached out and rubbed her shoulder. "Now, now, I'm sure we can find another solution."

"Please," Fabian said. "Because I don't like this idea of adding a second monster. We'd have to get rid of the basilisk, too. I bet they have their own special poison. So, it's not really an improvement."

"Ishtar's chariot is pulled by two basilisks," Ophelia interjected, sounding more alert now.

Fabian frowned at her. "And you're going to call her and borrow her pets?"

"It doesn't work that way," Ophelia laughed, apparently finding Fabian's pessimism amusing. "But with any luck, I might be able to summon a shadow basilisk."

"You know, I've always thought that the words 'luck' and 'basilisk' shouldn't be used together," Fabian mused.

Ophelia elbowed him, though she still chuckled. "Theoretically, it could work."

"Love the confidence."

Samantha couldn't help but laugh as well. What Ophelia was suggesting sounded ridiculous, but her mind was already racing to see if there was a way to work with it.

Meanwhile, Elda cautioned them. "Shadow magic can be very powerful but it's not the same as the real thing. The basilisk wouldn't be able to kill the spider."

"All it has to do is distract it," Samantha jumped in. "Remember, Ashuan's air is poisonous to it. The spider's surviving because it spun those webs, but they're magic. If I can get close enough to unravel them while a shadow basilisk keeps the spider occupied, it might actually work."

Fabian's eyebrows crept up his forehead. "You think this is a good idea?"

"Better than anything I've thought of in the last twenty-four hours. It's worth a try."

Ophelia preened in response.

Groaning, Fabian pushed himself out of his chair. "I can already see us all lying next to Lucille." But he was standing, ready to go.

"You know, it's no wonder the Emblem of Hope remains dormant," Samantha needled.

"Just being realistic," Fabian retorted. However, a spark in his eyes told a different story. There was still some hope in him. "And you know, you're always welcome to *change* my mind."

Samantha snorted and stood up herself, feeling energised by the simple presence of a plan. "Let's do this."

Elda sighed. "Be careful."

Matt

When Samantha called to update him their plan, Matt wished he could simply ditch Jan. The thought of Samantha taking on the Arachna alone was unbearable. The conflict with his brothers had already put her in danger once too often, especially after he'd almost killed her last week. Now she was in yet another dangerous situation.

Still, he didn't ask her to reconsider. "Be careful, okay?"

He'd be a dead man if he tried to stop her in the name of protecting her. Samantha was a competent witch and he loved that she could hold her own. Even against a demon.

"I'll take care of Jan... as soon as I find him." He hadn't seen Jan for a while now.

"You can't find him?" Samantha squeaked.

Matt sighed. "All the doors are locked and I've got the key. Neve froze all the windows, so he must be in the house. I just don't know where at the moment." What he didn't tell Samantha was the ominous feeling he had of being watched. "I'll see you soon."

He hung up and turned to find Neve watching him. "Did you find him?"

"Neve found him." Her voice was much softer than usual, as if she didn't want to be heard. Jan's previous attacks had frightened her, and Matt didn't know how much she understood about the spider infestation.

"Can you show me where?"

Instead of answering, the little girl pointed overhead.

"What the—"

Jan dropped on top of him from where he'd been casually hanging from the ceiling. The impact knocked Matt to the ground, cracking one of his ribs. His training kicked in a moment later.

He grabbed Jan and threw him to the side, then rolled on top of him. Unfortunately, Jan was also well versed in hand-to-hand combat and knew holds that Matt didn't understand until he found himself flipped onto his back. If this had been a fight with one of his brothers, he'd have found another counter, but this was his friend. Matt didn't want to hurt him.

Jan struck him in the neck with the side of his flat hand and Matt nearly collapsed from the pain. Instinct took over and he knocked Jan off his chest, but when he tried to get up, he found his lower body frozen to the floor.

"Sorry!" Neve shouted, already aiming at Jan again.

Matt groaned and tore himself free from the unintentional freeze. In the time it took him to break free, Neve had started chasing Jan along the wall with surprisingly well-placed icicles. There was already a row of them decorating the wall when Matt stepped in to stop her.

"Jan, we don't want to hurt you." Judging by the snow witch's growl, she was willing to do anything to protect her house. "We *don't*. Not you, not the spider, not your babies."

Jan glared at them, having retreated into a corner. As Matt watched, he placed his feet on the walls on either side and began to climb. There was no logical reason to explain how Jan could scale the wall like one of Fabian's superheroes. Matt shuddered just watching him.

"We're friends, remember? You and me, we're on the same side."

He didn't have much hope, but then Jan suddenly collapsed and fell from the wall, immediately curling up into a ball and whimpering. The spell the spider babies had cast over him had broken. At least, for a moment.

"Neve will make Jan some tea," she said, all sweetness and light again. "That will help."

"Good idea." Matt watched her fly into the kitchen, then took a step towards Jan. "Feeling any better?"

Jan shook his head. It took him the better part of a minute to raise it and look at Matt with haunted eyes. "I don't want this. In two months, I'll be all theirs. I don't want to be eaten and I don't want to hunt you."

Matt swallowed. "Samantha will find a solution. *We* will."

In front of him, Jan became still. Something like hope had taken hold of his features. "There's a solution."

"What is it?"

"You have to kill me." Jan's voice cracked as he fought his spider instincts. "Before seventy of those monsters hatch out of my chest."

Matt stumbled backwards, recoiling. A year ago, he would've agreed without hesitation. It was better to be dead than have this nightmare happen. He respected him for coming to this decision, but at the same time it hurt to be asked. His friends wouldn't understand. Samantha wouldn't. If he killed Jan, he might save lives down the road, but only the one taken would count.

He was better than this. Less pragmatic, but more emphatic. He had to hold onto that thought.

But Jan's eyes looked almost black in the dark room as he pleaded with Matt. "Promise me you'll kill me."

Rachel

When Rachel surfaced, she emerged from the water in a pretty little lake behind a Gregorian mansion. Annoyed, she climbed out and wrung out her clothes and hair. Since it was still the dreamworld, the mere act of doing so left her completely dry. What it didn't do was heal the slight scratch on her cheek.

"That's the last time I jump off a cliff," she muttered as she left the lake behind and entered the garden.

It was a meticulously tended rose garden, much more in keeping with the way Lucille felt like to her. If it hadn't been so extensive, it could easily have been attached to the Villa de Cerque. As it was, the house beyond the seemingly endless roses was big enough to house a school. It dawned on Rachel that this must've been the Swiss boarding school Lucille had attended before joining them in Greenvalley. Hadn't it been something with roses in the name?

But if it was a school, it was an eerily empty one—and huge. The garden just wouldn't end. Which meant...

Instead of trying to reach the school, Rachel looked around. It wasn't long before she spotted a circular flowerbed built like a sundial. In the middle, near the long wooden stick, was a ten-year-old girl in school uniform. She had picture perfect blonde ringlets, much like Cheryl liked to style her hair, but she was crouching and pulling the flowers out of the ground.

Rachel approached her cautiously. "What are you doing?"

The girl continued her wilful destruction, even though some of the flowers had thorns. She was even humming a little song Rachel couldn't quite place.

"Is that you, Lucille?"

As her name rang through the dream, the girl jumped. For a moment, a look of pure horror flashed across her face, but then she saw Rachel and relaxed. "It's you."

The girl's eyes were definitely Lucille's. This was how she'd looked before her rebellious teenage years. Rachel noticed the blood on her hands. "May I ask why you're tearing up the flowers?"

"It upsets her if I'm not perfect." Still rebellious, then.

"Who?" Rachel inquired.

"My mum," the little girl whispered.

"You mean Linda?"

No sooner had she said the name than the dream was shattered by an earthquake. Hedges shot out of the ground, quickly growing to several metres in height. Branches crawled across the ground like fingers reaching for them. The sky grew darker by the second.

Lucille sprang to her feet and took Rachel's hand. "You summoned her." Then she took off.

Rachel had trouble following her, but the dream was becoming more threatening, spurring her on. The branches were no longer crawling, but twisting and snapping like rattlesnakes, and the hedges grew until they'd blocked out the sky, turning the park into a vast maze, danger lurking around every corner.

A familiar clicking sound came from behind and the blood in Rachel's veins froze. Whatever they'd summoned wasn't Linda but something much more sinister.

"Lucille, you can't run from this!" She came to a halt, pulling on the little girl to stop her. "You have to fight the poison in your mind. You have to wake up."

"She's here." Lucille's eyes widened as she pointed behind Rachel.

Rachel turned and was knocked to the ground. Suddenly, she was lying in the street, aching all over.

Still disoriented, Rachel got to her knees, when she heard a car honking and tyres screeching. Bright lights blinded her as a car came straight at her. There was no time to run, no time to roll out of the way. All she could do was keep her head down and pray to whichever god was listening.

The light washed over her and there was a heart-stopping bang. When she dared to look up again, smoke was rising and there was glass all around her. She noticed scratches and cuts on her body and willed them to heal, but the marks remained.

A siren alerted her to the wreckage of a car just three metres from her. Had it swerved to avoid her? No, there was a van further down the road. She was just an observer in this dream—

Memory.

She wasn't in the dreamworld. She was in Lucille's subconscious, and this was one of her earliest memories. Now all she had to do was find her again.

The dirty blood on the road almost made her vomit. This was a bad accident. And indeed, the rescue workers were covering a person. They'd never talked about it in detail, but Rachel knew she was reliving the day Lucille's birth mother had died.

She found the little girl sitting on the pavement, clutching a worn-out teddy bear to her chest. Her face was bruised and she'd been crying, but now she was just sitting there, waiting for someone to take her out of this nightmare.

Even more cautious than before, Rachel approached the toddler and knelt in front of her. "What happened?"

She hadn't expected to relive this traumatic accident when she dove into Lucille's subconscious, but she knew they had to work through it if they were ever going to move on.

"I fell out of the car." She looked up as the paramedics pushed the covered driver past them. "That's my mummy."

Rachel whimpered. Her eyes filled with tears and she suddenly wanted to hug Lucille. No one should ever have to see their parents die, especially at this age.

A crowd had gathered around them, pointing and gawking at the two wrecks and body being wheeled past. A young man burst through the crowd, his eyes wide and searching. He saw Lucille for a split second before his eyes fell on the covered woman. As soon as he'd spoken to the paramedics, he collapsed in tears.

A young, emotional Bastien de Cerque, not the hardened businessman Rachel had met.

The scenery darkened and the sounds of the accident faded. Little Lucille began to cry again, clutching her teddy bear as if her life depended on it.

"There you are."

The voice sent shivers down Rachel's spine. She instinctively moved closer to Lucille, then looked up. A woman had appeared, looking somehow like Linda and not like her at all. A distorted nightmare version, like an ill-fitting suit worn by something not quite human. She also seemed to be floating.

Lucille immediately crawled behind Rachel, her small hands digging into her shoulders. "That's her."

"There's no need to hide, little Lulu. I'll find you anywhere," the fake Linda said, in a singsong voice.

This was it. Rachel was sure she'd found what was keeping Lucille in her dreams. She shook off the fear that had gripped her since she'd jumped off the cliff and stood up. "Leave her alone."

Linda cocked her head like a doll and narrowed her eyes. "You don't belong here." She fixed Lucille with a glare. "Lucille Vivienne de Cerque, I told you not to talk to strangers. Why can't you be a good little girl and listen? Come here."

To Rachel's horror, the little girl got up and walked towards Linda, as if in a trance.

"Lucille, don't!"

Lucille turned, but kept walking backwards until Linda's surprisingly long fingers grabbed her and pulled her towards her.

A tear ran down her cheek. "This is my new mummy. She loves me."

"No, no, she doesn't," Rachel blurted out.

With a ghastly smile, Linda wrapped her arms around Lucille. Her fingers turned into claws, and before Rachel could react, she'd stabbed Lucille in the stomach.

The teddy bear fell to the floor as Rachel screamed.

"You're too late, little dreamer," Linda sang, her voice both threatening and captivating. "No one escapes the spider's web."

Her body swelled as she wrapped Lucille in webs. Her limbs grew longer and more eyes opened on her forehead. Within seconds, Linda had transformed into the Arachna, and Lucille was nothing more than a puppet in her arms.

Jan

"Have you lost your mind?

Yes, Jan wanted to say. He'd absolutely lost his mind, and was losing it more and more every minute. Just keeping this conversation going was costing him all his strength. The spiders inside him wanted to climb the walls or snack on Matt.

"There's no coming back from this. Do you really think I want to give birth to seventy spiders from Hell and end up as food for them?" What a fate. Perhaps his father would finally believe him when he saw what was left of him. A small victory.

Matt held his hands tightly at his sides, as if afraid of accidentally fulfilling Jan's wish. "Of course not, but that's two months from now. Plenty of time to find a solution."

Jan took a deep breath before trusting himself enough to say what needed to be said, "Matt, I don't have two months. I can feel them inside me." Not each of them, but their collective interest in crawling and jumping and feeding. "I'm becoming a spider."

"Right now, you only have four limbs."

"That's not funny!" Jan snapped, then immediately pulled back against the wall, fighting the urge to rip Matt's head off. Was this how the half-demon had felt during his Blood Night, when all reason had left him and he'd become a slave to his deadly instincts?

Matt raised his hands in a submissive gesture. "I know. Believe me, I'm trying to help you, but killing you?" He grimaced in pain. "No, I'm done with that. I don't kill friends."

"Do I have to start something with Samantha before you'll consider it?"

Matt dropped his gaze and lowered his hands. He looked… he looked *hurt.*

Jan rubbed his chest, wincing at the tender, egg-sized swelling. He hated that he'd put Matt in this position. His friend had worked too hard to repent, too hard to be a better *human.* And now Jan was pulling him back to where he'd started. "I'm sorry."

"I'll do it," Matt said quietly, though he couldn't meet Jan's gaze. "But not now. Not until we've exhausted every other idea." Finally, he raised his gaze. "I promise."

Jan let out a shuddering breath of relief. "Thank you." At least he'd be spared this dreadful fate. And maybe Matt was right and they'd come up with another solution. One that didn't involve him—

"She's in danger." All his senses were suddenly on high alert. He couldn't even say what he'd just thought about, let alone spoken of.

The tasty half-demon asked him a question, but Jan didn't care. Within seconds he was back on the wall, crawling quickly towards the door. The mother of his children was in great danger and he had to protect her.

"Neve, freeze the lock."

The door slammed shut in front of Jan. He kicked at it but found it unyielding. "I need to get to her."

He whipped his head around and found a window. It may have been frozen shut, but it was very fragile. Armed with this new plan, Jan crawled towards the windows. One kick and the glass shattered.

Freedom, sweet, sweet free—

Someone grabbed him by the waist and dragged him back through abstract space. When they emerged from the slimy cold place, they were in the cellar. There was no door, no window, just books and old wine bottles.

A trap! Another freaking trap.

"Sorry, but your spider girlfriend will have to do without you."

Jan hissed and lunged at the half-demon who dared to get in his way, but he evaded him easily and Jan came up short. He spun around, letting the dark feelings inside consume him.

"The little ones are hungry."

If he was going to be trapped here with the half-demon, he would at least feast. Anything to grow bigger and stronger.

He jumped at the unsuspecting creature but missed again, landing instead on one of the wine racks. Bottles shattered around him, sweet and sour notes filling his nose. When he turned, the half-demon had a sword in his hand.

Something about the sharp edge of the weapon tore Jan from his instincts for a moment. This was it. If he could just hold onto his humanity long enough, this nightmare would be over.

"Do it!" he gasped.

But Matt the traitor shook his head. "It's not time yet."

Screaming, Jan lunged at him again. But where there should have been impact, there was nothing but air. The half-demon was gone, and he'd left him alone in this trap of a room while his mistress called for him.

He'd crawled every wall and ceiling a hundred times trying to find a way out. There was a window, but it was so tiny Jan couldn't even get his foot out. The door was not only locked, it was frozen shut. The need to join his mistress, the mother of the brood inside him, drove him almost mad.

Even though it wouldn't budge, Jan threw himself against the door again and again. He didn't care if it hurt or if he broke a bone. He just had to get out.

Then, on one attempt, he hit it so hard he heard something crack. The next thing he knew he was tumbling down the stairs, unable to keep his balance.

His head throbbed with pain and for a moment the agony cut through the fog of his senses. What was he doing here? The fact the spider was in danger was a good thing. It *should* be a good thing. It was his friends who were fighting it. Fighting to save Lu's life.

But Lu wasn't theirs to save. She belonged to *her* now. And so did he.

Jan tried to push himself upright as his fingers closed around a shard of glass. The sharp edges sliced into his hand and he gasped. Once more, clarity filled him, pushing aside the spider's needs.

And he knew what to do.

The first cut was the easiest. The brood didn't expect him to turn on himself. He hissed as the glass sliced through his shirt and skin just above the egg. But it wasn't enough.

Blood seeped between his fingers and ran down his chest. Jan tried to hold on to the shard, but it was getting slicker by the minute. Worse were the conflicting thoughts in his head. He held onto the pain because that was all him, while the rest of him was a screaming, panicked mess that wanted him to stop. Needed him to stop.

But he held on. And he cut deeper. Cutting and cutting until the egg-sized sac gave way a little. The spiders were scrambling, eager to reattach themselves. He had to do more if he was to be free, but there was so much blood he couldn't see where to cut next, and his fingers were stiffening.

Then there was someone else. Sword in hand, his dark, vengeful angel returned to him.

Jan tried to smile, but it faltered when he saw horror instead of determination. Matt wasn't here to set him free. In the end, he wasn't able to do it.

"You promised," he whispered. It didn't matter. His eyelids fluttered shut and he fell into blissful darkness. Free at last.

Rachel

Rachel ran like she'd never run before. She'd left the road behind and was now running through a forest that was both familiar and unfamiliar. She knew the paths, where they went up and down, and most importantly, where they led. But the forest didn't *feel* right. It was too dark, too twisted, too dangerous.

No matter how fast she ran, the Arachna was faster. Despite its massive body, it broke through the undergrowth, sending branches flying. Next it flattened a small tree, almost taking her out with it.

Rachel leapt over it, forcing the ground to meet her just at the right spot so she wouldn't twist an ankle. Instead of running, she willed the trees closer, putting distance between her and the Arachna, just because she wanted to.

Unfortunately, the Arachna seemed to weave dreams as well as webs. Where Rachel moved away, it moved closer, chasing her from one side of the forest to the other.

No, not from one side to the other: in circles. Rachel took a precious moment to assess the dream.

Webs. Everywhere the Arachna had gone, webs had appeared. While Rachel had been running for her life, the spider had been weaving her in. And now she was trapped, poised to fall into her web.

The Arachna landed behind her with a thud that nearly knocked her off her feet. It raised its front legs and clicked its claws. Although it had exposed its abdomen, Rachel knew there was no weakness to be found. The only weakness was in its eyes.

Suddenly, Rachel had her crossbow in her hand. She waited patiently for the spider to lower its legs again. The second it did, she fired. Just like in the real world, her shot was on target, and the bolt landed in one of its eight eyes.

The spider reared up, screaming in pain, and Rachel knew this was her only chance.

She couldn't leave the forest without running into one of its webs, but she could... *take the elevator?*

For some reason, there was an old-fashioned elevator in front of her. A flashing light told her its arrival was imminent. Then it beeped and the doors opened. To her surprise, Robert was inside, beckoning her closer.

With the Arachna charging at her, Rachel decided not to question it. Instead, she ran into the elevator, and not a moment too soon. The spider threw itself against the closed doors, causing the whole thing to shake, but it didn't break.

Rachel let out a shuddering gasp and sank to the floor, hanging her head between her legs to catch her breath.

"Looks like I came at just the right time," Robert said in his usual oblivious tone.

She didn't look up. It made absolutely no sense for Lucille to have a place in her subconscious for Robert. But he'd saved Rachel. Somehow, he'd arrived at just the right time to offer her protection.

"You realise I saved your life, right?"

"How? None of this is real. It's just a dream," Rachel said, more to herself than to Robert. It was what she had to believe to get out of here. Dreams couldn't harm—

Whack.

Sudden pain erupted in her head as Robert hit her with a cane and she finally looked up. "Why would you do that?"

"Does it matter? It's not real, is it?"

"It hurts." Her head throbbed.

"That's the subconscious for you. Go too deep and it'll hurt. You'll have those when you wake up." He pointed to the bruises and scabs she'd already amassed. The ones that wouldn't heal.

Rachel gulped. No dream had ever left a mark on her before.

"By the way, do you want to go down or up?" Robert asked, still sounding as cheerful as if they'd just run into each other in the city centre.

"Down," Rachel replied without thinking. "I need to go deeper." Going up was giving up, and she was *not* giving up on Lucille. Thinking of Lucille... "What brings you to Lucille's subconscious?"

Robert smiled obliviously. "Your brother sent me. He said you could use a familiar face. Someone you both know."

"Nico sent you?" No, Nico was dead. And if he were alive, he wouldn't know anything about the dreamworld. But the dreamer did. The one who was nothing but a dream. He'd helped her with what little he could.

"He did. He would've wanted you to go up. There's not always a way back from below, you know? Oh well."

There was another ping and the doors opened. Robert straightened and announced, "Basement. Lost memories and the inner self."

The landscape in front of her didn't look welcoming. Rachel had never been to Hell, but from what her friends had told her, it looked like it. Dark, yawning tunnels, whispers of danger.

"Looks creepy."

"You wanted to go down."

It wasn't too late to go up. She could still turn back and ask Nico to take her back to her dream meadow. Back to where she was the only one who made the rules. But she was on the right track. This was where she would find Lucille—in her innermost self.

Carefully, she stepped out of the elevator. "I'm in the right place."

Robert handed her his cane. "Good luck."

Rachel's hand wrapped around the smooth wood and she felt a little safer, as if this stick was more powerful than her crossbow.

She took a step into the darkness, and when she turned, the elevator was gone. Her safe way out was gone. From now on, her fate was tied to Lucille. If her friend didn't wake up, neither would she.

The cave system was completely silent. Rachel used the cane to check for webs because she didn't trust her own eyes. Not if the spider could weave magic. She walked down dark corridors and squeezed through narrow, twisting passages. It almost felt like she was walking through Lucille's brain, only it was cold, dark, and almost dead.

The corridor suddenly opened into a huge cavern. In the centre was a massive, pulsating, transparent cocoon filled with a clear red liquid. The floor was connected to the ground by glistening, sticky threads, and at the top sat the spider, pumping its venom into the cocoon.

Inside was Lucille. She was her normal age, but completely naked, her arms wrapped around her knees and her head tucked in, as if trying to make herself as small as possible. She didn't move.

"Lucille?" Rachel stepped closer, keeping a wary eye on the spider at the top. It didn't look like the Arachna, just an aspect of it.

Just before she reached the cocoon, footsteps sounded from a corridor near her. *Click-clack. High heels on the floor.* A moment later, Linda entered.

"You came back, I'm surprised." Her smile was ghastly. "But you're too late. The girl is mine. She has no strength left."

"You're lying. This is Lucille's mind, and she's far more powerful than you." She had to be. Lucille had to beat this.

As Linda's mouth moved, her voice seemed to come from everywhere at once. "Lucille has given up and dreams the sleep of the dead. She's with her mummy now."

Rachel swallowed. Would that be what Lucille wanted? To be with the mother she'd lost too soon? The one parent who'd loved her unconditionally?

She shook her head. Lucille had lived without her mother for over fifteen years. She was an adult now. A powerful witch in her own right, capable and compassionate, with a will to live. She was far too stubborn to give up.

"Lucille doesn't need a mother."

"She needs me," Linda hissed.

Suddenly, she lunged at Rachel, long fingers wrapping around her neck and squeezing. Her face quickly turned into the spider's, complete with bleeding eye.

"You're weak," Spider Linda hissed.

Rachel smiled up at her. "So you keep saying."

A moment later, the spider realised what Rachel had already known. The cane Robert had given her had been driven through her chest like a dagger.

"How is that possible?" Spider Linda asked, blood dripping down her chin.

Rachel freed herself and stood up. The spider woman fell to the ground. "This is still part of the dreamworld. Everything happens here because I want it to. And I want you to die."

Spider Linda glared at her, now foaming at the mouth. "This isn't your realm. It's hers." She pointed at Lucille. "And it belongs to the queen now."

"The queen?"

But the creature disintegrated, unable to answer questions.

Instead, the spider on the cocoon screeched. It jumped, just as the Arachna had jumped in the forest, and landed right in front of Rachel. The whole cave shook in response, reminding Rachel how unstable Lucille's mind was right now. How poisoned.

The only thing that distinguished this spider from the one she'd originally fought was a second bleeding eye.

"Why did I even ask?"

She stepped back, but not fast enough. The spider lunged at her, knocking her to the ground. Poison fell, missing Rachel by inches. She was trying to wriggle out of the way and crawl away from the spider when a leg struck her arm, pinning her to the ground.

Blood ran down her arm. Real, warm blood. Another wound she couldn't heal. Was she lying in her bed now, bleeding, while Hugo could do nothing but watch?

The subconscious could hurt her. It could also kill her if she let the spider succeed.

Think, Rachel forced herself. *What do you know about the spider? Her eyes are a weakness, but that's not the only thing that hurt her in the forest. There was something much more powerful.*

The spider's claws snapped closed when the first beam of light pierced the cave. Screeching, it crawled backwards, but Rachel called another beam, and then another. More and more light filled the cave, forcing the spider to retreat into the shadows.

Rachel jumped up and ran towards the cocoon. The spider immediately came for her. This time she didn't think and just swiped at one of its legs with her cane, breaking it.

The loss of a leg threw the spider off balance and it stumbled against the cocoon. The barbs on its hind legs tore a hole in the fragile structure, and red liquid gushed out. Lucille spilt out onto the floor.

Meanwhile, the spider retreated to the ceiling of the cave, eager to repair the holes Rachel had made. The light was fading.

Rachel ran to Lucille and shook her. "Lucille! Wake up! You need to wake up and fight."

But Lucille continued to sleep and the cave went dark again. Within seconds, the spider had repaired its deadly web. Now it was coming back for them.

"You must wake up." She'd destroyed the cocoon, what more did Lucille need. "I *want* you to wake up."

The spider was above her, its venomous claws glistening.

"Lucille!"

A groan behind her. The claws sinking. Venom dropping.

"Erit Lux!"

Bright light flashed through the dream, painting everything white as Rachel sank her cane into the spider's head.

Fabian

While they'd all been eager to return to the forest to test their theory, Samantha had forced them to sleep for a few hours. The rest had been welcome, but it hadn't been the main purpose. What they needed was daylight.

It was around six in the morning when they headed down the forest paths. Fabian yawned, somehow feeling more tired than before they'd gone to bed. He wasn't too worried, though. As soon as they came across the spider, he'd be wide awake.

Ophelia was by his side, her fingers intertwined with his. They were slightly sweaty, which told Fabian how nervous she was.

"You can do this," he whispered.

"I know," she said, in spite of her shaking voice.

Her job was to summon a shadow basilisk to distract the spider while Samantha entered her inner sanctum to unravel the web the spider had spun. All he had to do was support Ophelia and stop the spider from killing any of them.

Considering it had already struck down Lucille and impregnated Jan, Fabian gave them a five percent chance of survival.

"Are you sure you can destroy the webs?" If that part didn't work, the spider would get them sooner or later.

"It worked last time. They're just... *intricate.* They take time and concentration to untangle," Samantha explained. "Which is why—"

"You need us to distract the spider." Fabian held up his feather. "We'll cover you. Let's see how the spider likes wind and water."

Ophelia let go of his hand and took a step towards Samantha. "And a basilisk." She pulled a flat bowl out of her rucksack and handed it to Samantha. "Hold this."

Fabian was glad she hadn't chosen him when a dagger appeared in her hand. He loved her dearly, but he wished she'd shed all the snake cult stuff she'd grown up with. Only the tiniest of gasps told him she'd cut her palm.

"Nebit Ishtar ar Ischanen sedschim Iwadi no hinuk satesch! Accept my sacrifice, my goddess!"

As she whispered her incantation, the shadows seemed to flow towards them. Fabian gripped his feather tighter as they gathered around Ophelia and took shape. The black mass grew into a huge, serpentine creature, and his jaw went slack.

No wonder the spiders feared this monster. It wasn't just a giant snake, it was a giant snake on eight crab-like legs with a huge rooster head. *Everyone* would fear this monster. Everyone except Ophelia.

She stood there with glowing eyes, reaching for the basilisk's beak. As she touched it, a peal of laughter burst from her lips.

Leaves rustled behind Fabian and he spun around just as the spider burst through the undergrowth.

"Sam, go!"

As soon as Samantha moved, so did the spider. Fabian shot a stream of water at it, successfully distracting it enough for Samantha to slip away. Unfortunately, the spider was now coming for him.

"Take my hand!" Ophelia screamed.

Fabian whirled around and grabbed her outstretched hand. Immediately, a ribbon of shadows wrapped around them and carried them both up onto the basilisk. Fabian slipped into place behind Ophelia, trying not to think about the fact he was sitting two metres up on nothing but shadows.

The basilisk raised its ugly rooster head at the spider, who had paused for a moment.

"Isn't he beautiful?" Ophelia said, still laughing. She turned to Fabian and her face fell. "Choose your words wisely. Basilisks are incredibly vain."

He didn't have any words. Fabian swallowed hard, forcing the only compliment he could think of from his throat. "He's impressive."

Ophelia grinned and turned back. A moment later, the basilisk squawked in such a high-pitched tone Fabian slapped his hands to his ears.

The Arachna responded with a shriek of her own, and then the two went at it. Ophelia laughed with delight as the basilisk charged forward at breakneck speed. Trees whizzed past him, some barely within an inch of Fabian's feet. Nausea filled him and he almost threw up all over the shadows.

They dove deep into the dark web the spider had woven. Fabian tried to use his water, but all he could do was hold on and hope he didn't fall.

From time to time, he could see Samantha kneeling on the floor, her eyes closed as she untangled the webs with her fingers. At times they came too close, but Ophelia expertly guided the basilisk, and with it the spider, away.

A flash of light pierced the darkness as the first web collapsed. The spider shrieked and crawled towards Samantha. Fabian shot water after it, but all he managed to achieve was a wet floor. Meanwhile, Ophelia spun the basilisk around, making it move even faster.

They crashed around a tree, then another, when suddenly, the basilisk's beak closed around the spider's head. So much for not being the real thing.

"Remember, we need the poison!" Fabian shouted before the basilisk could crunch down and rob them of their only hope.

Ophelia nodded and the basilisk threw the spider into a tree instead. For a moment it curled up like Fabian had seen countless dead spiders do, but then it straightened and climbed up the tree, out of the basilisk's reach.

More light broke through the leaves and the spider fell with a screech. It tried to hide in the shadows, but in vain. The sky unravelled in a flash, which meant Samantha must have found the right thread to pull.

Fabian's chest filled with relief. He'd expected it to take longer. But the plan had worked. The webs unravelled and the spider died. And then they'd—

His heart stuttered. Steam rose from the now collapsed spider. But it wasn't just steam. The whole spider was disintegrating in the early morning sunlight.

Fabian dropped from the basilisk and ran towards it, horror seeping into his bones. "No, no, no, no, no!"

The claws glistened in the light, thick with poison. The very substance they needed to save Lucille. He reached for them, but they dissolved before he could grab them. The last drops of venom sank into the ground, killing the moss there, now lost forever.

"Where's the spider?" Samantha appeared beside him, looking exhausted.

Fabian stared at the empty space before him. Nothing but the dead moss indicated a giant monster had existed here just moments ago. "Gone."

"It's dead," Ophelia clarified from the top of her shadow basilisk.

"And the venom?" Samantha's voice faltered, mimicking Fabian's despair.

All hope was lost. There would be no magic antidote to save Lucille. "Lost. We lost."

Samantha

Samantha couldn't believe it. They'd beaten the spider and yet nothing would change the outcome. Lucille was still in hospital, still asleep. It had all been for nothing.

They'd gone straight to the hospital after making sure all traces of the spider had truly disappeared. It had been a stupidly beautiful morning, full of sunshine and birdsong. And all Samantha could think about was how Lucille would never experience a morning like that again.

"This is bullshit," Fabian muttered. The three of them were sitting in the lobby after visiting Lucille and finding her unchanged.

Samantha had no words for him. After two nights of little sleep and a morning spent unravelling magical webs, she was too exhausted to comfort her best friend. And he was right. Lucille in a coma *was* bullshit.

"Your phone's ringing," Ophelia said softly.

It took Samantha another moment to blink and realise what Ophelia had said. By the time she got her phone out of her purse, the call had stopped. But when she saw Rachel's name, she called back immediately.

"Has she woken up?" was Rachel's first question.

Samantha swallowed hard. Suddenly there was a huge frog in her throat and she was afraid she'd just start sobbing uncontrollably if she spoke. "No," she whispered, then realised she'd spoken too softly. "She's still in a coma. According to her doctors, nothing has changed."

There was a poignant pause on the other side. "Did you kill the spider? Did you get the venom?"

Tears burnt in her eyes. "We killed it, but the Arachna disintegrated before we could get the venom." The fact that they'd ruined their only chance by killing it prematurely tasted more bitter by the minute.

"That doesn't make sense," Rachel argued. "If you killed the spider in the forest, and I killed the spider in her dream—with Lucille's help—then she should wake up. There's no more poison in her."

Samantha tried to make sense of what was being said, but on what little sleep she'd had, Rachel sounded delirious. "You were in her dream, weren't you? But this is her body we're talking about. The poison is still inside her."

"No, it isn't." Rachel sighed. "The dreamworld or subconscious is connected to the body. Wounds there..." Her voice faltered. "The poison is gone. It must be."

"But it's still a dream." Samantha couldn't wrap her head around the alternative. Perhaps she was just too tired. "I don't understand how this works."

Again, there was a pensive silence. "Do you have a plan?"

Samantha's heart twisted painfully. Everyone always expected her to have a plan. "I can't make an antidote without the venom. I don't know how."

"Then I'll go back in."

"Rachel!"

But Rachel had hung up.

When Samantha put the phone down, she found Fabian and Ophelia watching her. "She thinks she can save Lucille in the dreamworld. Please don't ask me how."

The question was visible in Fabian's eyes, but he swallowed it and nodded, then hung his head again. Samantha noticed he was holding the Feather of Shitaten, his gaze lost in the endless blue. After a while he said: "If Rachel is still fighting, I won't lose hope."

Logic told Samantha it was in vain, but just like he had before, she kept her mouth shut, leaving Ophelia to comfort him.

Her gaze wandered around the lobby. She felt lost, unable to decide what to do next. Go to school? No, they were already late and there didn't seem to be any point. Hit the books in the hope of finding an already established antidote? What books were left when she'd already read so many? Or maybe she should ask Caspar, since it was one of his spiders and he knew a lot more about healing than he'd let on. Now *that* was an idea only a sleep-addled brain could produce.

Just then, the elevator opened and a familiar face stepped out in a blood-stained shirt.

"Matt!" In an instant, Samantha was running towards him. "What happened?"

He was as surprised to see her as she was to see him. "Jan took care of the brood problem himself."

In all the chaos, Samantha had almost forgotten about Jan. Now she was struggling to breathe. She couldn't possibly lose two friends in one day. "Meaning?"

"He cut it out of his own chest."

"Is it gone?" Fabian asked, joining them.

Matt's shoulders slumped with the same exhaustion Samantha felt. "If not, they'll cut the rest out during the operation. But if we're unlucky, he cut too deep."

It was too much. It was all too much. Samantha burst into tears. They poured out of her like a flood, too many to stop. A moment later, her nose was filled with the smell of dried blood and she found herself in Matt's arms.

"I know," he whispered, his chin resting on her head. "I know."

Lucille

It was a sunny day and the world was beautiful. Lucille was sitting in the garden, playing with her mother and giggling, oblivious to the worries of life. Everything was perfect. She felt loved and safe, basking in her mother's angelic aura.

Then a shadow fell on them.

Spooked, Lucille ran into her mother's arms and hid there. For a few precious moments she'd known no fear, but now she was afraid. Afraid of her peace being disturbed, afraid of harm coming to her, but most of all, afraid of losing her mother. Again.

"I know things were easier when you were young," a soft voice said. Lucille knew her as Rachel, but at the moment she'd rather forget her. It was a price she was willing to pay to have her mum back.

"When I was young, I liked my mum, too—and my dad," Rachel continued. She crouched next to the blanket and looked longingly at Lucille and her mother.

Her mother just smiled gently. She didn't speak, nor did she confront the intruder who'd threatened their happiness.

Lucille didn't remember more than her smile, more than her love. She didn't know how her mother would argue or what her mother would do, but... "She's the only mum I have."

Rachel shook her head. "That's not true. You've got Linda."

Lucille buried her face deeper into her mother, wishing she would do something, like fight for her. "Linda's not my mum. She doesn't want to be my mum."

"Doesn't she? Or don't you?" Rachel held out her hand. "Linda's made a lot of mistakes, but she's working very hard to be a better person. A better mother. She's fighting for you. Believe me. I know how it feels when they don't."

"She has Pascal now."

"That doesn't mean she doesn't want you, too."

Lucille sighed. Already the memory of her mother was fading, lost again to the undertones of her memories. "Does she?"

"Don't you feel it?" Rachel looked at her right hand.

Lucille followed her gaze. The right hand looked normal, but when she raised it to her cheek it was much warmer than her left. And she felt safe again. Safe and loved.

"She's there."

"Day and night. Just like a real mum," Rachel said quietly.

A real mum. She felt Linda's love in the touch of her hand. She felt her presence everywhere she couldn't feel her biological mum's, and tears rolled down her cheeks.

"I miss my mum so much."

Rachel pulled her into her arms and held her as she cried. "I know you do. But she's just a memory here. And there are people up there who love you, too. We love you very much. And so does Linda."

Lucille hiccupped as the words sank under her skin. Then she nodded. "It's time to go, isn't it?"

Slowly, Rachel stood and held out her hand again. "Yes, it's time to go home now."

Lucille woke slowly to the sounds in her hospital room. She couldn't see yet, but she could feel the group of people with her. Her family and friends. So many people who loved her.

Her eyes were still closed when she heard the door open and another person enter. Whoever they were, they were immediately greeted with, "How's Jan?"

"Better." The newcomer appeared to be Matt. "He'll recover. He's already awake and complaining about his mum making such a fuss about him."

How nice it would be to have a mother fussing over you, Lucille thought. Then she noticed the warm clasp around her right hand. *That's right. I have a mum like that, too.*

"Look!" That was Pascal's voice.

A second later, Lucille's eyes fluttered open. The light was a little too bright at first, and it took a moment to make out the various shapes in her room. There were Samantha and Matt, standing close together as usual. And there was Fabian and his new girlfriend. Philipp sat to her left, smiling with relief, while Pascal beamed at her from beside him.

And on her right was her mum. As soon as she saw Lucille had woken up, Linda burst into tears. "Welcome back, my dear."

Lucille blinked. The last thing she remembered was the spider in the woods and a bright light. And Rachel. For some reason, she remembered Rachel had been by her side, but her friend was nowhere to be seen.

"What are you all doing here?" Her voice was a little raspy, as if she hadn't used it for a while.

"Oh, you know, we've got nothing better to do," Matt joked, earning an elbow in the side, courtesy of Samantha.

Samantha told Lucille, "You had us worried. You just... wouldn't wake up."

"I'll go tell the doctor," Linda said, getting to her feet.

Lucille grabbed her hand. "Don't leave."

"Yeah, I can go," Fabian offered, slipping out of the room.

Stunned, Linda sat down again. She smiled and stroked Lucille's cheek. "I'm not going anywhere until your father gets here. His plane is due to land in an hour."

"You've been here the whole time." It wasn't her father she wanted.

Tears filled Linda's eyes again. "I've thought a lot about what you said over the last two days, and I'm so sorry, Lucille. You were right about everything. I failed you as a mother."

"I haven't made it easy for you." Not the way she'd clung to her birth mother and refused to accept this new woman her father had brought home.

"You were a child."

"I'm not a child anymore," Lucille insisted. She knew better now, knew what an impossible situation Linda had been put in and who she should have been angry at, even though *he'd* been put in an impossible situation, too.

Linda stroked her hair and smiled a little wider. "You will always be my child." Then she bent down and hugged her as tightly as she dared.

Soon, the doctor and a nurse arrived, and her friends filed out. Philipp went to look after Pascal, but Linda stayed. Her mum stayed.

Rachel

After that last dream, Rachel knew without a doubt that Lucille would wake. Her flower was blooming again, not a cobweb in sight. She'd succeeded, but she'd never been so deep into the dreamworld before. If you could call it the dreamworld at all.

"You made it back." Nico stepped up beside her and nodded at the flower. "And you saved your friend."

"If only everything could be saved like that." She'd learnt today how powerful dreams truly were, but there was a limit, and Rachel wasn't sure she liked it. "Thanks for your help."

She turned to him, taking in Nico's features. It was a good copy. He looked exactly like her brother. He'd even got the bright-white grin right. The one that always made her smile, no matter how bad she felt.

"It was all you."

Rachel took a deep breath. "It was, wasn't it?"

While Nico had sent her Robert and she'd used his cane in the fight, she could have easily made her own weapon. The only thing that had mattered was that she'd truly believed it would make a difference. It was her will which had defeated the Arachna. Hers and Lucille's.

Nico's smile faded a little, his expression more thoughtful than she'd seen him when he was alive, simply because he seemed older. More experienced. Wiser. "Do you think it's time to move on?"

She thought of Lucille and how many years she'd held on to the woman she barely remembered. It was the idea of her mother, the perfection of what she'd symbolised. Now, she realised she was doing the same. The man before her was an idealised version of Nico. The image she wanted to remember him by. Not his messy parts, not the fights they had, just the brother who'd always been by her side.

But like Lucille's mum, he was gone now and they were still here. They were alive, not only able to carry on, but obliged to. She was one hundred per cent sure that was what they both would've wanted.

Rachel sighed, then nodded to Nico. "I'm ready to let go."

He smiled one last time. "You and I will meet again. Until then, remember the lessons I've taught you. The dreamworld is dangerous if you venture too deep, but it can be worth it. Just remember you have something to come back for. Enjoy this life. It won't last forever."

As Nico spoke, he slowly faded away. A part of Rachel wanted to ask him to stay, to hold her one last time, but she knew it wouldn't be the same. She had to let him go and open herself up to the loved ones at her side and the life that awaited her.

The first thing Rachel felt when she woke up was pain. Life was a bitch. But it turned out dreams weren't much better. As Hugo floated towards her with a worried look on his face, Rachel scrambled out of bed and stood in front of the mirror.

She looked like she'd been in a fight. Her face was scratched and bruised, while a crust of dried blood covered her arm. It was the first time she'd seen the wounds, having only woken up long enough to call Samantha before that.

"You shouldn't have gone back inside." Hugo said, his voice full of concern.

Rachel raised her chin. "I had to help a friend."

"Did it work this time?"

She nodded, still discovering new bruises on her body.

Hugo breathed a sigh of relief. "I'm glad to hear that. I just wish you hadn't got hurt in the process."

"That's the price you pay for being alive." A smile crept across her face, the exact mirror image of Nico's. "Relax, Hugo. Lucille's alive, which makes it all worth it. Thanks for looking after me. It's appreciated."

The ghost seemed to grow three centimetres. "Always a pleasure, Miss Rachel."

"Alright. Let me get cleaned up and then I'll have a chat with my parents. It's time to face the elephant in the room so we can all move on."

After all, who was she to judge where her parents sought comfort? Nico wouldn't be forgotten, but she wasn't going to put her life on hold for him any longer. He deserved better. And so did she.

Part 3

Stress & Release

Fabian

After the drama of the past few weeks, the gang met in the Magic Circle to study together. Samantha had covered half the table with her infamous flashcards, folders, and textbooks, although she was currently out collecting yearbooks. Matt sat next to her empty chair, leaning back so far, he was balancing on the back legs, a geography book on his knees. Rachel was working on a mock maths exam, happily tapping numbers into her calculator.

They were all doing well, busy but on course for the finals, which started in two days' time.

Meanwhile, Fabian was about to lose his mind. He'd been staring at the same page in his physics book for a quarter of an hour and still couldn't make it make sense. The numbers on the page blurred and his brain ran in circles, reminding him time and again that he couldn't do it. He'd fail.

"I don't get it," he whispered.

Rachel leaned over. "What don't you get?"

"Heisenberg's Uncertainty Principle."

"Oh, that's easy. It just means you can only ever determine one value precisely, while the other becomes increasingly imprecise."

Fabian stared at her. "Oh, really? I understood *that* much." It was the maths that followed and the physical explanations he couldn't wrap his head around.

When Rachel just shrugged and went back to her mock exam, Fabian groaned and leaned over the table to grab Samantha's physics folder. It was beautifully organised, much easier to navigate than the textbook, and she'd written three pages on Heisenberg's Principle. None of which made any sense to him. His brain simply refused to understand it.

"I'm just not gonna go."

Just then Ophelia entered, a tray of drinks in her hand. "Does that mean we can go on a date instead?"

Fabian stared at her in disbelief. Not going to his exams wasn't really an option. He owed it to himself to give it his best shot. Even if his best shot was destined to come up short.

Ophelia placed the tray in the middle of the table and came around to put her arms around his neck. "Just kidding." She kissed his temple and squeezed him.

"You know," Jan entered, returning from work with a broad grin, "I've never been so happy that I don't have to deal with this shit."

Matt lowered his chair and raised an eyebrow. "As you've pointed out a dozen times. But don't worry, you're in training now, so you'll have your own exams sooner rather than later."

Jan snorted and pretended to shudder at the thought. He stepped aside for Samantha, who was carrying a heavy looking box. "Do you need help with that?"

Shaking her head, she looked every bit as stressed as Fabian felt. Rachel barely managed to get her mock exam out of the way before the box landed on the table.

"You were supposed to be back in an hour," Fabian complained. Surely Samantha could explain Heisenberg's Uncertainty Principle to him in terms his fried brain would understand.

She shot him a look that made him shrink in his chair. "Believe me, the last thing I wanted to do was spend two hours arguing with the printer about whether I'd even ordered the yearbooks."

"What?" Rachel asked.

"I know!" Samantha attacked the box and tore it open. "Finally, they managed to find a box." She pulled out a book and leafed through it, her gaze manically moving over the pages. Then she threw it back in, dropped onto the chair between Matt and Fabian, and groaned. "I can't believe it. They printed the old version."

Matt leaned in and fished the book out again, turning the pages much more slowly. "Looks great to me."

Samantha shot him another nasty look. "The voting results are wrong."

Matt skipped a few pages to find the categories and scoffed in amusement. "I see what you mean." He turned the page for Fabian and the others to see and pointed to his picture under the Mr Greenvalley election. "I didn't know my name was Robert."

Fabian immediately spotted the wrong name. According to the information on the left, Robert had won the election by thirty-four per cent. "Doesn't suit you."

"Ha!" Samantha snorted, still angry. "All the names are off by two categories. Robert won the Mega-Clutz category. And, unfortunately, you didn't win the Genius one with eighty-three per cent."

Matt flashed his teeth at her. "Maybe you just haven't noticed my genius yet."

Samantha's eyebrows arched and her face softened, then she suddenly burst into giggles, although they were slightly on the manic side. Unfortunately, the moment didn't last long before exhaustion returned. "Now I have to go back to the printer." She groaned.

"But not now," Fabian hastened to say, "I need you. Your folder just isn't the same without you."

Samantha sighed. She moved her chair closer to him and took a look at his work. "What are you working on?"

"Heisenberg's Uncertainty Principle."

"Still? Didn't we do that yesterday?" She rubbed her tired face.

Fabian winced. "Sorry. I'm just too stupid."

"No, you're not," Ophelia said with fierce determination and started to massage his shoulders.

"Lia's right," Samantha said. "You're really good at mechanics and you've got optics down, too."

Fabian snorted at her useless attempt to make him feel prepared for Monday's exam. "Do you really think Herbert chose mechanics?"

"Fine, back to quantum physics then."

Matt nudged her other side. "Do you have time to test me later?"

Samantha whimpered, looking like she was about to burst into tears. "When do I get to study for my stuff?"

"You've been studying since October," Fabian pointed out. "And you said the best way to learn is to explain it to someone else. Like me." He wouldn't have asked if he wasn't so desperate.

On her other side, Matt's megawatt grin was much more seductive. "There's a reason your picture is under Genius, even though you've been renamed as 'Marina'."

"You know, I could use some help, too…" Jan added just for fun.

Samantha cupped her ears and pretended to scream. She put her forehead on the table and buried it under her arms. "Just kill me now."

"Me too," Fabian sympathised, and a frighteningly large part of him meant it. "It'll be a mercy killing." There was no way he was going to make it through Monday unscathed, let alone the rest of the week.

Rachel

With only two days left before exams, Rachel and Jan went to the hospital to pick up Lucille. Her parents had paid for an extended stay to make absolutely sure she was in the best of health. It would've been annoying any other time, but Rachel suspected Lucille had appreciated the time off school to study.

Jan pulled into the staff car park and grinned at her. "Great perks, huh?"

"Parking?" Rachel scoffed. "I could've just walked to the hospital."

"And then you'll carry Lu home?" Jan's eyes widened mockingly. "Or do you expect *her* to walk too? In her heels?"

"Funny." After spending so much time in Lucille's subconscious, Rachel felt much closer to her friend than before, which was why she'd volunteered to pick her up.

In the hospital lobby, Jan offered to sign them in, leaving Rachel to watch the various people occupying the lounge. Most were relatives having coffee with their hospitalised loved ones. Others clearly worked there, easily identifiable by their name badges or scrubs.

A sudden burst of laughter made Rachel's head turn. A group of three men in blue uniforms were sitting at a table in the corner. One of them was middle-aged, but the other two looked to be in their early twenties.

The one who'd laughed was a brown-skinned man with dark curls and swirls of black ink peeking out from under his sleeve, hinting at a larger tattoo on his shoulder. He had an easy smile, his dark eyes sparkling above twin dimples.

Then their gazes met. For a split second, the stranger glanced across the room, his gaze instantly drawn to Rachel like an arrow to a target.

Hastily, Rachel lowered her eyes, embarrassment flushing her cheeks. How long had she been watching him like a creep?

"Are you coming?" Jan asked, already walking towards the lift.

Rachel hurried after him but couldn't resist glancing over her shoulder.

He was smiling. At *her*.

"What are you looking at?" Jan asked, pressing the button on the elevator.

"A bird." A *bird?* Rachel felt ashamed. Maybe the stress of the exams was finally getting to her, too.

The elevator arrived. She half expected Robert to be in it, but there were only more visitors and staff, who quickly cleared the space. As she and Jan took their places at the rear, she caught another glimpse of the stranger.

He was laughing again, not sparing her another look. But then his head turned—and other people stood in front of her, blocking her view.

The doors closed and the elevator began to move. Rachel tried to push every thought of the man out of her mind. So what if he'd looked at her? By the end of his lunch break, he'd have forgotten her. Just as she'd forget him.

"What do dark blue uniforms stand for?" Rachel blurted out, despite her rational thoughts.

"Blue?" Jan frowned. "I think those are the technicians."

"Technicians?"

"Well, do you think our machines are run by magic? They're an important part of the hospital's ecosystem." He grinned suddenly. "Not as important as the doctors, of course."

Rachel rolled her eyes. "You'll only be a paramedic."

Jan snorted. "Yeah, but I'll be the best paramedic they've ever seen."

"Because you're cheating," Rachel added smugly.

It wasn't until they were back in the lobby with Lucille she remembered the young technician. The seat he'd occupied was now empty, just as she'd known it would be. Still, she couldn't quite shake the pang of disappointment.

The next day, Rachel returned to the hospital lobby with her father, under the guise of a normal coffee date. Rachel had told him that she'd recently discovered how good the coffee was here—and the snacks—but what she was really looking forward to wasn't in the display case.

Nevertheless, she ordered a coffee and a large sandwich, which she planned to eat as slowly as possible. She tried not to look at her phone to check the time, knowing full well it was the same as yesterday.

"So, how are the exam preparations going?" her father asked as he sat next to where the technicians had been the day before.

Rachel sat across from him. "Good. I'm pretty confident." Tomorrow morning she'd have Physics. Then it was Maths on Tuesday, followed by Politics on Friday. "That's why I'm here. With you."

Not because of some guy she didn't even know. Who had time to think about guys when her finals were coming up? A break, however, was good for her. Fabian and Samantha may have been the type to cram until last minute, but she'd always done much better when she'd trusted the work she'd done before the exam. She'd earned a little distraction. After all, she just wanted one more look.

"So, what are your plans after this?" her father asked.

"Today?"

"After school," he clarified, with a smile.

Rachel managed to concentrate on him for a moment. "I want to study Maths in the autumn. Here in Greenvalley."

His eyes widened. "Really?"

She shrugged. "Well, I must have inherited something from you."

Mick burst out laughing. "Maybe. You know, the general consensus is you have to be crazy to study Maths."

Once again, Rachel looked over her shoulder. "Fine with me."

"Is that so?" A small smile played on his lips. "And where will this lead in the end? Got any jobs in mind?"

She rolled her eyes hard and glared at him. "Dad! How am I supposed to know? I'm sure something will come up when the time is right. I mean, did you know you wanted to be a professor when you started?"

He promptly snorted. "Absolutely not. I originally wanted to go into finance. You know, follow in my father's footsteps, but then I never managed to get away from university. Maths got me."

"Yeah, I get that." Again her gaze drifted away. And this time she was rewarded with his sight.

Like the day before, the curly-haired technician strode in with his two colleagues, chatting as they queued at the café. His laughter rang out, as carefree as the day before. When he looked to the side, he spotted Rachel, and his eyes lit up with recognition.

Rachel found herself smiling shyly, then sipping at her coffee.

The group of technicians ordered coffee to go, but instead of taking their usual seats, they made their way to the sunny benches outside. As he walked through the door, he raised his hand in a quick wave.

Rachel nearly burnt her tongue after accidentally inhaling the coffee. She sputtered and coughed, then quickly covered her mouth with a napkin. By the time she'd recovered, the technician was gone, walking down the street with his friends.

"Who was that?" her father asked, curiosity in his eyes.

"Who? I mean, no idea." Rachel dabbed at her lips once more, still trying to get over the fact he'd waved at her. What would Lucille say now? "I think he works for the hospital."

For some reason, her father grinned. "I see. Looks like he's a big fan of the coffee here, too." When she just stared at him in confusion, his grin widened. "Go on, Bug, run after him."

"What?" Her eyes widened. "I don't know him. I don't even know his name."

Mick just shrugged. "So? Ask him, then."

"Absolutely not." She wasn't going to make a fool of herself by running after some random technician just because he'd smiled at her. And waved.

"What if he's the love of your life?"

Rachel gave her father a flat stare. "I highly doubt it."

"Coward."

Instead of arguing, Rachel looked out the large glass windows, but the technician had already rounded the corner, and she realised she'd missed him again. Her father was right. She was a coward. But better a coward than a fool, so she stayed seated and enjoyed her mediocre coffee and her much-too-large sandwich.

Fabian

It was eight o'clock and Fabian was staring blindly at his folder and the notes he'd taken during his last study session with Samantha. Ophelia sat next to him, stroking his neck in the way that usually turned him on, but today was an unwelcome distraction.

"Don't you think it's time for a break?" she whispered in his ear.

As much as he wanted to throw everything to the wind and make out with his very sexy girlfriend, he couldn't. "I have Physics tomorrow."

"So, you want to study all night?"

Fabian sighed heavily. "If I have to."

"That's ridiculous. You'll just fall asleep tomorrow."

Another potential nightmare to add to his already bad dreams. "I'll go to bed. Just not with you in it. Sorry."

Ophelia let go but couldn't help rolling her eyes. "Do you want me to leave?" she asked with great restraint.

Fabian felt terrible, but he had to decide with his head, not his heart or any lower parts of his body. "It's only a week."

She sighed, put her arms around him, and kissed his head. "I understand, of course. But for what it's worth, you've got this. I believe in you."

"Thank you," he whispered, his guilty conscience churning in his stomach. "I promise I'll make it up to you."

"Don't worry about me. I'm just going to spend the week with Anne. We'll do some research on her goddess." She stood up slowly. "It'll be fun, but not as fun as it would've been with you."

Fabian looked at her wistfully. "Believe me, I'm no fun at the moment."

Ophelia laughed. "I've noticed. I'll put a pizza in your oven before I go, so don't forget to eat, and remember, you've got this. Good luck."

He was sorry to see her go, but for the next ten minutes he actually focused and felt like he was getting somewhere, much to his surprise. There would be no acing the exam, but that wasn't Fabian's goal. He just needed to pass so he could put the whole experience behind him.

The key turned in the door, announcing his parents' arrival. It only took a moment for Caroline to stumble into the living room. "I'm so sorry. We got stuck in traffic all the way to Wernigerode. Your grandmother sends her love and good luck for tomorrow."

She kicked off her shoes and put down her handbag. Behind her, his father hurried to the toilet.

"Damn, it's almost half past eight," she said. "Have you eaten yet? I still have to make you a lucky charm. I would have got one from the shop, but they sold out last Tuesday and I haven't got around to making another." She kissed his head, squeezed his shoulder, and went into the kitchen. "I will, though, right after I make..."

"Mum?" She'd fallen silent so suddenly alarm bells rang in Fabian's ears. Quickly, he got up and followed her.

He found her standing in front of the oven, looking at the freezer pizza bubbling in the heat, tears streaming down her cheeks.

Fabian was instantly transported back to when he'd found her crying in the shop. That had been half a year ago and nothing had changed. Any progress she'd made had been destroyed after she'd taken over the shop again. Her doctor had wanted to send her to a rehabilitation clinic by the Baltic Sea, but his mother had refused on the grounds of Fabian's exams.

"I'm so sorry," Caroline whispered. "I wanted to cook for you."

"That's alright. I can eat pizza *and* your food." Fabian tried to save the day before she had a complete mental breakdown. "Studying makes me hungry."

"But I promised to make you gratin. It's your favourite."

It was, but the gratin wasn't going to help him pass Physics. Fabian just knew it was important to her. "I still have Biology on Wednesday."

His mum started to shake her head. "Mum, it's okay. It's just a couple of exams. I've had exams before."

"It's your Abitur."

"But I'm old enough to look after myself. I don't need to be pampered. You're not a bad mum just because you don't make me my favourite meal before my Physics exam."

Caroline took a deep breath. Fabian knew she was trying to absorb his words and forgive herself. In his opinion, she was the best of mums. And to him, her mental health was more important than anything he had going on.

Gently, he took her arm and led her to the couch. "You've had an exhausting trip. I'm not going to starve in the next ten minutes. If you want, we can watch some TV and share the pizza. And then Dad can cook something for both of you."

He saw his father in the doorway, the worry he felt reflected in Joachim's face. When their eyes met, his father nodded. "I'll take care of it."

Fabian settled his mother on the couch and snuggled up next to her.

"But only for half an hour," Caroline said quietly. "I don't want you to fail your exam because of me."

"Don't worry about me. Sam prepared me. I've got this."

He didn't, but he'd be damned if he'd let his mother know. She already had enough to worry about.

The next morning didn't feel real. Only the Year 13s were at school, everyone else was on class trips or off, making the campus eerily quiet. Fabian leaned against the wall and tried to read through his entire folder one more time. Rachel was sitting on the stairs, waiting patiently, not even bothering to check her notes again.

Samantha arrived, a nervous smile on her face. "Good morning."

"Speak for yourself," Fabian muttered. He'd barely slept last night. First, he'd lain awake worried sick about his mum, then he'd been plagued by a series of nightmares. And to top it all off, his mum hadn't managed to make the lucky charm she'd promised him. Nothing about this morning was good. "I still have ten pages to read."

Samantha pulled down his folder, forcing him to look at her. "You're ready for this."

"Again, speak for yourself."

She rolled her eyes but left him to sit with Rachel. The two chatted quietly and it didn't sound like physics at all.

Five minutes later, Mr Herbert stepped out and motioned them inside. "You can come in now. Backpacks against the wall. I only want to see pens, calculators, and water bottles. If you need more paper, you can get it from the front. Now don't peek."

Fabian took a deep breath and joined the others in the room. White paper gleamed from the tabletops, making him feel nauseous. Each table was isolated to minimise the chance of cheating. As he made his way to a table near Samantha, he caught Mr Herbert's eye. Not wanting to risk an errant look getting him—or Samantha—into trouble, he chose a seat in the opposite corner.

Mr Herbert waited until everyone was settled, then looked at the clock alongside them. When it struck eight, he nodded. "You may turn the exam over now. You've got four hours. Good luck."

Fabian's hands were already sweating as he turned over the exam papers and began to read through the questions. Contrary to his and Samantha's belief, there was a small mechanics section. That part should be doable. He'd studied this.

On the other side of the room, Samantha was already writing on the provided pile of paper. Rachel took a moment to read all the questions, then started on what looked like the last block of questions: quantum physics. Of course, half the questions were about Heisenberg's Uncertainty Principle.

He went back to the beginning. Better to start with something he was good at.

Halfway through the first question, however, Fabian no longer felt confident about mechanics. The first result he'd gotten was complete rubbish. He checked the maths and came up with another even more outrageous than the first.

Deciding to come back to it later, he tried the next bit. And failed to get much further.

Pathways. It didn't matter if he got the right result. If he could just show his paths, maybe he could scrape together enough points to pass.

He drank some water, tried again, and tripped over another question. He jumped from question to question, trying to answer something, then striking it through when he realised how wrong he was. By now, half his work was crossed out, and even with his failing maths skills, Fabian knew he hadn't scored nearly enough points, if any.

Suddenly Rachel stood up. Fabian watched as she took her stack of papers and handed them in at the desk in front of the classroom. He watched in astonishment as she grabbed her backpack and left the room. A glance at the clock told him that they'd already been in the room for two and a half hours.

He glanced over at Samantha and found her looking *happy*. Happy and confident. Of course, there was a whole pile of neatly answered questions she was going through again to check her results.

Fabian drank some more water and rubbed his forehead. He only had to get fifty per cent right. Only fifty.

He hadn't even answered fifty per cent of the questions.

Drink again.

Another ridiculous result.

What was the formula?

More people handing in.

Time was ticking.

Drink.

Another try, another failure.

Fifty minutes left.

Samantha finished.

The water bottle was empty. Should he use his magic to refill it? Or maybe use his magic to break some pipes, like in that first class at the beginning of Year 12, so he could have a do-over.

He rubbed his temples, despairing at the crossed-out sections, the half-finished formulas, and his bullshit explanations.

The last student handed in twenty minutes before the end. Now it was just him and Mr Herbert. His teacher didn't say a word, but he seemed to be watching him every time Fabian glanced at the clock.

Only five minutes to go.

Still no water.

A lost memory and frantic writing.

Was it even the right answer, or had he mixed them up again?

Suddenly Mr Herbert was standing in front of him. One minute to go.

More writing, just for the sake of it. Maybe there was a point somewhere. There had to be.

"Time's up, Mr Bendtfeld," Mr Herbert said with unmistakable glee. "Pen down."

Fabian lowered his pen and tried his best not to make a face. Oh, how he wished he'd brought the pipes down again.

Mr Herbert picked up his exam, just glancing at the missing answers. "Looks like we'll be meeting again for the oral exam."

Great. A second chance for him to fail the exam. He grabbed his empty water bottle and stuffed it into his backpack before leaving the bloody room.

The sun was shining outside. A few students were still around, meeting up with friends. Rachel and Samantha were both discussing the exam, oblivious to his presence.

"I really thought there would be no mechanics, but that was basically twenty-five gifted points," Samantha exclaimed, sounding delighted.

Rachel rolled her eyes. "I suppose the exam board had more to do with it."

"Did you also get 55.7 metres per second on the last question?"

To Fabian's horror, Rachel nodded. He'd got fourteen, eighty-four with endless decimals, and *minus* seventeen. None of them even came close to fifty-five. So much for the mechanics part.

Taking a deep breath, he joined the two girls. "Hey."

Samantha turned to him with a broad smile. "Hi! How was it?"

"Don't ask."

Her face fell. "Oh dear. Did you manage to answer every question though?"

"Define 'every'."

"Well, every question." She laughed nervously. "The first block of questions was easy, wasn't it?"

Fabian sighed, already over this dissection of the exam. "No. Maybe. I don't know. Everything was hard for me. I…" He shook his head. "I don't think I got anything right."

"Well, you know the pathway is what really counts," Rachel chimed in. "Even if the result is wrong."

"Yes, but you need a pathway for it to count." Why wouldn't they just leave him alone? "I had a total blackout. Happy now?"

He put his hands in his pockets and walked away, unable to take their pitying faces any more than he had the previous, exuberant ones.

"Biology will be better," Samantha called after him.

He doubted it. And even if it did, it wouldn't matter if he failed Physics completely.

Matt

So far, finals weren't much different from usual exams. Sure, the written ones were longer, and they were weighted much higher, but it was still the same subject as it had been for the last two years. Matt couldn't understand why everyone was making such a fuss.

Geography had been really easy. His Physical Education exam had been a bit trickier, but not impossible. And as for Chemistry, he'd had the best teacher to get him through it.

The same teacher who was now sitting opposite him, grinning as she flicked through a box of German questions. Matt was confident that the oral exam, which wasn't due until the end of the month, would be just as easy, but he would never miss a chance to spend time with Samantha. Not even if it meant joining her rigorous exam preparation regime.

The two of them had met at Blackstone House, which unfortunately meant Jan was there too, doing homework for his paramedic training, and Lucille had also joined them in the spirit of study group. However, she was preparing for Arts, so she wasn't really part of the shenanigans.

"Okay, here we go," Samantha said. Her tongue slipped out, the tip pressing against her upper lip before flicking back in. The little tick had Matt's gaze glued to her lips, but if she realised, she didn't show it. "Name the three main themes of the Baroque period and interpret them in a modern context."

Although they'd done the whole Baroque period back in first semester, it was an easy question.

"Vanitas Vanitatem, the vanity of vanities. Memento Mori, remember you must die, and Carpe Diem, seize the day."

All three themes had been in vogue during the Thirty Years' War when whole regions had been depopulated, and both poetry and art had become obsessed with death.

Now all he had to do was figure out how to make death entertaining. It was almost too easy.

"Vanitas Vanitatem... obviously, I'm a very good-looking man." Matt hadn't even finished the thought before Samantha started to giggle. "You could say vain."

"Oh really?" Her eyes sparkled with unbridled joy as she brushed a lock of hair from her forehead. "I think eighty-three per cent of our year would agree with you."

Matt grinned. "Eighty-three isn't a hundred. Did you vote for me?"

Samantha put her elbows on the table and leaned forward. "Wouldn't you like to know?"

He was dimly aware Lucille was watching them over her art book, but he only had eyes for Samantha. He loved it when she got flirty.

"Unfortunately, mortality isn't really my thing."

Samantha gasped, but there was a twinkle in her eye. "Oh, wait a minute, let me just get my Torakh."

Matt quickly raised his hands. "Okay, okay. I probably wouldn't be able to take a step in Hescaryn without being fully aware of my own mortality."

Her smile was that of a well-fed cat, deliciously lazy and languid. "Much better. I just don't think the examiners will know what to do with Hescaryn."

She had a point. "Probably not, but maybe they'll give me fifteen points out of... deep *respect* if I tell them about the demons."

"Or zero and a referral to a psychiatrist."

Matt burst out laughing, drawing Jan's attention as well.

Samantha leaned forward even more. "And how are you going to seize the day?"

The answer was practically in front of him. "I could ask you out on a date."

"Will that impress the examiners?"

"Who knows?" Matt wriggled his eyebrows, not that he was interested in seducing any of the teachers at the school. "Does it impress you?"

Jan and Lucille's attention was now painfully obvious. Only Samantha seemed oblivious—or preoccupied. She leaned back and twirled a lock of her hair, pretending to think about it.

Matt held his breath. Despite the stress of preparing for exams and the other end-of-year events, Samantha had been unusually responsive to his charms lately. More importantly, she'd been the one flirting with him. When he saw her tongue again, he wondered if it was really as inadvertent as he'd thought or if she knew it was driving him wild and was enjoying the teasing.

He needed her to say yes so he could get her alone with that tongue and find out if it tasted as sweet as he'd imagined.

But before she could give him an answer, Hugo burst in, looking as if he'd failed every single exam he didn't even have to take.

"Hugo?" Jan asked loudly, completely ruining the moment. "What happened?"

"I lost her favour," the ghost said gloomily.

With a sigh, Matt shifted his attention. "You mean Rachel?"

The ghost nodded, deflating even more. "Yes. She no longer sees me. She's always talking about *him*. I can't take it anymore."

Samantha leaned over to Lucille. "Is he jealous?" she whispered.

"Sure is, but of who?" Lucille's eyes twinkled with curiosity.

"I really don't know what's so great about that rotting piece of meat," Hugo began to rant, much to everyone's amusement. "It's not meant to last. His brown curls will grow thin, and his dimpled smile will be hidden by wrinkles. But me, I'll be here forever. I'll always be there for her."

"Who are you talking about?" Jan asked annoyed.

There was a spark of anger in Hugo's eyes. "Oh, she doesn't know his name. She's never spoken to him, and she doesn't know anything about him and yet... here we are." He shuddered. "She told me he was doing something weird to her stomach. I advised her to see a doctor and she called me silly." The indignation of it all made Hugo snort. "I'm the silly one, but her obsession with this mortal man isn't silly?"

"Wait a minute." Samantha frowned. "Did you expect the two of you would..." She didn't even seem able to say it out loud.

Matt had no such qualms. The idea of Hugo being in love with Rachel was highly entertaining. "You have to understand, Hugo, mortality is irresistible. The immortal ones will always be there—we're literally eternal—but the mortal ones are only here now."

"I see," Samantha said, her gaze burning into his face. "So, it's my mortality that fascinates you so much?"

Her voice was all flirtation, no indignation, which made Matt grin. "Among many other things. What can I say? Memento Mori."

He was relieved when she chuckled in response. For once, he'd said exactly the right thing.

Unfortunately, Hugo was less amused. "I see, you think I'm silly, too."

Samantha's eyes widened. "Oh no, you have the wrong idea. We're very... um... So, Rachel has a crush on someone?"

"It's just fleeting, nothing serious."

Rachel having a crush was pretty serious in Matt's opinion. If you ignored her original infatuation with Fabian, she'd never shown much interest in anyone. Even during that ill-matched relationship she'd never seemed to be in love.

"But she hasn't spoken to him yet?" Lucille asked curiously.

"Not that I know of, although she plans to next time she sees him."

Lucille squealed with delight. "Oh, this is exciting. I must know everything. You know what? I'm going to call her."

"Don't," Samantha warned.

"I just want to see the man who can turn Rachel's head with nothing but an infectious smile," Lucille protested.

"And brown curls," Jan added, to fuel the fire. "He must be really special."

Hugo's face darkened even more. "He's not special at all. He's alive, just like everyone else here."

Matt couldn't help himself. "Yes, but we could all be dead tomorrow."

As expected, Samantha threw the study card at him, but her eyes sparkled.

It was too much for the ghost. Hugo pulled a face, raised his chin, and floated out of the house.

Lucille groaned in disappointment. "I wanted to know more."

"Well, from what we know," Jan said magnanimously, "she attracted Hugo, so this other guy is probably just as weird."

"At least he's alive," Samantha quipped, and all four of them burst out laughing.

Later that night, Matt sat down with his father to celebrate the end of the written exams. His time at school was coming to an end, and although he didn't mind the exams too much, he couldn't help but feel a little apprehensive about what was going to be a massive change in his life. Big decisions lay ahead of him and the last time he'd made one—coming to Greenvalley—it had changed everything. Most importantly, him.

"So, have you decided what you're going to do?" René asked after they'd toasted the exams.

"First, I want to enjoy the summer... if my brothers let me." That was definitely something Matt would have to deal with soon.

René winced. "And when summer is over?"

"I want to study." All his friends had plans to go to university. Even Jan had gone back to school, although his was much more practically oriented. "I was thinking about staying in Greenvalley and going to university like everyone else, but I have to admit the courses don't sound very interesting."

"What, no Tourism Management or Business Engineering for you?" René joked. As one of the few higher education institutions in the Harz region, the University of Greenvalley had a strong focus on the tourism sector. There were a few traditional subjects, but Matt had seen enough of those at school.

Rachel was going to study Maths, while Lucille was planning to study History. If he passed, Fabian would probably study Biology and

Samantha would continue with Chemistry, even though it wasn't her first choice. She'd really wanted to study Pharmacy, but the nearest university offering it was over a hundred kilometres away, and leaving Greenvalley was out of the question. At least for now.

As for Matt... The only reason he was toying with the idea of studying at Greenvalley was to spend more time with Samantha. But while they had enough chemistry to spare between them, he loathed the thought of having to study it.

"None of those subjects sound like they'd get me anywhere. I mean, I guess I could offer Hell Tourism."

René snorted. "A once in a lifetime experience."

Matt burst out laughing. "For sure."

When he'd calmed down, he decided to entertain the seed Chay had planted. "I applied to the University of Fader. No idea if I'll get in, but Chay said he'd put in a good word for me, and apparently, they love him. They have this huge department of Interglobal Studies." He shrugged, trying not to get his hopes up. "I thought now that I know Ashuan, I could get to know the next world."

"I see." René looked impressed, if a little sad. "It sounds exciting. I hope you'll come and visit from time to time."

"I'm not moving away," Matt said quickly. Unlike Samantha, he had options. "Fader or wherever, it only takes me a few seconds to get there. So, if it's not a problem with you, I'd like to... stay."

René's smile was full of the warmth Matt had come to appreciate in his father. "You'll always have a place here."

"Well, I hope there's a little place for me, too."

Both Traidous men's heads turned at the sound of the sultry voice. There, in the middle of the living room, was Melaney, wearing her usual wisp of nothing and smiling seductively at them.

Crumbs, who'd been dozing next to his food bowl, barked at her, startled by the sudden appearance.

"Mother?" Matt asked at the same time as René acknowledged her.

"Melaney."

She nodded coyly at them. "Good evening, gentlemen." She gave them a mock curtsy, then sat on the couch, crossing her legs so her already short dress slid up even higher. She leaned forward, giving them the best view of her cleavage.

Next to Matt, René swallowed hard. Matt, however, was more annoyed by her antics than aroused. Annoyed and worried. "What are you doing here?"

"What do you think?" There was a steel edge to her sweet tone. "I've come to visit my youngest after he shamefully ignored my invitations all year."

Definitely worried now. "I... uhm... I've been busy finishing my Abitur." When his mother just stared at him, uncomprehending, he explained, "My final exams at school."

"And?"

"Well, I think I've done well so far."

"Of course you have." Melaney snorted. "I didn't raise you to be an idiot."

Matt bristled at how quickly she'd dismissed him. He'd never had the same urgency to succeed as his human friends, but he'd worked hard for it. "It was actually Chay who took care of my education."

"The boring part, you mean. Numbers and reading and history about a bunch of people who never lived long enough to matter." Her eyes pinned him to the chair. "*I* took care of the most important part of your education."

Matt wished he didn't know what she meant. Uncomfortably, he rubbed his neck. "I wouldn't say it was the most important part."

Melaney gave him a flat stare. "Were you planning to ascend to Lust as a virgin?"

"Did you...?" René asked, suddenly horrified.

"No!"

"I have servants for that task," Melaney said, completely missing the point.

By sheer force of will, Matt managed to tear himself away from her gaze. He walked over to Crumbs and dug his fingers into his fur, using the dog as an anchor against the sexually charged atmosphere in the room.

He had to tell her. Maybe then he'd be able to enjoy the summer. "I don't want to become Archdemon." That wasn't so hard, was it?

As expected, Melaney's eyes darkened.

"To be honest, I don't think it would be a good fit." Somehow, he had to make his mother see she should take him out of her cruel game. "I haven't even had sex for..." He quickly counted the months in his head and surprised himself. "Almost twelve months."

Her eyes widened. "With anybody?"

"There just wasn't anyone I was interested in." The truth was that he wasn't interested in anyone *else* but Samantha. And since Samantha found her pleasure in Cian's arms, there hadn't been much action in his own bed.

René seemed to be aware of Matt's little omission, but he wisely stayed out of the discussion.

"What a waste." Melaney clicked her tongue. "As I see it, it's high time I took care of it."

"You're going to take care of it?" Matt asked, feeling his anxiety spike. This couldn't possibly mean what he thought it meant.

Melaney crossed her arms, looking displeased. "I'm not leaving until you've taken some time to reconsider your recent life choices."

Matt shot a worried look at René and found it reflected there. How the hell was he going to get out of this?

Samantha

Life after the written exams was surprisingly carefree. The only classes on her schedule were study groups and the voluntary oral exam preparation classes. All others had been suspended, leaving Samantha with a lot of time she hadn't quite filled yet. Barring any nasty surprises tomorrow, she only had one oral exam left to prepare for.

At least as far as her own exam load was concerned.

"I bet it went much better than you thought," she said to Fabian on the phone as she walked down the street. She'd just spent the whole morning helping him prepare for the compulsory Politics oral exam he still had to sit.

Unfortunately, it wasn't Politics that had kept him awake at night. "I failed, I'm telling you. I'd be surprised if anything I wrote down was correct."

Samantha rolled her eyes. "I highly doubt it. You're much better at Physics than you give yourself credit for."

"But not better than Herby gives me credit for."

"Herby's not the only one marking your exam." Even Mr Herbert couldn't take any points from him in this exam.

"But this time it's not Herby. It's me. I failed." By the sound of it, Fabian seemed to have collapsed on his bed. "I don't know if I can repeat the year if I fail tomorrow."

Samantha stopped, too upset to continue. "Fabian, listen. It's not over yet. If you fail Physics, you can make up for it in the Orals. You get a second chance."

"With Herby."

"Sure, but I'll be there every step of the way. And if"—she took a deep breath—"if you really don't graduate, repeating a year isn't the worst thing that could happen. You're not a hopeless case. It would probably be a good thing, because you're not a bad student at all, and you'll get better grades the second time around. Plus, you would have Physics with a different teacher. You'd probably be top of the class."

"As if." Fabian snorted on the other side. "I don't want to repeat," he whispered after a moment.

"Then you won't," Samantha said confidently, "because you will pass. We have two weeks. I'll design a Physics boot camp, if I have to."

"You'd do that, wouldn't you?" He didn't sound quite as desperate as before. "Thanks. I don't know what I'd do without you."

Samantha bit her lip to stop herself from saying the obvious. The truth was, she couldn't imagine going to university without her best friend, either. He wouldn't be gone from this earth, but she'd miss him dreadfully. "I've got you."

A sigh. "I know. Let's talk about something else."

"Your mum?" Samantha hadn't been able to check in with Caroline because of the exams, but from what she'd heard, she wasn't doing well. No wonder Fabian was struggling.

"No, silly things, please. Who are you taking to the ball?"

"No one?" Samantha laughed nervously. "I mean my grandma and my dad are coming, so I guess them?"

Fabian chuckled. "Sad, really sad. I thought you had too many admirers vying for your attention."

"Me and admirers?" Samantha snorted. "What are you talking about?"

"Well, are you gonna show up with Cian or are you gonna take pity on Matt?"

Samantha rolled her eyes. "That question right there is exactly why my date is going to be my dad."

"Boooring."

At least Fabian sounded a bit better now. Samantha decided to keep him entertained. "Let me guess, you're taking Lia to the ball?"

"Of course. She sent me pictures of the dress she bought with Anne yesterday. It's hot AF... I mean beautiful. Really beautiful." He coughed nervously.

Samantha laughed, amused at his inability to control himself. If there was one thing they didn't talk about in their friendship, it was sex, so this was big. He seemed completely smitten with Ophelia. "I see. Well, make sure you *actually* take her to the ball and not somewhere else when you see her."

"Unless I fail. Then we can skip the ball and hide away for the summer."

And they were back to exams. "You won't fail. I'll make sure you can take Lia to the ball without feeling sorry for yourself all night."

She'd arrived at her house and was looking for her keys while Fabian snorted into the phone. "I have to go now."

He took a deep breath. "It's going to be fine, right?"

"Right."

"Thanks."

Samantha hung up the phone and opened the door. "Hi Dad, I'm back from—"

She was only halfway through the door when she saw a leg hanging over the sofa. A female leg, and a very naked leg at that. And it wasn't her mother's.

Then her father appeared, his face flushed as he gave her a nervous grin. "Hey darling."

"Darling?" a woman's voice said. A moment later, the leg disappeared and a vaguely familiar woman looked over the sofa, her cheeks equally flushed. "You must be Ben's daughter."

"Yes, this is Samantha, my eldest." Her father ran a hand through his hair and had the audacity to chuckle softly. "This is... um... Christine. She works in the boutique across the street."

That's where Samantha had seen her before. She'd been running the shop for six or seven years and had never shown the slightest interest in her father, nor he in her, as far as Samantha could tell. And Samantha had spent many afternoons in the workshop.

It didn't make sense. "Are you two... Are you having an affair?"

Ben laughed. "You can't have an affair when you're single. It's nothing serious, darling, just a bit of fun." Meanwhile, Christine's arm snaked around Ben's neck, ready to pull him back down.

Samantha stared at them for far longer than she cared to. *Fun?* Was this how it was going to be? Her father bringing women home to have casual sex with in the living room? Not even the slightest bit embarrassed?

Christine succeeded in her manoeuvre and laughed with delight. The sounds that followed made Samantha turn on her heel.

"I have to go."

Lucille

Lucille was almost bursting with nerves as her entire year gathered in front of the stage. Today was the day they'd get their results, the day that would pretty much decide how well—and *if*—they'd passed or whether they'd have to sit additional oral exams.

She was standing with her friends, all of whom shared her excitement. All except Fabian, who looked like he was about to throw up. Lucille had heard about his disastrous Physics exam and gave him a moment's thought, but then her attention was drawn to their headmistress Mrs Renner as she took the stage.

It took less than half a minute for the students to quiet down. Mrs Renner smiled. "Hello everyone. I love seeing you all together for what may be one of your last times at this school. I want to congratulate you on your written exams and hope you're happy with what you've achieved. I'm very proud to tell you that we had twenty-three outstanding grades and only fourteen failures."

Next to Lucille, Fabian closed his eyes and took a shuddering breath. Meanwhile, Matt was grinning at Samantha. "What do you want to bet you can claim three of those outstanding grades?"

She elbowed him, but her eyes sparkled with the same nervous energy Lucille felt. Positive excitement.

Lucille crossed her fingers that she'd managed to get one of the outstanding grades. It was a possibility, though not a huge one.

"I want you all to look at your results and your other grades," Mrs Renner continued, "and decide if you want to add an additional oral exam. Remember that both results will be added together and you'll be rewarded with the average points. So, choose wisely. But do it by tomorrow evening. The form will be with your results."

Fabian groaned softly before leaning against Lucille. "If she doesn't hand out the results immediately, I'll fill the whole cafeteria with water."

"Don't. It will just smear the ink on our grades."

"I can't take this anymore," Fabian whined.

Fortunately for him and every other student in the room, Mrs Renner beckoned the tutors forward. "I'm going to hand your results to your tutors now, so if you could gather in your respective groups, please."

"Hopefully they won't be giving a speech as well," Rachel muttered as they shuffled to the right where Mr Zobel was leaving the stage with a pile of envelopes.

Robert joined them, grinning from ear to ear. "Exciting, isn't it?"

"Totally," Fabian replied sullenly.

"Alright," said Mr Zobel. "Let's get this over with so you can all relax. Barmer."

As Vanessa Barmer stepped forward, Fabian sighed with relief. "Thank you for your last name, Dad."

"Bendtfeld."

And off he went to get his results. The whole group waited with bated breath as he opened the envelope on his way back.

With one ear on Mr Zobel, Lucille nudged him. "And?"

Fabian looked up in pure misery. "Zero points."

"Shit," Matt cursed.

Lucille felt like she was going to be sick. It really was as bad as he'd thought. But before she could say anything comforting, her name was called. The last thing she heard was that the rest of his results were mediocre at best, none of them in double figures. Hopefully her own were better.

"Here you go, Lucille," Mr Zobel handed her the envelope and smiled.

After taking a deep breath, she tore the envelope open and gasped. Her Biology was only nine points, but her two main subjects were both in double figures and Latin was... "Thirteen!" she squealed as she returned to the others and fell into Samantha's arms. "I got thirteen in Latin." One of the outstanding grades *was* hers.

"That's great!" Samantha hugged her.

Matt clapped his hands as Rachel was called forward. Fabian crouched on the floor, his face hidden behind his hands, but he managed a tired, "Congrats".

Lucille looked at him sympathetically. "You can do it."

"I have to take the oral exam in Physics *and* Politics. I have to pass Politics, and I have to raise my Physics grade from zero, which means I have to get at least nine points in the oral. With Herby. I'm screwed. I'm totally screwed".

"No, you're not," Samantha said sternly. "Physics boot camp starts tomorrow. You're going to wish Herby was the one preparing you instead of me."

Fabian let out a tiny squeak, genuinely intimidated by the prospect. Even Lucille shuddered at Samantha's frightening declaration. Fortunately, she was interrupted by Rachel, who returned with new results to pore over.

"Twelve," Rachel complained. "I only got twelve in Maths. Ten in Physics," she said almost as an afterthought.

"Ten more than me," Fabian muttered, but he caught himself and added, "That's great, Rachel. Twelve is freaking fantastic."

Samantha was next, prompting Matt to extend his hand to Lucille. "So, are we betting?"

She snorted. "I'm not going to bet against Samantha when it comes to academic achievement."

Sure enough, when Samantha turned back around, her cheeks were flushed with joy. Her gaze caught sight of someone else, though, and Lucille followed it to Cian, standing two groups to the left. He was grinning from ear to ear and gestured with two full hands, then two fingers.

Samantha responded with a thumbs up, laughing softly, then showed him three full hands: the maximum points.

Lucille snorted. "There goes the first outstanding grade."

"Chemistry," Matt said, clearly having observed the same exchange. As soon as Samantha reached them, he leaned over. "Was I right?"

Coyly, she pressed her results to her chest and batted her eyelashes. She opened her mouth to reply, but then she caught Fabian's eye, and the smile fell from her lips.

Fabian sighed. "Come on, just say it."

"Thirteen. Same as my Politics." Her gaze met Matt's again. "You were right." As soon as the words were out, the grin was back.

Lucille squealed and hugged her before Fabian could bring it down again. "I knew it! That's so cool. Does that mean you've already secured your 1.0?"

"If I manage to get at least nine points in German."

Fabian snorted. "Any chance you won't?"

Samantha winced, but then caught herself. "At least we have a common goal now. Nine points. You and me. I'll come to your house every day until you're sick of me."

"There go my date plans," Matt joked.

Even Fabian couldn't help but chuckle, his cloud of doom lifting a little. It was finally Matt's turn to pick up his results, the stack in Mr Zobel's hands dwindling considerably.

Lucille realised she knew very little about Matt's grades. Samantha was always top of the class, and Fabian was always comparing himself to everyone else, but Matt never seemed to care whether his grades were good or bad. And he hadn't really started formal schooling until Year 12.

"How did you do?" she asked as soon as he returned.

"Alright."

Annoyed, she snatched the results from him and gasped. "You never told us you were a good student!"

All three grades were right up there. Two twelves and a fourteen.

Matt retrieved his results and shrugged. "It's not that—" Samantha elbowed him before he could make a fatal mistake and say *not that hard.* "—important," Matt said quickly. "It's not that important to me."

"Lucky," Fabian muttered. He finally stood up. "I'll probably have to repeat the year. Ugh."

"Don't give up yet," Lucille said. "I believe in you. Most of all, I believe in Samantha. You'll graduate with us, I know it."

There would be time to study for the final exam later. For now, Lucille wanted to celebrate.

Since her friends couldn't be persuaded to celebrate with Fabian's failure hanging over the results, Lucille met up with Philipp instead. Now *he* knew how to celebrate properly. They'd started with sparkling wine and barely finished their glasses before they'd tumbled into bed.

It was the best, most out-of-control sex they'd ever had, a celebration in more ways than one. Now they were cuddled up on the sofa, enjoying the rest of the meal Philipp had prepared for them.

His phone kept buzzing and he leaned over the table to grab it, a puzzled look on his face lifting the moment he saw who was texting him so eagerly.

"Who is it?" Lucille asked, too curious to wait for him to tell her himself.

"Um, Vivien. She's a good friend of mine," Philipp explained, taking a deep breath. "Full disclosure, we hooked up in our final year at university."

Lucille gritted her teeth. The last thing she wanted to hear about were the women Philipp had slept with before. She scolded herself for being so childish and asked him instead, "Why did you break up?"

He winced. "She went to Berlin, and I was more of a small-town reporter. We tried long distance for a while and found we liked each other, but didn't really miss each other when we weren't together. Not really the stuff of true love, if you know what I mean."

Lucille felt her heart blossom when she heard that. Sure, he hadn't necessarily said he was in love with her, but he clearly hadn't been with Vivien. "Her loss."

Philipp laughed. "If you say so." His gaze returned to the text messages. "She wants to come to Greenvalley for a week. Apparently, her magazine is doing a feature on the Harz's growing witch popularity.

And she wants to know if it's okay with me." He looked at Lucille warily. "Although the real question is whether it's okay with you."

Her first thought was "*Absolutely not*", but she quickly shot it down. Philipp hadn't beaten around the bush and had told her the truth about his relationship with Vivien, and he wanted to make sure she was on board. Besides, his friend was visiting for work, not him.

It was time to be an adult, and so she said, "Of course not. It's fine with me... unless you plan to hide me?"

Philipp tossed his phone behind him and leaned forward. "I could never hide you." Then he lowered himself on top of her to kiss her, while she giggled and wrapped her arms around his neck.

Who cared about his ex-girlfriend when she was his actual girlfriend?

Jan

Jan's new schedule certainly kept him on his toes. He had school three days a week, with lots of homework and tests, and two days of work experience at the hospital. Today was one of the latter. Compared to the theoretical classes, Jan loved the practical ones. Instead of crunching numbers and endlessly studying the names of bones, he was learning life-saving procedures and patient care.

Apart from the content of his course, he also liked the hospital environment better. The school was a bit stuffy and the teachers rather strict, as if they expected you to learn everything within a week. The hospital, on the other hand, was livelier. There was more laughter and more socialising—even the teachers were cooler. And they *loved* Jan.

Or at least they didn't hate him like some of his old teachers had. According to them, he was quick to pick up the proper way to deal with various injuries, and never had to be shown more than once or twice. For the first time in his life, Jan was at the top of his class. And he hadn't even demonstrated his healing skills yet.

"Are you coming down to eat with us?" one of his classmates asked at lunch.

"I'll come down, but I'm having food delivered." When his colleagues raised their eyebrows, he laughed. "Look, you know as much as I do. My friend just invited herself and promised to bring me a lunch box. It's never happened before." The friend in question was Rachel, and she had certainly surprised him this morning when she'd asked him to meet her in the lobby.

His colleagues whooped with delight when he mentioned it was a girl, and he laughed along with them. *As if* Rachel had taken a liking to him all of a sudden.

He walked down the stairs with them and accompanied them to the café, keeping an eye on the door. It wasn't long before he saw Rachel's trademark plaits. As promised, she was carrying a purple lunch box, but instead of looking for him, she was staring at someone else.

Jan followed her gaze and chuckled to himself. Next to the reception stood one of the technicians. Sure enough, he had dark curly hair and returned her gaze. His lips moved and Rachel froze.

By the time she'd regained control of her body, the technician was once again distracted by the receptionist handing him a file. Seizing her chance, Rachel rushed past him and straight to Jan, who could barely contain his glee.

"You really meant it about the lunch." He was aware his colleagues were watching them, but didn't feel too self-conscious. "So, is that him?"

"Who?"

"The technician. He greeted you, didn't he?"

She immediately glanced over her shoulder. "Oh, that guy. No, no, I don't even know him." But her gaze lingered on his back for a few seconds too long.

"If I remember correctly, he's a fine, rotting piece of flesh."

Rachel's head whipped around again. "Come again." Recognition flashed in her eyes. "Oh, no. You've been talking to Hugo, haven't you?"

"He came to us. Quite the jealous ghost, I must say. And all because of a hospital technician. That's why you asked me the other day." Jan couldn't stop grinning. "I see."

"Hugo doesn't know what he's talking about. If you ask him, I'm probably showing indecent interest in every man I look at for more than two seconds."

Jan laughed softly. "Of course."

"Jan, pleease. I don't even know who he is. I don't have a crush on him. Why should I? Just because he smiled at me and said hello?" As if controlled by a puppeteer, her head turned again. This time the technician looked at her at the same time and smiled, eliciting a soft sigh from Rachel.

"Sounds a lot like a crush to me," Jan commented dryly.

Rachel squeaked. "I don't even know his name." She shook her head hastily, then pushed the lunch box into his hands. "There's your food. Goodbye."

"Oh, come on." She was already hurrying away. "Does this mean I get food every day now?"

Jan snorted as she ran off. The lunch box had clearly been an excuse to see the technician.

Rachel stormed out of the building, too embarrassed to even look at her stranger. To Jan's delight, he noticed the technician watching her go. Whatever was going on between them wasn't one-sided. But if Rachel carried on like this, nothing else would ever happen. She definitely couldn't bring him lunchboxes every day just to have a reason to see this guy. People would have thoughts.

While she might be too shy to talk to the guy, Jan had no such qualms. He quickly crossed the distance and reached the reception just as the technician turned away from it with his folder.

"Hi."

Surprised, the man paused. Then his eyes fell on the purple lunch box in Jan's hands, and he frowned.

"Oh, don't worry. We're just friends. The girl you've been ogling and me, that is, not you and me... yet." Jan shook his head. "Let's try this again. Hi, I'm Jan, and I think my friend might have a crush on you."

Rachel was *so* going to kill him if she ever found out. Then again, she might die of embarrassment before he was in any danger.

The tech chuckled and rubbed his neck. "I see. Um, I'm Adam." He had a noticeable accent, as if German wasn't his first language, which made Jan hope he hadn't understood more than the gist of his ramblings. "So, your friend...?"

"Rachel. Her name is Rachel." Jan grinned at him. "Shall we have a little chat?"

Love was in the air. Adam and Rachel weren't the only ones to catch the bug. Jan didn't know whether it was spring in full bloom, the spectacular weather, or that hospitals were truly as raunchy as TV shows often made them seem. He'd already stumbled across two nurses making out in the on-call room, and a patient making the most of visiting hours today. And that wasn't counting all the longing looks and flirtatious chatter.

It made him miss Meg. They'd broken up a month ago, and the only reason he knew she still existed was because of Anne. They hadn't even stayed friends. It was a clean break, supposed to be painless. But it only seemed to work for Meg. Jan still found himself fantasising about how to win her back, reopening the wound every time it scabbed over.

He left the hospital a little later than he'd liked and almost ran into another couple. They were making out outside the hospital, not caring about being seen. As Jan walked past, hands slipped under shirts and into pants.

"Definitely spring in the air," Jan muttered to himself, then decided to take a little detour through the city centre to grab something to eat.

As he walked along the riverside promenade, he noticed quite a few couples, and even a throuple, taking advantage of the warm weather. And what an advantage. At least half of them were having sex for all to see.

Jan shook his head in disbelief and turned away from the river, heading towards the town hall. Every time he saw a screen in a shop, it showed erotic content. A young man in bright colours was handing out free condoms. Another was handing out flyers for sex clubs.

As Jan kept walking, he was almost run down by a scantily clad woman. She was followed by an equally unclothed man, squealing with delight as he caught up with her and pinned her against the wall.

"What the hell is—?" Jan stopped in front of his favourite Thai takeaway.

There was a party going on inside, but it wasn't just any party. Jan felt his pants tighten as he watched naked people shamelessly gyrating against each other. As he looked down the street, he saw several more brazen displays.

Greenvalley had gone mad, there was no other conclusion to be drawn. Whatever was going on was spreading like wildfire. He should probably get the others together and find out what was going on.

Or he could get over Meg.

Matt

Matt was relaxing on the couch, playing with Crumbs, while his father prepared his lessons at the table. He could almost pretend this was just another night in the Traidous household, were it not for the running shower. Even that unobtrusive sound made him hyper-aware of his mother's presence.

She'd made good on her threat to move in, and the apartment he shared with his father had felt electrically charged ever since. It had always been a little too small, but now it was almost suffocating. Not that Matt could think of a single room big enough to contain the force of nature that was Melaney.

The moment he heard the shower stop, his body tensed. A minute later, Melaney entered the room wearing nothing but a towel that barely covered her from chest to ass. Wet hair tumbled over her shoulders, dripping water onto the floor.

Matt noticed his father concentrating a little too hard on his lesson plan. His nostrils flared as she passed him. As if by accident, Melaney ran a finger along René's shoulders and the poor man clenched his teeth against what must have been an unasked-for wave of desire. She sat on the couch, causing Crumbs to jump off, and forcing Matt to scoot over.

He decided to give her plenty of room and stood up. "I'm going to bed."

That was how he'd survived the last few days with her around. Just never staying in the same room for too long.

Unfortunately, this time she decided to follow him into his room. Annoyed, Matt turned, stopping short when her towel fell away.

It wasn't the first time he'd seen his mother naked. Growing up in the Residence of Lust, it was an almost daily occurrence, but this was the first time her attention had been on him and him alone.

"What do you want from me?" he asked, panic making his voice a little shaky.

"What do you think?" A seductive smile played on her lips, almost impossible to ignore.

Matt swallowed hard. "Melaney... *Mother.*" He almost never called her mother to her face. It was the human way, but he hoped it would remind her of their relationship and how impossible it was for him to do what she'd asked. "Look, I don't want to kill you."

Melaney rolled her shoulders and shrugged. "Good to know." She approached him and put a hand on his neck, pulling him towards her. "But I won't miss out on having some fun with you."

"Fun?" This challenge she'd set was *fun* for her? For a year, his brothers had been trying to kill him and his friends, and Melaney thought it was *fun?*

Without warning, she shoved him onto his bed. Matt caught himself on his elbows and looked up at her in shock. It suddenly dawned on him she wasn't there to force him to kill her. No, what Melaney wanted was far worse.

Before she managed to join him on the bed, Matt jumped through space and reappeared on her other side. "You want to have sex with me?"

Annoyed, Melaney turned around. "Why are you acting so surprised? You know who I am and what I'm interested in. Have you really forgotten everything?"

"I'm... But I'm your son." Surely, she could see the problem here.

Melaney shrugged. "So what? Do you think Balthasar, Caspar or any of your other siblings made such a big deal out of it? No, they all came willingly, I can assure you." She smiled again and Matt felt his chest tighten.

This couldn't be happening. She was his *mother!* Matt backed away until his shoulders hit the cupboard behind him. His thoughts became more and more muddled the longer he looked at her. Growing up, the activity in Melaney's bedroom had often set the whole residence on edge. He attributed at least half of his hookups to her influence, but he'd never found himself the object of her desire before.

The worst part was how his body was responding to her. It knew how mind-blowing the experience would be. Had he been two years younger, he probably wouldn't have thought twice about it. Family ties were different in Hescaryn. Demons didn't value close relationships. They were just as likely to kill their family as they were to...

"Fuck." Matt moistened his lips and felt sweat beading on his forehead.

Melaney chuckled in a way that almost brought him to his knees. "Now we're talking."

Matt shook his head as if that would help him break out of his spell. "I'm not like my siblings," he heard himself say, then clung to the words as if his life depended on them.

"True," Melaney agreed. "You're better than them." She had him cornered in the room, her fingertips running down his chest, drawing a trail of fire across his skin. "Prettier."

She smiled again, and for a moment, all of Matt's thoughts dissolved into nothingness. Then she put a finger under his chin and pushed it up just enough to kiss his neck. "Better built."

Matt's breath caught in his throat. He blinked quickly, trying to clear the fog of lust that had settled around him.

Melaney was whispering in his ear, her hot breath robbing him of his mental faculties. "Hotter."

When he suddenly felt her other hand sliding down his body, nearing the bulge in his pants, he panicked.

Panting, he pushed past her and scrambled for the door. "I have to take Crumbs for a walk. Don't wait for me."

"You can't run away from this, *son*."

It turned out Matt could. At least for now.

Rachel

As Rachel washed the dishes, her parents were busy falling back into love. She watched them through the kitchen hatch as they giggled and kissed, no longer hiding what was happening between them. A month ago, the thought of her parents making out would have disgusted Rachel. Now, she smiled and wished Nico could've seen them like this.

As far as she could remember, she'd never seen them in love, not in real life. Rachel had known nothing but endless bickering and general avoidance. She'd never understood how her parents could've ever loved each other, but now she saw it. The two of them were acting like teenagers on their first date.

Love.

Rachel sighed happily, hung the towel on the rack, and gave her parents some space.

As soon as she entered her room, Hugo floated up. "Are you alright?" he asked, searching her face with a worried look. "You're not thinking about that rotting piece of meat again, are you?"

Ignoring his malicious tone, Rachel dropped onto her bed with another happy sigh. The mere thought of the hospital technician brought a smile to her face. "He said 'hi' to me."

"So?"

"And he smiled."

"He probably smiles at every girl," Hugo grumbled.

Rachel barely heard him, lost in her memory of the guy who'd caught her eye. She'd never felt anything like it. It was as if lightning had struck her and set her whole life on fire. If she stopped to think about it for a moment, she'd probably find it ridiculous, but who needed thoughts when they could see that dimpled smile in their dreams?

She took out her phone and stared at the message Jan had sent her this morning. Even though she hadn't asked, he'd managed to dig up some information for her. Most importantly, he'd sent her a name.

"Adam. Adam." She liked how softly it rolled off her tongue, as soft as the brown curls she wanted to sink her fingers into. "Adam Black." The last name was rougher, strong and determined.

"If you ask me, that's the least inspiring name I've ever heard."

Rachel laughed, taking no offence at Hugo's ramblings. Instead, she sat up and cocked her head, still smiling. "Did you know he was from New Zealand?"

"I didn't even know there was a new Zeeland."

"It's practically on the other side of the world." But he was here, in the same place as she was. What were the chances?

Hugo huffed. "Don't you think it's suspicious he's come all this way? For what purpose, I ask."

Rachel snorted. "He's studying abroad, combining it with a gap year. It's quite common where he comes from." At least if the internet was to be believed.

"So, he won't stay here?"

The hope in Hugo's voice pulled her out of her daydreams. "I guess not. He probably won't be here for long."

A smug smile spread across the ghost's face. "There you go. It wouldn't make sense to get attached if he's going to leave so soon. The other side of the world is far away."

"Very far." You couldn't possibly live further away from Germany. Rachel swallowed. She'd been on cloud nine for most of the afternoon, but now she realised how silly she'd been. "He's probably not interested in me, anyway."

"There are no guarantees in love," Hugo said wisely.

Rachel winced, reminded of her parents' divorce. "Don't I know that? You're right, I should forget him." The memory of his dimpled smile tasted sour now. "I don't know what I was thinking."

Hugo sat on her bed, looking a little worried now. "Miss Rachel, I didn't mean to upset you."

"No, no, you're right. There's no point for all this swooning and daydreaming if we don't really have a future. It's ridiculous. It just leads to heartbreak and isn't really worth it, is it?" Surely a friendly greeting wouldn't affect her that much. Within a week, she'd have forgotten all about him. "I think I'd like to sleep now."

Hugo rose again. "Of course." He floated away, watching her in silence as she got ready for bed.

As she was about to hit the pillow, he whispered, "For what it's worth, I'll never leave you."

Rachel smiled. "I know, Hugo."

The moment Rachel fell asleep, she found herself in an unfamiliar forest. There was a tension in the air that was unfamiliar to her. She felt adventurous, on the verge of something great.

Rachel looked around, noticing long silver trees and bushy ferns. The ground beneath her bare feet was covered with moss and smaller ferns that gave way a little with each step. Just beyond the forest, she could hear waves, but everything was so overgrown she couldn't tell which way the ocean was.

As she made her way through the undergrowth, a small grey bird with a fan-like tail flitted around her head, inviting her to play. It hopped from branch to branch, leading her deeper into the forest, until she came to a rushing river and a small waterfall.

Just below the waterfall, a man was pulling a kayak to the shore. He was wearing nothing but a pair of light shorts, the waistband resting on the strong muscles of his lower back. The sweltering heat made his dark skin glisten with sweat. Rachel's breath caught in her throat as she watched a bead run down his spine.

She'd never felt such pure carnal attraction before. She'd seen it in Fabian's dreams or when Matt watched Samantha's every move. She'd heard about it from Lucille when she gushed about her latest crush or every time her mother brought a man home over the years. But she'd never felt it herself, not when she was with Fabian, and not in her dreams.

The sheer lust with which she watched this stranger's muscles roll was foreign to her. Her gaze fell on the tattoo that stretched from his left shoulder down his arm and across a quarter of his back. She felt the irresistible urge to trace each line, first with her finger, then with her lips.

When he turned, Rachel forgot how to breathe. It was *him*. The handsome technician she'd spent all week fawning over. His dark eyes met hers like lightning had hit the ground. His lips curled up in his characteristic way, and Rachel could've melted into the ferns right there and then.

Her thoughts became reality as the dream world followed her wishes. Suddenly she was on her back in the ferns, Adam above her, his strong arms holding her at a delicious distance, allowing his gaze to roam over her body.

On any other occasion Rachel would have been horrified to find herself naked, but not in this dream. In this dream, she didn't think or worry, she simply existed in Adam's arms. Without the insecurities of reality, she wrapped her arms around his neck, burying her fingers in his soft brown hair.

The distance became unbearable, every molecule of air between them an unnecessary obstacle. In reality, Rachel would have been far too shy to initiate anything. Here, she couldn't resist the dimples and fire behind Adam's gaze. She pulled him close and sighed as his lips crashed down on hers.

It was a kiss like no other. It was made of dreams and hopes, honed in fire and heat. Her entire body melted under his touch, her muscles tensing. She arched against his body, pressing every inch of skin against his. His weight came down on her, enveloping her in him until there was nothing but the two of them. As their lips met, heat exploded from her mouth into every nerve of her body.

She was on fire, hungry for more of him. So much more.

Rachel woke up drenched in sweat and with an unfamiliar ache between her legs mid-morning. Before Hugo realised she'd woken up, Rachel jumped out of bed and stormed into the bathroom, almost knocking her mother over as she came out. A minute later, cold water poured down on her. Just like the waterfall—

"Damn it!" The dream still clung to her skin, warm and sultry, full of dark promises that frightened Rachel.

She'd been drawn into sex dreams before and usually left them as quickly as possible. With this one, she hadn't even stopped to think before surrendering to Adam. This wasn't her. It didn't feel like her.

As the cold water poured over her, taking an eternity to extinguish the heat on her skin, Rachel struggled to understand. What did it mean? Whose dream had it been? If it was his, did it mean he was thinking about her, too? Had she really made such an impression on him that he dreamed of her naked in the woods?

Or had it been her dream? Had she fallen so hard for him she hardly recognised herself? It couldn't be. She'd never felt these... desires. They were everything everyone always raved about, and yet so much more than she could bear. So strange and frightening. It couldn't have been hers... could it?

There was a knock on the bathroom door. "Hey, Bug?"

Rachel bit down on a curse. The last person she wanted to talk to right now was her dad. "What?"

"Um, there's someone downstairs for you. Said he didn't have much time."

Adam.

Suddenly Rachel was wide awake. She turned off the water and grabbed a towel. "Tell him I'll be a minute."

A *minute?* How could she make herself presentable in a minute? She couldn't even dry herself off in a minute, even if she patted herself like crazy. And make-up? Did she need make-up?

"Stop it," Rachel hissed at herself. She never wore make-up. Adam had dreamed of her after seeing her without it, so why was she worrying about make-up as if she was Lucille?

She groaned and hurried back to her room to find something to wear. How did he know where she lived? Had Jan told him when he'd questioned him yesterday? And how had Adam got here so quickly after she'd just woken up from his dream?

Unless it had been her dream, after all.

Another groan escaped her lips. It was so frustrating and confusing. He was just a man. The dream didn't mean anything. She may have been the dreamer, but that didn't mean her brain wouldn't cook up weird dreams of its own from time to time.

Finally, after less than five minutes, Rachel ran down the stairs. She didn't feel presentable enough, but she was too scared to miss him if she took any longer to get ready. A wave of disappointment hit her when she realised it wasn't Adam.

"Jan?"

He gave her a crooked, arrogant grin, as if he'd just had the best night of his life. "Hey there. I've got something for you." He opened his hand and held it out. It was a key pendant in the shape of a brown bird with a long beak. A kiwi bird.

"What's this?"

"I told Adam about your finals and that you still had an exam to go, so he gave me this. For good luck." When Rachel just stared at him, he added, "Are you gonna take it or not? I've got to go to school."

Rachel grabbed the lucky charm before he could take it away. "Thanks."

As she closed the door on Jan, she almost burst with happiness. A piece of him. She held a piece of him. He thought of her, cared for her.

She pressed the kiwi to her chest and squealed softly. This was better than any dirty dream.

Lucille

Lucille enjoyed the break she'd been given from school. With only one oral to prepare, there was relatively little for her to do—and all the more time to spend with Philipp. Today, they were going to meet his friend Vivien in a café, and Greenvalley couldn't have produced a more beautiful day.

They walked hand in hand along the promenade, enjoying the sunshine on their faces like so many others. Lucille was amused to see Jennifer and Björn making out so passionately they fell into the fountain. After a moment of shock, they just carried on as before.

Philipp snorted. "Almost makes me wish I had my camera."

"Almost." As amusing as it was, Lucille didn't want to waste any camera space on the two Elite idiots.

"For the paper, I mean."

Amused, she raised an eyebrow. "What do you want to report on? Spring came late this year, but it came hard?"

Philipp coughed, a delicious red flush creeping up his neck. "Um... you'll find this amusing, but our boss has four people working on this story."

"This story?"

"Look around you! Greenvalley is experiencing an absolute sex craze. No decency left. Everyone is just going for it." He pointed his hand off to the side, and sure enough, there were two men engaged in foreplay.

"Oh my." Lucille laughed nervously. "It *is* spring. Do you have to work too?"

Philipp shook his head. "Not as long as there are no monsters involved. Besides, I've got the day off." He took a step towards their usual café and held the door open.

Lucille curtsied flirtatiously, but her smile froze when she saw the erotic posters on the wall. She loved the café because it was cute, but there was nothing cute about the new decor. If anything, it gave her a lot of ideas about what to try with Philipp once they were done with this meeting.

"There she is." Philipp waved to a black woman with a gorgeous head of curls.

As soon as she saw Philipp, her eyes lit up and she stood up. Lucille couldn't help but admire her figure-hugging style. She was exactly what Lucille imagined when she thought of a sexy big city reporter. Vivien looked like she wasn't taking any prisoners.

The two embraced like the good friends they were, then turned to Lucille.

"Lucille, this is Vivien," Philipp said with a big smile. "Vivi, that's my Lucille."

Vivien's smile was even bigger than his. She leaned in to kiss Lucille's cheek and her perfume hit Lucille's nose. A hint of something sweet and spicy. "Hello. Philipp has told me so much about you. I feel like I know you already."

As they all sat down, Lucille put a hand on Philipp's thigh. "Do you really talk about me so much?"

"Not that much," he said, laughing nervously.

"All the time." Vivien cackled and clapped her hands. "He's got it bad, Lucille. Really bad. And I can see why. You're a beautiful girl. Love the bag."

Lucille felt the heat rise in her cheeks. "So are you." She blushed and quickly turned to Philipp to stare into his pretty eyes. "I've got it pretty bad too."

Philipp didn't even blink. Instead, he leaned forward and a moment later they were kissing. Lucille wrapped her arms around him while he slipped a hand into the small of her back as the kiss went on and on. She could barely let go of him and when she did, she was gasping for breath.

She expected Vivien to be offended, but the woman just grinned. "Don't let me stop you."

Still, Lucille cleared her throat and tried to focus on her for a moment. "So, Vivien. You studied with Philipp?"

"Sure did. We always fought over the work placements."

"Vivien always won," Philipp pointed out, putting an arm around Lucille's shoulder, which didn't stay there for long, instead dropping until his hand was on her butt.

Lucille retaliated by putting her hand back on his thigh and pushing it up until it rested in his lap. What she felt there made her smile. "How do you like Berlin?" she asked Vivien.

"Oh, I love it," Vivien said passionately. "Lots of people, but that's the great thing about it. You can listen to the most fascinating characters just by travelling from one end of the city to the other. And it's such a vibrant city with people from all over the world, each bringing their own culture."

"That sounds"—Lucille's breath caught in her throat as Philipp started to massage her through the fabric of her pants—"really exciting. Look." She gasped a little. "I need a moment to freshen up. It's quite... *hot* out there."

She managed to slip out of her chair and quickly found the only toilet at the back of the café. Just as she was about to close the door behind her, Philipp ducked in and closed the latch behind him.

"What about Vivi?" Lucille asked breathlessly, already undressing him with her eyes.

"What Vivi?" Philipp joked, then his hands were on her face and they continued the kiss from before.

Lucille's knees buckled and she sank into his embrace. Philipp spun her around and pressed her back against the door, his hands slipping under her top as he kissed her neck.

"I've never done it in a public place before," Lucille confessed, not the least bit worried.

Philipp let out a raspy laugh. "Don't give me any ideas." He pulled the top over her head, breaking their skin contact for a torturous moment. Then his lips were back, kissing up her nape.

Eagerly, Lucille tugged at his shirt, almost tearing it in her efforts to get him out of it. "I'm open to anything."

His eyes sparkled before he kissed her again.

Samantha

Samantha had barely returned from Fabian's when she found Rachel on her doorstep. "What's going on?"

"I need to talk to someone. Someone alive who isn't my parent."

Chuckling, Samantha opened the door and let her in. "Is this about your mystery man?"

Rachel's eyes widened and she gasped. "Gosh, how many people has Hugo told?"

"He came to us during study group," Samantha admitted, then chuckled. "He was extremely jealous. I have no idea what he thought was going on between you two before. Iced tea?"

She went into the kitchen, took out two glasses and filled them with iced tea from the fridge.

"Thanks." Rachel leaned against the counter and sipped the drink. "Hugo and I don't have a relationship."

"He's fond of you."

"And I'm fond of him, but I'm not in love with him, and I have no desire to kiss him or even get close to him."

Samantha raised her eyebrows. "But you do have those urges when it comes to your mystery man?"

"Adam," Rachel blurted out. "His name is Adam. Jan asked him... I mean..." She put a hand in her pocket and pulled out a small kiwi bird charm. "He gave me this. Adam, that is. After Jan told him about our exams."

"Cute." Samantha narrowed her eyes. "Wait a minute. What does Jan have to do with this? Is he your wingman?"

Rachel looked absolutely horrified. "No, he... He took it upon himself to ask Adam his name because they both work at the hospital. He's a medical technician there and he's from New Zealand. Isn't that cool?"

"Very," Samantha said, grinning as she watched Rachel gush. "So, let me ask you again, do you have certain urges when it comes to Adam?"

The question darkened Rachel's cheeks so much Samantha almost burst out laughing. For some reason, her friend was dying of shame. Samantha was surprised she cared at all as Rachel had never shown much interest in sex, not even when she'd been in a committed relationship.

"Oh my god, what is it?"

"I had a dream," Rachel whispered, her breath catching in her throat. She put her glass down, as if afraid she'd break it. "We... There was Adam... in the forest and then... we... we had sex."

Samantha started to giggle, then quickly clapped her hand over her mouth and swallowed. It took her a few breaths to regain enough composure to ask. "Was it good?"

Rachel looked at her as if she'd been slapped. "It was horrible!"

"Oh dear."

"Not the sex. I mean... Gosh!" Rachel clenched her jaw and groaned. "It was good. Surprisingly good, but I don't... that's not what I want. I don't know what's happening to me. This isn't normal."

Samantha took a step closer and held her hand. "Rachel, it was just a dream. These things happen."

"They don't happen to me! Besides, I don't even know if it was my dream or his."

"Does it matter?" Samantha wriggled her eyebrows.

Rachel let go of her hand to bury her face in her hands. "I've never had a sex dream before. Not one where I was part of it."

"But it was good?"

"It was perfect. Like... like a dream. Now I want to go to New Zealand and repeat it in person."

Samantha laughed. "Maybe you should give Adam a test drive here first. The tickets are expensive."

Rachel's eyes widened and her mouth fell open. "Test drive? Sam, I haven't said a word to him."

"We'll have to change that." She took Rachel's hand and pulled her along. "Let's go to the hospital and make your dream come true."

"No way!"

"Come on! You like him. And he seems to like you, too." When Rachel resisted, Samantha added: "I'm not asking you to have sex with him. You can wait until you get to know each other a bit better." One look at Rachel's face made her chuckle. "Or not."

"I don't know."

"I can hold your hand. Not during the sex, though."

"Sam! I don't even know if he's working today."

"If not, we'll just go and see Jan."

Rachel pulled herself free. "No. If I go, I'll go alone."

Samantha chuckled. She didn't want to push Rachel any harder than she had to. "I want a full report, though."

"O-okay."

At least it seemed like Rachel was ready to face her crush now. She even followed Samantha willingly to the door. Just as they passed through the living room, the front door opened and slammed against the wall as her father stumbled in with a woman in his arms.

A key clattered on the floor. The two of them were locking lips, not even bothering to close the door. By the time they got halfway up the stairs, they had lost half their clothes.

Samantha stared at them, dumbfounded. The woman wasn't Christine this time. This one was a total stranger to her and yet...

"My mum used to do that all the time."

Samantha swallowed. She'd known about Annette's reckless behaviour. There had been many nights when Samantha had comforted Rachel after she'd escaped the sexually charged tension in her home. But never in a million years had she thought her father would turn out like this. And with no regard for his daughter living in the same house.

"Dad!" She hurried up the stairs. If this was how it was going to be, they needed boundaries. And fast.

But her father didn't even hear her. He and his mystery woman smashed into the walls, unable to be even an inch apart. In their blind fervour, they searched for the nearest door, which happened to be Samantha's room.

"Dad!"

"Not now, sweetheart." And with that, they stumbled into her bedroom.

Stunned, Samantha stood in the hallway, staring blindly at the open door. Every sound that followed made her stomach clench tighter. They were doing it in her room. In her bed.

"Yep, definitely like my mum," Rachel commented dryly.

Samantha couldn't even answer. She felt sick and betrayed. Violated.

She spun on her heel and ran down the stairs, almost overwhelmed by the need to throw up and the urge to go as far as her feet would take her. Suddenly, she couldn't bear to stay in her house for another second.

Matt

"What do you mean, she wants to sleep with you?"

In his hour of need, Matt turned to René for guidance. For better or worse, they were both trapped in the small apartment with Melaney. Matt had tried talking and he'd tried avoiding her, hoping she'd get bored waiting for him, but his mother was nothing if not stubborn.

The way he saw it, he had two options: sleep with her or kill her. Unfortunately, he was no longer sure which one his mother was after.

"She came into my room naked."

René frowned. "I thought she wanted you to kill her. Not that I want that either. For you or for her."

"I'm not going to. Do you think that's it, though? That she's trying to get on my nerves until I snap and kill her?" Was it all just a deeply upsetting trick?

"I don't know *what* to think. Especially when she's in the room." Horrified, René shook his head. "Please forget I said that."

"Consider it done." The last thing his father needed was to fall into Melaney's trap again. She'd already stolen enough years from him.

René sighed. "Knowing her, she won't give up until she gets what she wants. You can't give in, understand? She's your mother."

"It's not like that in Hescaryn."

"It is here."

As if he didn't know. Matt groaned. "I don't want to sleep with her, trust me. But she's the Archdemon of Lust. Her power can..." His mouth went dry as the true extent of her power crossed his mind. If she really wanted to sleep with him, there was no way he could resist her. Even if he hated every minute of it. "You feel it, don't you?"

"Matt, your mother—"

"Are you two talking about me?" Melaney appeared in the middle of the room, wearing a negligée that revealed much more than it concealed. "If it isn't my two favourite men."

Matt swallowed hard. "Men?"

In a flash she was in front of him, a hand on his cheek. "My dear, you don't think I'd put them all aside just for you, do you?"

"Y-you could set me aside," Matt offered, feeling his throat tighten.

She bit her lip and smiled seductively, her hand tracing a line from his cheek down his neck. "You're my masterpiece. I could never."

"You're my mother!" Matt clung to the words, ignoring the way his body was reacting. He wanted to pull away from her touch, but his feet wouldn't move.

"And the best fling you'll ever have," Melaney said in a deep, sultry voice that did something funny to his stomach—and the regions below.

Helpless, Matt turned his eyes to his father. The words "help me" caught in his throat when he saw René's glassy eyes. Melaney's desire had completely captivated him.

He was still looking at his father when he suddenly felt her lips on his neck. Hot breath blew on his ears and his skin burnt where she sucked it between her teeth. For a moment, every nerve in his body was attuned to that little spot, his own thoughts lost in a whirl of lust.

It wasn't until René let out a soft gasp that Matt's brain kicked in again. Not knowing what else to do, he simply disappeared.

Jan

Renovating an old house was a hell of a job. Doing it with a snow witch was a test of patience in more ways than one.

"Neve likes paint!" the little snow witch exclaimed, her dress and face covered in splashes of sky-blue paint.

Jan winced. "Jan likes it, too, but I prefer it on the walls." The only good thing about Neve's 'help' was the thin layer of ice that protected the floor—much better for the environment than layers of plastic, though not that great on the floorboards upon thawing.

The doorbell rang and Neve promptly floated across the room and down the stairs. A minute later she was back. "Samantha brought luggage."

"Luggage?" Jan put down the paint roller, wiped his hands and headed downstairs, careful not to slip on the ice.

Sure enough, Samantha was standing in the hall, a large backpack on her shoulders and a sleeping bag in her arm. The sight of her filled Jan with dread. People didn't just turn up with sleeping bags if everything was fine.

"I hope I'm not intruding," Samantha said in a small voice.

"On me and Neve?"

The little snow witch floated forward to hug Samantha's leg. "Neve likes Samantha. Did Samantha bring food?"

"No, but I can cook."

Jan took a step forward and wordlessly offered to take the sleeping bag off her. "Come in. Maybe we should start with why you're here, because you look like you're going camping."

Samantha handed him the sleeping bag and closed the door behind her. "Well... not camping per se." She took a deep breath, her eyes a little too wide. "I wanted to ask if I could move in."

He almost dropped the sleeping bag. "Excuse me?"

Her nostrils flared slightly, and he noticed the redness in her eyes. Still, she forced a smile. "I mean, the garden is mine, isn't it?"

Jan laughed. "True... I guess."

"Alright, here it goes: I feel terrible about it, but I can't deal with my dad dating again. You know, when my parents were together, the most they did was kiss—they probably haven't had sex for years—but now he has a new woman over every day and I... I suddenly wish I'd moved to Cologne."

Now that was something Jan could sympathise with. "I can only imagine. Parents kissing is disgusting, but watching them flirt or whatever your father does—"

"He's having sex," Samantha blurted out. "In my room."

"Yuck!"

"So, can I move in with you? At least for a bit until I find something of my own? I'd normally go to Fabian, but I don't want to impose on Caroline."

Jan found himself nodding before he'd even processed the question. "Sure, if you don't mind the leaky roof and dodgy stairs." It would be a long time before Jan could make the whole house liveable.

"I could help you renovate. Not that I know what to do."

"Neither do I," Jan joked, feeling a wave of despair coming over him as it often did when he thought of the house. "But you can cook, which is a big plus. I'll take a roommate over ramen any day."

Samantha giggled and he felt the cloud of doom lift a little. "I can do that."

"Samantha's food every day?" Neve asked, then cheered. "Neve loves new roommates." And with that, she floated back upstairs.

"Well, she changed her mind quickly, didn't she?" Samantha said, giggling.

"She's extremely bribable." So was Jan now that he thought about it. Ironically, he rather enjoyed having Neve around. And as much as he cursed all the extra work the Blackstone House had made for him, he wouldn't consider selling it for anything. "Alright, let's get you settled in."

He mentally went through the rooms in his house and decided on the study. It was bare and a bit dusty, but at least it was dry.

Just as they were about to go upstairs, Matt appeared in front of them. His eyes were a little wild and he was panting. Before Jan could even ask if he was alright, he blurted out, "I need to move in with you."

"Uh…"

"Has something happened?" Samantha asked, immediately concerned.

"My mother's in Greenvalley."

Jan felt his throat tighten. The last time he'd seen Melaney, she'd ripped Malcolm a new one. "Oh."

"She wants me to sleep with her."

"What the—" Jan's eyes widened. "Did I hear that right? She—" He shook his head. "Have all the parents gone mad?"

Matt winced, looking like he'd been tortured with a hot iron instead of… Jan couldn't even finish the thought. As hot as Melaney was, she was Matt's *mother*. Torture with a hot iron was far preferable.

"Please. I can't stay there. It won't be for long, I promise. I hope."

"Oh well…" Jan looked at Samantha, considering how complicated their past had been. "If that's okay with you?"

Samantha seemed rather amused. "Well, we can't send him home to that." She shrugged. "It'll be fine, I'm sure."

Jan decided "fine" was one way to describe this new living arrangement. He was in the kitchen making breakfast while Samantha enjoyed a cup of tea when Matt walked in, wearing nothing but a pair of boxers.

The moment he saw Samantha, a crooked smile appeared on his face. "Morning."

"Good morning," Samantha replied coyly, her gaze fixed on her teacup.

Matt completely ignored Jan and walked towards Samantha, only to grab a teacup from the cupboard. Samantha had to move a little to avoid him brushing up against her, but when he reached for the kettle, he had her effectively pinned in place.

"What are you doing?" Samantha asked, a question Jan desperately wanted an answer to as well.

"I'm pouring tea." That was, indeed, all he was doing, but there was so much tension in the air Jan couldn't look away. Matt settled against the counter, shoulder to shoulder with Samantha. "Did you sleep well?"

Samantha looked as if she was going to shrug but thought better of it. "It was a bit uncomfortable. Even with a mat."

"You're welcome to join me on the couch tonight."

Jan nearly choked on his cereal while Samantha gasped. "You want me to sleep on the couch next to you?"

Matt put his mug down and turned to Samantha, still completely ignoring Jan in the kitchen. "Or *with* me."

"Matt!"

Her cry only seemed to spur Matt on. He looked deep into her eyes and Jan saw the moment Samantha's indignation vanished. She was completely enthralled, which was only made worse when he raised a hand to brush a strand of hair behind her ear.

As if to protect herself, Samantha raised the teacup to her mouth, a tiny obstacle between her lips and Matt's. He never broke eye contact. On the contrary, he placed his hands on hers, then tipped the cup to his own lips. Samantha stared helplessly into his eyes as Matt lowered the cup between them.

Jan cleared his throat. He'd been watching them for far too long, suddenly aware of how wrong it felt to be in the same room as them. "Um, can I have some tea, too?" He immediately closed his eyes. Was that the best he could do? He may as well have asked if he could join them.

But it had worked to some extent. Broken from the spell, Samantha turned away from Matt and pushed her mug into Jan's hand. "I... I need to go. Fabian will be... I have to study with him. Now." Then she hurried out of the kitchen.

Gulping, Jan turned to Matt, expecting him to glare or worse. But his friend just sighed, looking more lovesick than angry.

Jan took a deep breath as he came off his own heightened libido. "Everything's going to be fine."

Or not, if just being in the presence of these two had such an effect on his own body.

Fabian

The monotonous work of restocking the shelves at the Magic Circle wasn't nearly enough to keep Fabian's mind from wandering. He knew he should have been at home preparing for the two exams he still had to sit, but it all seemed so pointless. He'd probably pass Politics, but whether it would be good enough to lift his average out of the gutter remained to be seen. As for Physics, he had little hope. Even with Samantha's boot camp, he still had to face Mr Herbert, and the oral exams weren't nearly as impartial as they pretended to be.

Some days, Fabian wondered why he even bothered. He could just stop torturing himself and spend time with his girlfriend. Lately, that seemed to be all he could think about. He didn't know if that was his brain telling him he needed a break or if he just wanted to forget everything.

His mother came over after the last customer had left. "Shouldn't you be studying?"

"Shouldn't you be recuperating by the Baltic Sea?"

Caroline frowned, clearly unhappy with his snappy retort. "Fabi, I told you I wouldn't leave during your exams."

"I'm not going to pass. You can be there next year when I try again." Despite his words, the thought of repeating his entire final year without his friends by his side made him feel physically sick.

"Fabian!" His mother's voice was like steel. "Giving up is not an option. I want you to do your best."

Fabian threw his head back and groaned. "I'm doing my best... for you. Your health is more important to me."

"Not at your expense, darling," Caroline said quietly. She put her hands on his shoulders and massaged them gently. "Please." When Fabian didn't give in, she added: "If it helps, then do it for me. Seeing you graduate this year will do wonders for my health."

Fabian narrowed his eyes and turned to her. "Low blow, Mum."

Caroline smiled apologetically. "Whatever gets you through the day."

The wind chime above the door went off as the door was pushed open and Samantha burst in. "There you are." She sounded fairly angry.

"Sam," Caroline turned with a warm smile. "Please take him off me. It's been one of those days."

Samantha cocked her head. "Thinking about throwing in the towel, are we? Not on my watch. Come on."

"You two are terrible!" Fabian complained, glaring at them both. With a heavy sigh, he abandoned the shelf. "I'm tired." The thought of having to go back home to study was crushing.

"You're not the only one, believe me." The harshness vanished from her face as she forced a smile. "We're going to mix things up today and go for a walk. I don't know about you, but I need some fresh air."

Fabian frowned. "We're going for a walk?"

"Don't worry, I don't need cue cards to ask you physics questions."

"Of course you don't," Fabian muttered.

"Be nice," Caroline said. As usual, though, she smiled at Samantha. "Thanks for taking such good care of him. Now, off you go." She shooed them towards the door. "Oh, and if you see your father—"

"I won't," Samantha snapped.

Fabian's eyebrows crept up. Samantha didn't snap at his mother, especially not since the diagnosis. But before he could ask her what was wrong, she'd pulled him out of the shop and onto the forest road. It wasn't until they reached the edge of the woods that she let go and breathed a sigh of relief.

"You want to tell me what that was about?"

"No." She sighed and waved him off. "It doesn't matter. What matters is that we get you ready for orals."

"I don't know why you're even bothering. Herbert won't miss the chance to send me out with another zero."

She stopped short and gave him a heavy frown. "Can you stop? Firstly, there are two other examiners in the room, and secondly, he can't give you zero points if you show a basic understanding of physics."

"Which I don't have," Fabian pointed out.

"I know you do."

Her voice sounded strained, and he knew he was pushing it. Still, he couldn't stop himself from doubting.

"What if I have another blackout? What if I'm standing there in front of him and can't get a single word out?"

Samantha whimpered, looking almost as desperate as he felt. "Fabian! I can't teach you how to open your mouth. All I can do is teach you physics—and politics. But I know you've got this. You're not half as stupid as you think you are."

Fabian shook his head. "You don't get it. I break out in a sweat. I wake up at night because all my formulas are rubbish, and when I try to answer, I can't because my mouth is sewn shut. And that's if I have a good night's sleep." The last two weeks had been brutal.

"I'm sorry, Fabi." Samantha rubbed his arm. "I know how hard it is for you." When he snorted, she took a deep breath. "I see you. You're my best friend. Don't you think I know how much you're struggling with everything? You had a bad day that Monday, but you have to let it go. I know you've got this. You can easily get eight, nine points, maybe even ten, but not if you drive yourself crazy like this."

"It's not like I'm doing it on purpose."

"I know. Just... Maybe you need a day off. We can ask Rachel to deal with your anxiety dreams."

Why hadn't he mentioned this before? The solution had been right in front of him, and instead of admitting how bad he felt and getting help, he'd just muddled through, feeling worse every day. Suddenly, Fabian knew exactly how his mother felt. And what he had to do to help her.

Later at home, he sat his mother and father down in the living room. They looked up at him with thinly veiled apprehension, probably expecting some grand announcement about him giving up. As if that was a viable option.

"What's this about?" his father asked.

"I have a preposition for you. You probably won't like it."

"Fabian." His mother looked absolutely devastated, her breath quickening. "We can do this. We—"

"There is no 'we' in this." Fabian winced as he saw her eyes widen. "What I'm saying is: you have to go. More specifically, *you* need to go to that clinic. Tomorrow." He raised his hand before his mother could react. His father was strangely quiet. "I'm fine, Mum. I've got Samantha here to drill me, and Lia to make sure I'm eating well and all that, so you can go. Please go."

Tears swam in his mother's eyes, just as he'd known they would. Fabian hated how harsh his words sounded but figured it was the only way to get her to actually leave. "Please, Mum. You need this, and so do I." Not because it would distract him from his exams, but because he couldn't cope with the guilt he felt about her putting her health on the line for him.

His mother tried to speak, but the tears stopped her. Instead, his father put an arm around her and smiled gently. "Come on, Caro. You waited so long for the place."

"I can wait longer," she whispered.

"But I don't want you to," Fabian said. "I want you to go and get better so you can be the great mum I know you are. I'll be fine, really." He probably wouldn't be, but he'd give it all for his mum. Failure wasn't an option.

"It's six weeks, Fabian," Caroline argued. "I'm going to miss everything, not just your exam. Your graduation, the ball. All of it."

And that would suck, but not as much as losing his mother to this disease. "There will be videos and photos, and yes, I know it's not the same, but none of that matters to me as much as you getting better."

"We might be able to take a break for graduation weekend," Joachim chimed in. "Come on, let the boy concentrate on what's important. I can drive you up in the morning."

"What about the workshop?"

Joachim shrugged. "Ben can handle it. He'd push for you to go, too. You know that."

Fabian held his breath as he watched his mother. She bit her lip and blinked quickly, trying to hold back the tears. Her gaze met Fabian's again. "Are you sure about this?"

"I've never been more sure of anything in my life." He could already feel the relief washing over him and let out a huge sigh. "I've got this. I'm focused, I'm prepared. Don't worry about me."

She pushed herself up and bridged the distance between them to place a hand on his cheek. The smile may have been tearful, but it was genuine. "I know you do. Write it down and say it to yourself every night before you go to sleep. Eat well and take breaks. They're important, too."

"I know."

"Of course you do." Caroline took a deep breath, then pulled him into a huge hug. "Thank you."

Fabian closed his eyes and savoured the touch, drawing as much love and encouragement from it as he could. When he opened his eyes again, his father was nodding at him, his face filled with gratitude. It told Fabian he'd made the right decision. Now he just had to keep his side of the bargain and pass.

They talked a bit about logistics before Fabian went upstairs to study. Merle skulked around his legs, and he crouched down to scratch her ears. "The two of us are going to have so much fun together."

He stood, opened his door, and did a double take. "Lia?"

Ophelia was sitting on his bed, wearing nothing but some tempting lingerie. She smiled at him wickedly. "I've been waiting for you."

Her voice immediately went down to Fabian's nether regions. Merle tried to get in, but he practically slammed the door. A protesting meow could be heard through the door.

"What are you doing here?"

She patted the bed. "I'm here to look after you."

Fabian's throat tightened and he tugged at the collar of his shirt to catch his breath. "I need to study."

"I can help with that."

"Like that?" he croaked, wanting nothing more than to forget all about Politics and Physics and go straight to Biology instead.

Ophelia smiled darkly, her eyes full of delicious promises. "How about a reward system? You get one answer right and I'll let you touch me."

"T-touch...?" Fabian swallowed hard. He knew this was a terrible idea. Somewhere his brain was trying to tell him to be reasonable, but his brain was no longer in control of his body. That role had moved far down his spine. "You know what? I think it's time I took a break."

Who needed study time when they could fall for lust instead?

Rachel

While Rachel was supposed to be preparing dinner with her dad, she wasn't really doing much apart from playing with the little kiwi bird charm. She'd dreamed about Adam every single night for the past few days, and each had been objectively hotter than the one before. The whole thing still felt a little wrong, but she was slowly getting used to the idea that this was what desire felt like. Not her silly infatuation with Fabian, but real desire. Hadn't people always said: "You just haven't found the right person yet"? Adam was right in every single way.

"I still haven't found the courage to talk to him."

Embarrassing as it was, she was talking to her dad about it. Mick snickered with amusement, which only made it worse. "What are you waiting for, Bug? He's obviously interested in you. Otherwise, he wouldn't have given you that charm."

Rachel hid it behind her back. "He only did it because I have exams. He's just being nice."

"Really?"

Rachel sighed. "What am I supposed to do? I can't just go over and talk to him."

"Why not?"

The truth was the thought frightened her. The sexual dreams only made it worse. Whether he had the same dreams or not, they'd be all she'd be able to think about. Besides, telling the object of her infatuation hadn't exactly worked out last time.

"Because... because... it doesn't work like that. I don't even know him." For all she knew, he could be boring or a total ass.

Her father chuckled. "That's why you're getting to know him." He lowered the heat under the pot he'd been stirring. "Rachel, here's the thing. Adam isn't going to wait forever. He made the first move. Now it's your turn to make the second."

"Maybe Jan could give him my number or something." Jan seemed to have little trouble getting to know new people.

Mick shook his head. "He probably could. But that would be the cowardly thing to do. Unless you want Jan to be part of your future relationship, too."

Rachel's eyes widened and she stammered, "N-no. Of c-course not." It was embarrassing enough Jan was involved at all.

"There you go. Why don't you invite him to the ball?"

"To the ball?" Rachel squeaked. "That's, like, next week. I can't go to the ball with someone I've just met."

"Can't or won't?"

When Rachel glared at him, Mick laughed.

"That was a joke. I was actually hoping you'd take us."

"Us?" Rachel nearly dropped her charm. "Like you and Mum?"

The question seemed to amuse Mick. "Well, we can't leave her home alone, can we?" The smile faded from his face, and he looked at her with a stern expression. "Rachel, your mother would like to come."

She recoiled at once. "She's never had any interest in my education. She hasn't even been to a single parents' evening."

Mick sighed. "I know your mother could have—*should* have done more. But the same goes for me. I didn't go to a single parents' evening either."

"You were living in LA."

"Sure, but that doesn't change the fact you needed me and I wasn't there."

Rachel's throat tightened and her eyes stung. With his mere acknowledgement, her father had brought up a world of pain. But she refused to let it drag her down.

"It's too late. I've finished school—almost. I'll start university in the autumn and live my own life."

She was an adult now and no longer needed her parents as much as she had before.

Mick smiled softly and nodded. "All true. So, will you allow us to attend this last event of your childhood? Please."

Rachel found she didn't care one way or the other. If they missed it, it would be business as usual. If they came, their presence wouldn't add anything to the evening. "Sure. If I don't have to ask Adam."

"You should still give him your number."

Spurred on by her father—and another sensual dream—she decided to visit the hospital. How hard could it be to give her number to a guy who'd already said hi to her once? If her nerves could be trusted... way too hard.

The road to the hospital was littered with couples, as if to mock Rachel. Here people were unabashedly making out in broad daylight, while she couldn't even manage to talk to her crush. She shook her head and told herself to get on with it.

Rachel was ready to walk into the hospital and hang out in the café until Adam came down for his break. It would give her time to calm her nerves and think about what she'd say to him. Maybe they could even share a coffee.

It wasn't to be. She was walking past the large glass windows towards the entrance when she spotted him inside. Worse, he saw her, too. Their gazes met through the glass and she froze, unable to so much as blink.

His eyes were so dark, like the deep pools of cold water in the rainforests of her dreams. She scraped her teeth over her bottom lip, heat blooming in her stomach. Adam's throat bopped as he swallowed, then his eyes dropped to her lips, and Rachel inhaled sharply.

There was something between them she had only experienced in her dreams. Like an elastic band, it drew her closer and closer to him. Before she knew it, she was standing at the window, her breath fogging the glass. He stood on the other side, still watching her with thinly veiled desire.

As her body pressed against the thin barrier between them, Rachel gasped. She wanted Adam, wanted him here and now. And it felt wrong. Unnatural. Scary. This wasn't her.

Forcing herself to blink, she broke eye contact. His mouth opened as if in question, but Rachel spun around and all but ran away.

It wasn't until she was a kilometre from the hospital, Adam far behind her, that she stopped, huffing and puffing. The intense look in his eyes replayed endlessly in her mind, turning her insides to liquid fire. The desire was still there, unyielding and overwhelming.

Rachel slapped herself hard, then again and again until the fire died down. Panting, she slumped to her knees and stared at the floor, wondering what the hell was wrong with her.

Matt

Living at Jan's place was surprisingly fun. There was a lot more room in the house, Crumbs and Neve got on like old best friends, and the human company was excellent. Best of all, there was no demon mother trying to seduce him.

Matt spent his days studying for his German exam and helping Jan renovate the attic they were turning into Samantha's room. They'd already repaired the roof and were in the process of laminating the main area. The little turret she'd fallen in love with would have to wait until her more pressing needs were met.

As Jan knelt on the floor, measuring and lining up boards, Matt helped as best he could, but his mind was on Samantha. "So, she's moving in for good?" He still didn't know how this decision had come about.

"Looks like it," Jan murmured before setting down a board and aligning it as if he were trying to pass a maths test.

"You two together?" There was a question in there somewhere, one Matt tried his best not to say out loud.

Jan looked up and pulled a face. "There's nothing going on between us, if that's what you mean."

"I know," Matt said a little too quickly. Lately, whenever he thought of Samantha, he was overcome by a violent wave of desire. He'd gotten along so well with her, giving her all the time she needed while telling himself he'd accept it if it never happened, but these days he was truly struggling. "I'm just surprised, that's all."

Jan snorted. "You and me both. Apparently, her dad is enjoying the single life a bit more than she's comfortable with." When Matt raised an eyebrow, Jan readily expanded, "He's trying to sleep with half of Greenvalley."

"Oh." Matt still didn't see the problem. Her father was single and free to sleep with as many people as he liked. Matt assumed it had something to do with people's general squeamishness about sex.

"Still, better than your own mum trying to sleep with you, right?"

Matt shuddered. "Don't remind me."

"Look. I wouldn't exactly kick your mum out of my bed if she came to me, but she's not *my* mum, so there's that."

"Thanks for sharing," Matt said in a strained voice. It wouldn't surprise him at all if his mother slept with his friends, just to make a point. And then they'd be as fixated on her as his father still was. He wouldn't wish that on his worst enemy, let alone the people he cared about.

Jan rubbed his neck, a blush creeping up his neck. "You'd think she'd have other things to deal with. Like her impending death."

"Melaney has no other priorities. And as for her death, I'm beginning to doubt she was telling us the truth. If the Council really ordered her to arrange her own death, they've been extremely lenient with the timeline. And frankly, she doesn't act like someone willing to die at my hand or my brothers'."

"So, you think—"

Jan was distracted from what he'd wanted to say by the sound of the door downstairs. Then they heard singing, the notes as beautiful and magical as the owner of the voice. Matt felt his pants tighten before he even had a chance to see her.

"Are you up there?" Samantha interrupted her singing to call up.

"Yes," Jan called back before Matt could find enough saliva to open his parched mouth. "If you're lucky, you can sleep on laminate tonight."

"The couch offer still stands," Matt muttered.

Jan gave him a strange look before their attention was drawn to the stairs. A moment later Samantha appeared, and Matt lost the power of speech again. She was wearing a pair of shorts that left most of her toned legs bare. The skin shimmered slightly, a sheen of sweat thanks to the warm day. Over that she wore an oversized shirt that looked like it hadn't come from her wardrobe.

Matt's jealousy flared, but he fought it back. At least one of them was getting some relief.

"How's Fabian?" Jan asked.

Samantha twirled a lock of hair around her finger and smiled. "Oh, he's studying with Ophelia now. She seems to know the right motivation."

When she winked at them, Matt almost came undone. Maybe they could study a bit, too. He'd teach her all about Carpe Diem while he wrote poetry on her skin.

Jan's sharp laugh pulled him out of his daydreams. "I hope he knows what he's doing!"

"Don't we all?" Samantha asked coyly.

She certainly wasn't upset about the new arrangement, which had given her time to pursue other things. Matt hated to think why that might be.

"You'll probably be able to move in properly tonight," Jan said. "We just need to figure out how to get your bed up here."

"I can do that," Matt blurted out. "I know my way around beds."

Jan gave him a long glare. "Oooookay."

Samantha just laughed—the sweetest sound in all the worlds—and turned back to the stairs. Her shirt had ridden up a bit, giving Matt a glimpse of her well-formed ass in those forbidden shorts. "Alright. I won't get in your way. I'll make lunch." Then she took her incomparable perfection down the stairs.

"I love living with her," Jan said, a cheesy smile on his face.

"Same," Matt said, catching his breath at the same time.

Confused, Jan looked at him. His gaze fell on the tight package in his pants. "Whee. Um... Good you're not staying long."

Matt just whimpered. He knew he loved Samantha, but she'd never driven him mad like this before. If he didn't control himself, he could lose everything they'd built in a moment of unbridled passion. As much as he wanted to press Samantha against the kitchen cupboard, maybe even put her on the counter where she could wrap her legs around him, he couldn't risk it.

"I need to take Crumbs for a walk."

Jan nodded. "Good idea. Walk it off, buddy. I need my house to stay intact."

Matt wasn't sure if he was hinting it would be destroyed during the epic sex he and Samantha were about to have or when she inevitably tried to disembowel him. Either way, it sounded delightful.

The fresh air and the sight of Crumbs frolicking in the meadow helped his out-of-control desire a little. He took a deep breath and tried not to think about Samantha waiting at home. Or Samantha in those shorts. Or Samantha at all.

It was quite warm outside and lots of people were enjoying the park. Crumbs met some puppy friends, barking happily at them, and they played fetch until the fog of lust in Matt's head was replaced by pure joy. Whenever he took the stick from Crumbs, he gave him a big hug and praised him endlessly. "Who's a good boy?"

"Not you, for sure."

Matt's head shot up and he groaned.

Melaney had found him. A sharp line of displeasure between her eyebrows was the only mark on her face. "You can't run from me, Melchior."

He pulled himself up and began to walk. "I can certainly keep trying."

Naturally, she wasn't going to give up that easily and fell into step beside him. "Why are you fighting this so hard?"

"Because you're my mother. No one sleeps with their parents by choice." Why was it so hard for her to see that?"

"Demons would."

There was that. Matt sighed, then shrugged. "Yeah, but I'm only a half-demon."

Her eyes narrowed dangerously. "I'm well aware. Your human side seems stronger than ever right now. But that's not who you are. You have a demon side, too, and you can't ignore it forever."

His demon side, the one that only ever got him into trouble and hurt the ones he loved.

"I'm not ignoring it. I love jumping through space and all the other perks it gives me. Especially the healing powers." The physical attributes were all he loved about it lately. Everything else just made his life in Ashuan more complicated.

Melaney grabbed his arm, her sharp nails digging into his skin. "We live in sin, Melchior. Don't ever forget that. I didn't give birth to you so you could play human."

Matt swallowed hard. "It's not like you gave birth to me on purpose." She made it sound like he owed her for what was a simple consequence of her lifestyle.

"You were destined for greatness. *I* destined you for greatness." Her eyes burnt into his own, wiping away all thoughts. "It's time for you to return home and fulfil your destiny. Be mine."

Matt cleared his throat. "If we're talking about destiny, it's here. My destiny is here." Even without Samantha, the prophecy had chosen him. Chay had chosen him.

He tried to shake her off and continue on his way, but Melaney pulled him around, almost ripping his arm out of its socket. Crumbs barked in indignation.

"Shut up!"

Melaney raised her hand, black magic pooling in her palm. Just before she could shoot Crumbs, Matt pushed her arm away. The energy went past Crumbs and hit a tree. A naked couple who'd been hiding in the bushes squealed and ran off.

"Crumbs, run!"

The dog just whimpered, his tail between his legs. Before Melaney could shoot at him again, Matt punched her in the stomach. Or at least he tried. Melaney matched each punch, faster and harder than the one before. Matt was hit in the chin, in the chest, in the shoulder. One punch broke his nose, blood spurting all over his face.

The next thing he knew, he was thrown through the air and landed hard on his back. The impact made him see stars, and for a moment he couldn't breathe. Just as he tried to sit up, her foot pressed down on his chest, the heel of her shoe digging into the soft tissue just below the ribs.

Matt cried out in pain, feeling like he was being stabbed in the heart. Then the pressure faded, only to be replaced by Melaney's weight as she straddled him. Before he could catch his breath, she was kissing his face and neck, sucking on his skin, and pulling up his T-shirt.

"Look at that. There's still passion in you."

Matt was overcome by two different kinds of pain. The one from his injuries and the sudden need between his legs.

"I don't want to sleep with you," he ground out between his teeth. He knew what was happening. Melaney was using her archdemon powers to make him succumb.

"I can feel that lie, darling."

She shoved her body between his legs and wriggled on top of him until he couldn't help himself and moaned.

Samantha, Matt thought as hard as he could. *That's who I want. Her, only her.*

It didn't help. His body was at Melaney's mercy, responding in kind when all he wanted to do was throw up.

Suddenly she screamed in pain. Anger flashed across her face, and she whirled around, hand outstretched to where Crumbs had sunk his teeth into her leg.

Matt used her momentary distraction and the loosening of her grip to push her away. Then he grabbed Crumbs and jumped away with him. When he reappeared in the Blackstone house, he almost buckled under the weight of his unfulfilled desire.

Neve floated by. At first, she was delighted to see Crumbs, but when he didn't give a happy bark in return, cowering in Matt's arms and whimpering instead, she began to worry. "What does Matt need?"

"Ice. Lots and lots of ice."

Lucille

No one Lucille knew cared about exams any more. Certainly not Lucille. As far as she was concerned, she was as prepared as she was ever going to be, and now it was time to celebrate. Luckily, she knew exactly how and with whom to do so.

She arrived at the Greenvalley View office building in a tight-fitting mini dress, chuckling as she saw the headlines in today's morning papers: 'Best entertainment in town: a guide to the hottest deals'. On closer inspection, it seemed every story the Greenvalley View had covered was sexually charged.

Lucille chuckled softly, then sauntered over to the reception desk. Leaning on her elbows, she squeezed her breasts together, creating an even more enticing cleavage. "Hello there. I'm looking for Philipp Vendenberg."

The woman behind the counter looked at the swelling of her breasts without even trying to disguise it. She clicked her tongue. "He went down to the archives half an hour ago." She pointed to an elevator behind her. "Go down to the second floor and you should find him." She wriggled her eyebrows. "Have fun."

Strangely, Lucille wasn't offended, but rather pleased by the insinuation. "Oh, I will. Thanks."

Swaying her hips, she walked towards the elevator, well aware of the receptionist's gaze following her. Once inside, Lucille checked her reflection in the wide mirrors around her. She looked absolutely fire. Philipp was in for a treat.

There was a ping and the doors opened again. Lucille stepped out and orientated herself. The archive was full of shelves and unsorted boxes. To her left were two desks with computers and large scanners. A few newspapers were stacked there, but no sign of Philipp. She was about to call for him when she heard unmistakable moaning.

Her heart pounding in her throat, Lucille slowly turned towards the sound. She passed shelf after shelf until she came to the end of the room where another set of desks stood. And there she found her boyfriend, entangled with his ex-girlfriend Vivien. Sweat was running down his bare back.

"Philipp?"

He turned his head at the sound of her voice. His eyes widened and he immediately let go of Vivien and came to her, stark naked as he was. "I can explain," he rushed the words out, still breathing heavily. "I just wanted to show her my work."

"Your work?" Lucille didn't know where to look. Her gaze kept dropping, but when she looked past him, they found Vivien instead, sprawled on one of the desks, not appearing the least bit disturbed—or guilty. "And while you were doing that, you lost your clothes."

Philipp tried a rueful smile. "Something like that." Then his breath caught and his eyes widened again. "Lucille, I didn't plan it. It just... it just happened. I don't even know why or how."

"Because she's very sexy," Lucille said, her gaze still glued to Vivien.

"Sure, but I love you. Only you."

He tried to kiss her, but Lucille pushed him away. Vivien grinned as she saw her coming, well aware of how amazing she looked draped across the desk.

"You're friends, right?" Lucille's voice caught in her throat. "Very good friends."

"I didn't want this," Philipp insisted, following her.

Lucille glanced over her shoulder. "Is that so?"

He gasped, his face blushing the most delicate colour. "Perhaps a little. But I really just wanted to—"

Lucille stopped him with a finger on his lips. Somewhere in the depths of her mind she was hurt and embarrassed, but that wasn't what she felt as she looked from him to Vivien, both drenched in sweat and smelling of sex.

Her handbag slid to the floor. "Honestly, I thought it was hot." She stared at Vivien, scraping her teeth across her bottom lip. "Care if I join?"

Instead of answering, Vivien took her hands and pulled her in, placing them on her hips. Then she kissed Lucille, her lips impossibly soft and giving. With a choked moan, Lucille opened up to her. A heartbeat later, she felt both Vivien's and Philipp's hands on her.

Samantha

It was impossible to avoid Matt in the Blackstone house. He was there when Samantha made dinner, stepped out into the hallway at the same time as her, and casually hung out in whatever room she went into. It was as if he had a supernatural sense of where she would be. It made the house feel crowded, despite its abundance of space.

For the last half hour, she'd escaped his presence by weeding the far corners of the garden. Adrianes' hell plants were thriving, but that didn't stop more mundane weeds from taking up residence. Samantha harvested some for potion ingredients, others she simply threw into the bucket beside her.

The crack of a small twig alerted her to someone approaching from behind. Even before he opened his mouth, Samantha felt her body react to his presence.

"There you are."

"Matt."

There was another reason why Samantha was running from Matt. Lately, whenever she saw him, she wanted to drink from what he offered so freely. She lay awake at night thinking of him sleeping beneath her, so close and yet so far. And half the time she wished he wouldn't let her go, that he would grab her and force them together.

They were like magnets finally reversed, only held back from each other by sheer will. Maybe it wasn't just Matt who had a supernatural sense of *her*. Perhaps she chose to enter the rooms he was in, tempting fate.

He came closer, stalking her like the apex predator he was, lithe muscles and danger in his eyes. Samantha just sat there, holding her breath, waiting for him to pounce.

"Let me help you with that." He crouched behind her, then extended his arm. The weight of his limb rested on her arm, his fingers wrapped around hers as his hot breath brushed the back of her neck. His lips almost touched her ears as he whispered, "Do you know how much I want you?"

"Matt..." Samantha swallowed.

Her eyes fluttered shut and her body leaned back just enough to touch his chest. His muscles didn't give in, hugging her as if they were always meant to hold her.

She let out a breath that was more gasp than anything else and pulled away. "I'm not ready for this." Her body, however, was very ready.

Unfortunately, Matt seemed to know exactly how heightened her libido was. "Are you sure?" he asked, slowly moving his fingers up her arm, goosebumps following in his wake.

"Yes, absolutely."

Samantha knew better than to give in to him. It was spring. Her hormones were going crazy, enhanced by the warm weather and stress of exams. That was all this was. Nothing she wanted to take a chance on.

Matt nuzzled his nose into the nape of her neck and breathed in as his other arm wrapped around her, his fingers spread across her stomach, right between her breasts and the ache in her legs. "I know you want me."

Samantha's eyelids fluttered. For a moment, she wished his fingers would move down. When his lips touched her neck, her breath caught in her throat. His other hand moved from her shoulder across her face, tipping it gently towards him. Their gazes met and Samantha forgot how to breathe altogether.

She had to cling to every mental faculty she had left to resist him. But when she opened her mouth, all that came out was, "I want you."

Matt's lips curved into a smile. His normally brown eyes went dark with desire.

"You're a very handsome man and you know it," Samantha continued, her breath brushing his partially opened lips. "And for some reason I find it almost impossible to resist you."

"Then don't," he whispered.

Samantha sucked in a breath from his lips, almost faltering. Then she shook her head. "I don't want to."

He lowered his gaze for a moment, disappointment washing over his face. But when he looked up again, his eyes were still full of desire. Even more than before.

"If you want me," he said in a low voice, his fingers running from the edge of her cheeks down her neck, "and I want you... if we both can't resist the pull any longer..." He tilted his head and followed the trail of his fingers with feathery kisses. "Why shouldn't we just give in?"

He made some excellent points, both with his words and with his lips. Samantha's skin grew hot under his touch, and she felt incredibly lightheaded, as if she'd been sitting in the heat for too long. She lifted her arms and moved them towards him. But instead of wrapping them around his neck and pulling him in for a kiss, she squeezed them between them and pressed against his chest, gaining some life-saving distance from his lips.

"I don't want it like this. I don't want to be one of your many conquests. I..."

She struggled to find the words to say what exactly it was that was holding her back. There was no denying he wanted her. He'd been obsessed with her for the better part of a year, maybe longer, but she knew what he used to be like, where he'd come from, who his mother was, and what sex meant to him. And somewhere in the middle of it all, Samantha was afraid that if she gave in to him, he'd get what he wanted and move on while her heart was still tied to his. He was half-demon, after all. Unfamiliar with love, even if he thought otherwise.

And maybe she was wrong. Maybe she didn't give him enough credit, couldn't trust him after he'd hurt her so much, then struggled to understand why she felt the way she did. All she knew was she wasn't ready to give in, even if her body thought otherwise.

"I can't."

She couldn't look him in the eye, unable to face either his disappointment or desire. Even without seeing him, she felt him watching her.

He drew in a sharp breath, his muscles tensing under her touch. Then he pulled back and stood, quickly putting a few steps between them. "I'm sorry. I didn't mean to push you." He shook his head, as if clearing cobwebs. "I don't know what's wrong with me."

"I do."

Samantha jumped as Chay appeared between the hedges and joined them in the garden. Seeing the half-demon was rarely a good sign. Sometimes Samantha thought he didn't like her very much, but today she was glad. Whatever brought him here would help distract her from her treacherous body.

Slowly, she stood, ready to face the interruption. Surely a monster hunt or the end of the world would set her straight. "What's wrong with him?"

"Oh, it's not just him," Chay said, flustered. "It's you, too. And your friends. All of Greenvalley's affected. Have you been to town lately? Everyone old enough to have sex is having it. Doesn't matter if it's at home or in public."

Matt's frown mirrored hers. "Wait, what? Are you saying this surge of desire I'm feeling right now isn't unique?"

Chay snorted. "The only thing unique about it is that you're hyper-focused on her." He nodded at Samantha, who swallowed.

Unlike Matt, she'd gone looking for relief elsewhere. Even though she and Cian had agreed to end things weeks ago, it hadn't stopped them from reigniting their affair. Maybe it really was her.

"Melaney's in town, isn't she?" Chay asked, his voice softening. "And she wants to have sex."

"Yes, with *me*!" Desperation clouded Matt's beautiful features. "I won't do it, Chay."

"Which is exactly the problem."

Matt gasped. "Are you saying I should just do it?"

"Matt, don't."

While Samantha knew demons weren't half as squeamish about relationships between close relatives, she was. And the thought of Matt succumbing to his mother disgusted her enough to clear her head.

He gave her a pained look, letting her know he felt exactly the same. "I don't know why this is a problem for everyone else," he said to Chay.

"She's the Archdemon of *Lust*, Matt. Everyone in town is under her spell. The sexual tension in Greenvalley is thick enough to cut with a knife, and yet they all fail to find relief long enough to last. It won't as long as Melaney doesn't get what she wants.

"You mean sex?"

"Oh, I'm sure she has sex. Just not with the one she desperately wants to have in her bed. You." Chay took a deep breath. "You need to do something about this before the people die of sheer exhaustion."

Samantha held her breath. She hadn't realised how sex-crazed the city had become. Her own desire had blinded her to what had been going on, but now she saw the signs. Matt's intense flirting, Rachel's atypical sex dreams, Fabian's sudden disinterest in studying, her own disinterest in helping him. And most of all, her father's sudden sexual activity.

"What do you want me to do?" Matt asked, sounding incomparably tortured. "I can't sleep with her. She's my *mother!*"

"Sleeping with her would be the easiest solution to your problem," Chay admitted.

Samantha immediately picked up on his words. "The easiest, but not the only."

Chay winced. "I don't envy you if you want to do it the hard way."

"Tell me," Matt insisted. "The hard way seems to be the only way I ever get anything done."

"You have to convince her to leave Greenvalley without getting what she wants."

Matt barked a laugh, then ran his hands over his face. "That's impossible."

"I wouldn't tell you if I thought it was. Matt, you're going to have to deal with this one way or another. Samantha"—Chay wouldn't look at her when he spoke about her—"won't be able to resist you for much longer. You don't want that. Neither of you want this, believe me. Not like this. Not under Melaney's spell."

He was right about that, Samantha thought, though she still felt personally attacked. It was an unreasonable thought, but one she couldn't shake. "You don't have to do this alone, Matt. We can talk to her to—"

"No! Absolutely not." Matt shook his head vehemently. His face hardened. "I'll talk to her. Alone. You're not going anywhere near that woman."

Samantha bristled at his tone, but then she saw the pain on Chay's face and suddenly she was terrified. If Melaney wanted Matt and Matt only wanted her, then her life was forfeit the moment the archdemon found out about her.

"Well, I'll leave you to it." Chay took a step back and for the first time since interrupting them, he met Samantha's gaze. "Be careful."

Fear knotted in Samantha's stomach. She'd survived Balthasar's vicious attacks and Caspar's wild rage, but she doubted she stood a chance if Melaney's wrath turned on her.

Chay was gone, but Matt was still there. "I'll get her to leave. One way or another, she'll be gone by tonight." He swallowed hard. "And if I have to kill her... Anything to keep her away from you."

Samantha nodded, even though she felt like she was about to faint. "I believe in you." But if not, now was a good time to stock up on protection spells.

Matt

Despite Chay's warning and all the tension he'd noticed between them earlier, Matt was surprised to catch his parents red-handed when he jumped home. Those were images he'd never wanted to see. He stumbled backwards, sending a vase flying. It crashed to the floor, causing Melaney to look up. Her eyes glistened and she immediately pushed René away.

"You came," Melaney said in a breathless whisper.

Matt swallowed, the hope they could get through this without harm fading. "Can we talk?"

Melaney waved at René. "You may go."

"This isn't your residence," René snapped, glaring at her.

Before Melaney could answer either way, Matt grabbed her arm and dragged her to his room. He pushed her towards the window and slammed the door. "My father?"

"You know how you came to be, don't you?"

"Yes, of course I do, but..." Matt struggled for the right words. The truth was he was very protective of René. He'd loved Melaney as only humans could and had been robbed of everything: his love and the child he'd loved even more. And if that wasn't enough, she'd ruined him for any other woman. Matt owed him so much and he hated that Melaney had ensnared him again, just because she was bored.

Melaney stepped up to him and ran her fingertip down his cheek. "I had to entertain myself while I was waiting for you, didn't I?"

"Could you please cover up? I said talk, not fuck." He picked up one of his shirts from a neat pile on the desk and handed it to her.

Melaney looked at it. When he offered it again, she rolled her eyes. "Very well. Let's *talk*."

Even though Matt was taller than his mother, the shirt hugged far too much of her features and was barely long enough. He'd probably burn it afterwards.

"You're driving the whole town crazy with lust."

"So?"

Exasperated, Matt groaned. "You need to stop. Please, go back to Hescaryn."

Melaney narrowed her eyes. "I'll go back as soon as I've led you back into my realm of lust."

"I won't sleep with you." Whatever else was going to happen, Matt wasn't going to budge on that.

She shrugged and sat on his bed, crossing her long legs seductively. "Then I'll stay here. You won't be able to resist me forever. Or rather, *escape* me forever. I could tie you up, if that's what you prefer."

Matt's throat tightened, but he pushed through it with enough anger to spare. "You're my mother."

"And isn't a mother's *love* the most natural thing in all the worlds?"

"That's not the kind of love I'm looking for, I'm afraid."

Her eyes darkened and Matt suddenly remembered how dangerous she was when she was displeased. "You mean the way you love your little Samantha?"

Blood rushed from Matt's face, rendering him dizzy. "How do you know about Samantha?" he asked breathlessly.

This was exactly why he hadn't wanted Samantha to come. His mother wasn't allowed anywhere near her if he had anything to say about it.

Melaney rolled her eyes, already bored with the subject. "Balthasar. Your father. Everyone seems to be convinced you're obsessed with a little human girl, like a complete idiot."

"I'm not an idiot because I love her."

"Debatable." She clicked her tongue. "So, tell me. What does this girl of yours have that I don't? It can't be this." And with that, she tore off his shirt and threw it at his chest.

Matt was too slow to catch it, still stunned at how aware she was of the role Samantha played in his life. He swallowed before forcing the words out, his gaze drawn to her despite his convictions. "It's not about sex."

"Really?" Melaney arched an eyebrow. "Are you saying that because that's what's expected of a human or because you haven't been able to sleep with her yet?" When Matt didn't answer, she snorted. "You're a disappointment, Melchior. A massive waste of my qualities."

As hurtful as the words were, he could take them. "Disappointing enough for you to leave?"

The eyebrow crept higher, withering him on the spot. Then she snorted and simply vanished.

Matt let out the breath he'd been holding and rubbed his face, as if that would clear his head. As much as it stung to be called a disappointment, it was far better than either of the alternatives. Let his mother ignore him as much as she wanted to. He'd rather be forgotten than have her wreak havoc on his father, his town, his friends. Or worse, Samantha.

Maybe in a few decades she'd forget the slight and he could show his face in Hescaryn again. For now, he was content to stay right where he was.

Rachel

"I know you don't like him," Rachel said to Hugo as she paced her room. "But I do. I can't stop thinking about him." After the awkward eye contact at the hospital, Rachel had been able to keep her distance, but now her resistance was wearing thin. She needed Adam like she'd never needed anyone before.

Hugo stared at the floor. "I hear the noises you make at night."

Heat filled Rachel's cheeks, and she coughed heavily. "Hugo!"

Since she'd asked him to stay, it had never occurred to her he might be privy to what she did under the sheets, but then again, she'd never really done that before.

"I need to meet him. I'll go over there, and this time I won't run away. It's not like we're going to have sex right away. Although I wouldn't mind." The heat from her cheeks moved south. "I wouldn't mind at all if we ended up in bed or in the elevator tonight."

"Miss Rachel, please!"

Just then her phone buzzed with a group message from Samantha.

"If its physical love you desire, so be it. Very well, he shall have your body, as long as your mind is mine."

"Hard pass." Rachel read the message and felt like she was going to be physically sick. "Of course it's not real." Disgusted, she threw the phone on her bed before collapsing into her chair. "Matt's mother's in town. That's why I'm having so many erotic dreams and can't think of anything else."

Hugo frowned. "I'm afraid I don't understand."

"She's the Archdemon of Lust."

"Lust is a sin," Hugo lectured immediately.

Rachel rolled her eyes. "Deadly sin." She took a deep breath and allowed herself to wallow for a moment. "I can't talk to Adam while this is going on. My feelings—and his—may not even be real. It's all because of her."

"Of course they're not." Hugo nodded eagerly, though he still seemed to struggle to understand what had changed. "None of it is real."

"Like you said, it's just physical love."

"And the most shameful kind."

She snorted. Of course Hugo would find premarital sex shameful. "You really need to get with the times, Hugo. There's nothing wrong with sex. It's just... not a big interest of mine. Usually." Thanks to Melaney, her own body was now betraying her. Fun times.

Samantha

To distract herself from her unnatural sex drive, Samantha moved her books in, sorting and re-sorting them on the shelf Matt had transported for her. It had saved her having to organise a big move and pay someone. If he ever needed to make a lot of money, starting a moving company was definitely an option.

And just like that, her thoughts had returned to Matt and what might have been in the garden. Despite the cold shower, she could still smell him on her skin, still feel the light touch of his kisses. If she could go back and do it all over again, she probably wouldn't have been able to resist.

All thanks to Melaney. Samantha groaned in frustration. Unfortunately, Chay's prediction had been right. She wouldn't be able to keep her distance if this went on any longer. A part of her thought about visiting Cian just to get it out of her system, but she immediately hated herself for it. It was horrible for Cian and horrible for Matt. Not when the latter, who had far fewer scruples about casual sex, had been able to hold back for her.

The temperature dropped when Neve came in. "Strange woman wants to speak Samantha."

"I didn't hear the bell." Then again, she was up in the attic, high above the door.

"Woman is strange. Woman doesn't need bell."

Samantha felt the blood drain from her cheeks. "Oh. That woman." There was only one group of people who didn't need to knock or ring, and only one woman who'd be interested in visiting Blackstone House.

"Are you sure she's not looking for Matt?" They must have missed each other.

Neve shook her head. "Woman wants Samantha."

"Wonderful."

Samantha took a deep breath and reached for the strands of magic, quickly finishing the woven web of protection to throw it over herself. Melaney had come for her and Matt wasn't there. She thought about calling him, but before she could act on the thought, Melaney appeared in front of her, wearing nothing but a thin see-through dress.

"Found you."

"Neve, you need to—"

Before Neve could react, Melaney reached out and shot energy at the little snow witch, sending her tumbling down the stairs. Melaney watched her coldly before closing the door. "She would've just got in the way."

Samantha swallowed, stunned by the casual cruelty. "What do you want from me?"

"I was told you were clever."

"Matt." Samantha closed her eyes and took another deep breath. The magic was wrapped around her, woven as tightly as she could.

"My son, Melchior," Melaney corrected her. "I've heard you're responsible for turning him away from me, for ruining him. And for what? You're wasting his youth. Soon you'll be dead and forgotten. Let's just skip ahead, shall we?"

Even though she'd been expecting the attack, Samantha jumped when she saw the black magic flying at her. She threw herself onto the bed, but it was too late. Energy crackled around her shoulder with a dull thud. Not an ounce of pain followed, proving the efficiency of her woven shield.

Slowly, she recovered from the shock and set her fingers to work on a counterattack.

Melaney's eyes narrowed. "Right, you're a little witch. That's how you put a spell on him."

"I didn't put a spell on him. His feelings are true."

The net came together around Melaney. Just a few more strands and it would tighten. It was the same kind of spell she'd once learned from

Malcolm's anti-magic band, a powerful device that not only blocked a demon's powers but also drained them.

"He has no feelings for you." Melaney laughed coldly. "He's just confused. He feels lust, not love, though for what, I can't possibly fathom."

She regarded Samantha with a withering glare that reminded her of Cheryl, only many times worse. Samantha was nothing compared to Melaney. Just an ugly, insignificant, short-lived human witch. But a witch who knew how to deal with arrogant demons.

The web was almost finished when Melaney's eyes narrowed. "You think you're safe behind your spell? I'll show you the true power of lust."

Suddenly Samantha doubled over, her need multiplied by a hundred. The magic unravelled between her fingers as she found herself moaning. And then, even without touching herself, she was rocked by a massive orgasm that threw her to the ground, leaving her seeing stars and panting as if she'd run a marathon.

"And again."

"N-n-no."

The next wave rolled over her head, sweeping her under. Melaney just stood there, watching as every muscle in Samantha's body tensed and shook with the intensity of her next orgasm.

Pain and disorientation followed the release. Samantha found her hands clawing into her palms and struggled to release them before Melaney attacked again. Sweat dripped down her forehead and her mouth was parched. Her whole body ached, strangled by orgasm after orgasm.

There was no time for embarrassment, no time for shame. If Samantha felt anything in the throes of insatiable lust, it was sheer terror. Melaney may not have been able to attack her with black magic or weapons, but she could drain her, and Samantha was unable to gather her wits long enough to even attempt a counter spell before the next orgasm made her scream.

"Sam!"

Suddenly, Matt was there. The door slammed against the wall as he burst into the room, panting heavily.

"Hello, Melchior."

For a moment, Melaney let go of Samantha. Now was the time to finish what she'd started, but all Samantha could do was moan and gulp down as much air as she could to replace what she'd lost to her unbridled lust.

"What are you doing to her?"

"Showing her what happens when you cross the House of Lust." Melaney's gaze met hers again.

Samantha whimpered and tried to crawl away. She wanted it to stop. She didn't want it to happen in front of Matt. But it was happening. Mercilessly, Melaney drove her towards another release.

"Cross you?" Matt roared. "Samantha hasn't done anything to you. She's innocent."

"No one's ever innocent. Can't you hear her?"

Tears streamed down Samantha's cheeks as she was forced to come again and again. She tried to speak, but her mouth was too dry to form words.

"You're killing her." Matt's voice broke.

Melaney was more interested in her perfectly manicured nails. "Can't say it's a loss to me."

The sick smile on her face made Samantha cry even harder. She tried to fight the supernatural hold the archdemon had on her, but her body was already convulsing again. Then Matt was there, holding her as she came apart in his arms. He swallowed, his eyes darkening as he fought his own desire.

"Please," Samantha formed with her cracked lips, managing a breathless whisper.

"You're welcome to take her place, you know?"

Matt looked at his mother. "Will you let her go then?" His voice had hardened as he protected himself from the inevitable.

Samantha tried to shake her head, but she was too weak. Her muscles shuddered and she struggled to breathe.

Meanwhile, Melaney was smiling triumphantly. "Possibly."

"You have to promise to let her go," Matt insisted. "If you do"—he took a deep breath before forcing the words out—"I'll do whatever you want."

"Look who's come crawling back to me."

Matt's eyes flared. "Make no mistake. I don't want this. But I will have sex with you before you have to die. Not now."

Melaney's face darkened. "Not now?"

Immediately Samantha felt her body react. She couldn't do it again, couldn't bear the force of what Melaney was putting her through. Her heart rate was all over the place, her muscles shaking like crazy until they tensed.

"Stop it!" Matt roared and the tension eased a little. "I can't do it now, because I have to take care of her. You think I can leave her like this? What good would it do if she dies, anyway?"

"Oh, she will die, my sweet Melchior. All humans do."

He rolled his eyes, but Samantha saw him gulp. "So do demons. You're already planning your death. Either way, I'll do it. I swear."

"Swear it on your life."

"I swear it on my life," Matt said, all too willingly. "Just let her go."

Melaney snorted, but then she clicked her fingers and released Samantha from her grip. "There. She's all yours. Come find me when you're done with her, but don't leave me waiting too long." And with that, she was gone.

Samantha collapsed into Matt's arms, overwhelmed with relief but exhausted to the bone. The pain that followed was excruciating. Her whole body felt sore from her neck down to her toes. Her breathing was shallow, and her heart rate was racing.

Matt held her, gently brushing the sweat-soaked strands of hair from her face. "I'm sorry," he whispered. "I'm so sorry."

"Wa-wat..."

He nodded sharply before scooping her up in his arms and placing her on the bed. "I'll be back in a second."

And indeed, less than half a minute later, Matt was back with a bottle of water. He slipped one arm under her shoulders and held the bottle to her lips.

Samantha's eyelids fluttered as she slowly sipped the water. "Thanks." Her mouth felt a little better and her breathing had calmed. "I..."

"Ssh. Just drink. Then we'll wash you, and you'll sleep."

"We have exams tomorrow." It was the most pointless thought she could have had, but it felt like her brain was returning after a week in a fog.

"I'll wake you up in time. Don't worry."

Samantha took a deep breath. For a moment she wasn't sure she'd be able to stay awake long enough to take a shower. She wasn't even sure she could stand under the shower with her aching legs. But now that the fog had lifted, the enormity of what had happened caught up with her.

"How did she do that? I had a spell." Now that she thought about it, the shield was still intact. Melaney hadn't broken it, and yet she'd almost killed her.

Matt sighed. "Every archdemon has a special ability related to their sin. Some are closely guarded secrets, but Melaney... My mother can bring anyone to their knees with her lust. She uses it to punish and control, sometimes to protect." He bit his lip. "She's never used it on me."

"Because she wants you to come willingly."

He winced. "It's not really willingly when it's a deal I've made, is it?"

"I'm sorry."

Matt shook his head, puffed up his cheeks, and let out a breath. "It's not your fault, it's mine. I should've been here. I should've stopped this. All of this. I'm the one who's sorry for dragging you into my mess."

Samantha put a hand on his, which was as much as her body was capable of. "Don't be. The only ones to blame are your family. You don't have to deal with this alone." She swallowed, remembering what he'd promised his mother. "We'll find a way to get you out of it."

A whimper escaped his mouth as he laid his forehead on hers and took deep, shaky breaths. "I don't want you to get hurt again."

"Neither do I. I don't want *you* to get hurt either and this *will* hurt you. It's hurting you now." She yawned, deep exhaustion claiming her muscles. "We'll get through it. Just like we got through everything else and will get through everything in the future. We're the Six, aren't we? Getting hurt is part of the job description."

He laughed softly, his head vibrating against hers. "True." Then he was still for a moment. When he opened his mouth again, his voice was just a whisper. "Do you think she's right? That it's only lust that draws me to you? That I'll never know what love is?"

Her heart fluttered. She tried to raise her hand to lay it on his cheek, but her arm refused the exercise. "No. I don't think that's true."

Once, she'd been convinced of it. She still feared it was true, but then she thought of Caspar of all people and her heart calmed.

"Demons aren't immune to love. Your society teaches you otherwise, but that doesn't mean you're without feeling, without pain. You just push it aside in order to survive."

"I don't think I can survive this," Matt whispered. "It's too much."

"It's not a weakness, Matt. It's a strength. It gives us something to fight for. Something to *live* for, not just survive."

He took a deep, shuddering breath, as if inhaling her words. Then the arm under her shoulders tightened. "Alright, enough of that. You need to sleep, so let's get you cleaned up."

Samantha smiled as he lifted her into his arms. "You know, if you keep this up, I really might not be able to resist you much longer."

"I'm not going to force something that isn't there," he said, ignoring the joking tone of her voice.

But there was something. Even if Samantha couldn't fully trust it, it was undeniable. *Matt* himself was undeniable to her. This dance around each other had to stop sometime. Either she had to let him go or she had to let him in.

"Hey, Matt."

He looked at her as he kicked open the bathroom door. "What is it?"

"After we both pass tomorrow"—it should be a given if she didn't sleep right through it—"take me to the ball, okay?"

The smile on his face made Samantha's heart skip a beat. She might not have admitted it out loud yet, but she was his, through hell and back.

"It would be my pleasure."

Lucille

It was a rude awakening for Lucille when she finally came to her senses. Somehow, she'd caught her boyfriend cheating on her, and instead of getting angry, she'd just joined in. She'd never been interested in threesomes before, but that hadn't stopped her. And as for Vivien, Lucille had experimented with girls at boarding school, but she'd never taken it this far. What had begun as a wonderful experience had ended in shame and regret.

Vivien was the first to dress. She grabbed her bag. Unable to look Philipp in the eye, she took a moment for Lucille. "I'm terribly sorry, Lucille. I have no idea how this happened. I..." She shook her head at a loss. "I'm not that kind of person. Sorry."

With another helpless shrug, Vivien ran out of the archives.

Lucille picked up her phone from the floor and checked the latest messages. The first one was a doozy. Tears threatened to well up in her eyes, but all she could do was laugh.

When Philipp looked at her worriedly, she wiped her eyes. "It's nobody's fault. Well, nobody's fault but Matt's mother's. We were all under the influence of her deadly sin. Lust."

Philipp frowned as he buttoned his shirt. "Are you saying we had no choice?"

Lucille still felt like she was about to cry. "We did. In a way. All we had to do was resist temptation."

She hadn't done so, but neither had Philipp. Quite the opposite. While she'd come here with the clear intention of finding *him*, he'd already found someone else.

"Lucille..."

"I mean, a threesome with you and your ex?" She winced, then said sarcastically, "How could I not resist *that?*"

Philipp gave her a wry smile. "If it helps, it was extremely hot." When Lucille stared at him wide-eyed, he quickly lowered his gaze. "It doesn't help."

"No, no, it doesn't. Philipp, you slept with another woman."

"So did you."

Lucille swallowed as the truth hit her. She hadn't expected him to throw it back in her face, forcing her to confront it. "I mean before I arrived. You couldn't resist your ex-girlfriend, and I understand. She's gorgeous."

Gorgeous and incredibly sexy. Even now, no longer under Melaney's spell, Lucille could admit that. She hadn't even hesitated for long. Which must've meant her relationship with Philipp was a lot less secure than she'd previously thought. And not only on her part.

"What do you want from me?" Philipp asked. "It's magic, right? Irresistible magic? If half the stories we printed last week were true, the whole town had fallen victim to it. I didn't stand a chance. You, a *witch*, didn't stand a chance."

"Well, yes. But most people slept with the people they'd always wanted to. Unless they were single. You—"

"And you."

She took a deep breath and let it out through her nose. "Yes, and me. We were just having fun. I mean, you obviously still have a thing for Vivien, and I... I just had a thing for fun."

"And what's the problem with that?" Philipp's voice was strained. "If you had fun, then we're good, right?"

"It's just made me realise we're not serious," Lucille blurted out. Once she'd gotten it off her chest, she was able to breathe easier.

Philipp rubbed his eyes and took his time. Finally, he looked at her, completely taken aback. "So, what now?"

"Well, I'm going home. Then I'm going to take a hot shower—or a cold one—and then I'm going to study for my exam, which happens to be in less than fifteen hours." How could she have forgotten about the exams?

"None of that includes me," Philipp pointed out.

Her eyes began to burn with unshed tears. "No, no, it doesn't. Because I don't think we're meant to be together."

Philipp threw his head back and groaned. "You can't be serious. You really blame me for this?"

"I'm not blaming anyone," Lucille replied angrily. "This was fun, but it's not that deep. And I want deep. I want..." *What Matt and Samantha had,* even if they hadn't admitted it to each other yet. "I'm sorry, Philipp. You're a nice guy—"

"Oh, shut up, please." He shook his head. "This is stupid. Did it ever occur to you it might be a bad idea to make such a massive decision right after such a big spell? But sure, if that's what you want, fine by me. Go on. You've got an exam to prepare for."

The fact he'd let her go just like that cemented it. Maybe he was right and she should at least sleep on it, but the fact remained they'd been together for almost six months and he'd slept with his ex without thinking twice. And she hadn't cared. Still didn't, really.

Lucille was well aware she was most likely the problem here. She couldn't even put her finger on what it was that had bothered her so much. The only thing she knew was she couldn't bear to stay in this relationship after what had happened. The threesome had left her with more questions than answers, and it was time she found out some of them. Alone.

"Goodbye, Philipp."

He just snorted, clearly not pleased with how the day had gone. Neither was Lucille, but as she stepped outside the Greenvalley View and breathed in the fresh air, she knew she'd made the right decision. Somewhere out there, the right guy was waiting for her.

Or girl.

Fabian

When Fabian woke up the next morning, tangled up with Ophelia, exhausted but strangely satisfied, it took him a few moments to remember where he was. The room was unbearably hot, the air stale. His skin felt sticky, which immediately made him want to take a shower.

Carefully, he extricated himself from Ophelia and climbed over the bed to open the window. Grabbing some fresh clothes from his drawers, he tiptoed out into the hall.

An angry meow awaited him. Merle glared, her eyes full of reproach, as if he hadn't fed her for weeks. With a sigh, Fabian abandoned his plans for a shower and headed to the kitchen. The smell of the litter made him gag, and there wasn't a crumb of food in the dispenser.

"I'm sure I fed you. I..." He scratched his head. "What day is it?"

Merle meowed loudly, reminding him she didn't care about the date. She was hungry *now*.

As he filled her drinking bowl with water, his gaze fell on the oven timer. 9:43. So he'd slept in a bit after a night filled with—

"Lia!"

The water sloshed from the bowl as he spun around. Hastily, he set it on the floor, ignoring Merle's complaints, and ran back upstairs. "What day is it?"

Ophelia groaned, half asleep, as he burst into the room, frantically rummaging through the clothes on the floor for his phone.

"What are you doing?"

Melaney

Ever since her return to the residence, Melaney had been seething with anger. She'd tried her usual methods of relieving stress, but none of her many playmates could satisfy her. They were all boring, less perfect than the one she wanted. The longer she waited, the less she understood how she could've let him go. She should've forced him to leave his stupid human girl instead of accepting a lacklustre promise.

Annoyed, she pushed her mate Frennys away from where he'd been busy between her legs. He wiped his glistening lips and looked at her with adoring eyes. "Would you like to switch things up?"

Melaney stood, flicking her sheer robe in his face as she moved. "Switching is exactly what I want to do." She poured herself a glass of firewine. "You bore me, Frennys."

He winced. "My apologies."

Frennys had been at her side for nine hundred years and was used to her mood swings. A little *too used* to them for Melaney's taste.

"It's not your apologies I want. It's *him.*"

"Melchior." As her chosen mate, he knew all about her plans and desires. "I told you, there's too much human blood in him."

Melaney rolled her eyes. "Can't you see it's spicing things up? I want him, not Balthasar, not Caspar, not *you.*"

Once more, Frennys flinched. He was an exceptionally handsome man, dark skin and sharp angles all over. His cheekbones alone were to die for, the look in his hazel eyes smouldering, even now. And yet he had nothing on Melchior. Not when he was in demon form. In his demon form, Melchior was perfection.

In his human form, he was beginning to annoy her.

"Surely a demon would be much better suited to dedicate his life to lust," Frennys continued. "Balthasar—"

"Balthasar got his reward," Melaney snapped. She threw her glass to the floor in front of Frennys, shattering it and splashing wine in his face. "He's the head of the Small Council and he has them completely in his pocket. Caspar is the General of Terror, leading the Black Guard from one bloody victory to the next, so he shouldn't complain about not having enough power, but Melchior"—her voice became a hiss—"Melchior is a *high school graduate* now. And maybe he'll start *university* in the autumn. Isn't that great?" She rolled her eyes at his lack of ambition. "Does he want the pleasure I'm practically throwing at him? No! Does he want to be my mate? NO!" Furious, she grabbed the flagon of fire wine and smashed it against the wall, almost setting fire to the tapestry. "No one refuses me. Especially not an unworthy half-demon like him!"

Suddenly, Frennys was behind her, his body moulded perfectly to hers as he wrapped his large hands around her shoulders and whispered in her ear, "Forget him. He's not worth your desire."

Melaney swatted him away like an annoying insect and started pacing again. "It's that girl of his. He wants her, but she's playing hard to get. He's so obsessed with her he can't think of anything better." She snorted, the very thought amusing her. As if she didn't have a hundred of lovers in her arsenal who were more suited.

"You mean he's deluding himself?"

"Do you think an ordinary human girl could compare to *me?*" She'd seen the girl. There was nothing special about her, nothing that could explain why she had such an inextricable hold on him.

An appreciative smile curved Frennys' lips as he devoured her body with his gaze. "Not in the least."

Melaney basked in his attention for a moment, but annoyance was already creeping back in. "Samantha has to go. Her and all his other little friends. That's what's keeping him in Ashuan. Once they're gone, Melchior will see he belongs here. By my side."

"Your side." Frennys swallowed, then forced a smile. "He might take it the wrong way. Get angry. I hear humans are like that. Humans and wrath demons." He laughed at his little joke. Slowly, he made his way back to her. "You may have to kill him, too."

"Not until I get what I want." The thought of killing Melchior if he continued to irritate her was rather sweet, but that would mean defeat, and it wouldn't change the fact he'd rejected her. Besides, she had bigger plans for him. "You may be right."

Frennys was directly in front of her, but she turned again and walked over to the bed. "He might get a little too angry if I kill Samantha. He deserves it—she does too—but he's too obsessed to understand why. He'll be spoiled, and that would only lead to disappointment. If I wanted angry sex, I'd ask Caspar. I want Melchior to *want* me. It can't be that difficult, can it?"

"Everybody wants you." Frennys gave her a naughty little smile. "*I* want you. Let me sweeten the time until he inevitably answers your call. I could summon some of the demons in your service." He shrugged. "Why don't you leave him a few more years? He's only nineteen, practically a baby. I'm sure, given some time to mature, he'll see there's so much more here than there ever could be in Ashuan. Humans are notoriously fickle. He'll have forgotten all about this girl in a decade."

"Oh, but don't you know he *loves* her?" Melaney said.

"Love," Frennys spat, "or lust? Didn't you say she was playing hard to get? Of course he's obsessed with her. He's like you in that way."

The realisation hit Melaney and her face lit up. For the first time since her return from Greenvalley, she felt elated. "Oh, Frennys, dear." She jumped in front of him and immediately cupped his face. "You're right. I know how to get him to come here willingly." Excitement rushed through her body, setting her nerves on fire. "Oh, we're going to have so much fun."

Frennys put an arm around her and pressed her body against his. "Don't we always?"

Melaney grinned. "You simply know how to make me happy."

She kissed him passionately, raking her nails through his hair and down his neck. Pushing him away, still giddy from her plan, she turned to her bed.

She dropped her sheer dress and looked coquettishly over her shoulder. "I liked your orgy idea. Get me a good selection, will you?"

Frennys' eyes darkened. "I'll be back at once."

As Melaney sank into the pillows, savouring the feel of silk against her naked skin, she imagined her plan coming to fruition.

Soon, my dear. Soon you'll be all mine.

Part 4
Giving & Taking

Samantha

The bus made its way up a steep mountain road. The suspension squeaked, and for a moment, Samantha thought they'd just roll back down the hill, but then the gradient eased, and they rolled into a car park and came to a stop. A collective sigh of relief went through the bus, accompanied by the snap of the seatbelts unfastening. Within moments of the door opening, the aisle was filled with students and backpacks.

Samantha nudged Rachel, who'd fallen asleep on her shoulder. "Hey Sleeping Beauty. Stop dreaming about Adam and get up."

Rachel rubbed her cheek and gave her a dirty look. "I wasn't dreaming about him."

"But you wish you were," Samantha teased.

"He's not asleep," Rachel admitted. She squeezed into a space between the students in the aisle as they slowly shuffled off the bus.

Samantha's backpack greeted her as she stood to follow Rachel. Behind it, Matt smiled. "There you go."

She laughed softly. "I could've reached for that myself, but thanks."

"And where would've been the fun in that?" Matt replied good-naturedly. He waited until she'd slipped into the corridor in front of him, like a gentleman, then helped her put on her backpack.

Together, they joined Rachel, Fabian and Lucille at the side of the bus where their luggage was being distributed by the driver. This was their graduation trip, which meant the whole car park was full of excited graduates, their luggage, and four buses. Samantha looked up at the steep mountains around her and smiled. Greenvalley's Witch Hump had nothing on the peaks of the Austrian Alps.

Once everyone had collected their luggage and the buses had made their way back down into the valley, the students followed a weathered signpost up a winding footpath through the alpine forest.

"You know, if you really want to be a gentleman, Matt, you could carry my bags," Lucille said, five minutes into the hike.

Matt looked over his shoulder and snorted. "Why did you bring two bags of luggage for a single week?"

"Are you sure you want the answer?" Lucille asked. "There's clothes, toiletries, a hairdryer, four different pairs of shoes—"

"I do *not* want the answer," Matt said as the others giggled. "Give me your bag."

Lucille smiled triumphantly, then winked at Samantha, who'd insisted on carrying her own. The joke was on her, for a minute later the path opened up to a wide clearing in front of a crystal-clear mountain lake. Rustic wooden huts were scattered around, surrounding a picnic area, a fire pit, and a sports field.

An old woman, hunched over with age and with a face so wrinkled her eyes nearly disappeared, greeted them. "Welcome to our serene realm of nature. There's room for eight people in each hut. I believe a list has already been made. The keys are over there. Showers and kitchen are on the right, and rubbish collection is behind the reception. Please keep things tidy and have a good time. If you have any questions, come find me."

Her last words were drowned out by the clamour for keys and excited chatter.

Fabian emerged from the crowd, holding up a key victoriously. "Cabin number three for us!"

Happy to be away from the rest of the class, Samantha and the others followed as Fabian led the way across the clearing.

"You know, when the committee told us they'd booked an alpine campsite, I was a bit... upset," Lucille said, "but this place is breathtaking. It's so beautiful. I don't even mind there's no pool."

Samantha laughed. "As if you haven't already booked your trip to Bali."

"Besides, there's a lake," Rachel pointed out.

"Lakes aren't really my thing," Lucille said. "There might be fish and a mucky bottom." She shuddered. "I'll wait and see before I test those waters."

"Suit yourself." Fabian led them to a hut by the lake and put the key in the lock. "As soon as we've unpacked, you'll find me in the water." He pushed the door open. "Here we go."

Lucille rolled her eyes. "Water mages."

Giggling, Samantha stepped inside. The inside was as rustic as the outside. Almost everything was made of wood, and quaint embroideries of forest animals adorned the walls. Fresh flowers greeted her on a cosy-looking bench and table, and a selection of well-worn board games, jigsaw puzzles, and old books spilled out of the only cupboard in the living room.

A small butler's kitchen was attached to the back of the house, just big enough to make coffee and a light snack. The larger one for cooking was opposite the fireplace. On either side of the kitchen were two rooms, each with four bunk beds.

Matt leaned over to her. "You know, if I slept in your bed, we could all fit in one room."

Samantha slapped him on the shoulder and snorted. "And what do you dream about at night?"

"You, only you."

"Get out!" Fabian complained, much to everyone's amusement. "No, but seriously, there are eight beds, so I guess we can spread out however we want."

Just then, they heard noises coming from the living room, but as they went to investigate, they stopped when they saw Robert come in, grinning. "You found it."

"Um, yeah," Matt said carefully.

"How do you like it? I think this is the nicest one of all, best view of the camp."

Lucille and Fabian shared a confused look, prompting Samantha to say, "Robert was on the travel committee."

"Exactly." Robert beamed. "Don't tell the others, but I thought I might as well take advantage and get us the best cabin."

"Right," Fabian said slowly as he realised they'd be sharing with Robert. "You got the best hut, the best group of people... anything else?"

Robert nodded. "Oh yes, Cian and Shayna."

"Cian?" Matt blurted out, suddenly looking a little tense.

"Yes, we worked together in Chemistry for two years, didn't we, Sam?"

Samantha couldn't decide whether to be scared or amused by Matt's reaction. "Mhm."

"I don't know Shayna that well," Robert continued, oblivious to the potential drama he'd caused, "but I do know the two are friends."

"Not just the two of them," Rachel muttered.

Meanwhile, Lucille put a hand on Matt's shoulder. "That's right. I don't think the Elite Idiots will be able to tear themselves away from the bee queen. They'll insist on sharing a hut, I'm sure."

There was a knock at the door. A moment later, Cian's head appeared. "Hello?"

Robert turned. "Welcome to Chalet Robert!"

Amusement won out and Samantha covered her mouth to hide the giggle that was breaking from her lips. As soon as Cian had dragged his bag into the cottage, Matt looked at him darkly. Cian returned the look sullenly, and the atmosphere in the living room went from amused to charged.

Behind him, Shayna entered, a twinkle in her eyes. "Oh, hello, everybody. This looks like it's going to be so much fun!"

Fortunately, the camp was too beautiful and offered enough distractions to prevent any confrontation between Cian and Matt. As soon as Shayna and Cian had moved in, they'd joined their friends, while the rest of the group explored the campground and the nearby forest. Fabian had gone swimming as promised, but judging by his grimace, the water was a little colder than expected.

Later that night, the graduates partied loudly. Music blared through the woods, and Alan had organised more than enough cheap beer to last them six weeks. Lucille was chatting to some girls from her drama class, while Fabian and Robert were playing table tennis under the floodlights with a few others, at least half of whom were too drunk to hit the ball.

Rachel had removed herself from the situation and retired early, while Matt and Samantha sat on the edge of the jetty, far away from the hubbub, looking up at the magnificent night sky. The milky way stretched across the lake to the peaks on the other side.

Matt glanced over his shoulder and shook his head when very loud and very off-key singing arose. "I'll never understand these wild parties."

Samantha snorted. "Are you telling me demons never party?"

"Rarely. Except maybe in the House of Gluttony. At least no one gets drunk like that."

"Is that because your healing powers instantly remove the alcohol from your blood or because it's too dangerous to get drunk in Hell?"

"Ha-ha, very funny."

Samantha elbowed him lightly. "What's the matter? You're not usually so stuck up."

"I'm not being stuck up!" Matt protested.

"Yes, you are." She laughed at him. "It's our graduation trip. We'll never see most of these people again, at least not regularly. They're just celebrating one more time."

"I don't see you celebrating."

Samantha rolled her eyes at him. "Because I'm *such* a party animal." She could count the parties she'd attended in her teenage years on one hand.

Smoothly, Matt put an arm across her back, close but not quite touching. He leaned in. "You know, there are other ways to celebrate our—"

He was interrupted by a small horde of students running towards them, squealing and giggling. They both turned their heads to see them stripping in the darkness and jumping into the water.

"Skinny dipping," Matt said under his breath. "Now that's a party I'd enjoy."

His gaze met hers and she suddenly felt too hot in her own skin. "Oh no. Absolutely not! I—"

She squealed as Matt scooped her up in his arms and threw her into the lake. Samantha tried to flap her arms, as if she could stop the fall that way, then she crashed into the water. The shock of the cold waves made her gasp for air. She pushed herself off the ground and surfaced, ready to give him a piece of her mind.

On the jetty, Matt had taken off his shirt and was unbuckling his belt. The light behind him painted the sides of his muscular torso, and Samantha swallowed, suddenly no longer interested in complaining.

"I'll get you back," she said, nevertheless. Her body was already adjusting to the temperature. Maybe because Matt was heating it up.

He gave her a lazy smile, almost invisible in the backlight. Then he slipped out of his pants and Samantha held her breath. Fortunately, he stopped there. Instead of taking off his boxers, he raised his arms and dove headfirst into the water over her head.

Samantha was ready. Interlocking her hands, she pushed down on his head the moment he emerged. Matt went back under, but he wrapped an arm around her, pulling her with him.

There was nothing but his touch in the darkness beneath the lake, which was both disorienting and strangely exciting. Samantha could feel the knotted muscles of his shoulders under her fingers, his nose buried in her stomach. His arm was locked around her hips, making it impossible for her to move away until he wanted her to.

Which was when he kicked off the ground with his feet, catapulting her backwards out of the water. Samantha crashed back into the water, squealing and laughing, then quickly returned the favour by splashing a wave at him.

Surrounded by drunken classmates and under a veil of stars, the two engaged in an all-out water battle, forgetting all their worries and complicated feelings for a few precious moments.

Later, lying in bed, her hair still slightly damp, Samantha almost wished they'd stuck with their original rooming plan.

Rachel

Rachel didn't care much for the rest of the graduating class and had only signed up for the trip to travel with her friends, all of whom turned out to be much more sociable than she was. Last night, she'd tried to read for a bit, but the party outside had made that difficult, so she'd gone to sleep, spying on Adam from the fringes of his dreams. His dreams were interesting and nowhere as sexually charged as they'd been under Melaney's influence.

She didn't dare enter them, lest he notice her, but oh, she was tempted. These dreams showed a completely different world, with places she'd never even seen pictures of. She was half-convinced he knew about magic. Once she was back, she'd have to find the courage to approach him, but the things that had happened to them because of Matt's mother still weighed on her. She'd need more time before she could look him in the eye and not see what they'd done in her dreams.

With the others still asleep, having probably gone to bed in the early hours of the morning, Rachel slipped out to take a walk in the woods while everything was quiet and peaceful. As she stepped out of the hut, she swallowed hard.

The tranquil campsite they'd arrived at yesterday had been practically wiped out. There was litter everywhere, mostly bags of crisps that had flown into the bushes or floated in the lake, and empty beer bottles, some of them smashed. A couple of young trees were bent and broken, while someone had hung lengths of toilet paper between the branches of another.

Disgusted, Rachel crossed the campsite and ducked into the woods until she had left the fields of rubbish behind her. She breathed in the fresh air and began her walk, instantly at peace within the beauty of nature.

Dappled sunlight fell on the forest floor and a fresh breeze sang through the leaves. Rachel closed her eyes, listening to the sounds of the forest, when she suddenly heard breathed words.

"Wretched humans. Defilers of the forest."

Rachel opened her eyes and looked around for what she thought was a demon, but there was no one.

"Someone must make them go away!" the hissing continued. "Human plague!"

She looked up at the trees and saw the leaves swaying in the wind.

"Parasites! Murderers! Blood! We want their blood!"

Stunned, Rachel stopped. She tried again to catch the speaker but came up short. The hissing was carried away by the wind.

As she moved on cautiously, she saw the old woman who'd greeted her yesterday walking through the forest. She kept stopping and bending to the ground, as if picking mushrooms, but her fingers only brushed stones and always came up empty.

"Good morning," Rachel called.

The old woman straightened and smiled at her. "Good morning, child. Awake so early?"

Rachel had no idea how early it was as she'd never bothered to check. "I went to bed early." She hadn't quite forgotten the evil whispers yet and decided to ask, "Did you hear something?"

"I hear the wind in the leaves, the chatter of the birds, and the buzzing of the insects. What do you mean?"

"That's an aggressive wind, if you ask me," Rachel said. She wondered if she'd imagined it.

The woman shrugged. "The wind is a moody child. Sometimes it whispers, sometimes it storms and tears the branches from the trees. Don't listen to it."

Rachel frowned. There seemed more to those words than the wisdom of an old woman. "Who should I listen to, then?"

"Oh, every being has a story. Some are short, some are long. The stories of the stones are the longest, though even they face the end eventually, like everything in this mortal world, until they're reborn."

Definitely something more. "You want me to listen to the stones?"

"You young ones are always too impatient to listen to the old ones, but that's the cycle of life. One day you'll understand." She nodded at Rachel and walked on.

Rachel quickly followed, fascinated. "I've never heard the wind talking back home."

"Ah, I suppose a lot of people live at *home*?"

"Compared to here, sure."

Greenvalley wasn't a big city, but it was a city, whereas this area seemed deserted when there wasn't a graduating class ravaging it.

The old woman sighed. "People often silence all other things." She stood and surveyed a pile of rubbish dumped at the edge of the forest. "They destroy so much without thinking."

"It's bad, I know." Rachel felt an immense weight on her shoulders, as if she were solely responsible for the state of the campsite.

"Nature always has to give, but one day it won't just stand by and watch man tear it down."

A shiver ran down Rachel's spine. The old woman continued her walk, soon disappearing behind the trees, the same trees that now looked a little ominous, as if the branches would come crashing down on her if she didn't take care.

Deciding to heed the warning, Rachel picked up the rubbish and made her way back to camp, picking up as much as she could carry on the way, using a crisp bag for smaller pieces. At the edge of the campsite, she ran into Cheryl and Ani smoking cigarettes.

"Are you the cleaner around here?" Cheryl sneered when she saw the pile of rubbish in her arms.

Rachel raised her chin. "We're just guests here."

Ani huffed. "Relax. There's nobody here."

"That's no reason to trash the place."

Cheryl gave her a haughty laugh. "Trash the place? How dramatic." She shrugged. "Oh, well, I won't keep you from your new hobby. In fact, I'll make it more challenging for you."

And with that, she flicked the stump of her cigarette into a bush and left with Ani. Rachel half expected the bush to catch fire, but the cigarette just burnt out, buried too deep in the bush to retrieve it.

Above her, the wind began to hiss again. "Disrespectful. Hateful. Hate them."

Rachel turned her face up, feeling immense guilt again. "I'm so sorry."

Matt

When Matt had heard about the trip, he'd imagined long walks in the woods and nights under the stars with Samantha, a series of romantic dates, and then a kiss—and maybe more. The reality, however, was they'd be sharing this paradise with almost a hundred other teenagers. Even worse, *he* had to share a room with Cian, the guy who'd snuck in when Matt hadn't been looking and claimed a part of Samantha she wasn't ready to give him yet. Matt was fine with her taking her time. He was also fine with her having a sexual relationship with Cian—she deserved whatever made her happy. What he wasn't fine with was having to see the guy every day, let alone sleep in the same room.

To make matters worse, Cian had picked a fight with him in the morning, as if he'd never heard of self-preservation.

"I told you, I don't snore," Matt replied to Cian's accusation, then marched into the kitchen, where Samantha was pouring herself a cup of coffee.

"How would you know?" Instead of leaving him alone, Cian followed. "You were asleep."

"Only I wasn't, because *you* were snoring so loudly."

Cian snorted and rolled his eyes. "Hardly. I was up all night."

"Are you trying to be funny?"

"It's not funny," Cian countered.

Samantha stepped between them, a cup of coffee in her hands. "Look, I don't want to interrupt this tantalising discussion, but you're both innocent. It's Robert who snores."

Matt glared at Cian, who returned the look sullenly, before they both snorted. Annoyed, he asked, "Why are you even here? Don't you have your own friends to stay with?"

Cian just shrugged, seemingly unwilling to reveal his reasons, which only made Matt assume it was because of Samantha. But before he could call Cian out, the boy turned and left the hut.

"Hey, I'm talking to you!"

"Matt, please," Samantha said quietly.

For once Matt ignored her. There was something about Cian that kept tugging at him. He wasn't a rival or anything, but he was annoying.

In an instant, he'd followed him outside. "Are you running away from me or what?"

Sure enough, Cian kept his head down and walked away with hurried steps. A pinecone fell from the trees and hit him on the head, making Matt snort. Cian spun around. "What the hell, Matt? I'm just going jogging with Alan. Do I need your permission for that?"

Matt snorted and turned. He'd taken three steps when another pinecone hit him in the head. Enough was enough. Matt clenched his fists and lunged. "You're asking for it."

Cian stumbled back, but then his stubborn streak got the better of him and he raised his hands to defend himself. Matt was about to grab his collar when a barrage of pinecones came crashing down on them. The pain was instantaneous, and they both leapt under the awning of the nearest cabin. Frowning, they looked up at the trees that had relieved themselves of their entire load of pinecones.

A door opened behind them and Alan came out, dressed in shorts and a shirt. "Did you knock?" he asked, confused.

"The wind," Matt said, still in shock.

Cian nodded sharply. "Yeah, it blew a lot of stuff down."

Alan raised an eyebrow before glancing at the carpet of pinecones at their feet. "I can see that." He shrugged, already losing interest. "So, shall we get going?"

Oddly, Matt felt himself included in the "we". "Um..." He caught Cian's amused look and felt challenged. "Sure, why not?"

The three jogged away, as they'd often done during PE or football training. As usual, the two Elite Idiots chatted at the front, talking about footballers and game results Matt had little interest in, but it felt good to move his body, and strangely, he didn't hate the company.

As nice as it was, there was something underfoot. On the last stretch around the huts, Matt noticed several odd accidents. One boy fell over a tree root that wasn't really sticking out that much. Two girls walking along the lake slipped and fell in. Two other students were nearly killed when a huge branch fell. A girl reading on a blanket suddenly slammed her face into the dirt for no reason. And when a group of graduates started a volleyball match, a swarm of wasps sent everyone running.

"See," Alan commented with a sour grimace, "that's why I voted for Ibiza, but no, it's *nature* for us."

Matt thought they had enough nature in Greenvalley, but their surroundings at home had never been as hostile as this.

Jan

Jan felt the absence of a hundred of his peers in the city keenly, especially his friends. Due to his training, he hadn't been able to join them. Not that he had the money to indulge. It would've been a boring week if Anne hadn't forced herself on him.

His little sister had pinned him down and used her doe-like eyes to draw him into her priesthood research. Now they were sitting in his living room with a pile of books and scrolls she'd collected from the Magic Circle, Elda's library, and Samantha's personal notes. Jan had organised the snacks.

"I miss Samantha," he said, looking at the seemingly insurmountable pile of research material.

Anne had bought a neat little notebook and was doing some calligraphy on the cover, as if she was going to hand in her work at the end. "You don't have to help me. I know you don't like research."

Jan snorted. "That's an understatement. But hey, my little sister wants to find out what it means to be the priestess of an actual goddess. Of course I'm helping."

"Neve is helping, too." The little snow witch floated horizontally above their heads.

Jan tilted his head back. "Can you even see the letters from up there?"

"Neve doesn't know letters."

"Perfect." Jan laughed and looked at Anne. "I hope you know what you're getting yourself into."

His little sister didn't share his amusement. "Honestly, I have no idea. You and your friends all have special powers. I have *potential*. But for what? What does it mean to be a priestess, and why did Hanna choose me? How does she even know I exist?" Anne wrinkled her nose. "Or does she?"

Jan wished he had an answer but he was as clueless as she was. "I'm still having trouble accepting there's such a thing as real gods."

"Same."

He nodded at the books. "Let's find your answer in there."

Anne smiled. "You're right. Let's get started." She picked up the thickest book and began to read.

Jan tried to follow, picking up a red book called *Pantheons of the World*. Instead of reading from cover to cover, he flipped through the pages, not quite sure what he was looking for. There was no Hanna in the Norse, Greek or even Native American pantheons, and the glossary at the back only confirmed it.

He picked up another called *Daily Rituals and Prayers* and thought it was all a lot of hokum, but he kept trying.

Snow fell on the pages. He brushed it away and looked up at Neve. "What did I tell you about snow in the living room?"

"Neve is bored."

You and me both, Jan thought, but kept his mouth shut. "How about Neve goes outside and makes a snowman?"

"With Jan?" The snow witch's eyes twinkled.

Jan's eyes fell on Anne, who was giggling, though she tried to hide behind Chay's *Circle of Magic* book. "Jan will join you later."

His heart was heavy when Neve flew out to have fun in the garden while he was stuck inside. But a promise was a promise, and Jan was determined to keep it.

He and Anne read in silence for a while. The more Jan learnt about the different pantheons and their rituals, the less confident he felt. It was one thing to believe magic and monsters were real—both were hard to deny when they spat in your face. But gods? Jan had always found it hard to believe in some all-powerful, invisible beings who had nothing better to do than play around with people's lives and answer prayers when they felt like it. His recent encounter with the cult of Ishtar hadn't exactly improved his opinion of gods—or their priests.

"Do you think this Hanna is real?" he asked, still unable to find any mention of her.

Anne was deep in her reading and blinked. "Magic is so why not gods?"

Jan shrugged. "There's no proof they exist is there?"

"I think that depends on your point of view. Some people would say there's plenty of evidence in all the beauty of the world. Like Hanna being a goddess of life. You could probably see her in every blooming flower and the cry of a newborn baby."

"I'd just call that life. No goddess needed." Seeing Anne's face drop, he quickly changed tack. "I mean, I could be wrong. I'm not a biologist or anything, and maybe there's a divine plan behind all this. It's just..." He sighed. "Why do you want this so much? You've never believed in god or anything like that."

Anne put the book down. "I never believed in magic either and look how that turned out." She sighed. "All my life I thought I knew everything. Not literally, of course, but I thought I was on the right track. Magic wasn't real, everything was subject to common sense and logic. But I was wrong. I should've believed you."

Jan winced. He'd spent years trying to convince his family that the monsters he saw were real, and they'd called him crazy. Anne might not have said it directly, but she'd been the shining example for Jan to measure himself against.

"You showed me the truth, and now I want to know everything. I want to be a part of your life. Of this." She pointed to the book. "Do you understand how big this prophecy is? There's going to be a war. A magical, all-encompassing, multi-world war. And my brother will be right in the middle of it."

"About that..." Jan had never really thought about the prophecy. It was as unreal to him as the gods, something that didn't quite make sense. "I don't really think any of it will happen."

In his opinion, they'd already defeated the Greedy One. His friends might disagree, believing Chay over common sense, but he'd long since given up worrying about the distant future. Whatever happened would happen, and he'd react to it when it did, rather than worry about prophecies or the hidden agendas of long-forgotten gods.

Anne shook her head vehemently. "It all fits. You're chosen, Jan, and one day you'll carry the weight of the world on your shoulders."

"No, thank you." That didn't sound like him at all.

"I know you don't think you can do it, but I do. And I want to help in whatever way I can. That's why I want to find out as much as possible. Maybe I'm meant to be a priestess of Hanna, maybe I'm not, but if there are gods, it would be good to have them on our side, right? You'd want to have the goddess of life on your side, wouldn't you?"

"If it means she'll keep me alive, sure."

Anne smiled, as if his joke meant the world to her. "And that's why I want to see where it takes me. I want to be part of your world."

It always made Jan feel bad when she adored him so much. He hadn't been the greatest big brother, often putting her down and blaming her for their parents' failures, but Anne had looked up to him anyway. For so long he'd resisted the call. Now, he wanted to live up to it.

"You know, why don't you ask Lia? She may not know much about Hanna, but she's had dealings with priests and priestesses, and worships a goddess."

Anne's eyes lit up. "I didn't know that! Oh, I'll have to ask her at school tomorrow." She leaned forward and surprised him with a hug. "Thanks for being so supportive."

Jan patted her back awkwardly. "Glad I could help."

After all, this goddess business was harmless. Anne could've insisted on going on their monster hunts, but she'd happily found something else to fixate on. Jan would do anything to protect her.

It turned out researching her future priesthood was the opposite of keeping Anne safe. Jan was working a shift at the hospital when Anne and Ophelia found him. He knew there was trouble when he saw Anne's worried expression. The real injury was to Ophelia, who was much more relaxed, and held up her hand to show him a rather deep cut.

"I cut myself."

Jan stared at her. "Why would you do that?" He was well aware of Ophelia's past and that she used blood in some of her shadow spells, which did the opposite of calming his nerves.

"We were testing to see if Anne could heal like you."

His gaze shifted from Ophelia to Anne. "When did you start pulling shit like that?"

Anne's eyes widened, but before she could answer, Ophelia stepped in again. "She didn't do anything. It was my idea. Anne was against it."

Jan commended her for taking responsibility, although it didn't look like Anne appreciated it.

"You were just trying to help. We were attempting to find out if my potential included any special powers."

"So, are you going to heal me or not?" Ophelia asked. "Because it hurts."

"You know, I should send you to a real doctor for that much stupidity," Jan grumbled.

Ophelia raised an eyebrow, but her nostrils flared a little, and the look in her eyes wasn't half as confident as she wanted it to be. Cutting her hand probably didn't look good in her guardian's record.

"Yes, I'll heal it." After all, he was hardly one to judge.

While he was healing her, he noticed how close Anne was standing to Ophelia. It seemed as if the two had become fast friends after Meg had left. The development worried him a little, knowing what he did about Ophelia's past. He wanted to give her a chance for all the chances he'd been given, but he also wanted Anne to be safe, and Ophelia seemed just the kind of person who'd get her into trouble. He knew the kind, because he'd *been* that kind.

"All done." The cut had taken him barely five seconds.

Ophelia clenched her hand and twisted it, testing the new skin. "Perfect."

The three were interrupted as a technician approached. Jan recognised him immediately. "Hey, Adam."

"Hi." The curly haired guy gave each of the girls a friendly nod before looking at Jan. "So, um, I'm having a party on Friday." He handed Jan a small card with an address on it. "It's my farewell party, so if you don't have anything else to do, please come. You can even bring... friends."

One friend in particular, Jan thought. The New Zealander was as infatuated with Rachel as she was with him. "Wait a minute. Farewell party?"

Adam shrugged, evidently having mixed feelings. "My internship is over. I'm flying home this weekend. So..." He nodded at him. "Think about it, okay? Please."

"Of course."

With a final smile, Adam walked off, leaving Jan to be besieged by two curious girls.

"Who was that?" Anne wanted to know.

"Adam Black, one of our technicians. Rachel has a crush on him, and he seems to like her too, but..." It was obvious to Jan that Adam was hoping to see Rachel one last time. "She's only coming back from their trip this weekend." A day too late to say goodbye before she could even say hello. "Damn."

There had to be something he could do.

Fabian

Fabian was about to make himself a snack after swimming all morning when Shayna burst in. She slammed the door behind her and leaned against it with her arms outstretched, as if to hold it fast.

"Are you okay?" Fabian asked, his toast raised halfway to his mouth.

"Pinecones," Shayna huffed. "They're lining up for attack."

His confusion only deepened. "Okay?"

"Don't look at me like that! It's the truth. Nature's gone mad."

Fabian had no idea what had gotten into her. Then again, not much of what she'd said made sense, either. "Did you smoke something?"

Shayna was unimpressed. "Do I look like someone who takes drugs?"

Not knowing how to answer, Fabian just shrugged.

"I *don't*."

"Good. So... were the pinecones carrying weapons?"

She gave him a flat look. "Funny, really funny." Carefully, she let go of the door and crossed the room to join him. "Can't you just hug a girl and comfort her when she's scared?"

Fabian almost choked on his toast. "Excuse me?"

Shayna nudged his arms. "Arms." She pointed at herself. "Girl."

Heat rose in his cheeks at the thought of hugging Shayna. "I can't hug you."

"Is that a motor problem or an emotional one?"

"I have a girlfriend!" Fabian protested, making Shayna giggle.

"Oh, Fabi, it's so easy to mess with you." She stood on tiptoe and kissed his cheek before he'd even realised what she was doing. "Keep doing you." She walked into the bedroom.

Fabian's face was on fire. He knew if he looked in the mirror he'd be tomato red. "Hey! What about the pinecones?"

Shayna grinned. "I know you'll protect me if need be."

She closed the door behind her, leaving Fabian confused and embarrassed. It was the second, if not third, time Shayna had caught him off guard. It unnerved him. He knew she was probably just teasing him so she could laugh about him with her friends. It didn't mean anything, and yet he always blushed hard. He hated how easily she was able to mess with his head. He wasn't an idiot, so why did he act like one?

After three days of unusual freak accidents, Alan called all the graduates to an emergency meeting at the notice board. What should've been planned activities was now a collection of everything that had happened in the last seventy-two hours, with Alan presiding over the proceedings.

Fabian and his friends stood on the fringes of the meeting. None of them had contributed an incident, and judging by the looks of his friends, they found Alan's power play as ridiculous as he did.

Robert was the last to hand Alan a Post-it. While he'd stuck every other one on the board without question, he raised an eyebrow at Robert's. "The mud threw itself in your face?"

"Yes," Robert said, his face still dirty from whatever had happened to him.

"Explain."

Robert gladly complied. "Well, I was walking in the woods behind the huts, and suddenly I was lying face first in the mud."

"You fell?" Alan barked, obviously at the end of his tether.

More than a few students giggled or snorted.

"No! The mud threw itself in my face," Robert insisted.

"Fine!" Alan snatched the post-it out of Robert's hand and aggressively pinned it to the board. "Alright. Apparently, some people here think they're very funny." Alan's gaze shifted to Fabian and his friends.

Matt snorted. "What are you looking at me for? I don't find it funny at all."

Alan ignored him, his eyes scanning the group in front of him. "My team and I are going to start questioning everyone to find out what's happened here. We'll find out who's behind this, and I can tell you, it's not going to be pretty."

"Oh, you and your *team*," Matt called out. "Could you be any more biased?"

"Shut up, Traidous," Alan shot back. "This is a police matter now."

Fabian rolled his eyes. Alan and his police fetish.

"Maybe we should call them, then," Lucille said, earning a few chuckles of her own.

"That would be ridiculous." Alan groaned and shook his head. "You all know what I mean. I want everyone in their huts until my team gets to you. Got that?"

Almost no one cared about such an arrangement. They all waved Alan off and either went to their huts because they wanted to or did the opposite and picked up their abandoned table tennis and volleyball games.

Fabian and his friends shuffled into their hut to talk.

"Man, I hate Alan so much," Fabian said, sliding onto the bench. "He always thinks he can order everyone around just because his dad is the Chief of Police."

"Frankly, I wouldn't be surprised if the Elite Clique were behind this," Lucille said, sliding onto the bench next to him.

"I don't think so," Rachel said quietly. "It's ghosts or maybe nature spirits, taking revenge for all the chaos we've caused."

Fabian stared at her, stunned. "Excuse me?"

"The wind whispered death threats."

The blood drained from Fabian's cheeks. "Death threats?"

Rachel nodded, her eyes dark with worry. "The wind is very angry. And I mean, I get it. This place looks like a garbage dump. I'd be angry, too."

"Since when can you talk to the wind?" Samantha asked.

"It wasn't the wind, it was the nature spirits."

They all exchanged puzzled looks.

Fabian, who kept his thoughts to himself, was amused. Leave it to them to go on vacation and attract a monster. "So, what now?"

"Can we talk to them?" Lucille wondered aloud. "I'd like to try the diplomatic version before confronting the whole forest."

Fabian snorted. "What would you say to the *wind*? Hey, wind, could you please refrain from killing us? Thanks?"

As if she hadn't heard him, Rachel spoke over him, "The old woman might be able to help. She told us to find her, and when I spoke to her the other day, she seemed to be well acquainted with the spirits."

She was about to say more when the door opened and Cian, Shayna, and Robert entered.

"Ah, Alan's trusted team," Matt called out, "here for an unbiased round of questions. Am I right?"

"Oh, shut up." Cian seemed in a foul mood.

"Did something happen?" Samantha asked.

Unlike earlier in the day, there was no cheeky amusement in Shayna's face now. "Cheryl's disappeared."

"Disappeared?" Fabian clarified. "Or has she gone into hiding because she's responsible for all this mess?"

"No one's seen her since this morning."

Lucille

Lucille volunteered to accompany Rachel, not only because she wanted to see if the stories about a talking wind were true, but also because she'd wanted to ask for more details about the new man in her life.

"Have you spoken to Adam yet?"

Rachel stared at her as if she'd said "to a stone" instead of Adam. "No. I told you, it was just Melaney messing with us."

"I thought we'd established she only increased the natural attraction, made us forget our morals, and—"

"Is that what happened with you and Philipp?"

Lucille stopped. She hadn't talked to anyone about what had happened between the two—or three—of them, only that they'd broken up.

"You know, he was a nice guy," Rachel probed gently.

"And you think I broke his heart?" Lucille was well aware of how disastrous her track record was. "You know he cheated on me?"

Rachel turned, eyes wide. "He did what?"

"I caught him in the archives with his ex." *And then I joined them.* Lucille pressed her lips together, not ready to share that detail with anyone. Rachel was right. Melaney *had* been messing with them, and it had left her confused and hurt at the same time. "The truth is, Philipp was a nice guy, but our relationship wasn't that deep. I don't even miss him."

What she missed was the affection and being in a relationship, but not the man himself. Not really a testament to her relationship. "Sometimes I wonder if there's something wrong with me," she confessed. "I want nothing more than to be in love. I love the flirting and the thrill of a new relationship, but then I find myself wanting more. Like, I want it all. I want that big screen love, that deep connection and commitment. I want a guy to look at me the way Matt looks at Samantha." Or maybe a girl.

She bit her lip, then took a deep breath. "Every time I find myself in a relationship and the first few weeks or months of excitement have passed, I feel like something's missing. Like they're not the one."

"You think Matt is Samantha's one?" Rachel asked doubtfully.

Lucille nodded. "One hundred per cent. Honestly, the only ones who need to realise that are them."

Rachel pursed her lips, looking doubtful. Then she shook herself. "Don't take this the wrong way, but I think you're projecting."

Stunned, Lucille gasped. "Come again?"

"You just said it yourself. You believe in great fairy tale love, but in my experience, that kind of love doesn't exist. People are attracted to each other and something clicks, and then they're together for a while, but given enough time, no relationship lasts."

It was a hard pill to swallow for Lucille. "So, you think every relationship is doomed?"

"Not doomed, no. I think relationships are just what they are, and we should appreciate what we have when we have it, instead of always looking to the future and measuring it against some impossible standard. I understand that Philipp cheating is a no-go, but you dumped Fabian for no reason, and you dumped Dion and—"

"I told you, there's something wrong with me," Lucille cut her off before she could go any further. Maybe Rachel was right and her expectations were too high, but the alternative was just too bleak to accept. There was so much magic in the world, why not in this part of her life?

"If there's something wrong with *you*, then there's definitely something wrong with me."

Lucille frowned, not used to Rachel being so open about her own feelings. "What do you mean?"

Rachel looked up at the trees as if to take courage. "Well, I've been thinking... Melaney's spell made me feel things I'd never felt before."

"You mean lust?" When Rachel nodded shyly, Lucille began to understand. "You've never been sexually attracted to anyone before."

"Part of me wants the same thing you do," Rachel confessed, though she didn't meet Lucille's eyes. "Like, I thought I wanted Fabian's love and devotion, because the way he used to feel about Samantha was the kind of love every movie or book tries to convey. He was the same with you, and now with Ophelia. He's always all in, and I'm, like, the opposite."

"Fabian comes from a loving family. His parents are high school sweethearts and so supportive of each other and of Fabian. It's different with you and me."

Rachel nodded thoughtfully. "We're broken because we come from broken homes. You're desperate to be loved and I'm reluctant to fall."

"Gee, you make us sound awful." If Lucille hadn't felt bad about her love life before, she certainly did now.

Rachel chuckled. "Well, look at me. There's a guy who's actually interested in me and I'm interested in him, and—thanks to a certain archdemon—I feel something for him that I've never felt before, and yet... I'm just waiting for the feeling to pass."

Determined, Lucille took Rachel's hands. "You can't let life pass you by like that. What if he's the one?"

"I don't believe in stuff like that."

"But what if he is?"

Rachel swallowed, her gaze lost in Lucille's. "You really believe that?"

"Like you said, I'm desperate, even though I like to think of myself as a hopeless romantic. I don't want to give up on love, and neither should you. Especially not when it's practically throwing itself in your face. Promise me you'll give Adam a chance."

"You know Nico said the same thing?"

Lucille frowned. "About Adam?"

"About letting life pass me by." Rachel sighed. "It wasn't the real Nico, just a dreamer wearing his face." She waved her hand. "Forget about it. I promise." Her voice gained some strength. "I may need some help, but I will give Adam and me a chance. He won't be the one, but..."

"...he'll be someone."

Rachel smiled softly. "Yes. Someone." Then her face changed to one of determination. "But first we need to figure out how to appease the nature spirits."

"Yes, please. This week was supposed to be a big party." Instead, every fun activity had been inevitably ruined when nature attacked, whether it was sinking sand on the volleyball court or the frequent pinecone attacks.

"Honestly, I could do without everyone else," admitted Rachel.

"But it's our last time all together."

"Fortunately." Rachel sighed. "I know I'm supposed to enjoy this, but I've never really liked these people. I mean, look at the way they treat this place. And we're supposed to be the generation who cares about the environment."

Lucille chuckled softly. "Now *you* sound like a nature spirit." They reached the reception hut and knocked on the door. When Lucille tried to open it, she found it locked. "No one home."

They walked around the hut and looked in the window. Suddenly, Lucille felt a little dizzy. "Do you see what I see?"

Rachel's face was slightly ashen. "You mean an empty room and dusty shelves?"

No one had used the reception for ages. "Where exactly did the old woman say we should find her?" Lucille's voice jumped a little. First the weathered signpost, now the deserted reception. "And what kind of haunted camp did Robert book us into?"

Fabian

It seemed Fabian couldn't get away from Shayna on this trip. She would watch him when he came back from swimming, pretending to paint her toenails in the sun, and always happened to enter or leave the room he was in. He'd spent about five minutes in the communal kitchen, cooking dinner, when she walked in and came straight for him.

"Hungry?" Fabian asked, bracing himself for whatever she might throw at him this time.

Shayna smiled sweetly. "Are you offering to cook for me?"

There was more than enough spaghetti boiling to feed the whole hut. "What do you want?"

"Alan wants me to question you."

"Me specifically?"

Shayna nodded. "Yep. He thinks you're the weakest link in the chain. Actually, he said 'the weakest member of your group', which made me ask him how he'd know if you've never showered together."

And there it was. The predicted heat crept into Fabian's cheeks, making him all flustered. "You wanted to ask me something."

She looked like the cat that got the cream, her eyes sparkling with amusement. She hopped onto the counter beside him and crossed her legs. "Alright. What did you do to Cheryl?"

"I wouldn't touch Cheryl with a ten-foot pole."

"Understandable."

Fabian almost dropped his spoon. "It is?"

"Well, it's not like she's gone out of her way to maintain a good relationship with you."

"Quite the opposite."

"Unfortunately, that makes you a suspect."

Fabian groaned. "Really?"

Shayna put her hands up in defence. "I'm just passing on what I've been told."

Fabian shook his head. He let go of the wooden spoon, leaving the sauce to simmer, and leaned against the counter next to her. "Is that all you do? Alan or Cheryl say jump and you jump?"

This time, he'd managed to catch her off guard. For a moment Shayna stared at him, indignation creeping onto her face, but then she relaxed and a cheeky grin took its place. "Look at that. Someone's discovered their backbone."

"At least one of us needs to have one, don't you think?" Fabian had no idea where this had come from. He'd spent years defending himself or Samantha from the Elite Clique, but he'd never dished it out.

Shayna seemed to revel in it. She clapped her hands and giggled gleefully.

Fabian frowned. "You're making fun of me, aren't you?"

"A bit."

"Why?"

"Because I think you're cute when your face turns red. It's adorable."

Immediately Fabian felt the heat rise in his face. He knew it must've been bright red with embarrassment, but Shayna just giggled.

Jumping off the counter, she brushed his side as she sauntered back out. She paused at the door and looked over her shoulder. "I'm looking forward to the dinner you've offered to cook me."

Unable to find the words, Fabian just stared at her in disbelief. When the door closed behind her, he gasped, releasing the breath he'd been holding the whole time. His face was burning, and his stomach churned with all the wrong feelings.

Annoyed, he shoved at the counter. That damned Elite Clique. Even now, they couldn't stop messing with him and his friends. Just a few more days and he'd be rid of them. He could hold out for that long. He had to.

Fabian wouldn't allow anything to jeopardise his relationship with Ophelia. And certainly not a girl from the Elite Clique who toyed with him out of sheer boredom.

Samantha

Samantha took advantage of the fact it was broad daylight and everyone was out and about to talk to Cian about the whole Cheryl thing. They sat shoulder to shoulder on his bunk bed, speaking in low voices.

"I think Cheryl's behind her own disappearance." Samantha knew she wasn't the reason nature had gone mad, but she doubted the queen bee had been abducted by pinecones. "Maybe she wasn't getting enough attention."

"She certainly didn't get the attention she wanted at the ball." Cian grinned at her. "You looked amazing."

Samantha's cheeks warmed and she giggled. "Stop that."

"I mean it. Cheryl was furious."

She sighed. Cheryl had always hated it when Samantha succeeded at anything. Seeing Samantha steal her moment at the ball was exactly the kind of thing that would drive her to pull a prank like this. "Furious enough to fake her own kidnapping and ruin camp for everyone?"

Cian leaned his head against the wall and sighed as well. "Definitely. But she doesn't usually do these things alone. Ani would be involved at the very least, and she says she doesn't know where Cheryl is."

"Ani could've lied." Samantha knew better than anyone it wouldn't have been the first time.

"I don't think so," Cian said, wincing. "She was pretty upset. Of course she's sure you're behind this. And as dutiful as he pretends to be, Alan has put you at the top of his list of suspects." He rolled his eyes, letting her know what he thought about that.

Samantha patted his thigh sympathetically. "You don't think I'm involved, do you?"

He put his hand on hers and held it. "You've got more than enough on your plate, hunting monsters and demons and whatnot, to pull magic tricks on the graduating class."

"I hope you didn't say that to Alan."

Cian laughed. "Of course not. I just flipped him off."

"You did?" Alan and Cian were as close as Samantha was with Fabian. They argued as friends did, but never anything serious.

When she looked at Cian's face, he seemed angry. "He started talking bullshit, like you wanted to get back at Cheryl or something."

"Oh yeah. After not doing anything like that for nine years, I had to cram it in quickly before it's all over. I'll be glad if I never have to see her again."

Cian chuckled and laid his head on her shoulder. "Are you also happy you won't see me again?"

"Why? Are you not planning to visit your mum when you move away? Besides, Bielefeld isn't that away." Although Samantha quietly thought part of his decision to study chemistry in another city was to get away from her.

"Will you come and visit me?" Cian asked quietly.

"Maybe."

Just then, the door opened. Cian and Samantha jumped, causing Cian to hit his head on the bed above them. Any thoughts of visiting him fled from Samantha's mind as she saw who'd entered the room.

"Matt?"

His face darkened as he took them in. They were still sitting a little too close to each other on the bed, but they were fully dressed and hadn't done anything more than cuddle a little.

"Nothing happened."

"It did."

Samantha stared at Cian. Had he gone mad? Had he forgotten who it was he was talking about and what he was implying? "No, we…"

"We were talking as friends," Cian continued, on his self-destructive path, "and I won't apologise for that." He looked at Samantha. "And you shouldn't have to, either."

"I didn't... I mean..."

Cian groaned and got up from the bed. "I'm done with this."

"You're done?" Matt asked, his voice dangerously deep.

But Cian ignored him, his attention focused solely on Samantha. "He loves you, and you love him."

"Cian..."

"You told me so."

"She did?" Matt asked.

Cian still ignored him. "I know you still have doubts and there are some very good reasons for them, but I don't want to be one of your reasons. I'm done being your safety cushion. It's time for you to take the leap or let it be. I'm out."

He turned to face Matt. For a moment it looked as if Matt was going to strangle him and Cian swallowed, finally realising the risk he'd taken. Samantha felt like she was going to be sick. Then Matt stepped aside and let Cian go, leaving her alone with him.

"Is any of that true?" Matt asked.

Samantha couldn't look at him. "Some of it."

"Which parts?" Matt demanded. "You'll have to be a bit more specific."

She looked up, anger coursing through her veins. "Do I?"

His face softened. "Please."

Behind the stern demeanour was a vulnerability that took her breath away. Seeing her with Cian had hurt him. But knowing that only raised walls inside her.

"I'm... I'm sorry," Samantha began, not quite sure what it was she was apologising for. "I—"

A terrible crash in the living room made them both jump. Without so much as a glance at each other, Samantha and Matt ran outside.

The first thing they saw was the tree. Branches and leaves were still shaking. The top had crashed into the living room, smashing the window and the table with the old jigsaw Robert had been trying to solve. Robert himself was sitting on the floor among twigs, puzzle pieces, and broken glass, a trickle of blood dripping down his face from a gash just below his hairline as he stared at the tree.

"What happened?" Samantha asked.

On the other side of the corridor, Shayna emerged, a pair of headphones dangling from her neck. Then the cabin door flung open and Cian burst back in, followed by Fabian.

"Is everyone okay?" Cian's gaze met Samantha's, quickly checking she was unharmed.

Curious onlookers stood in the doorway behind him, already gossiping. Samantha grabbed a handkerchief from the box on the shelf and went to Robert, just as Alan, Ani, Jennifer, and Björn pushed their way inside.

"Are you okay?" Samantha asked, pressing the cloth against Robert's head.

"Will people believe me now when I say the tree attacked me?"

"Of course." Samantha patted his shoulder and looked up at Fabian and Cian who must've seen the tree fall. "What happened?"

Cian's face was still lined with concern. "One minute it was standing over there, all peaceful, and then suddenly, *crack*, it fell on the house."

"Trees don't just decide to fall," Alan protested.

Fabian snorted at him. "They do if they've got a rotten core."

Alan narrowed his eyes. "Shut up, Bendtfeld. Though, you're right about one thing. There's something rotten here."

"Nature's fighting back," Robert whispered, still stunned by his near-death experience.

"Something like that," Samantha said quietly.

Apparently, she hadn't said it quietly enough, because Ani raised her voice. "What are you saying, Sammy? Are you confessing? Did you cast a spell on the forest?"

"Sure, and then I used it to blow up my own shelter."

"There!" Ani pointed, looking for approval from the crowd outside. "She admitted it. This whole mess is her fault!"

Before she could go any further, Cian stepped in, his face distorted with anger. "Stop that nonsense, Ani. Samantha has nothing to do with the attacks and certainly nothing to do with this tree."

Robert, however, stared at her wide-eyed. "You know real magic?"

Samantha rolled her eyes.

Meanwhile, Ani had an aneurysm. "You again! Don't you see how stupid you look, Cian? Just because she opened her legs for you once, you follow her around like a lovesick puppy."

Samantha held her breath and quickly checked with Matt. He had his arms crossed and was staring at everyone but her with a murderous gaze. She couldn't tell if his anger was directed at Cian, Ani, or simply everyone.

"The only one who looks stupid is you, Ani." The unexpected support came from Samantha's left. Shayna grimaced. "'Samantha's cast a spell on nature,'" she mimicked. "Come on! I thought you didn't believe in all that magic nonsense."

"I don't." Ani immediately bristled. "Why are you defending her? Cheryl would—"

"Cheryl isn't here," Shayna snapped as Lucille and Rachel made their way in. "And if she was, I couldn't care less what she had to say or *do*. I've already wasted far too many years of my life giving a flying fuck about whatever nonsense Cheryl's said."

While Ani gasped, Fabian seemed surprisingly impressed.

"Is that why you didn't want to share a hut with us?" Jennifer asked, sounding a little hurt.

"Among other things." Shayna shrugged. "I just wanted to have some fun outside of our oh-so-great clique. I really didn't need a week of Cheryl bitching about everything and everyone. Honestly, I don't need it at all. For all I care, Cheryl can stay lost or in hiding or whatever it is she's doing."

Ani narrowed her eyes. "Oh, you're *so* done. I'm going to tell Cheryl everything you said."

"Good. Then I won't have to repeat myself."

While the battle lines seemed to be drawn between Shayna and Cian on one side, and Ani, Jennifer, and Björn on the other, Alan seemed a little overwhelmed. "Okay, so you don't like Cheryl anymore, but I'm still worried about her disappearance."

"Then maybe you should start looking for her instead of playing camp police," Matt said.

Alan's face darkened instantly. "Nobody asked *you*, Traidous."

"But he's right," Cian insisted.

Ani threw her hands up. "Oh god, now another one's lost his mind. Come on, let's go." Without looking back, she left the hut, Jennifer and Björn on her heels.

"Are you coming, Alan?" Björn asked.

Samantha almost felt sorry for him. Alan seemed genuinely heartbroken about his clique falling apart around him. Helplessly, he looked at Cian.

"I'm not going to join your witch hunt. I already told you."

Alan's expression hardened, his decision made. "Fine, if you insist on making a fool of yourself for Samantha." Then he stormed off.

Slowly the crowd in front of the hut dispersed and things settled down inside. Shayna made a big show of letting out a sigh of relief, obviously not the least bit bothered by what had just happened.

"The air was so thick you could've cut it up and put it on a sandwich."

"Can somebody tell us what's going on?" Lucille asked, looking around. "There's a tree in the living room."

"It fell over," Matt said, loosening his threatening stance. "And as far as I understand, Shayna and Cian just handed in their resignations from the Elite Clique."

Worried, Samantha looked at Cian. The others might not have meant that much to him, but Alan was his best friend. "I'm sorry."

"It's not your fault."

To her surprise, Shayna agreed. "Believe me, this was long overdue." Seemingly losing interest, she made her way over to Fabian. "See, I have a backbone, too."

"I saw," Fabian said surprisingly seriously.

"Now that I'm practically homeless, can I move in with you?"

All confidence vanished from Fabian's face and his cheeks darkened. "Your family owns a hotel."

"So, you'll move in with me?"

As Fabian turned bright red, Shayna laughed. Surprisingly, it wasn't a mean laugh like Samantha had heard so often from Cheryl or Ani. Shayna seemed genuinely amused by Fabian, despite that making no sense at all.

"I don't have to understand that, do I?" Lucille asked as she slid next to Samantha.

"Nope." Samantha's eyes fell on the tree. "But we really need to do something about the nature spirits."

Jan

Anne's quest to find out more about Hanna had not only brought her closer to Ophelia, but also meant the two were spending far too much time at the Blackstone house. Jan had already given up on ever really calling it his home. While he was the official owner, Samantha now lived upstairs, and everyone and their sister—specifically his own—used the house as a meeting place.

Such was the case on Wednesday afternoon, when Jan had been looking forward to an evening of beer and football on the couch. Now, it was covered in research material and two teenage girls were huddled on it, expecting him to serve them lemonade or something.

"Did you find out anything about Hanna, at least?" he asked, setting down a pitcher of raspberry cordial and two glasses.

Anne wrinkled her nose. "Nothing really helpful in terms of her divinity, but she was an impressive woman. She was the only heir to her father, the King of Amain, and was engaged to Draken's son, Roric."

"'The Greedy One' Draken?"

"Mhm, that evil dark mage. But marriage was the last thing on her mind. She liked to dress up as a boy and train with soldiers. Legend has it very few were good enough to challenge her. And then she met Kairos."

"Let me guess, he was better than her?" Ophelia said, with a roll of her eyes.

Anne shrugged. "It doesn't say, but she saw potential in him, stole the Sword of the Gods from her father's treasury for him and helped him flee the city. She even stood up to her betrothed."

"Draken's *son*." Jan still couldn't quite get over the connection. He'd been under the impression the heroes of old had no connection with Draken and his descendants.

"Roric, yes. They met again later, and Hanna managed to kill him, even though he was an exceptionally talented mage. And then she defended the stairs of the Black Tower all by herself while Kairos fought Draken."

Ophelia whistled, suddenly much more appreciative. "Not bad. Hanna was badass."

Jan had to admit, the warrior princess had been quite something. Matt must've got his sword skills from her.

But Anne made a face. "Yeah, sure, but none of that helps. She didn't become a warrior goddess, she became a goddess of life, but all I can find out about that is how she kept Kairos alive for a while, which I assume means she had healing powers. Which I don't have."

"We'll find something for you," Ophelia promised. "Don't worry."

Anne leaned back, pouting slightly. "I should just forget about it. Who cares what kind of potential a demonic mass murderer sees in me?" She shuddered and grimaced. "I don't know why I'm even entertaining this."

"Because you want to help," Jan reminded her. "And Caspar may be a psychopath, but he wouldn't say something like that lightly. Growls and insults are more his style, not positivity."

Ophelia nodded and jumped in. "Jan is right. You have potential, but maybe you should start with something small. You won't develop powers overnight. That's not what priests do. Eresta... The main task of any priest is to nourish the faith. There are no Hanna temples in Ashuan, but why don't you make up a little ritual just for yourself?"

"I wouldn't even know where to start."

"Here." Ophelia put her hand over her heart. "You start here. Sure, there may be some traditional rituals with lots of meaning, but the most important thing is intention. Take an aspect of Hanna and build a little ritual around it."

Jan saw his own doubt reflected in Anne's face. "I don't know."

"Just try it. Worst case, nothing happens. Best case, you make a connection between you and your goddess."

Anne tested the words on her lips. "My goddess." Then her expression hardened in determination. "I'll think of something. Maybe I can grow a plant or something."

Jan kept his thoughts to himself and smiled painfully as the two girls made their plans. People grew things all the time and none of them found their calling as a priest of Hanna. But Anne seemed happy with the flimsy excuse for a plan, excitedly drawing up ideas for her new ritual, and brainstorming words for her prayers.

"I've been honouring Hanna all day by learning how to save lives. Do you think she'd mind if I relaxed on my couch now?"

Startled, Anne gathered her research. "I'm so sorry. Has your game already start—?"

Someone was banging on the door.

Jan groaned and headed for the entrance. He was halfway across the living room when the door burst open with a bright flash and crackling black lightning. *Demon energy.*

"Hide!" Jan shouted, ducking behind the wall for cover. He glanced behind him to check on Anne and Ophelia.

Both girls had taken cover behind the sofa, with Ophelia gathering her shadows around her. That made her better equipped than Jan.

Meanwhile, the demon slammed the rest of the door open and entered. "You go upstairs. I'll check downstairs," a male voice said.

Jan bit his tongue. *Two demons.* He put his fingers to his mouth and gestured for the girls to keep their heads down. Patiently, he waited near the door, listening for the footsteps. Their only chance was to take the demons one by one, which meant he had to wait until the second one was upstairs before he attacked the first. Thanks to the age of the house, the stairs creaked under their footsteps.

The other demon entered the living room. Unfamiliar to Jan, he was dark-skinned with muscular arms in a sleeveless vest. "I know you're hiding," he said in a deep drawl. "I heard you."

He turned his face towards the couch and Jan didn't wait a second longer. Pushing himself off the wall, he kneed the demon in the back, then brought the edge of his hand down on his neck.

An unsuspecting human would've collapsed under the impact. The demon just stumbled and groaned, then turned and caught Jan's arm before he could land a third blow. With a twist of his body, he spun Jan around and threw him into one of the chairs, which immediately fell apart beneath him.

Jan struggled to his feet, a fatal disadvantage against any demon. But there was no energy, no second attack. Instead, a wall of shadows rose in front of him, slowly closing in on the demon.

Jan used the distraction to drop back to the couch. "Go out the back door," he whispered to Anne.

"I'm not leaving you."

"I can't worry about you."

"Then don't," she hissed, a little too loudly.

Energy tore through the shadows and whipped across the couch, sending stuffing flying. Jan threw himself flat on the floor, although it had already missed him.

Anne whimpered and pressed her body into the corner behind the couch and the wall. "Please, Hanna, if you can hear me, please keep us alive."

Jan winced. Divine intervention would be nice, but he'd learnt long ago he had to take care of these things himself. Luckily, he had Ophelia at his side, whispering in her shadow-snake language and raising several of her signature creatures.

The demon tried to fend off the snakes, but his blows went right through the shadows. Meanwhile, the snakes *were* biting him. With a thud, the demon fell to the ground.

"Is he dead?"

"Just knocked out," whispered Ophelia.

Jan scrambled to his feet and grabbed the thickest book he could find. Just as he was about to bring the almanac down on the demon's head, the second appeared right in front of him: a pale woman with dark painted lips.

With a flick of her hand, she shot energy at him. Jan raised the book in front of his face, bracing himself for the impact, but it never came.

Confused, he peered over the edge of the cover. The woman seethed and fired again, but her energy crackled and fizzled against a blue shimmering wall. A shield.

"Please protect us, Hanna," Anne whispered behind him. "Please keep us safe and protect our lives from these harbingers of evil."

"Whatever you're doing, keep doing it."

Jan slowly backed away and the shield followed. Either it was tuned to his presence or it was already shrinking.

It didn't help that the demon kept attacking, as if she expected the magic to break apart eventually. Her partner groaned and began to move again.

"How long can you keep this up?"

"I don't know. I don't even know what I'm doing." There was palpable panic in Anne's voice.

"Keep praying!" Ophelia snapped, her face tense.

Another burst of magic hit the shield, making Jan jump. "I'll get a knife from the kitchen." In the future, he'd put strategically placed daggers all over the house. "Lia, you keep them at bay."

The next blast of energy hit the wall panelling instead, undoing all the work Jan had done. As he crawled into the kitchen, a window shattered. Jan hated to leave Anne and Ophelia alone, but he needed a weapon. As he quickly rifled through the drawers before settling on a paring knife, he heard more and more damage in the living room, punctuated by the panicked squeals of the girls.

He ran back, knife in hand, as the room fell silent. "Anne? Lia? Are you—" He stopped short when he saw the two demons frozen in the living room. *Literally frozen.* "Neve."

The little snow witch hovered behind them, her face distorted with anger. "Nobody gets to break Jan's house. Nobody."

Jan felt his heart flutter with relief. "You're the best. Make sure they never thaw, will you?"

"They'll make lovely statues for Neve."

"Nice. Are you okay?" Jan turned to the girls.

Anne was shaking. The blue glow was gone and Ophelia had an arm around her, talking to her reassuringly. "It's over. You've survived your first battle. Neve saved us." Then she smiled. "Actually, you saved us. Or rather, the goddess you prayed to."

There was no denying someone had heard Anne's prayer and decided to intervene. Maybe Hanna wasn't half as bad as Jan thought.

"What did they want?"

"They were looking for something," Jan remembered. "Or someone."

Matt

While the others were distracted making plans, Matt had grabbed Cian by the arm and dragged him away from the camp and into the forest. Cian was protesting and trying to free himself, but Matt's grip was relentless. He only let go when they were well away from the huts and Samantha. He checked to see if anyone had followed them before turning to Cian.

Cian's eyes were wide, his breath shallow, and he held his arm as if he was injured. Through his fingers Matt could see bruises.

"Sorry about that."

"You're sorry?" Cian repeated in disbelief.

Matt nodded. "I didn't realise I'd grabbed you hard enough to bruise."

"No problem," Cian said, despite his voice dripping with worry. "What's going to happen next?" He glanced over his shoulder, realising how far away from everyone they were.

"What do you mean 'next'?"

Cian stared at Matt's feet, his breathing still all over the place. Scared, Matt decided. Cian was scared, though he didn't understand why.

The boy seemed to gather some courage and raised his eyes. "Well, aren't you going to kill me?" The last two words were whispered. He narrowed his eyes, as if he expected Matt to strike him right there.

A terrible weight settled in Matt's stomach. "You think I want to kill you?"

"You don't?" There was a sliver of hope in his voice

"You mean because I caught you and Sam in the same room?"

Cian shrugged cautiously. "Yeah?"

Matt snorted, the sound leaving a bitter aftertaste. "No. No, Cian, I'm not going to kill you." It hadn't even occurred to him to do that, although he could see perfectly well why he might think that. Or why Samantha did. He swallowed hard. "Did you really think I'd drag you into the forest to get rid of you?"

"It's not that unlikely, is it?"

"I've learnt from my mistakes. A lot has happened since then." Matt bit his lip. The weight in his stomach was growing. "Is that what Samantha thinks? That I'd kill you given half the chance?" He'd thought they were past that. He'd known about her relationship with Cian for half a year and hadn't so much as laid a finger on him.

"Maybe," Cian admitted. "I don't think it's what she really believes, but the doubts are still there."

The confirmation almost took Matt's breath away. "She still hasn't forgiven me."

"She has. I think she has, actually. It's just..." Cian groaned, looking terribly conflicted. "It's complicated. Sam is complicated."

"That didn't stop you sleeping with her."

"That's what makes it so complicated." As he went on, Cian began to relax, and the smell of fear faded. "I usually have healthy boundaries. It's not like there aren't other great girls who'd be more interested."

"Yeah, I know." Matt leaned against a tree and let Cian's words sink in. Suddenly, he knew exactly how the other felt. Hopelessly in love with a wonderful girl who was unable to commit to anything deeper than the surface for fear of losing him.

Cian frowned at him. "So why *did* you drag me into the forest?"

Matt snapped out of his depressing thoughts, suddenly nervous. "Um... well, you said Sam... loved me." Cian raised an eyebrow. "How... how do you know?"

"Oh. Oh!" Cian's lips curved into a superior smile. "I see. That's what's going on here. Well, because she told me."

"Sam told you she loves me?"

"And now you want to know exactly what she said, don't you?" When Matt just shrugged, Cian snorted. "I don't remember. It was when she broke things off with me. You know we had some kind of deal?"

"Yeah, sex and friendship." As much as it had bothered Matt, he'd never tried to take it away from her.

Cian nodded thoughtfully. "But never love. She wasn't ready for that when we started dating. And after I found out why"—the guilt weighed heavily on Matt—"I gave her space. And even though she told me right away that she'd never love me, I had hopes that things would change. I thought one day she'd get over losing Daniel, and when she was ready for a new love, I'd be there." He snorted bitterly. "And well, she eventually fell in love again. It just wasn't with me. I don't know why, but for some reason she can't stay away from you."

Hearing that should've made Matt's head spin. It was everything he'd ever dreamed of. And yet the guilt on his shoulder and the weight in his stomach made it impossible to find any joy in it.

"If that's true, why did she go back to you and not me?"

During his mother's ill-fated visit, Samantha had rejected his attentions and found relief in Cian's arms instead.

Cian sighed heavily. "Because you're still the one who killed Daniel."

The twin weights crushed Matt's heart between them.

"She has feelings for you, but she hates herself for them."

Matt's head shot up. "She hates *herself*?"

Cian shrugged. "Well, any normal person would run as far away as possible, wouldn't they?"

"I'm not a normal person." Person usually meant human, and even after two years, many of their ways still confused Matt.

"Right. Well, most people wouldn't understand how anyone could ever develop feelings for someone who'd caused them so much pain. I couldn't live with myself." Cian lowered his voice. "And Samantha seems to have the same problem."

So, it was hopeless. Forgiveness or not, human morality kept her from following her heart and would continue to do so. "I see. So that's what's standing between us."

"It's definitely not me," Cian said. A bitter twitch of his facial muscles accompanied the words. "I've come to accept that it'll never be me."

"I wish I could give up on her that easily."

Cian grimaced in response, but Matt chalked it up to the depressing truth.

"What I want is... Honestly, I don't even know what I want."

"You want to be with her," Cian said, surprisingly gently. "You want to be the reason she laughs. You want to look in her eyes and see an adventurous glint inside, promising to change your life. You want her to be happy. Really happy, without a guilty conscience."

Matt stared into Cian's face. The words strangely moved him. It was as if Cian had plucked them straight from his mangled heart.

"That's pretty accurate."

Cian smiled softly. "I must be crazy to encourage you. Thing is, unlike me, she actually has feelings for you. You two have been through so much, with so much more to come. I can't compete with that. You're bound to each other. She just needs a little more time."

Matt appreciated the vote of confidence, but he wasn't quite ready to hope again. The truth was he wanted Samantha to be happy, not conflicted. And if all he was ever going to bring her was pain, he didn't want any part of it.

"You know, for an Elite Idiot you're not so bad," he admitted.

He realised now he'd never given Cian—or Alan, for that matter—a chance after being introduced to them as part of the Elite Clique. If he'd had, they might have even become friends.

Cian snorted, then laughed. "You know, you're not bad for a bloodthirsty half-demon either."

"That was *one* night!"

"Sure it was," Cian said, but he didn't sound serious.

Any trace of the fear he'd felt earlier had completely vanished, leaving behind two idiots in love with the same girl. Matt boxed him in the shoulder and Cian retaliated with a quick jab in his side before they both broke into a grin. Although the conversation hadn't yielded what Matt had hoped for, he'd come out of it feeling a little wiser. There was no point in forcing Samantha's hand. The ball was in her court now and she could either pick it up or kick it away.

Whichever made her happier.

Fabian

"We've got to do something," Lucille said, stepping away from the shattered window.

Fabian was busy picking up the remainders of the table. "But what?"

"Find whoever's responsible," Lucille said immediately.

"You mean Cheryl?"

Lucille shook her head and opened the door for Samantha and Rachel, who'd returned with a map of the campsite. As the table was broken, they spread it out on the floor instead.

"So, if I were a nature spirit, where would I hide Cheryl?"

Fabian pointed to a round mark. "I'd throw her in that well." And it would've brought him a lot of joy.

Suddenly, someone grabbed his arm and snuggled against his shoulder. "Then let's check it out together," Shayna said, with a cheeky grin.

Mortified, Fabian looked at her. "You're still here."

"Did you think I'd let you have all the fun without me?" Shayna giggled.

Across from him, Fabian saw the girls sharing a look.

Samantha smiled at him with that mischievous glint in her eye that told him he wouldn't like what she had to say. "That's a fantastic idea. You and Shayna check the well, and then maybe the shore." She traced a path around the lake with her finger.

"The entire shoreline? That'll take two hours."

"Not if you find Cheryl first," Lucille said, in an equally sweet manner.

Fabian narrowed his eyes. "Seriously?"

Samantha stared him down. "Please."

"Fine. If I have to." Fabian knew when he was being sacrificed. He just thought it wouldn't involve spending more time with Shayna.

"Come on. Two hours will be over in no time." Shayna said, with a wide, cheeky grin that spelt a lot of trouble.

He glared at Samantha and Lucille for good measure, but Shayna didn't give him much of a choice as she pulled him towards the door.

"Have fun, you two!" Lucille dared call after him, earning herself an even dirtier look.

It didn't take long for Shayna to ignore his boundaries yet again and link her arm with his. From past experience, Fabian knew there was no point in trying to shake her off. So, instead of protesting, he made polite conversation.

"Are you planning to study in the autumn?"

"Not really. How about you?"

"Biology."

Shayna cringed. "Ugh, no. I mean, you do whatever you want, but I dropped Biology as soon as I could."

Fabian almost sighed with relief that she wasn't going to suddenly show up on his course. "Really? I thought Biology was the girls' subject."

Almost every girl in their year had chosen Biology out of the three sciences for their final two years.

Not Shayna, apparently. "No, I'd much rather do Physics. It's basically just maths with more practical applications."

Despite himself, Fabian was impressed. It was one thing for Samantha and Rachel to be good at science, but Shayna was such a girly girl he hadn't expected her to have a head for numbers. "Well, fair enough. So, if you're not planning on going to university, what *are* you going to do?"

"I don't know. I'm thinking of taking a gap year, but I can't decide where I'd like to go. My parents aren't big fans of the idea, either. But I still have a few months to decide. Worst case, I work for my parents at the B&B and figure things out." She smiled, not the least bit worried about her future. "We just spent thirteen years at school. Why are you so eager to go back to it? *Live a little!*"

"Maybe."

Fabian had never really thought about anything besides studying. Samantha had always planned to go to university, so he'd planned to follow her as usual, and just picked a subject he was interested in.

A gap year sounded cool, but Fabian knew his parents could never afford the travel costs involved. Besides, he couldn't leave his friends to defend Greenvalley alone. And he happened to look forward to studying Biology. The lectures sounded cool, the field trips even more so.

Before he could think of a better answer, Alan crossed their path, walking around the lake in the opposite direction.

He immediately pulled a face when he saw them. "What the hell, Shayna?"

She let go of Fabian with a sigh. "Alan," she said, sounding terribly tired.

"Are you two a thing now, too?" Alan asked, his voice bordering on disgust.

"Fabian has a girlfriend."

Alan snorted and spat on the forest floor. "Doesn't look like he's thinking about her." He shook his head. "Man, I don't know who's more embarrassing. You or him."

Unlike with Ani and the others, Shayna actually seemed to care about Alan's words, her usual smile lost to his mockery.

Fabian couldn't bear it. "If I may give my opinion, right now, you're the one embarrassing yourself."

"Nobody asked you, Bendtfeld!"

Fabian raised his hands, taking a relaxed stance, even though he was seething inside. "Fine. I'll just stand here and listen to you rant about me."

"You got a problem with that?" Alan growled.

"Yeah, sort of. Not that it ever bothered you."

Fabian was so over the other guy's constant posturing and casual bullying. His actions over the last week alone had been the final straw.

Alan snorted. "Let's go, Shayna. Bendtfeld thinks he's a big boy now."

"Oh, but why? I want to see how this pans out," Shayna said. "There's no popcorn, but don't worry about me."

Annoyed, Alan groaned. "Really?" He turned to Fabian. "Fine. Bendtfeld, get out of my sight."

A dangerous calm settled over Fabian. "No, thanks." He was far too old to let Alan walk all over him.

"Do you want me to clip your ears?" Alan asked, already clenching his fists.

"Is that what they do at home to you?" Fabian sighed as Alan's face darkened. Apparently, he hadn't been too far off with his comment. "Fine, *Aster*. School's over. You can keep your weird ass threats. Nobody cares about your detective daddy or you."

Shayna almost clapped, grinning from ear to ear, while Alan couldn't decide whether he was angry or confused.

"I'm warning you, Bendtfeld. One more cheeky remark like that and I'll end you."

Two years ago, Fabian would've been shaking in his boots. With Björn and Cian at his back, Alan had given him a lot of trouble when they'd been younger. But now he didn't seem so big anymore, just a little guy who'd peaked in high school. Compared to the demons and monsters Fabian had to deal with on a regular basis, Alan was nothing to be afraid of. Not with an entire lake behind him.

"Okay, let's put an end to this."

Alan's eyes almost popped out of his head. "You want to fight? *You?*"

Fabian didn't deign to answer. Alan rolled his neck, not needing to be asked twice. Fists clenched, he lunged at him. Fabian wasn't a fighter like Jan or Matt, but he'd learnt to dodge monster attacks for years. Alan had anger issues and experience in scuffles enthusiasm, but he was much slower than a demon. One step aside, and Alan almost ran into the water.

Fabian decided that cooling off was exactly what Alan needed. Taking advantage of all the freak accidents lately, he reached for the water, causing a wave to crash onto the shore, grabbing Alan, and making him fall flat on his belly in the surf.

"You!" Water dripping down his skin, Alan glared at him.

"What?" Fabian asked innocently. "Are you saying I cast a spell on the water?"

Behind him, Shayna giggled.

Alan's eyes blazed. "Oh, you'll pay for that." But as he tried to stand, the water gave way beneath him, and he fell back into it.

"Oh dear," Fabian taunted. "Looks like I'm not the only idiot tripping over his own feet."

One embarrassing stumble in eighth grade had sealed Fabian's entire high school career.

Shayna burst out laughing, earning a helpless look from Alan.

"Shayna!"

"Sorry, Alan, but you deserved that one." She linked arms with Fabian again, far too happy for someone who'd just seen a friend humiliated. "Come on. We still have half a lake to go around."

With Alan practically speechless in the water, Fabian didn't even mind having Shayna on his arm. In fact, he felt great, wishing he'd stood up to Alan years ago.

"Beautiful day, isn't it?"

"Perfect for a swim," Shayna said with a broad grin.

Fabian mirrored her grin, feeling far too pleased with himself.

Rachel

With Shayna out of the way, Rachel led Lucille and Samantha into the woods to where she'd last seen the old woman and heard the wind complain. But when they arrived, nothing stirred.

"I can hear a little rustling of leaves," Samantha said, "but no words. How about you?"

Rachel shook her head, while Lucille said, "Nothing. Can't you summon the ghosts?"

"They're not really ghosts; they're nature spirits." Rachel had already tried to summon them and had come up short.

"What about the old woman?" Samantha asked, looking a little nervous. "You said you met her here."

Rachel pointed over her shoulder. "She came from over there, picking mushrooms and—" An idea suddenly struck her. "She told me all beings have a story, and that the story of the stones is the longest."

Lucille frowned. "I'm afraid I don't follow. What's this about stories?"

"Well, so far we've only been attacked by plants, right?"

"Thankfully," Samantha quipped, a little helplessly.

Rachel didn't care for her stone-filled horror visions. "We have to find the stones. They're older, more mature."

When the other two still didn't understand, Rachel simply started walking.

As before, the forest was beautiful. Mottled sunlight covered the ground, and they saw two squirrels chasing each other up and down the trees. There were few stones, but Rachel kept walking in the direction she'd seen the woman coming from, and ten minutes later they came to a glacial boulder. A fairy ring of mushrooms grew around it like a last layer of protection.

"This is it."

Lucille tilted her head. "What is it?"

"Watch out!" Samantha called, but it was too late.

A rustling in the leaves above them alerted them to the trees' movement. As one, the mighty pines raised their roots and took a step closer, encircling them. They dropped their branches until they pointed at them like swords, the message clear. Rachel swallowed as even the air began to taste hostile.

While Samantha quickly wove a shield, Lucille summoned her fireball. Panicking, Rachel grabbed her wrist. "Don't!"

Lucille glared at her. "I'm not going to get impaled by a tree."

"They're not attacking. Not yet, anyway."

"Not yet?" Samantha asked, understandably nervous.

But Rachel was sure of it. "They're guards."

"Guards? For whom?"

"There's no one here," Lucille said, fireball still in her hand.

Rachel scoffed. "There's so much here. Trees, the earth, rocks, leaves."

"Well spoken, child," said an ageless voice with a slight echo.

Samantha took half a step back, almost impaling herself on a branch. "Okay, I heard *that*."

In front of them, the boulder peeled away like the skin of an orange. The stone itself turned into old, bent people, including the woman who'd greeted them at the campsite. She smiled at Rachel and nodded in appreciation.

In the middle of the boulder people was a golden bush. Only it wasn't a bush at all. The branches moved, revealing themselves to be part of an elaborate magical dress worn by a beautiful ageless woman. She had long auburn hair, covered with a crown of golden leaves. There was a lump at her feet.

"Cheryl!" Samantha called.

It took Rachel a moment to recognise the sleeping queen bee, though she was quickly distracted by the awe-inspiring woman. "Who are you?"

The woman smiled at her with such warmth, as if she were summer herself. "I am the Queen of the Forest. I reign over this piece of nature."

"Does that mean you ordered the attacks on us?" Samantha asked.

Angry voices rose around them and the wind blew in their faces. "Impudent humans! Make them go away!"

The queen raised her hand. "Be calm, my dears. Don't frighten our visitors. They don't know any better."

Before Lucille could throw her fireball or Samantha could accidentally offend the spirits any further, Rachel took a step forward. "But we'd like to know better. We're willing to learn."

The queen looked at her thoughtfully, as if testing the truthfulness of her words. "You have upset the balance of nature. It's about giving and taking, but you have only taken, and now my people demand a price."

"And the price is Cheryl?" If so, Rachel was tempted to just call it a day.

But Samantha took a stand beside her. "Is there another way we can make up for what we have taken? We can also give."

The queen pondered her words for a while. Then she nodded. "There is a way, I believe. It's not too late to undo most of what you've done. Are you willing to put in the necessary work?"

Lucille joined them, and Rachel noticed she'd given up her fireball. "Tell us what needs to be done, and we'll do our best."

The queen smiled warmly. "Cleaning the forest would be a start."

Rachel almost groaned. She shouldn't have needed a spirit queen to tell her that they needed to take better care of the grounds. "Consider it done."

"Will you let her go once we're done?" Samantha asked tentatively. Despite the years of torment she'd endured at Cheryl's hands, she was still worried about her safety.

"Her actions directly threatened the forest. She almost burnt it all down."

Rachel remembered the cigarette Cheryl had flicked into a bush. "We'll ban smoking near the trees." These were all sensible measures. Even her party-crazed peers would have to see that.

"Very well." The queen nodded at them. "We'll let her go as soon as you've kept your promise."

The trees retreated and lifted their branches once more. The queen covered herself, returning to her shrubby form, and covered Cheryl as the rock people took their places to protect her.

Rachel, Samantha, and Lucille didn't dare speak until they were well away from the wondrous place. Rachel wished they could've spent a little more time with the nature spirits, but they had a job to do today. Maybe there'd be time after they got Cheryl back.

"How are we going to get everyone on board?" Samantha asked.

Lucille grinned. "Oh, all we need is a little incentive."

Matt

While Matt had been busy with Cian, the girls had brokered a deal with the local nature spirits. Lucille had turned their demands into a friendly competition between the cabins, offering the winners a pizza and crate of beer. Suddenly, everyone was in a hurry to tidy up the campsite and fill as many rubbish bags as possible. "No smoking" signs had gone up, and Matt was sure they'd have the woods cleaned by sundown.

He deposited his full rubbish bag outside their cabin and grabbed another bag as Samantha joined him. He marked her interest with a raised eyebrow, but didn't get an answer until they were well away from the others.

"I see Cian's still alive."

Matt didn't find it very funny. "Did you really think I'd hurt him?"

"Of course not," she said, a little too quickly. "Okay, maybe I was a bit worried, but obviously for no reason."

"You had plenty of reason." He sighed and bent down to pick up a dirty bottle. "All you see when you look at me is the man who killed Daniel."

To his surprise, she bent down beside him and put her hand on his arm, whispering, "That's not all I see. Not by a long shot."

Matt held his breath until she let go and stood back up.

Samantha looked up at the trees and tucked one of her black curls behind her ear. "I shouldn't look past what happened. I don't want to, but it happens. More and more often."

Slowly, Matt rose. "Why?"

"Because I can see how much you've changed and how much effort you've put into it. I know... or rather, I can imagine it hasn't been easy to turn your life upside down. It's a fact you were raised by demons and brought up with a completely different code of morals. And I'm really impressed by how you've examined and dissected that to find your own values."

There was a strange new feeling in his chest, a warmth that was neither love nor lust. It took him a moment to realise it was pride. Not the nasty, arrogant kind Hel and her house practised, but one of accomplishment and recognition. He felt seen by the only person he cared about.

Matt didn't quite know how to respond. It felt too important, but also wrong, to thank her for it. He *had* put a lot of work into it, perhaps more than he realised. But he hadn't done it because he was such a great guy. There was only one reason why he'd worked so hard to become a better man. That reason was standing next to him, her face so pure and vulnerable. Acknowledging his efforts while navigating her own complex feelings took just as much, if not more, effort. And while Matt had quickly discovered it would all be worth it, Samantha had no such guarantee. She was risking her soul for him, and Matt could only hope one day he'd be worth it.

"You know this is your fault, right?" he said awkwardly, not exactly the smooth response she might've expected.

Instead of bristling, Samantha laughed. "It's a fault I gladly own." She cocked her head and frowned slightly. "Are you alright?"

Startled, Matt shook his head. "I'm fine. I..." He quickly swallowed the automatic answer.

The fact was, he wasn't fine at all. Today had been a bit of a rollercoaster. From seeing Samantha and Cian together, to hearing how much she was still struggling and that in developing feelings for him she was effectively betraying the values she believed in, to having his own struggles acknowledged. He felt bad because it seemed that while she was making him better, he was making her less than she was.

It all fed into his guilt. Matt had thought making amends would lessen the torture he felt over Daniel's death, but every day, it grew. And it wasn't just Daniel. It was his fault Samantha had to compromise herself, and his fault she was constantly in danger. He didn't deserve her, and loving her felt selfish. It *was* selfish, but unlike Cian, Matt didn't know how to let her go.

"Matt?" Samantha's voice was full of concern. "Talk to me."

"That'll only make it worse," he blurted out.

She blinked in surprise. "Talking will make it worse?"

"No, I don't want to burden you any more than I already have. It seems I only cause you trouble."

Samantha took a deep breath. She took a step towards him and gently took the rubbish bag from him so she could hold his hands. She searched his face until he held her gaze. "I may not be ready quite yet, but you're not just trouble for me. I don't have feelings for you just because you're extremely handsome and charming."

"You don't?" Matt couldn't quite fathom what else there was.

"I mean, those are definitely pluses, but I..."—she stumbled over the word, as if she was struggling to admit it—"I *love* you because you care so much. And yes, I said you've changed a lot, and you have, but you've always cared. You're incredibly brave, and you fight for those you love—which, for some wild reason, happens to be me—even to your own detriment. Would a demon risk his own life over and over again for someone else?"

His breathing slowed and he felt lightheaded. "You'd do the same for me. We do this for each other."

She nodded. "We do, yes. And you're kind. When you came to Ashuan, you could've easily been a complete asshole. Cheryl and co. would've loved to have you in their clique, but you chose us."

"You were the only ones who believed in magic."

"Maybe, but I remember the early days. I remember when you came to me after Nico died. You'd seen so much death in your life, it didn't affect you the way it did us."

Matt rolled his eyes. "Yes, very caring."

Frustrated, she pushed him a little. "You *came*, Matt. Yes, his death didn't mean as much to you, but you had enough emotional intelligence to notice how it affected *us*. You looked after me, because even if you didn't understand, you knew *I* was struggling and you helped me. You were my rock when I was struggling to breathe. And what you said to me then has got me through so much in the last two years."

"What I said?"

Matt remembered finding Samantha at her grandmother's, struggling with the enormity of what had happened, and the role she'd played in Nico's death. He'd been so impressed by what she'd achieved in such a short time and hadn't been able to see her beating herself up when she should've been celebrating her success. But the words of their conversation eluded him.

Samantha nodded, her gaze as intense as ever. "You've put it all into perspective for me. We've fought so many battles over the last two years, most of which we've won, otherwise we wouldn't be standing here. But sometimes we lose, and it hurts, but it doesn't mean the fight itself was in vain. Because we keep on fighting, even when there's no hope. Because as you said back then, sometimes, even against all odds, we win. You and I—all of us, really—we don't give up." She smiled softly. "Just like you never gave up on me."

"I..."

Matt struggled to breathe. He wanted to take her in his arms and kiss her right there. Part of him was almost convinced Samantha would even welcome it. But the guilt weighed too heavily. Despite what he'd done, she believed in him. She believed he could be a better man. And Matt wasn't nearly so sure.

He hung his head in shame. "I haven't changed as much as I should've."

"What do you mean?"

"Well, for one thing, I actually like being half-demon. My natural powers, the freedom. You say I'm brave, but I thrive on the thrill. The fight for survival gives me life. I'd be bored to death if I had to live in Fabian's dream world."

Samantha chuckled softly. "I think I'd be, too."

"See, and that's why I... *love* you. You're so much braver than me because none of this comes naturally to you. You're not super strong or heal easily, but you still fight, and you don't do it for yourself, but for those you love."

"So, like you."

Matt protested, "No, I just..." He narrowed his eyes. "I see what you mean."

She raised her eyebrows, her lips quirking. "You think I don't remember you covering me with your own body when Caspar attacked us on the way back to Ashuan, or when Balthasar sent those crows? Or..." She swallowed suddenly. "The promise you made to your mother."

Reality struck him in the face. Over the past few days, Matt had almost forgotten about his oath. He'd gladly taken it to save Samantha, but that didn't mean he was looking forward to fulfilling it. "I don't want to do it."

"Good," she said, a noticeable tremor in her voice. "I mean, I know demons are different, but it's just wrong. She's your mother."

"Anyone who isn't you would be wrong."

Maybe in another life Matt wouldn't have minded so much. In another life, he'd even have enjoyed the fierce competition with his brothers and would've gladly killed *or* slept with his mother. But that life wasn't his anymore. It hadn't been his since the day he'd seen this human witch, who hadn't even discovered her own powers yet, working herself to the point of exhaustion to save a friend.

Samantha stared at him, breathless for once.

Matt laughed softly. "Why are you so shocked? I love you, remember? You're the only one I want. I'd give it all up for you: the power, the thrill. If I could become human, I would." He had no idea where that had come from, but as soon as he'd said it, Matt knew it was true.

"Don't." With a sudden urgency, Samantha let go of his hands and moved even closer. She cupped his face and searched his eyes. "Change is good, Matt, but I don't want you to lose all that you are. You're not human. You're half-demon, and maybe I shouldn't, but I love you just the same."

"But you really shouldn't," Matt insisted. "There's too much darkness in me. Too much depravity."

She scoffed at that, and suddenly there was a wicked gleam in her eyes that did something sordid to him. "Perhaps instead of fighting it, what I really need is to embrace the darkness in myself."

A wonderful shiver ran down Matt's spine. Suddenly his hands were on her hips, and he pulled her towards him with a sudden jerk. As their bodies collided, Samantha let out the most delicious gasp.

"Maybe you should," he said in a low growl.

"There you are!" Lucille's voice rang out from behind them.

They flew apart, searching for random pieces of rubbish as their three friends approached.

"Huh," Lucille said, looking far too pleased with herself. "Well, if you're not too busy, and you can totally say no—just putting it out there—Rachel said the spirits are ready to receive us now. We'll be on our way, but if you want to stay and continue whatever—"

"We're coming," Samantha blurted out, dashing any hopes Matt might have held. "And for the record, we were just talking."

"Oh, yeah," Lucille nodded eagerly, "that totally looked like talking. I always have my hands all over the people I talk to."

Fabian and Rachel snorted behind her.

Flustered, Samantha gasped. "Oh my god, will you stop?"

Grinning, Lucille linked arms with her. "Not until you tell me all about it. For your information, I'm planning on living vicariously through you."

Samantha glanced back at Matt helplessly, but he just laughed. Judging by the reactions of the others, they were the only ones making such a big deal out of it. Maybe Samantha was right and there was still hope for them. Even with the odds against him, she was worth the fight.

Lucille

Within five hours they'd cleaned up the camp and the nearby forest. Bottles had been retrieved from the shallows of the lake and the bushes. Every last cigarette butt had been collected, and smoking was only allowed near the water for those who couldn't abstain. A group of them had also done their best to restore and protect the young trees near the campsite.

When it was all done, Lucille and her friends returned to the Queen of the Forest. It was as wondrous as the first time, and Lucille couldn't wait to tell Linda about her dress of gossamer silk and golden leaves. This time the trees didn't interfere, and the air felt much less hostile.

"We did the best we could," Rachel reported.

The queen gave them an affectionate smile. "The wind told me already. You did well. I will return your friend, on one condition."

"Another?" Lucille asked. They'd already spent the whole day cleaning. Not exactly the fun holiday they'd planned.

"Take care of these woods while you're here."

Lucille breathed a sigh of relief and smiled back. "Gladly."

The ground itself rolled Cheryl out. Matt bent down and slung her over his shoulder.

"She won't remember a thing," the queen promised.

"Thank you," Rachel said.

"Just remember to respect nature and always give as much as you take. Do this and we will treat you well."

And with that, the queen took her place again. As before, Lucille marvelled at how she could look human one minute and like a bush the next. A moment later, the boulder people had covered her, and the trees parted behind them.

Lucille turned, eager to return to camp, and came face to face with one of her classmates. "Robert."

Robert stood there, eyes wide open, mouth agape.

"What are you doing here?" Samantha asked, her eyes reflecting the panic rising in Lucille.

Had Robert seen the Queen of the Forest? Had he seen what had happened to Cheryl?

He opened his mouth, but at first nothing came out. When he closed it, he shook his head, and his gaze fell on Matt. "You found Cheryl."

Matt nodded happily. "We did. Looks like she partied a little too hard. Once she's slept it off, she'll be as good as gold. Come on, I want to go for a swim before it gets dark."

One by one, they walked past Robert, ignoring what he might have witnessed earlier. Robert stood motionless for another minute, but soon they heard him running after them.

"I love swimming! Shall we have a water fight?"

Samantha and Lucille exchanged glances. Either he hadn't seen anything or he had an admirable ability to compartmentalise.

"Sure, all against Fabian," Matt suggested.

"Hey!"

They all burst into giggles, while Robert grinned like an idiot, completely oblivious to the joke.

On their last night, they sat around the fire pit, drinking and toasting marshmallows and bread on sticks. Ready-made rubbish bags ensured nothing landed on the ground. The nature spirits had kept their word and the last two days had been wonderfully peaceful.

Now, around the fire, a cosy atmosphere, thick with nostalgia, enveloped them like a warm blanket. People were telling stories from their school days, remembering events from long ago. Most of them were new to Lucille, but she loved hearing them anyway. Pictures were taken and a few tears were shed, but mostly people were having fun and enjoying their last moments together.

There were also a few surprising hook-ups, but not the one Lucille had been impatiently waiting for. Although Matt and Samantha sat next to each other, they seemed to do nothing but talk and toast bread on their sticks over the fire. The only thing they had going for them was the fact they didn't have eyes for anyone else.

Lucille noticed Cian watching them with a forlorn gaze and felt terribly sorry for him. He was good boyfriend material, but compared to Matt there was really no competition. Not when Matt had grown so much for Samantha. Luckily, Cian had good friends, and soon Alan came and pulled him up to kick a ball around with a few others.

To Lucille's surprise, Shayna squeezed into the small space between her and Fabian.

"Excuse me," she said cheerfully to Lucille, before giving her full attention to Fabian, who seemed much more comfortable around her than before.

"You're still persona non grata?" Fabian asked, nodding to the other side of the fire where Cheryl was entertaining Ani, Björn, and Jennifer.

Shayna shrugged. "I haven't really tried to change that. I meant it when I said I'd had enough of their childish crap."

"Well, Alan and Cian made up quickly."

Shayna rolled her eyes. "They always do. I'm telling you, there was a lot of embarrassing crying and hugging involved. Alan even apologised, but don't think you're going to get the same treatment any time soon."

Fabian snorted. "I'll be happy if he leaves me alone."

"Oh, he'll give you a wide berth from now on."

"Good," Fabian said grimly, making Lucille curious to know what had transpired between them.

Her desire only grew when Shayna grinned. "But don't think you'll get rid of me with a little water play."

Fabian's eyes widened, while Lucille's mouth dropped. Had he revealed his powers? Was that what had changed between them?

Lucille was bursting with curiosity and just had to ask, "What happened?"

"Oh, Fabian and I were enjoying our little walk around the lake when Alan tried to pick a fight," Shayna said in her best juicy gossip voice, fulfilling all of Lucille's needs. "Fabian tried to put him down easy, and by 'easy' I mean he had some absolute zinger clap-backs, but Alan has never been one to back down. So, the fight starts and before Alan can even land his first punch, he slips and belly flops into the water. He tries to get up and falls again. It was humiliating. Just what he needed. And I'm saying this as a friend."

Behind Shayna, Fabian grimaced in pain, making it clear those slips had been anything but accidental.

Good for him, Lucille thought, grinning. "I would've loved to have watched that."

"I should've recorded it. Damn." Shayna patted her knee, then turned back to Fabian. "Well, give my regards to your girlfriend. She's a very lucky girl." She leaned down to kiss his cheek, then stood again and waved to Lucille before joining Cian and Alan.

Lucille laughed at Fabian's confused expression. "So, Shayna Richards has a crush on you?"

He grimaced. "Don't be ridiculous. She's just messing around."

"Sure, if that helps you sleep at night." Lucille knew when a girl was into a guy.

"I don't sleep at night. I've got a girlfriend," Fabian said smugly.

Lucille gasped. "Fabian!" She punched him in the shoulder and turned to Rachel. "Can you believe this guy? Flaunting his relationship in front of us."

Rachel snorted and shook her head. Her gaze found Cheryl. "She got over it quickly."

Lucille rolled her eyes. "She's probably telling everyone how she saved the day or something." A wave of nostalgia and excitement for the future washed over Lucille and she put her arms around Fabian and Rachel. "From tomorrow on, we'll never have to deal with her again. Isn't it wonderful?"

Fabian grinned. "I can't wait. No more Elite Idiots, no more Robert, and no more Herby. I love graduating."

Giggling, Lucille let go and had another glance at Matt and Samantha. Their stick bread was done, and Samantha was breaking it up and feeding it to Matt, while he'd casually put an arm around her back.

"Do you think those two will ever seal the deal?"

"I'll probably be with Adam before they do."

"Rachel!" Lucille chuckled. "Does that mean we're going to *talk* to him?"

Rachel gave her a withering look. "*I'll* talk to him. He's going to have to like me for who I am, not what you think he might like."

"Fair enough." Lucille shrugged. "But with Fabian in a committed relationship, Matt and Samantha hooking up, and you dating Adam, I'll be the only one single."

"Jan's single," Fabian pointed out.

"Oh great, maybe I'll date him." Lucille shuddered. She looked into the fire and nodded to herself. "We'll be at university soon. That's a whole new dating pool."

Rachel snorted at her, then leaned forward to share a look with Fabian. "We should warn the university."

Fabian nodded eagerly. "Maybe posters? 'Beware of this woman'."

"You're horrible friends. Horrible, horrible!" Lucille said, but when they burst into laughter, she willingly joined in.

Whatever the future held, she couldn't wait.

Jan

Friday night came and Jan had fended off three demon attacks. Since the first, he'd been carrying a dagger wherever he went, hoping he wouldn't suddenly have to reveal it in class. He'd been lucky so far, but he still felt like a psychopath going to Adam's farewell party with a concealed weapon.

Part of him was afraid he'd accidentally lead the demons to the party and cause a massive massacre. Normally he wouldn't bother—although the promise of free beer and snacks was tempting—but this time, he owed it to Rachel. It sucked she couldn't be here to do it herself. He hadn't even been able to tell her because there was no reception at the campsite.

The party was in a shared flat, which was absolutely packed when Jan arrived. People were even standing in the hallway chatting. The kitchen was overflowing with pizza boxes, salad bowls, and buns, and the selection of alcohol was promising. A man Jan didn't know handed him a bottle of beer without even asking who he was.

Jan drank a few sips as he carefully made his way through the flat, looking for Adam or a hidden demon. There were a few people he knew from his training or from the hospital. He had no idea if they were all there for Adam, but if they were, he'd certainly made a lot of friends during his time in Germany.

After ten minutes of searching, Jan finally spotted the familiar curly head in one of the bedrooms. Adam was sitting on the floor in a group of people, laughing at a friend's story. Next to him was a small pile of presents, mostly photos and German sweets.

Jan didn't know anyone else in this group, but he approached them anyway. "Hey."

Adam looked up, not recognising him at first. "Hi, um…"

"Jan, but I'm not important." He pulled a note out of his pocket and handed it to Adam. "That's Rachel's number. She's out of town, so she couldn't come."

"Rachel?" Adam frowned, then his eyes widened in recognition. "Oh, Rachel! Thank you." As his friends looked at him in confusion, he smiled adorably. "Just a girl I met."

"What?" the guy next to him asked, laughing. "You didn't say anything about a girl."

Adam tried to downplay the whole thing, but quickly admitted to having a bit of a crush. Within seconds Jan was forgotten. He nodded to himself before leaving.

On his way out, he grabbed two slices of pizza and drank his beer. It was a shame Adam's time in Greenvalley had been so limited. Jan hardly had the chance to talk to him more than once or twice, but found him easy to like. He felt sorry for Rachel that she'd never have the chance to get to know him properly, but hopefully the exchange of numbers would help a little.

It was all he could do for her.

Samantha

The journey home was far too long and noisy. When the buses finally pulled into the car park at Greenvalley train station, Samantha breathed a sigh of relief. One by one, the graduates disembarked and milled around the heaps of luggage, saying tearful goodbyes and promising to keep in touch.

Samantha craned her neck to find Cian, who'd ridden on another bus. When she saw him with Alan, lifting luggage off the bus for everyone, she made her way over. "Hey."

Alan gave her a dirty look but got out of her way while Cian smiled. "Hey, are you leaving?"

"No, not yet. Um, I just wanted to apologise."

Cian's eyes widened. "Don't, please. You've been honest with me from the get-go. I'm the one who can't get over you." Before she had a chance to react, Cian grinned. "Just kidding."

She chuckled politely, not quite convinced he was joking. "I bet you'll meet lots of girls in Bielefeld, all begging to be your girlfriend."

He threw his head back and laughed. "I don't think so, but I like the idea." He sobered up a little. "We'll keep in touch, right?"

"Of course."

"Come here." Cian pulled her into a friendly hug before he grabbed his bag and left with Alan.

Samantha returned to her friends, only to see Rachel running off without her luggage. She made it to the bus just in time and squeezed into the closing doors, looking distraught. Turning to look at the others, Samantha saw Jan and an upset Lucille. Fabian was busy with Ophelia, who'd jumped into his arms and was kissing him like there was no tomorrow.

"What just happened?"

"While you were gone, Adam had his farewell party," Jan explained. "I gave him Rachel's number just in case, but she's hoping to catch him at the hospital before he leaves."

"He's leaving?" Samantha asked in dismay. "That's a shame."

Jan nodded. "Yeah, he's a nice guy. So, how was the trip?"

"Surprisingly exciting," Matt said, slipping into the spot next to Samantha, as if it were his natural place.

"We met the Queen of the Forest," Lucille said, a twinkle in her eye.

"Did she eat too many mushrooms or what?"

Samantha laughed. In retrospect, it was rather surreal, but there was no doubt the nature spirits had been real. "There really was a Queen of the Forest. She was beautiful. Her people, though... Let's just say it was an interesting time." A little softer, she said, "And Robert may have seen a little too much."

"That Robert?" Jan pointed at her classmate, who was kissing Anne. He didn't seem to give a single thought to what he'd seen. "You know, I haven't missed him all week."

Lucille snorted. "Lucky you. We had to bunk with him." She craned her neck. "Well, I can see my ride. Matt, shall I give you a lift?"

Matt shook his head. "I'll walk with Sam."

His words amused Samantha. "I didn't know I was walking."

"Well, you do now. Let's put yours and Rachel's luggage in Jan's car and get going."

"Oh, I'm glad I came out here to pick up everyone's luggage," Jan protested, but then shook his head with laughter. "You two go, have fun. It's not like you haven't just spent a whole week together."

"He's got a point," Samantha said as she walked away with Matt. "We did spend a whole week together."

"Yes, surrounded by a hundred of our former classmates, in a cabin with six others, while being endlessly harassed by nature spirits." Matt had a point, too. "Besides, I don't think I'll ever have enough time with you."

And there it was again, the big open question. Should they dare it? "So, now we're walking?"

"How about catching a movie at the cinema later tonight?"

"Is there anything good on?"

"Sam!"

She giggled. "What?"

Matt looked a bit like a lost puppy, desperate for her attention. She decided to throw him a bone.

"You're not going to try and take advantage of the darkness and the intoxicating taste of caramel popcorn, are you?"

His eyes were glued to her lips. "Tell me more about the intoxicating taste of caramel popcorn sticking to your lips."

When she laughed, he seemed much more relaxed.

"So?"

"Not tonight. I'm exhausted and need a bit of rest. But later this week, yes. If I get to choose the movie."

Matt snorted in amusement. "I don't care one bit about the movie, so sure."

"And no popcorn," she said sternly.

"Look, I also like the taste of nachos on your lips. Anything really."

Samantha rolled her eyes but couldn't help laughing. A movie date sounded nice, though. Normal. Human. Just what their relationship needed more of.

Unfortunately, when she got home, the fridge was noticeably empty. Jan persuaded her to order some Thai food, but the first thing Samantha did the next morning was go shopping. After what Jan had told them about the random demon attacks, she'd hidden her Torakh in her handbag and put her flowers in her hair.

The shopping itself was uneventful, but on the way back she thought she heard something. Samantha looked over her shoulder. Even though she was prepared for it, she was startled by the sight of two demons who'd appeared.

She immediately dropped her shopping bags and grabbed the Torakh from her handbag as she reached for the magic around her. Just then, three more demons appeared behind her.

Two demons were a challenge, but *five?* As one of them reached for her, Samantha sliced her arm with the Torakh. The woman hissed as steam rose from the wound.

Despite their aversion to the weapon, two more advanced. Samantha whirled around, slashing without looking as she drew enough magic to throw a ball of pure pain at one of her assailants. Within seconds, however, one had an arm around her, while another grabbed her wrist and twisted it until she screamed in pain and dropped the Torakh.

"Matt!" Samantha called out loud as she kicked and scratched. "Melch—"

One of the demons clamped a hand over her mouth and yanked her head back violently. Samantha saw stars while tears shot to her eyes. They jumped through the cold, smooth dimension that connected the worlds. When they reappeared, she was thrown forward and hit rough stone.

No immediate attack followed. Samantha tried to weave her magic into a shield, but the strands eluded her. It was as if a wall had been erected between her and the source, closing her off so completely she couldn't even see.

Panic had her in a chokehold, but she forced herself to breathe evenly and assess the situation. There still hadn't been another attack, which didn't fill her with relief, just more and more dread.

Slowly, Samantha raised her gaze and stared directly at Melaney.

Part 5

Lust & Love

Samantha

Samantha was in Hell. And not just any part of it, but right in the heart of the Residence of Lust, and alone with an archdemon and her followers. The throne room was cast in obsidian. Hidden lights shone behind the glassy surface, like trapped spirits in the wall. Luscious plants with gigantic red flowers emitted a sweet, sensual smell.

Melaney was half sitting, half lying on a majestic chaise longue with golden legs and embroidered cushions. Next to her was a heartbreakingly beautiful man wearing nothing but tight leather pants. There were also scantily clad guards and what Samantha thought were playmates, all watching her with a kind of excitement that reminded her sharply of Cheryl and her cronies.

"Welcome to my humble abode," Melaney said in her sultry voice. "I've been waiting for you, my dear. Have a seat." She pointed to a suspiciously comfortable armchair behind Samantha. "Sit!" she ordered sharply when Samantha hesitated.

Cowed, Samantha perched on the edge of the chair. As soft as it was, it felt like a trap, as if there were hidden nails under the covers.

Melaney stood up in a languid motion. "You must be exhausted, dear." Her voice was deceptively sweet again. "You look a bit rough."

Samantha resisted the sudden instinct to check her hair. She could feel her ponytail was in disarray and hoped the flowers were still in place, but didn't dare draw attention to them. Her arms were covered in bruises and scratches, and, judging by the way her face was burning, she knew it looked the same.

"I've made you a drink," Melaney said. She held out her hand and the unfamiliar man at her side handed her a silver goblet. She offered to Samantha. "Drink, my dear."

Having learnt from her previous command, Samantha took the goblet and examined its contents. The liquid was a little thicker than water and golden in colour. There was no smell to indicate what was inside. She didn't know if it was a demonic drink, a magic potion, or just plain poison.

"Drink!"

The harsh tone of Melaney's voice startled Samantha, and she took a small, cautious sip. The liquid was surprisingly warm, but when it went down her throat, it burnt and made her cough. Suddenly Melaney's hand was in her hair, nails raking over her skin as she pulled Samantha's head back and poured the drink into her mouth.

Half the liquid ran down her chin and cheeks as Samantha coughed and spluttered. Her throat was on fire and her whole face felt like it was filled with pins and needles. She was shivering, sweat pouring down her forehead.

Melaney just smiled. "I knew we'd get along well. Now that's done, I want you to meet someone." She waved the leather-clad man forward. "This is Frennys, my mate. He's my companion, my counterpart, and my favourite playmate. You see, lust is not a sin to be indulged in alone. My son Melchior seems to have forgotten this. Since he likes you so much, you'll have to help me remind him."

The burning in her throat had subsided enough for Samantha to speak. It hadn't been poison, but she'd be foolish to assume it was harmless. Melaney had an agenda. Either this was a sordid game or a devious plan. Samantha struggled to decide which. Only one thing was clear: Melaney wasn't going to kill her. At least not yet.

Samantha looked at Frennys again, trying to understand what it meant to be the mate of the Archdemon of Lust. Someone dedicated to the sin, no doubt.

"Are you saying you want me to be his... *mate*?"

"Something like that. This special potion will help you find the lust within you."

All the blood drained from Samantha's face as the words sank in. She didn't know how the liquid did that, but she could've sworn she could still feel its heat in her stomach.

"What if I don't want to be his mate?" she forced herself to say. "I have a mind of my own."

Melaney stroked her hair almost affectionately. "Then we'll have to break it."

As Samantha stared at her, speechless, Melaney took a step back and leaned into Frennys as if to kiss his neck. "Why don't you show our guest to her room. I'll take care of her later."

"Take care of?" Samantha squeaked.

Before the words were fully out of her mouth, Frennys grabbed her arm in a vice-like grip and yanked her to her feet.

Melaney sank back into her pillows, looking very pleased with herself. "Well, someone needs to make sure you meet my requirements for lovers."

Samantha's breath caught in her throat and her eyes widened. She swallowed, but before she could even begin to form words, Frennys dragged her away into a tunnel-like corridor that soon turned into a maze of passageways.

She was still struggling with the enormity of what Melaney had planned for her when Menuha crossed their path. "Menu."

The demon's eyes widened in surprise, but she didn't make a move towards them. Soon, she disappeared around a corner.

While most of the rooms were either walled off or opened up from the tunnels, the one Samantha was dragged into had a door. A large black rune was carved into the wood, and when Frennys placed a hand on it, it swung open. The first thing Samantha noticed was the huge canopy bed in the middle of the room. Red silk curtains were lavishly draped over the posts, and numerous pillows were piled up on it.

Next, Samantha's gaze was drawn to the walls. Instead of windows, colourful paintings framed by heavy curtains depicted scenes which would've put the Kamasutra to shame. Below them were heavy drawers, the sinful contents of which Samantha could only guess at. A few phallic objects on top were hint enough.

She quickly looked away and found a table near the door. It was laden with fruit and nuts. A silver pitcher and matching goblet reminded Samantha of the potion she'd been forced to drink. She sincerely doubted that this one's contents were any different.

Frennys let go of her arm to run his hands down her sides until they came to rest on her hips, causing Samantha to freeze. He leaned forward, his hot breath close to her ear. "We're going to have a lot of fun together."

When he let her go, Samantha's knees almost buckled, and she shivered from head to toe. Frennys gave her a smirk before he left. The door closed behind him and the light of a magic seal flashed once. Samantha knew without having to check she'd been trapped.

Suddenly the room began to spin, and she found herself on the floor trying to catch her breath. Tears formed in her eyes as her fear took over.

"Melchior," she cried desperately.

Nothing.

Whatever rune had sealed the room, it hadn't just cut Samantha off physically, but magically as well. She was alone among demons who wanted to turn her into their puppet, with no way to escape or call for help. There was no magic, and her Torakh was lying on the streets of Greenvalley between the contents of her shopping bags.

Startled, Samantha touched her hair. Coming up empty at first and almost screaming, she found her flowers dangling precariously from the bottom of what had once been her ponytail. She gently plucked them from her hair and cradled them between her hands. With the rivers of magic blocked, she was unable to use their pollen, but it felt good to have something familiar with her.

Now all she had to do was survive long enough for someone to find and rescue her. But when Samantha looked at the paintings on the walls, she feared survival wouldn't be the issue.

Rachel

If the world ended tomorrow, Rachel wouldn't care. Even though it was the afternoon, she was sitting on her bed in her pyjamas, listening to the sappiest songs on her playlist, and filling dozens of tissues with her tears. Sometimes she tried to tell herself how pathetic she was and would snap out of it, but then she thought of Adam and the many chances she'd had to talk to him, and would start crying again.

"Rachel," Hugo said, in a stern voice, "a woman shouldn't let herself go like this. No man is worth so many tears, especially not a scoundrel who couldn't even find the courage to court you outside of your dreams."

"How was he supposed to know I was interested?" Rachel blubbered. "I couldn't even say a word to him."

"I didn't hear him say anything, either. When I was alive, it was the man's duty to court someone, not the other way around."

"But your time is over," Rachel said bitterly. "This is my time now, and here you have to seize the day instead of always dreaming of the future." Nico had warned her time and again that this would happen. But had she listened? *No!*

Hugo shook his head. "You're being too hard on yourself. He made eyes at you when he knew he didn't have much time left in this country. It wasn't fair of him to give you such hope."

Rachel gave the ghost a flat stare. "He can't read minds."

"Too bad."

"No, no, no." Tears welled up again. "I'm the problem. You know, it's not just Adam. It's *me*, every time. I didn't say anything when my mum was horrible to me. I couldn't bring myself to tell Fabian I loved him until it was over. We wouldn't even *have* gone out if it weren't for other people, like Samantha and Lucille."

Hugo frowned. "You're in love with Fabian?"

"I *was*. For six years! And... and... it's me, me, me. I'm the problem."

"I see," Hugo said, though he still looked like he was struggling to understand. "So, this isn't really about Adam?"

Rachel stared at him. "Of course it's about Adam. What if he was *it*? What if he was my only chance. My Mr Right?" She'd told Lucille she didn't believe in such things, but her friend had gotten into her head since then, and now she was panicking that she'd blown it. "What if he was my only chance for true love?"

"That's a ridiculous assumption that leads to nothing but pain."

Which was exactly how Rachel felt. "No one will ever love me!" Her throat tightened and she threw herself into her pillows, crying bitterly.

Resigned, Hugo patted her shoulders. "Now, now. That's not true. Your friends and I love you very much."

Each word made Rachel sob harder and harder. She'd had her chance with Adam, but instead of taking it, she'd found excuse after excuse not to talk to him. Maybe it would've never led to anything, especially with him on the other side of the world, but now she'd never know. It could've been everything, and now it was nothing.

As soon as she fell asleep, Rachel tried to find Adam's dreams, but his flower was lost in the meadow, no longer blooming near her. With such a big time difference, it would take a miracle for them to be asleep at the same time. Then again, Rachel had months of endless summer ahead of her. She could easily change her sleeping habits. And then what? Adam would dream about her, wondering why he couldn't forget a girl he hadn't even known?

Rachel sat down on her meadow with a sigh, wishing Nico was there to cheer her up, but the dreamer who'd worn his face stayed away.

He'd said they'd meet again one day, but that day was clearly not today. She was toying with the idea of drowning herself in a dream when she noticed a wilting flower beside her.

There was something familiar about it, but she couldn't put her finger on it. All she knew was that it contained a nightmare.

Self-loathing made her touch the flower anyway. After all, a nightmare may have been the only thing strong enough to distract her from the one she was living.

The dream was unlike any Rachel had ever experienced. There was no dreamer, at least not at first. Instead, it was a dark room with flames blazing alive and dying here and there. Every time the light flickered, distorted images of copulation and despair flashed. Doors slammed shut and everything was plunged into darkness, then a golden liquid poured into the dream, startling Rachel. The fires rekindled and enveloped the room. It grew smaller and smaller until it burst and distorted faces appeared in its place. Their laughter sounded like nails on a chalkboard.

Rachel was about to stumble out of the madness when she came across a little girl with dark curls sitting on the floor crying her eyes out. A mirror appeared in front of her, but when she looked into it, a grotesque monster stared back.

A prolonged scream jolted Rachel awake. It took her a few seconds to realise she was screaming along with it.

"Bug?" Her father was standing in the doorway, panting. "Did something happen?"

Rachel had to catch her breath before she could answer. "It was just a dream, Dad. A nightmare." Whoever had dreamt it was in serious trouble.

Mick's face softened. "Because of Adam?"

It wasn't until he mentioned Adam that Rachel remembered her heartbreak. She immediately teared up. "Maybe."

She'd gone to bed practically hating herself. Maybe that was why she'd searched out the darkest nightmare she could find.

"Oh, Bug. If I tell you this will pass, it won't really help, will it?" Mick smiled gently.

"Not really."

She knew it would pass, but what frightened her wasn't the fact she'd lost Adam, but that it might always turn out like this.

Her father nodded wisely. "Try to get some more sleep."

As he closed the door, Rachel sank back into her pillows. Torn between the horrible images of her nightmare and the heartbreak of Adam, she called softly to Hugo, "Could you hold me while I sleep?"

The ghost floated closer. "That wouldn't be very decent."

"Please."

"Of course, Miss Rachel. Whatever you need."

Apparently, Hugo had his own ideas about what she needed. When Rachel woke in the morning, he was gone, and half an hour later, Lucille was in her room, telling her they were going out. Rachel knew when she was being set up, so she sulked all the way to the park, while Lucille chattered on and on.

"My dad practically forced me to send an application to Oxford. I very much doubt they'll take me, big donation or not, which is really for the best. I can't be in two places at once like Matt, can I?"

Annoyed, Rachel gave her a flat stare. "Hugo asked you to take me for a walk, didn't he?"

"Are you a dog?" Lucille joked, but then her smile faltered. "There may have been a ghost hovering over my bed when I woke up this morning—you can tell him that's not exactly a decent way to wake a woman who's been out clubbing till one. Anyway, he told me you could use a little cheering up because of your... heartbreak?"

Rachel huffed. "I'm not heartbroken. If I'd known ghosts were such big gossips, I wouldn't have asked Hugo to stay."

"Don't shoot the messenger." Lucille laughed. However, she quickly sobered and asked Rachel in a softer voice, "Do you still feel lonely?"

"No, I mean, sometimes, but I know it's a me problem."

"A *you* problem?"

Rachel nodded. "Yes. I keep waiting for people to make the effort to be around me instead of doing it by myself. And it doesn't matter if it's my friends..." She had to catch her breath as her throat tightened again. "Or if it's Adam."

"Oh, Rachel!" Lucille pulled her into an embrace and held her tight.

For a few moments the world was right again. Then she saw movement in the bushes behind Lucille. "Watch out!"

Lucille whirled around and together they stared at the demon who was already raising her hands. "Scutum Protecto!"

The amulet around her neck glowed red and a shield formed in front of them just before energy hit it. As the magic fell apart, Lucille grabbed Rachel's hand and ran.

More shots missed them by inches as they ran down the path they'd just taken. Just as they thought they'd escaped, a second demon appeared in front of them, causing Lucille to scream.

"Do something," Rachel urged.

Lucille threw her fireball straight at the new demon's face and the smell of burnt flesh filled the air.

This time it was Rachel who pulled her friend into a small grove. To her relief, they stumbled over a fallen branch. Rachel picked it up and turned to face the hunters. Lucille also made a stand, taking a brief moment to go through her spell list.

Something stirred in the bush in front of them. "Sageat ne—"

A demon appeared right behind Lucille. Grabbing her shoulder, she was about to hit her with black magic, when Rachel brought her stick down on the demon.

Immediately, she let go of Lucille and turned on Rachel instead. Blood flowed from a wound above her ear. As Rachel tried to hit her again, she caught the branch in the air and ripped it from her hands. She smashed it into Rachel's hip, sending her flying sideways and crashing into a tree.

Something burst at the back of her head and when Rachel touched her hair, her fingers came away slick with blood. Suddenly dizzy, she fell.

"Sageat negru distrugere!" Lucille shouted.

Her arrow of black magic hit the demon from a short distance, and she went down screaming.

Lucille ran to Rachel. "Thanks for—"

"We have to leave!" Rachel shouted, noticing the second demon. His face showed signs of burns, but they were already healing.

She was still a little dizzy and her vision was filled with black spots, but she pulled herself up with Lucille's help. "I'm no good like this."

Lucille breathed heavily. "I've got you." She closed her eyes and inhaled deeply. "Gradus in umbra!"

A vortex of dark magic appeared beside them. Rachel had no idea how this was going to help them, but as Lucille pulled her towards it, she began to panic. Lucille's spells were notoriously experimental, and jumping into one seemed like a good way to die.

Instead, the vortex spat them out on the other side of the park, out of sight of the demon. While Rachel stumbled over a bush, Lucille managed to stay upright, looking quite pleased with herself.

"That was lucky."

"You call a demon attack *lucky*?" It was one thing for Jan to tell them about the random attacks, another to experience them.

"Oh no, we're lucky the portal opened in open space and not in, say, a tree."

"I'd kill you if you hadn't just saved our lives."

Lucille gave her the ghost of a grin. "Let's go before he comes back for us."

Fabian

A pile of letters awaited Fabian when he returned from his trip. His mother was still away, and his father had apparently forgotten to empty the letterbox. Most of them were advertisements or bills for his parents, but there was also a letter from Greenvalley University.

Suddenly full of nerves, he returned to his room where Ophelia had slept last night with him. "This came back quickly." He'd only applied the week before they'd left.

Ophelia's eyes lit up. "From the university? Did you get in?"

Fabian took a deep breath and opened the letter, eagerly searching the text for the information he needed. "I didn't."

It didn't really make sense. The application deadline hadn't even passed and yet there it was, in black and white: 'Unsuccessful'.

"Will you apply somewhere else?"

"I don't want to go anywhere else." He dropped onto the bed, still staring at the letter in disbelief. "They didn't even put me in the lottery. Now I have to wait at least half a year before I can start university." After all the work he'd put into his exams, it felt like a slap in the face.

Ophelia climbed up behind him, wrapped her arms around him, and tucked her chin into his shoulder. "No lottery?"

Usually, if an application was unsuccessful, there was still a lottery to fill the last few places. Fabian had never heard of anyone being denied access to that pool of applications.

"It's a straightforward no. There's no small print, no explanation. And it arrived months before they usually send them out. They don't want me. They don't want me at all." So much for waiting half a year.

"I don't believe that. You just happened to be the first one they looked at."

Fabian snorted. "Right, and they knew straight away there'd be a hundred better candidates than me. They don't even have a minimum grade average requirement. It doesn't make any sense."

"Maybe it's a system error?"

Annoyed, Fabian groaned and stood up. He couldn't believe that, after all the drama with Herbert and Melaney, the university wouldn't even take a second look at his application.

Ophelia wasn't going to let him off that easily. She climbed out of bed and came over to him. She cupped his face gently. "It's not the end of the world, Fabian."

"But it feels like it. I bet they'll admit the others right away." Universities would fight over Samantha if she'd applied to more than one.

"I agree it sucks, but you'll find something else. And until you do, I'll help you pass the time."

The prospect of spending the whole summer in bed with his girlfriend instantly wiped the rejection from Fabian's mind. He put his arms around Ophelia and kissed her. She giggled and pulled him back into bed, making him forget all about the letter of doom.

Later, when he was working at the Magic Circle, Fabian called Jan and told him about the rejection. Normally, Samantha would've heard the news first, but he knew he couldn't bear her helpful advice when it was so clear she didn't have to worry about it happening to her. Jan, on the other hand, was the only one of his friends who'd never thought about university.

"Yeah, I'm sure I'll think of something," Fabian admitted after he'd told him about the situation as he restocked the shelves. "Guess, I could take over the Magic Circle."

Jan snorted on the phone. "At least until your mum gets better. But hey, don't think too much about it. Maybe Biology would've been a bummer. You're still helping out in the garage, aren't you?"

Fabian rolled his eyes. "Oh yes. Herbert will throw a party when he hears I became a mechanic after all the trouble."

"Forget that guy! Being a mechanic is a good job."

"Sure, it is, but then I'd have to spend every day with my dad and Ben." It wasn't like he was going to open his own garage and become a competitor.

"Ew."

Fabian chuckled quietly. At least Jan understood him. "Exactly. How's your training going?" Jan was on a special course in Braunschweig.

"Pretty boring, to be honest. I thought I'd left school behind me, but there's still so much to learn if I want to save lives the traditional way."

A movement behind his shoulder distracted Fabian. He thought it was a customer who'd somehow bypassed the doorbell, but when he saw a wing, he cursed and dived to the ground. Energy shot over his head, hitting the potion bottles on the shelf.

"Shit!" Fabian let go of the phone and formed a delta with his fingers.

"Fabian? What's going on? Hello?"

Water shot from between Fabian's fingers as the demon leapt forward, grabbed his shoulder, and slammed him into the shelf. The water disappeared through the cracks in the floorboards as Fabian groaned.

"Fabian?" Jan's voice called from the phone.

The demon pressed his arm against his windpipe, pinning him to the boards. Fabian gasped for air and dug his fingers into the demon's arm, but no matter how hard he pulled, the demon was so much stronger than him. Black spots danced in front of his eyes as he sensed water close to him. As desperate as he was for air, he called the water to him.

Suddenly, the demon was trying to get away from him, loosening his grip, but Fabian held on. Then he saw what was happening. Under his fingers, the demon's skin was drying out at an alarming rate. Taking a deep breath of fresh air, he desiccated him.

Gasping and coughing, Fabian dropped to his knees and crawled away from the demon's mummified corpse. He grabbed his mobile phone.

"Fabian?" Jan was still there.

"I'm fine," Fabian croaked, "I'm still alive..." He looked at the demon he'd somehow drained of all his water. "For now."

Matt

Not knowing what to do with himself now that there was no school, Matt had taken Crumbs for a five-hour walk. He'd hoped to turn up on Samantha's doorstep, but neither she nor Jan had been home. So he'd taken Crumbs into the woods instead, then all the way over the Witches Hump, and back home. The dog had loved it, although he'd been just as excited to be home, and had run straight to his water bowl.

Matt took a little longer to take his shoes off and walk into the living room, but he still caught his father pushing a pile of books aside and looking suspiciously interested in a cup of cold coffee.

"What are you doing?" There was a book on the floor. Matt crouched down and picked it up. "*Gate to Another World?*" He turned it over and read the back. "*Demon Summoning?*" What the hell was going on?

"I'm not trying to summon anyone," René said hastily.

"Glad to hear it." Matt still wasn't convinced. "So, what is it you're researching?"

It was subtle, but René definitely swallowed. "I'm going to help you. I want to talk to your mother."

Matt snorted. "Uh... Melaney is in Hescaryn." He looked at the book's title again. *Ashin — The Gate to Another World.* "You want to go to Hescaryn?"

"I'll convince her to leave you alone."

"How?"

René lowered his eyes and seemed to stumble over his words. "Well... so... I'll... I'll offer myself in your place."

"In my…" Matt's eyes widened as the realisation hit him like a bolt of lightning. "You want to sleep with her. Really?"

"It wouldn't be the first time."

Matt scoffed at him. "You don't say." He'd caught them sleeping with each other during her last visit. As amazing as René was when she wasn't around, he had no resistance when she was. "Don't take this personally, but if she was that interested in you, she'd visit more often." There was no question who Melaney had come to see.

René's eyes darkened. "I may not look as good as you, but there's a reason she spent so much time with a simple human. I held her attention for two years."

"Woah… Is this a pissing contest?" Matt didn't understand what was going on. René was uncharacteristically nervous, his behaviour so erratic… as if he was hiding something.

And now he even got angry. "I had her first."

Matt did a double take. "Holy shit! You're not interested in helping me. You want her back." And suddenly he knew exactly why.

"So what? You'd benefit from it."

"Don't you get it? She has you under her control. Whatever hold she had over you before has doubled and tripled since she soaked this city in lust. This isn't you."

René stood up and snorted. "I've only ever loved her."

"For twenty years. Even though she left you and kept your child from you, you never looked twice at another woman."

"Yes, Matt, that's what we humans usually mean when we say we're in love with someone." He snatched the book from Matt's hand and dropped it on the table where more books about demons and Hescaryn were stacked.

Matt shook his head. "This isn't love. It's a curse. She's the Archdemon of Lust, Dad. You're bound to her for as long as you live… or she does."

"I won't let you kill your mother," René hissed.

"And I'll have to tie you up if you won't be reasonable. Look, Dad, going to Hell—to her—will be your downfall. And you wouldn't be the first person to be ruined by her." Matt softened his voice. "She doesn't want you."

The slap came so quickly Matt didn't see it coming. His cheek stung for a few seconds, during which he just stared. This was wrong. Really wrong. Maybe tying René up hadn't been such a bad idea after all.

Before he could find words or do anything, Menuha appeared. She looked around curiously and frowned. "What's going on?"

René lowered his eyes and retreated to his room, taking his books with him.

Matt swallowed, still at a loss for words.

"What are you doing here?"

Startled, Menuha said, "Um, I came to warn you."

"Warn me?"

"Don't come to Hescaryn. Under no circumstances, okay? It's a trap."

The day was getting stranger and stranger. "What kind of trap?"

"Melaney has..." Menuha forced a painful smile. "I'll take care of it, Matt. Don't worry, just stay where you are. Promise me!"

Matt had no idea what he was really promising. "I have no plans to go to Hescaryn."

"Good." Menuha looked relieved, but before he could press her for details, she was gone.

Confused, Matt rubbed his nose. He had no idea what this quick visit from Menuha was all about. His cheek no longer hurt, but there was still a phantom sting. His father had never laid a hand on him. To do so now was most unlike him. And here he'd hoped to have a mature adult on his side.

The door to René's room opened again and Crumbs barked. Matt looked up and almost took a step back. René had been remarkably busy while he'd been talking to Menuha. He'd put on a jacket clearly designed for demon hunting, with all sorts of weapons readily available. Matt saw the metallic glint of his pistol and the telltale hilt of a Torakh. He was also wearing a backpack that seemed to have been ready to go before they'd even started talking.

"And where do you think you're going?"

"I'm a grown man, Matt," René growled. "I can make my own decisions."

"Not good ones, apparently." Matt casually placed himself between his father and the door. "You're clearly under her spell. How do you expect to survive long enough to see her?"

René sneered at him. "I used to be a demon hunter."

"In training," Matt shot back. "And you fell in love with the first demon you met."

"Don't worry about me."

Matt's voice rose in exasperation. "But I do!"

The sneer turned into a warm smile, and for a moment it seemed as if René was back. "You've changed a lot, you know. The day you knocked on my door—"

"Don't," Matt warned, as the sappy words threatened to overwhelm him. "This isn't goodbye forever. In fact, it's not goodbye at all because you're staying here."

The smile faded. "So I can watch you go off and become an archdemon? Your mother has to die for that. By your hand." The more he said, the more agitated René became.

Matt swallowed hard. "Do you think I want that?"

"I don't know, Matt. You tell me."

"You're crazy. Completely insane." Matt felt the desperation grow inside him. He refused to believe René was so far gone he'd run to his own doom. "Why can't you just forget her?"

"There's no woman like her," René explained, with all the passion he could summon.

Matt gritted his teeth. He'd heard enough. "You're staying here." He grabbed his father's upper arm and dragged him back to his room.

René protested, but he had no chance against Matt's superior strength. Once inside, Matt closed the door, locked it from the inside, then jumped through the abstract space back into the living room, with the key.

"Matt!" René pounded the door with his fists. "Let me out! Let me out of my bloody room!"

Matt didn't like it. He didn't like any of it, but it was the only thing he could think of to keep his father safe.

Lucille

It quickly became clear they were all being attacked by demons. Judging by the lack of other reports, the attacks were certainly targeted. Lucille and Rachel made their way to the Blackstone house to meet with the others and come up with a plan. In Lucille's opinion, the first thing they needed to find out was *why* they were suddenly being chased by demons. Were they looking for something or had they been ordered to kill them? It was clearly personal, and Lucille's thoughts went straight to Matt's brothers. Caspar was still banished from Ashuan but could've easily sent his Black Guard in his place.

When they arrived at the Blackstone house, Fabian, Ophelia, and Anne were already there, knocking on the door.

"What's going on?" Lucille asked.

"Neve froze the door again."

When Fabian turned to her, Lucille immediately noticed the dark bruises on his neck. They matched the ones on her shoulder.

"Let me. Hiantes qetes mensura."

The heat under her hand melted the ice in the lock. Lucille cast another protective spell before opening the door, thanking her foresight as five razor-sharp icicles flew at her.

"Neve, it's us!"

The little snow witch appeared in a flurry of snow. "Finally."

Cautiously, Lucille stepped inside. "Finally?"

"Jan's not here. Samantha's not here. Neve had to defend house all by herself."

"Were there many attacks?" Lucille looked around and immediately saw the splintered wood and shattered windows. "Oh dear."

The others came in behind her. Anne covered her mouth with her hand. "Oh no. Jan put so much work and money into this."

Lucille still felt a little bad that she'd been the one to coax Jan into buying a house that needed so many repairs just to be liveable. "We can worry about that later. First, we have to deal with the threat."

"Hey, Neve," Fabian said, "I know Jan is at his training, but why is Samantha not here?"

The little snow witch threw her hands up in the air. "Neve don't know. Everyone gone."

"Since when?"

When the snow witch didn't answer, Lucille pulled out her phone. Sure enough, Samantha hadn't said anything in the group chat. Her icon was even higher, indicating she hadn't read a message since yesterday afternoon. Matt wasn't much better, but at least he'd checked in this morning.

Lucille's heart fluttered. "She could be with Matt." And if she was, she certainly didn't care about her phone.

Fabian gave her a long look. "While we're all being attacked by demons?" He snorted. "We're lucky to be alive, but it's nice to know they're having fun."

Lucille raised an eyebrow and dialled Samantha. When the call immediately went to voicemail, she stared at the display in surprise. "Caller unavailable. Looks like her phone is dead."

"How convenient."

Fabian went upstairs to check while the others shuffled into the living room. Rachel and Ophelia picked up some of the broken bits and pieces and put them to one side, while Anne turned around, her eyes full of dismay.

"Why are there so many demon attacks? Is this normal?"

Rachel shrugged. "It's probably Matt's brothers."

"I agree," Lucille said, before carefully sitting down on the dusty couch. "This screams of Caspar and his army. We know he's not in prison anymore, but he's still banished. He could've—"

She was interrupted when Fabian almost fell down the stairs in his haste to get back to them. "Samantha's room has literally been trashed. I didn't see any blood, but it's a mess."

Neve nodded wisely. "Demons evil. Just wanted Sam."

A shiver ran down Lucille's spine and she suddenly sat up straight. "They wanted Sam?" Suddenly she *wished* Samantha was off somewhere with Matt.

"If I wanted to get to Matt, I'd go for Samantha, too," Rachel said, her voice shaking slightly. "When did we last see her?"

"At the station," Fabian said promptly. His whole face had gone white. "She went home with Matt while Jan took her luggage."

"I'll call Matt." Lucille switched contacts and tried calling again. His phone rang, but he didn't answer either. "Nothing." Panic crept into her throat. "What's going on?"

Fabian stared at her with wide eyes, as if he expected her to have all the answers. When she couldn't think of anything to say, he started pacing. With every step he took, the air felt a little muggier. Lucille glanced helplessly at Rachel, who shrugged, but then opened her mouth. "Would now be a good time to tell you about my nightmare last night?"

Lucille groaned, unsure if she could take any more bad news. "Was it prophetic?"

Rachel shrugged. "It didn't feel prophetic, but it felt familiar and yet completely alien." As everyone looked at her expectantly, she launched into a description. "It was a little girl's dream, though I can't be sure because I barely saw her in it, which is highly unusual."

"Poor child," Anne commented. "What did she dream about?"

"It wasn't necessarily a child. Young children can often appear in dreams set in the past, or they're symbolic of complete withdrawal. The dreamer feels helpless, powerless. Like a child."

Lucille was still waiting for the point. She knew Rachel wasn't suddenly going to start babbling about someone else's bad dreams.

And indeed, Rachel bit her lip. "I didn't pay much attention to it at first—I haven't slept well the last two days—but now I think it was Samantha's dream."

"What? How?"

"I told you, it felt strangely familiar, and the girl... she had a head of black curls. I didn't see her clearly enough to be sure, but it could well have been Samantha as a child." Rachel looked at Fabian as if he might be able to identify the dream image she'd been the only one to have seen.

Fabian's gaze was glued to Rachel, hanging onto every word. He swallowed. "Wouldn't you recognise Samantha's dream?"

"That's why I'm not sure. If it was, then something big's happening. Someone has done this to her."

Lucille told herself to stay calm and solution oriented. "Well, if she's not with Matt—" Just then her phone buzzed with a message. "Speak of the devil."

Matt: I'll be there in an hour. I have to deal with René first. He's... A crazy smiley face followed.

"Guess she's not with Matt," Fabian said, tense.

Lucille swallowed. "Like Rachel said, they'd use Samantha to get to Matt. Balthasar tried to use her several times. He or Caspar could've kidnapped her to lure Matt to Hell, just like they did on her birthday. As soon as Matt finds out, he'll jump to Hell and bring her back."

"I sure hope so!" Fabian growled. "What does he mean, he'll be here in an hour? If Caspar hurts Samantha, I'll go to Hell myself and kick his ass."

"I don't think Caspar would hurt Samantha."

Everyone turned to Anne in disbelief.

"Have you met Caspar?" Lucille asked sarcastically.

If Caspar had gotten his hands on Samantha last night, there might not be much left of her friend to save. On the other hand, she'd had at least one night's sleep, according to Rachel's dream.

"Twice," Anne said, her voice growing more confident. "I was alone in the room with him when he healed her. Unlike the school shooting, he was... different with her. Gentle. Caring. I think he likes her."

Lucille and Fabian's eyes met in disbelief. If there was one thing the demon general didn't like, it was a human like Samantha.

Caspar

A heavy bolt of energy slammed Caspar into the wall of Melaney's throne room. He was bleeding from several wounds, struggling to stay upright, and all he had to show for it were a few already fading scratches and a bit of tousled hair on Melaney.

His mother glared at him with blazing eyes. "I did not permit you to touch me."

"You wanted to die!" Caspar hissed.

"Not by your hand."

Caspar snorted. "One of us. You said it would be one of us. But you've already made your choice. And you've also decided who'll be his mate."

His heart threatened to burst at the thought of Samantha. He'd learnt from Menuha that Melaney had captured a human and was trying to turn her into a playmate for her son Melchior. *Jeyne*, a playmate for *Melchior*. Caspar spat.

Ignoring his outburst, Melaney studied her immaculate fingernails. "You always lacked patience, my dear."

"I'm not your dear!" Caspar roared.

Melaney's gaze shot up and he suddenly felt as if he were withering on the spot. "Go!"

The power in her voice forced his legs to carry him out. He was halfway down the corridor when his knees buckled, and he spat blood. Quick footsteps alerted him to Menuha who'd come running, fussing over the wounds that were already healing.

"Why are you doing this to yourself, Casp? You know you don't stand a chance against her."

"I lack 'patience'," Caspar repeated, followed by an ugly laugh. "As if she's going to change her mind when she's already obsessed with Melchior."

"Oh, Caspar."

Caspar grunted and pulled himself up on his feet. His body was still in pain, but it was nothing he couldn't handle. "He's not even twenty years old and she's practically *handing* it to him." Furious, he spun around. "She didn't even care I was gone for decades."

"She killed our father because of it," Menuha pointed out. "Gruesomely."

"Sure, but did she try to find me? No!"

Menuha gave him a cautious smile. "You were strong enough to find home on your own."

"Strong enough."

The words tasted bitter. The human mage his father had sold him to had enslaved him, then tortured and abused him for thirty years. And on top of that, the other humans had killed the only person who'd ever really cared for him.

"And shouldn't Melchior be strong enough to come here on his own? But no, he's not even demon enough to tell Melaney to her face that he doesn't want her lust."

His mother was delusional if she thought Melchior was ready for the power and responsibility that came with the position. Melchior didn't want to be the Archdemon of Lust. All he wanted was Samantha.

"Maybe he hasn't made up his mind yet."

Caspar snorted and continued. "That's *his* problem. Or at least, it should be. But no, little Melchi is being spoiled by our dear mother, and now she's even handing him Samantha on a silver plate." The more he thought about it, the angrier he became. "He's half human! And Melaney doesn't just tolerate it, she supports his bloody humanity!"

Menuha struggled to keep up with him. "We have to save Samantha."

"Why would I do that?"

"So he doesn't come here," Menuha said, her patience wearing thin. "That's why Melaney brought her here, to lure him to us. If we rescue her and take her back to Ashuan, there's no reason for him to come here. Melaney will realise he's strayed too far from his demon origins, and will be open to other suggestions. To you."

Caspar's eyes narrowed as he considered her argument. He knew Samantha was the lure. He had no idea why Matt hadn't already come to rescue her, but he knew he'd stay as far away from Hescaryn as possible once she was safely back home. But that didn't mean Melaney would suddenly choose Caspar. Besides, Samantha would be out of his reach again.

He quickened his pace and strode off. "Nice try, sister."

Menuha ran after him, then jumped in front of him when he wouldn't slow down. "Don't you understand?"

"I understand you're trying to manipulate me."

"No, I..." Menuha rolled her eyes. "Please. I want to free her, but I need your help."

Caspar gritted his teeth, considering her plea once more. They were close to the room where they were holding Samantha. Where she was being prepared to become the mate of the new archdemon...

"No. Samantha stays here."

Samantha

Samantha had done what she could to make the room appear a little less intimidating. The suggestive pictures were all hidden behind heavy curtains, and she'd stuffed the extra cushions under the bed then hidden her flowers behind them. One look at the drawers had confirmed her suspicions and she'd never touched them again afterwards. As for the potion, she'd ignored it and quenched her thirst with the grape-like fruit on her table. They were rather tart, but at least they were bursting with liquid. So far, she hadn't noticed any side effects.

From time to time she reached for the magic but always came up against that mysterious wall. She could feel magic all around her, but her access to it was blocked. Not even her flowers responded. It didn't matter which demon she summoned—not even when she used blood to strengthen her call—none came to her aid.

After several hours alone, Samantha had fallen asleep. Not that it had provided her much rest. No one had come to replace the food or check on her. They all knew she couldn't escape on her own.

When the door finally opened, Samantha grabbed the nearest object and threw it at the intruder.

The demon caught the phallus deftly, looking at it with interest. "Is this your choice?"

"No!"

He looked younger than Melaney's mate. If he'd been human, Samantha would have thought he was about her age, which in demon terms must have meant he was around a hundred years old. Like all Melaney's lovers, he was exceptionally handsome.

Not that Samantha cared. Seizing her chance, she tried to push past him through the open door. He immediately threw an arm around her hip and held her without so much as a struggle.

"Let me go!" Once more Samantha reached for her magic, only to come up short. She was nothing more than a weak human girl, powerless in the face of demons.

He laughed hoarsely. "You don't give me orders. Melaney does."

"I don't want to." To her annoyance, Samantha's voice rose, and her breathing quickened. "I won't let you turn me into a mindless sex slave!"

"You'll enjoy it."

"Absolutely not!" His presence was suddenly overwhelming, his body too close to hers. Heat blossomed in her core. "Let me go!"

The demon laughed again, his breath hot on her neck. "Not until you've drunk your potion."

To thwart him, Samantha kicked the jug off the table. The golden liquid seeped into the lush carpet.

"You think you're very clever, don't you?" There was a sudden edge to his voice that made her hair stand on end. Her heart pounded in her chest, her ribs aching as she refused to answer.

The demon let go, only to pull a bottle of the same potion from his clothes. "Let's get this over with."

Shocked, Samantha stumbled away from him as he uncorked the bottle, but he leapt across the distance and grabbed her chin. His fingers dug into her jaw, forcing her to open her mouth as he pinned her against the wall. Without further warning, he poured the drink into her mouth and held her until she was forced to swallow.

Tears ran down her cheeks when he finally let go. He dropped the empty bottle carelessly and left the room, locking her in again. Fire blossomed in Samantha's stomach, and she sank to her knees, sobbing.

The potion was more than just an aphrodisiac. It was changing her very being, turning her into something she didn't want to know.

Samantha was still crying when the door opened hours later. She threw the bowl of fruit and managed to hit Melaney's dark-skinned mate in the stomach.

Instead of grunting, he chuckled. "Have we got a bit of a temper?"

"Go away!" Samantha shouted. "Before I cast a spell on you."

Frennys laughed outright, a booming sound that vibrated in her bones. "If you're really a witch, you must have noticed you can't cast spells in her residence. A security measure. I'm sure you understand."

She swallowed, aware of the wall blocking her. Stubbornly, she wiped away her tears and stood. "You can tell Melaney I won't play her game."

"No one refuses Melaney. Me least of all." Frennys ran his eyes down her body, appraising her. "Let's get this over with, shall we?"

Samantha's eyes widened and she quickly retreated to the back of the room. "Oh no! I'm not having sex here. With you or anyone."

When Frennys kept coming, a predatory smile on his lips, she raised her hands.

"Stay away from me."

He stopped a metre away, looking amused. "Why? Are you afraid you might be tempted otherwise?"

The worst thing was that part of her *was* very tempted. It was the part that had been set on fire by the potion. The part that didn't feel like her. She trembled at the thought of what it meant for her future.

As Frennys approached again, Samantha pushed away from the wall, ducked under his arm, and ran for the door. She let out a whimper when she found it locked.

"I see, you want to play first."

He came at her with the patience of a predator who knew he had his prey cornered. Still, Samantha ran, too afraid of what would happen if he got his hands on her body.

Their cat-and-mouse chase came to an abrupt end when Frennys used his jumping powers to appear right in front of her. His hands landed on her hips, and he pulled her close. "Got you."

As he lowered his head to kiss her neck, Samantha pressed her lips together. Her stomach grew hotter, and her breath came short and sharp. Panting, she tried to pull away, but Frennys' fingers dug into her hips, holding her close.

"I thought..." Annoyingly, she had to catch her breath. "I thought lust was..." A moan escaped her lips and she almost burst into tears. "Lust was voluntary. Not forced."

His hands moved slowly up her body. "Oh, trust me, I'll only do what you want."

Samantha didn't trust him at all. Still, it took far more effort than it should have to pull her arms up and put her hands on his chest to create some much-needed distance between them. "I don't want this."

Frennys let go of her abruptly. "Then you're not ready." A bottle of the golden potion appeared in his hand.

Samantha barely noticed its presence. She was too fascinated by the feel of his skin under her fingers, still clinging to him though he no longer held her.

"Are you sure you don't want this?"

Startled, she blinked and dropped her arms. Her cheeks felt hot, and her breath was still ragged. "What are you doing to me?" she asked, in horror.

"It's the potion," Frennys admitted. "It's lust bottled up. Sooner or later, you'll be begging me to touch you."

Samantha felt like she was going to be sick. "That's terrible."

"On the contrary. It's pure pleasure. You'll serve lust for the rest of your life—until lust is finished with you." The last part was said with a distinctly sour note.

Eagerly, Samantha clung to this tiny bit of information. She needed something to occupy her mind so her body wouldn't betray her. It was obvious he was conflating Melaney with the sin of lust, but what did it mean she was done with him? Was there more to him being her "mate"?

"If she dies..."

"I die," Frennys said, his eyes darkening. "Yes."

"I'm sorry."

"Drink."

He offered her the potion, but Samantha shook her head. In an instant, he was behind her, his body pressed against hers. With his empty hand, he caressed first her arm and then her stomach, stoking the fire within. Samantha held her breath, both fearful and eager to see where his hand would go next.

Drops of fiery liquid fell into her open mouth and she swallowed absentmindedly, too focused on the gentle pressure of his hand. Soon it would sink beneath her stomach, following the direction of the heat.

Gasping, she jerked his hand away from her, just inches from her waistband. "Don't."

Frennys laughed softly. "Look at this. All empty."

Samantha's gaze focused on the bottle in his other hand. Her throat burnt, but it wasn't as bad as it'd been a day ago. She was getting used to the potion. To the fire. To the touch. Tears streamed down her cheeks, and she choked back a sob that broke from her throat.

"We'll see how you feel about this in a few days," Frennys said, his voice full of dark promise. He left without another look.

The sobs came harder and faster as understanding dawned on Samantha. In a few days, there'd be nothing left of her. The fire would consume her, and she'd belong to the House of Lust. For the rest of her meagre life.

Rachel

"We're going to stay at the Blackstone house until the situation is resolved," Rachel explained to Hugo as she packed her backpack with essentials, especially her dreamweb. "I don't want any demons showing up here. Besides, we're stronger together."

The ghost nodded seriously. "I will accompany you, of course."

"Thank you."

"I'm glad you seem to be feeling better. Life goes on... For you, at least."

Rachel took a deep breath. Despite running for her life and fearing for her friend, she hadn't completely forgotten about Adam. "It's over. I missed my chance, and I have to hope I don't make the same mistake next time. It wouldn't have worked out, anyway. I mean, he lives in New Zealand. That's not exactly around the corner, and unlike Matt, I can't teleport."

Hugo nodded proudly. "You're absolutely right."

Just then Annette knocked on the door and Hugo faded into invisibility. "Oh, hey. Going to a sleepover?"

"Yes." A potentially lethal sleepover, but a sleepover, nonetheless.

"Lucky I found your phone, then."

"My phone?"

Annette nodded. "It was on the charger downstairs, and someone's been texting you nonstop you then. Look, this came for you today."

Rachel assumed the situation had worsened and her friends had been texting for help, but then she saw the messages came from an unknown number. Confused, she unlocked her phone and scrolled back to the start.

Hi Rachel, this is probably super weird, but your friend gave me your number at the party and I simply had to text you. Sorry, if that's too forward... Oh, this is Adam, btw, from the hospital.

"It's from Adam!" Rachel squealed. Excited, she hugged her mother, then eagerly read the rest of the message.

It wasn't until Hugo appeared next to her that she realised her mother had left. "He wrote?"

"He wrote," Rachel confirmed, giggling happily. "He says he's angry at himself for not talking to me earlier, but that he can't stop thinking about me. He also told me a bit about himself and asked if I'd like to chat when he got home. He's currently at the airport, you know. Gah! I have to look for flights to New Zealand."

Hugo frowned. "Maybe you should answer his messages first."

"Yes, yes, of course." Rachel's fingers hovered over the keys.

"And then there are the demons."

He sure knew how to spoil things. "I know!" With a sigh, she locked the phone. There was no point in replying to Adam if she didn't know whether she'd be alive tomorrow. Still, Rachel pressed the phone to her chest and another wave of giddiness washed over her. "He wrote to me!"

Hugo just sighed heavily.

Half an hour later, Rachel had to push all thoughts of Adam aside as she rejoined the others at Jan's house—fortunately, he'd be flying for two days, giving her some time to resolve this particular drama. When she arrived, Matt was already there, getting an update from Lucille and Fabian.

"What do you mean she's gone?"

"We think Caspar took Sam. Anne thinks he's in love with her or something."

It wasn't only Matt who frowned.

"And he wants to lure you to Hell."

Matt shook his head. "It's not Caspar."

"You're sure about that?" Rachel asked.

While the thought of Caspar having a thing for Samantha was disturbing, she wasn't so quick to dismiss it. Samantha had told her Caspar hadn't even tried to kill her when he'd *actually* kidnapped her on her birthday.

"Firstly, he doesn't like Samantha, and secondly, it doesn't look like him. If he was responsible for her absence," Matt's breath caught on the word, "he would've made sure I knew about it by sending me a finger or—"

"That's more than enough detail," Fabian said hastily. "Thanks."

"So, Balthasar then?" Lucille mused.

Matt sighed. "I think it's worse than that. Menuha came by earlier today. She told me it was a trap and that she'd take care of it, which makes me think my mother's the one behind it." Bitterly he added, "Unfortunately, Menu forgot to mention it was Samantha I wasn't supposed to be worrying about and shouldn't go to Hell for under any circumstances."

"She knows you well," Rachel commented dryly. And apparently Melaney did, too.

"So just because your sister tells you to stay out of it, you leave Sam in your mother's hands?" Fabian asked, sounding agitated.

Matt's eyes narrowed. "I didn't know she had Sam until two minutes ago."

Rachel rolled her eyes and huffed. "I'm sure a fight is just what we need right now."

"My mother wants me to kill her!" Matt said loudly. "I'm sorry if I'm not exactly keen on it!"

"Matt…"

As usual, Lucille tried to fan the flames, but Fabian jumped up. "Your mother's trying to kill *us*! Since last week, demons have been crawling all over the place, attacking us. And Sam…" For a moment he was too overwhelmed with worry to speak. "Who knows what your mother's doing to her?"

Matt crossed his arms and glared at him. "Let me know when you find a way to turn back time so I can stop her before it happens."

Rachel groaned. "Can you two stop it? Your fighting isn't helping Sam."

Fabian's jaw twitched as he swallowed his anger, still glaring at Matt. "Go to Hell, Matt, and get her back."

"I told you, Menuha will take care of it."

The anger bubbled up again, making Fabian tremble in its grip. "You'd better pray to all your nasty gods that Samantha is still alive or I swear I'll deliver you to your mother myself."

Matt's face darkened, but instead of retorting, he simply disappeared.

Lucille sighed and collapsed on the sofa, burying her face in her hands. Five seconds later she shook her head, determination in her eyes. "I think we should start with Plan B. Just in case."

"I'm gonna kill him," Fabian said darkly, falling onto the sofa next to her.

"Do we have a Plan B?" Rachel asked, "We're at a serious disadvantage here. None of us can jump through space or go to Hell on our own. So, what can we really do?"

Matt

Hearing about his mother taking Samantha away from him was almost enough to send Matt over the edge. Depending on how she'd treated Samantha, he was convinced killing her suddenly wouldn't be such an issue for him. Last time she'd nearly killed Samantha with endless orgasms, now the girl he loved was in Hescaryn, alone among demons. No matter how hard he tried to protect Samantha, his family always found ways to hurt her in his place.

With anger and fear fighting for control of his body, Matt jumped straight into his father's room. "By the way, the woman you love so passionately kidnapped—"

The room was empty. René was nowhere to be seen.

Confused, Matt tried the door, but it was still locked. Then he noticed the open window. He leant out of the window in disbelief, but didn't see anyone on the pavement below. Looking to the side, he found the gutter just close enough to reach for someone leaning out of the window. Still, it was at least twelve metres from their floor to the ground.

"Not bad."

Perhaps he'd underestimated his father's abilities. Either way, René was long gone and halfway to Hescaryn, if he wasn't already there.

Matt looked around and found a letter addressed to him on the book of interdimensional portals. His hands felt cold as he unfolded the letter and read it.

Dear Matt,

I'm sorry I can't resist the desire to be with your mother. I didn't fight for her seventeen years ago and I've regretted it ever since. It's hopeless, I know. You're probably mad at me, and rightly so.

Don't follow me. You're so much stronger than I ever was. Hold on to your beliefs and don't be so hard on yourself. You're perfect just the way you are.

Love, Dad.

"This is a bad joke, isn't it?" A bitter taste filled Matt's mouth as he read the letter again. "You're setting a hell of a bad example, you know?"

He jumped back into the living room and sat on the couch, book and letter still in hand. Crumbs came over and laid his head on his lap, whimpering. Matt dug his fingers into the dog's fur as he read the letter again and again. Each time, the words hit harder and deeper.

He cared for René. Cared for him far more than he'd ever cared for his mother. René had opened his home to him and taught him so much over the past two years. Matt had been able to talk to him about anything, and René had helped him navigate the intricacies of humanity with love and patience. Even when he'd been at his worst.

And now he was gone. A victim of Melaney's siren call. It wasn't right. René deserved the world. He deserved a woman as kind and warm as he was, not one who'd chew him up and watch him die while he fought for her love.

And Samantha... Matt swallowed hard. What was Melaney doing to her? What had she already done while Matt sat here in Ashuan, waiting for her call. He'd been to her house this morning and hadn't even noticed she'd already gone missing.

Matt buried his face in Crumbs' fur and counted his heartbeats which felt unnaturally loud and fast. If something happened to Samantha... If he lost her... If his mother...

"Chay," he whimpered. "Chay, if you can hear me, please—"

Before he could finish the sentence, his friend arrived. "You called?"

Shaking, Matt looked up at him, a painful hope surging in his heart. His friend would know how to fix this. He always fixed things. "I need you. I... I don't know what to do. My dad... Sam... Melaney took Sam and..."

Crumbs slinked away as Chay crouched in front of Matt. "I know."

Tears filled Matt's eyes. "She wants me to kill her, but I can't. I can't kill my own mother."

It wasn't just the fact she was his mother, but that killing wasn't as easy as it used to be. Taking someone's life was a huge, momentous thing, with all sorts of consequences. In self-defence, yes, but outright murder?

Chay smiled weakly. "You don't realise how likeable that makes you."

Matt swallowed his tears. "But I have to help Samantha. Menuha said—"

"She's going to fail."

"What?" Shock vibrated through him as he absorbed Chay's premonition. "Menuha can't save her," he repeated quietly. "That means I have to go." To Hescaryn, to his mother—the one to whom he'd promised himself. "If I do this... if I give my mother what she wants, there'll be no... there'll be no coming back from it."

He couldn't possibly hope to be with Samantha after he'd bedded his mother. But if that was what it took to get her home safely...

"You're stronger than you think."

Matt drank in the words, trying to take strength from them. "It's a trap. You want me to knowingly walk into a trap?"

Chay shrugged, his mouth a bitter line. "You wouldn't be the first half-demon to do so." When Matt cocked his head, Chay waved his hand. "Another time. Matt, I know you'll do the right thing. I know that better than anyone. Trust yourself." He looked to the side and saw René's book. "Mind if I borrow this?"

"Sure. It's not like my father needs it anymore."

"Don't give up on your father just yet. He's tougher than you think. The world will be different when we meet again." And with that ominous farewell, Chay vanished.

Matt dropped his head between his legs. There was far less comfort in Chay's words than he'd hoped. If Samantha died at his mother's hand, the world would be a very different place, indeed. If he killed Melaney and ascended to the Archdemon of Lust, it'd be different, too.

A young, confused part of him wanted to stay and let destiny unfold, but that was not a part Matt had ever given in to. It didn't matter what might happen to him. All that mattered was he had to save Samantha.

Samantha

Unsettled, Samantha paced her room. From time to time, she would stop and lift the curtains to peer at the lewd pictures hidden behind them.

"Like what you see?"

Startled, Samantha dropped the curtain and spun around. As usual, the archdemon was dressed alluringly, revealing far more than she was hiding. Heat blossomed in Samantha's stomach and her cheeks flushed. "How long are you intending to keep me here?"

"As long as it takes."

"Meaning?"

Melaney strolled over to the small table and ran a finger over the silver pitcher that had recently been refilled. "Not long now, and you'll want to stay here."

Instead of protesting, Samantha focused on the slender finger and potion that stoked the fire inside her. The potion she hated and now craved.

Melaney sat down on the bed, crossed her long legs, and patted the mattress beside her. "Come here!"

Samantha shook her head, but her legs followed anyway. Against her will, she approached the bed, then forced herself to sit as far away from Melaney as she could.

Melaney smirked, but didn't insist on closing the distance. "Let's get to know each other better. I take it you're not a virgin."

Although Samantha had no interest in having the sex talk with the literal Archdemon of Lust, her mouth opened. "I had my first time with fifteen... four years ago."

"And how many partners have you had since?"

"Three... only two I've had sex with." She hadn't been with Daniel long enough to ever cross that line.

Melaney sighed. "All men or...?"

"All men." She shook her head, seizing a rare moment of clarity. "Why do you want to know?"

"I want to know how much work we have to do."

"Work?" Samantha squeaked.

"Come closer."

Against her will, Samantha moved a little closer. Melaney was only an arm's length away.

"I'm going to teach you the art of pleasure. If my son wants to have sex with you, he should at least enjoy it, don't you think?" Melaney moved closer and placed her hand on Samantha's cheek. "You don't want to disappoint him, do you?"

Samantha fought to keep a clear head. The thought of having sex with Matt was overwhelming. "I... I don't want Matt to... I don't want to sleep with him." Her body, however, disagreed and she sudden found herself wishing Matt would come find her for all the wrong reasons.

"Look, I'd prefer if you didn't sleep with him either, but he's like me in that way. Once he's obsessed with someone, he won't let go until he gets what he wants."

Until he gets what he wants. There was no denying Matt was obsessed with her, but was he obsessed because he was in love with her or because she wouldn't sleep with him? Samantha wanted to believe the former, but she'd always feared the latter, and now, here in Melaney's realm, confronted with demonic desire, doubt crept in. Matt had tried to be human for her, but he had a demon side, too, one that wasn't too different from his mother's.

When she blinked, Melaney was suddenly too close. The hand on her cheek slid down to her neck, pulling her close. Samantha tilted her head back, which only exposed her neck to Melaney's lips. The flames in her belly ignited and the fire coursed through her veins until the heat almost consumed her.

Think, Samantha, think. With her body under Melaney's control, her mind was the only defence she had left. What had they talked about? Matt! They'd talked about Matt and his love for her.

"He's not," Samantha swallowed hard, "like you." Her breathing became ragged as Melaney planted kiss after kiss down her cleavage. "He's... different... better... human."

Suddenly, Melaney pushed her onto her back and climbed on top of her. Holding Samantha's arms in place with one hand, she followed the trail of kisses with the nail of her index finger, slicing the skin. A different kind of fire erupted in its wake as Samantha gasped in pain, panic rising in her chest.

"He's my son," Melaney hissed. "If he were human, as you claim, wouldn't he be here by now?"

The last time she'd been taken to Hell, Matt had followed within half an hour. Now, a full day had passed and there was still no sign of him.

"Did you really think you meant anything to him? That he loved you?" Melaney looked down at her and snorted. She lowered her head until her hot breath blew across Samantha's skin. "All. He. Wants. Is. Sex."

Tears welled in Samantha's eyes as Melaney seemed to confirm her worst fears. She wanted to believe it was different, but trapped here, caught in the thrall of desire and lust, it was hard to believe anything else mattered.

He hadn't even come for her. And now she was at his mother's mercy.

Jan

So far, Jan had avoided any demon attacks on the training course. He'd heard the news from Greenvalley, of course, and was concerned not only for his friends but also his sister. Anne was just beginning her journey into the supernatural, and while Hanna seemed to be blessing her, those blessings were a little too unreliable to put Jan's mind at ease. And now Samantha had been kidnapped while he was in Braunschweig. It had made it incredibly difficult to concentrate on the actual content of his course.

Apart from that, Jan loved his training. This two-day course was his first real exposure to emergency scenarios. As a paramedic, he not only had to provide first aid in the field, but also often had to rescue patients from unsafe situations. Most of the time firefighters did the actual rescuing, but there were situations where Jan had to get involved. He learnt all about stabilising patients and making sure they could be moved, whether from crushed car wrecks or collapsed buildings.

It was a lot of fun and Jan excelled at the physical exercises. The theoretical aspects of his training were another matter, but he found it much easier to study for something he was interested in than all the stuff he'd had to take at school.

He was about to get a coffee from the break room when a window next to him shattered. Jan jumped, spilling his coffee all over the table. He put the cup down and looked sideways. Nothing moved.

A hand fell on his shoulder. Jan grabbed the arm, turned, and threw the attacker onto his back. Only then did he realise it was one of his colleagues—André or something.

His eyes widened in panic as he stared up at Jan. "What are you doing, Kerscher?"

Jan reached out and pulled him back up. "Sorry. I had a fright. Are you okay?"

André patted the dust from his trousers, still breathing heavily. "Sure, but damn, where did you get those moves?"

"Karate." Jan glanced at the broken window, nervous the demon would choose this moment to appear. "I have to take a call. There's an emergency at home. Can you tell the others I'll be a bit late for the next session?"

André eyed the broken window and swallowed, clearly judging him for it. "Okay, sure. Hope everything's alright." He backed away quickly.

"Thanks!" Jan called as he started down the corridor. As soon as he was out of sight of the break room, he opened a window and jumped out onto the grass. He landed in a cat-like manner and looked around.

Something hit him in the stomach, sending Jan sprawling. The attacker kicked at him, but Jan caught the leg before it hit his ribs, and twisted it to throw them to the ground.

The demon looked at him in surprise. Jan pulled a pocket knife from his shoe and flicked it open. But before he could use it, she attacked again, this time shooting energy at him.

Jan ducked just in time, rolled to the ground, and regained his footing. The demon jumped at him. A series of quick blows and jabs and flying energy followed. Jan defended himself as best he could, ignoring the occasional hit to his arms or legs. Then his hand moved forward, and he plunged his knife into her belly. The demon retreated and disappeared, probably to heal before trying again.

Exhausted, Jan leaned against the wall behind him and took several deep breaths, praying his asthma wouldn't kick in. There were still three hours before he could go home. That was if he wasn't killed by demons before then.

It was already dark when Jan arrived at the Blackstone house to find his friends and sister in the living room. Before he could say anything, Neve flew into his arms and hugged him tightly. "Jan is back! Neve was so scared."

Anne snorted in amusement. "Neve can handle demons better than any of us. How was your training?"

"Exciting. I learnt how to rescue people from accidents and how to run away from demons. How about you?"

"The demons are after all of us," Fabian said exhausted. "Apparently Matt's mother wants to cut off all his connections to Ashuan." Bitterly he added, "Or move them to Hell, instead."

Jan assumed he was referring to Samantha's abduction, then noticed Matt wasn't here. "Did Matt go alone?"

Fabian's face darkened. "Oh no, Matt suggested we stay put while Menuha rescued Samantha." He shook his head. "We're going to Hell. As soon as we figure out how to get there."

"Which is kind of a big deal," Lu chimed in. "Unfortunately, there's no railway station or airport in Hell."

"But something very similar."

Everyone jumped as Chay suddenly appeared among them. Jan found himself holding the pocket knife again. Embarrassed, he hid it behind his back. "Um, hello, Chay."

Chay nodded at them, then handed a book to Rachel, standing closest to him. "You can't wait for Matt to do something. You have to save Samantha yourself. More specifically, there's more at stake than Melaney's possible death. You have to get to Samantha before Matt does."

Lu breathed a sigh of relief. "Does that mean Matt is on his way?"

"I hope so," Fabian grumbled, then frowned. "Why does it matter who reaches her first?"

"It will affect events more direly in the future. Trust me. Now, how to get there: the worlds are linked by gates."

"Gates?" It was the first time Jan had heard of it.

Chay pointed to the book in Rachel's hands. "Did you think demons were the only ones who could cross worlds?" He shook his head. "The rivers of magic don't just flow through one world, they also flow between worlds. Anyone who can use magic in any form can enter at the gates. One such gate is here in Greenvalley, and fortunately, it leads directly to Lucin. Among other places."

"Among other places?" Ophelia asked.

"It's a bit complicated. You travel through abstract space, and it's called abstract for a reason. Basically, it's like taking a bus. You get off at the right stop. It's just... the rivers don't stop there, nor do they announce the stations beforehand."

Fabian crossed his arms and frowned. "So how do we know when to get off?"

"As soon as you're close to a gate, you'll see glimpses of the world. As soon as you see Lucin, you get off." Chay nodded at the book again. "The exact procedure is described in this book."

"Can't you just take us there?" Lu asked.

"Unfortunately not. You need time to prepare and sleep, and I need to set things in motion. I'm sorry, but that's all I can do for you."

Lu swallowed. "Okay, thanks for the book, then."

Fabian nodded. "Yes, at least we can do something now. The waiting's been killing me." He smiled sadly at Ophelia when she squeezed his shoulder in comfort.

"You should be fine if you leave early in the morning. It's going to be a long gruesome day." With a final nod of encouragement, Chay disappeared.

The others shared uncomfortable looks. "Looks like a holiday in Hell is in order," Jan tried to joke. He'd have to call into work and continue the family emergency line of excuses.

Lu took a deep breath and clapped her hands, a determined look appearing on her face. "Rachel, you're going to read the book or at least the part about travelling between worlds."

"Already on it."

"The rest of us will make a plan for what we need. Weapons, potions, anything protective. Also..." She swallowed. "We need to make arrangements in case we... in case we don't come back."

Fabian paled, but nodded, if a little frantically. "Samantha needs us."

"What can I do to help?" Anne asked.

Jan shot a glare in her direction. "You're not coming. You're my arrangement in case I don't come back."

Anne groaned. "The demons attacked me as well. I have some powers, and I care about Samantha, too."

"It's too dangerous." This was one thing Jan didn't want to budge on.

"It's also dangerous for all of you." There was a treacherous gleam in Anne's eyes. "I don't want to be the one waiting at home alone while you all risk your lives. Besides, what if the demons keep attacking?"

Jan hadn't thought about that. Anne might be safe because she wasn't one of the Six, but what if she wasn't? What if Melaney decided family members were fair game, too?

"There's safety in numbers," Ophelia said. "If we stay together, we should be fine... right?"

For a moment Jan toyed with the idea of tasking Neve with keeping Anne safe in the Blackstone house, even against her will, but then he relented. That way he could personally make sure she stayed safe. "Fine. But we stick together. No solo adventures or exploration."

"Agreed," Fabian said. "We've got this."

If only it were that simple.

"Alright." Lu nodded to each of them. "Let's make a plan."

Fabian

The leaves were covered, and wisps of mist hung low in the forest as Fabian and his friends walked to the Spring of Magic. They'd learnt from the book that all the river's junctions doubled as gates. If the demons didn't already come and go as they pleased, he would've been worried about having a back door. Now, he was glad it was so close.

They all had backpacks packed with essentials and had done what they could to protect themselves. And they'd made arrangements.

"I've closed the Magic Circle and left a letter for my parents on the counter in case of... Oh, well."

Ophelia squeezed his hand, but even she had nothing encouraging to say. They were going to Hell to try to break into an archdemon's residence and get out alive, after all. The chances of them all doing so were frighteningly slim.

"I told Albert," Lucille said. "He wanted to stop me, of course, but he realised there was no changing my mind. He promised to give me three days' grace."

"Guys, can we stop the doom planning, please? This is a simple mission. We go in, get Sam, get out," Jan declared.

"I prayed to Hanna last night. Maybe she'll help us," Anne added.

Jan changed his tune instantly immediately. "It would help me more if you stayed here."

"I thought it was a simple mission," Rachel wondered.

Jan snorted and kept his mouth shut.

Despite their eerie mission, Fabian couldn't help but feel his heart lift at the beauty of the place. As usual, it was exceptionally lush, still wet with dew, and with a surprising amount of wildlife, including small creatures which appeared to be dragonflies, but were probably magical. They put down their backpacks for a moment and breathed in the fresh air.

"Alright," Lucille began, "let's go through this again. We're obviously going to encounter first- and second-class demons. I don't know how many third- or fourth-class demons there are in Lucin, but I assume most of them will be humanoid. Unless they have pets. Then—"

"Just assume everything you see is trying to kill you," Jan joked.

Fabian rolled his eyes. "We're so going to die."

"No, we're not," Ophelia said confidently, pulling him to her. "And if we do, at least we'll be together." When she kissed him, he felt a bit better about the whole thing, even if her outlook was a little too Shakespearean for him.

"Alright, shall we?" Jan asked.

Fabian pulled away from Ophelia and sighed. "Goodbye, Greenvalley. It was nice knowing you."

"Can you please pull yourself together?" Lucille sounded exasperated. "We'll be back."

"So you say."

"Are you always this optimistic before battle?" Anne asked, looking back and forth between them.

Jan grinned. "We try our best."

"We're not going to die," Rachel explained, matter-of-factly. "I've got holiday plans for New Zealand."

"In that case, we'll refrain from dying," Lucille promised, a sparkle in her eyes.

Fabian shook his head and pulled himself together. "Samantha needs us. We can't die."

"That's better," Anne commented, giving him a broad smile.

Jan nodded at him. "Then let's get this over with. Fabian, you're first."

Startled, Fabian stared at him. "What? Why me?"

"Easy. You're still the strongest of us. But don't worry, we're right behind you." Jan grinned at him with what he probably thought was encouragement.

Ophelia leaned against his shoulder. "You can do this." She gave him another little kiss. "See you in Hell."

"Just remember," Lucille said. "Concentrate on the magic and get off the river as soon as you see Hell."

"So simple," Fabian whined.

He'd thought they'd all go together. Safety in numbers and all that. Now he was the vanguard, possibly stumbling straight into a nest of demons.

Jan clicked his tongue in annoyance. "Come on! Go. We haven't got all day. Remember, this is for Sam."

Fabian sighed. He would do almost anything for Samantha. She'd been in Hell for two days already. He couldn't even begin to imagine the horrors she'd endured. The sooner they got there, the sooner they could all go back. "You can all go to hell," he muttered, then turned towards the spring.

"After you, darling." Ophelia smiled and gave him a gentle nudge.

With another sigh, Fabian stepped into the centre of the spring, trying to feel the magic that burst from the ground here. Before he could formulate another thought, the current swept him away.

It was a bit like riding a real river, except there was no bank or bottom. Fabian floundered at first, but soon found his flow and swam along, looking for glimpses of other worlds that crossed the river. Sometimes he saw things moving in the river beside him, sometimes he was alone, surrounded by magic and stars. The first place he saw was a snow-covered citadel on a mountain. The next was somewhere tropical. So far, they looked like they could be anywhere on Earth.

The third gate he glimpsed was suffused with purple light and frequent flashes of lightning. Neither Earth nor Hell. Then, Fabian saw something familiar. Dark tunnels with a distinct red glow and a silver line running down one wall. Not silver, but *sylver*, the dominant liquid in Hell.

He reached out, trying to find something to hold onto. Instead of grabbing hold of the magic, he simply stumbled out into an empty corridor. Once he found his footing, he looked around. Definitely Hell.

And thankfully, deserted.

With a sigh, Fabian stepped aside and waited.

And waited.

Almost ten minutes passed before the next person appeared. Jan fell out of thin air and crashed to the ground before quickly climbing to his feet. "Woah. What a trip."

"Man, that took forever," Fabian complained. If there'd been any demons around while he'd been waiting, the others would've only found his body.

"Where are the others?"

"You are the others."

Fabian didn't like the way Jan grimaced and almost took a step back. "No," his friend said. "I was last to leave. The others should've been here by now."

Only they weren't. He and Jan were the only ones inside the Dûr Lôrac. "Why do I have a really bad feeling about this?"

Lucille

"This is bad," Lucille said as she and Rachel hid behind a stall of foul-smelling mushrooms. The gate was right in front of them in a busy marketplace in the middle of Hescaryn's shining city. Countless demons were milling about, but none of them paid them any attention. For now.

"Something's gone terribly wrong."

She couldn't see Fabian and Ophelia, who'd gone first, nor Anne and Jan, who should've arrived after Rachel.

"Wonderful," Rachel said, swallowing hard. "Just wonderful."

They only dared wait a few more minutes, for the longer they stayed, the more looks they attracted. "Let's go find the residence. Hopefully the others will join us there."

They walked across the bustling market, pretending to be mildly interested in the various wares, as if they knew exactly where they were going, while listening for clues as to where to head next. Lucille would've thought that appearing in such a large group of demons would've meant her immediate death, but no one seemed to notice they weren't first-class demons themselves.

Slowly, Lucille relaxed, and her curiosity grew. There was a surprising amount of respect for the stallholders. No money changed hands, but she saw other goods being exchanged. Some demons paid by promising work or favours, and some stalls—most of the food ones—seemed free to all. Lucille assumed there was some sort of government-run agricultural scheme that provided enough food for everyone.

Her tongue itched with questions she couldn't ask. How did demon society work? What had the Council of Seven decreed? What did Balthasar's Small Council do? What happened when anyone could be killed at any time? The very fact all these demons were peacefully going to market intrigued her.

They had almost reached the big staircase at the end of the market when they heard a familiar name.

"If Balthasar doesn't show his face in the Council soon, the Red Blade will take over." The speaker was an antsy blonde woman in a group of four.

Another curly-haired woman grimaced. "I hope not. I liked Balthasar. No one else ever pulled the strings as skilfully as he did."

"True, but with that talent it was only a matter of time before he'd reach for something bigger," a freckled young man said. "I think it's high time he stabbed Melaney in the back. Without his help, she'd never have got her hands on lust."

The blonde huffed. "Don't dismiss the General so quickly. He won't put up with it. I heard Volac's throwing a massive tantrum because Caspar refuses his call. He's planning something."

A third woman shook her head. "Maybe, but Melaney's bed is not a battlefield. Who knows if he's even up to the task? I heard he killed the last person who tried to flirt with him."

The curly haired woman leaned against the wall and sighed. "A man in her position would certainly be a change. We haven't had a male Archdemon of Lust for three thousand years. Though, if it were up to me, I wish the General would stick to his Bloodriders."

"Yes, I don't want him in the Council of Seven," the freckled man said. "It would be like having two wrath demons, and we know how that'd go. Balthasar, on the other hand, would be a boon to any Council."

In Lucille's opinion, the man was completely besotted with Balthasar.

The blonde scoffed at him. "He's too cunning. Too much power and in a few centuries he may long for the Black Throne."

"What about that mysterious half-demon boy Melaney seems to favour?" the third woman asked.

"Ugh." The curly-haired one grimaced. "Who wants a half-demon on the Council of Seven? He'd be dead in a week."

The man nodded his head. "Agreed. Let's see if it's even true Melaney is planning her demise. I can't imagine she'd give it up voluntarily."

The blonde rolled her head, and her gaze met Lucille's. "What are you looking at?" she asked aggressively.

"Just wondering if Bal—"

Rachel pulled her away. "He's there! Look."

Lucille turned but couldn't see anyone.

"Where?"

"Nowhere." Rachel said, sounding annoyed. "What were you thinking getting involved with them?"

"I was just asking for directions."

"And exposing us?" Rachel huffed. "Remember, everyone will try to kill us."

Lucille clicked her tongue as she followed Rachel up the stairs. "They don't know what we are."

"Well, they'll soon find out if you behave so... undemon-like."

"What should I do? Attack them?"

Just then, a burst of energy shot past them. Lucille and Rachel ducked behind the railing at the top and looked down, only to find they hadn't been the target of the attack. Instead, a fight had broken out below. One demon smashed another into a food stall, sending pastries flying everywhere.

The other demons made sure to stay out of the way, but unlike humans, they didn't pay much attention to the fight.

"I hear the Seer is in town," a black-robed demon said to two others as they passed. "It's been years since he spent any meaningful time in Hescaryn."

His pale companion scoffed. "I don't trust him. His loyalty to the Council wavers constantly. Who's to say he really sees the future and isn't just making it up?"

The third, much taller man shrugged. "He prophesied Malcolm's death and Iyaga's surprise succession."

"Lucky guess," said the first.

Lucille and Rachel exchanged glances, but this time Lucille held her tongue. How anyone could call such an accurate prediction luck was beyond her, but that was no reason to get involved.

"Surprising how well informed they are without any media." She'd never have guessed demons were such gossips. "Fascinating."

Rachel huffed beside her. "Yeah, oh so fascinating."

"Is everything okay?"

The look Rachel gave her was subantarctic.

Lucille quickly found something else to focus on. "Let's get as high up as we can so we can see Lucin from above."

Getting around Lucin was incredibly frustrating. While there were more than enough stairs, they often ended in a dead-end with no way to get to the next level, unless you could fly.

As Lucille absorbed all the fascinating details of life on Hescaryn, Rachel seemed to grow more and more frustrated with each step.

Finally, Lucille tried again. "What's going on?"

"Are you honestly asking?"

"Yes?"

Rachel rolled her eyes hard. "We're in Hell, Lucille. Just the two of us."

"I noticed." And with just the two of them, a fight was the last thing they needed. "The others can't be far."

"They're not here." Rachel made a sweeping gesture towards the city, which was a maze of multi-storey buildings, half streets, and open squares.

Defensively, Lucille crossed her arms and watched the hordes of demons as if her friends would suddenly appear among them. "But we know where they're going. We just have to get to the Residence of Lust and wait for them there."

Rachel laughed dryly. "Fine. Lead the way."

The truth was Lucille had no idea where to go. Matt had told them all seven residences were arranged around a large square, but she didn't see anything like that in the city in front of her. Not that they'd managed to find a single unobstructed view. There may have been a system to the buildings and streets, but if there was, it was based on people being able to either fly or jump, and they couldn't do either.

"Why are you so mad at me?" she asked, suddenly feeling defeated.

"I'm not mad at you," Rachel admitted, her voice a little softer. "It's just that for the first time in my life I have something to look forward to. Adam contacted me and I want to go see him. I don't want to die here."

Last night, before they'd fallen asleep in Samantha's bedroom, Rachel had confessed about the texts she'd received. Lucille had encouraged her to look into flights, to have something to hold onto if things got tough. But as much as she liked her friend exploring this new relationship, now wasn't the time.

"I don't want to die, either. Maybe I don't have Mr Right waiting for me at home, but I want to go to university in October and maybe meet a nice guy. I want to learn more about magic and..." Lucille took a deep breath, realising she was panicking. "The thing is, Sam wants all that, too. She has as many plans for the future as we do, probably more."

Rachel giggled. "Sam probably has more than the two of us put together."

Things were starting to go right again, and Lucille relaxed a little. "She needs us."

"I know she does. She's my best friend. It's just that... I really like Adam." When she said it this time, it sounded more desperate than angry. "I already missed my chance with him once. I don't want to... I want him. I want to know what we could be."

"Come here!" Lucille pulled her into a hug. "We'll find the residence and we *will* rescue Samantha. And then we'll all go home, you'll fly to New Zealand to meet your Adam, and everything will be fine."

While Rachel was only able to force a smile, Lucille took what she could from the hug. "We won't die here. Promise?" She held out her little finger.

Rachel snorted at first, but then wrapped her own around it. "Promise."

"Cute," a deep voice said suddenly, close to them.

Startled, Lucille didn't even wait to see who it was. "Scutum Protecto!"

Energy hit her shield seconds after it went up. Lucille grabbed Rachel's hand and ran. Several shots hit the walls around them as they ducked behind buildings and ran down stairs. At one point, Lucille managed to throw a fireball, but she didn't check whether it hit its target.

They ran on and on until they had lost the demons—and their way.

"Where are we?" Lucille asked, panting.

Just then, a black-haired, winged demon in leather armour with a sword strapped to his back appeared in front of them and Lucille screamed.

Rachel's eyes widened. "Matt?"

Matt

Matt had lain in wait, looking for René, but his father must've made it to Hescaryn moments before him. As he searched the streets, he'd listened for any sign of fighting. Then, someone had called out "humans" and his heart had skipped a beat. But instead of his father, he'd spotted Lucille and Rachel.

He grabbed both girls by the arm and carried them through the abstract space to a quieter part of Lucin, not too far from the residences. "What are you two doing here?"

"It's a long story," Lucille said, still panting from her involuntary sprint and subsequent fright.

"Your mother abducted Samantha," Rachel said. "Did you really think we were going to sit at home and twiddle our thumbs?"

Matt shook his head, instantly feeling guilty. His shoulders relaxed slightly as he ran a hand through his hair. "Sorry. It's just... it's dangerous. You almost got yourselves killed out there."

"Trust me, we noticed," Rachel snapped.

"Where are the others?"

"We travelled the rivers of magic," Lucille explained. "Apparently there's more than one way into Lucin, and the others must've used other exits." She studied him once more. "What are you doing out here? I would've thought you'd go straight to the residence."

Matt rubbed his neck. "I was hoping to catch my father. He must've gone through the gate, just like you."

"Your father's here?"

He nodded grimly. "Yes. René's got it into his head that he's madly in love with Melaney and has to save her life."

When Lucille's eyes widened in surprise, he sighed.

"It's some kind of curse. He's not acting on his own free will. Not really."

Matt had never slept with Melaney, but he'd seen the devotion that followed. Few demons moved on from the Archdemon of Lust. A human wouldn't stand a chance.

"We haven't seen René," Lucille said softly.

Matt closed his eyes for a moment and breathed deeply. "Then he's probably in the residence. Let's go there. Maybe we can save him *and* Samantha." Though his words sounded hopeful, he couldn't shake the deep fear he felt at the thought of their fate. And the guilt.

If he hadn't refused to answer his mother's call, René's passion wouldn't have been reignited. And as for Samantha. Everything bad that had ever happened had been the direct result of his own actions—or inactions.

He took Lucille and Rachel with him as he jumped to the edge of Residence Square. There, in the shadow of the great gate, he pointed out his mother's residence.

Normally, only two scantily clad guards stood at the entrance. Now, there was a full cohort of eight guards guarding the residence with blood on the ground at their feet. A lot of blood. Someone had died there.

As they watched, a runner from the Council of Seven came up to the residence. Before she could open her mouth, the guards shot her. Next to Matt, Lucille gasped, and Rachel retched.

"How are we going to get past them?" Lucille whispered.

"They've probably been instructed to let me through, and I have enough authority to order them to let you in as well." He knew at least six of them by name and they'd all know who he was—and alert his mother.

Rachel eyed him carefully. "But you don't want to."

"Correct."

"I suppose I could come up with an illusion."

Matt wished Lucille didn't sound so uncertain. An illusion that could hide them as they entered the residence would've been perfect, but the guards were all standing shoulder to shoulder.

With a sigh, Matt stepped back from the square. "There must be a second entrance."

"Is there?" Rachel asked.

Matt was already searching the streets heading away from the square. One of them led straight into the Dûr Lôrac. The cave system ran past at least five of the residences. "I'm almost sure. Come on."

This close to Lucin, he wasn't afraid of anything lurking in the shadows. There was a reason why the residences were built high above the rest of Lucin but so close to the cave system. There had to be a secret entrance—or rather an emergency exit—somewhere in this maze.

"What do you think of a frontal attack?" Lucille asked.

"Do you want to kill us?"

"What Rachel said."

Before Lucille could protest, Matt put his hand on her arm.

Another demon appeared right in front of them. Fortunately, she had her back to them as she hurried down the corridor. Matt thought he'd seen that long honey-blonde hair before, but he couldn't quite place it.

To his surprise, the demon walked straight through a wall. She didn't jump or anything, she just turned left and moved through the stone. Excited, he followed her and found a small crack right at the back of the Residence of Lust. It was a bit of a squeeze, though, especially with the sword on his back.

When he emerged, he found himself in a small chamber that seemed to serve as a storage room. The strange demon was standing at the door, spying on the corridor.

Matt recognised her now. Anger rose in him, and he leapt forward, grabbing the unsuspecting demon and pinning her against the wall. She immediately raised her hands in surrender.

Matt wasn't fooled. No demon would give up this easily. As Rachel and Lucille entered the room behind him, he hissed, "You're Alecia, Pyke's Devotee." And not just any Devotee of the Archdemon of Envy, but his first ranked.

Alecia shrugged and smiled at him. "And you're Melaney's human son."

"Half-demon."

"Half of Hescaryn speaks of you."

"Envious?"

"Um, Matt?" Lucille said carefully. "Or rather, Melchior. Who's this?"

Grumbling, Matt let go of the demon. "She's a spy, that's who she is. And that's how she knew about the back door."

Alecia seemed mildly amused. "You could seal it when you become archdemon."

"I don't want to be archdemon."

She grinned. "Then we don't have a problem." With an annoyingly relaxed shrug, Alecia turned towards the door.

Matt grabbed her and slammed her back against the wall. "What does Pyke want?"

For the first time, Alecia's smile faded a little. "What do you think? He wants to know what game Melaney's playing."

Lucille touched Matt's shoulder lightly. "Why do you care so much what she's doing?"

"She doesn't belong here."

"Neither do we. We don't have time for a turf war, Matt. Samantha needs us."

Alecia perked up. "Who's Samantha...?" Her gaze met Lucille's. "You're human."

Matt growled. The last thing they needed was the House of Envy getting into their business. He let go and entered the corridor, quickly finding his bearings.

"Melaney's throne room is this way," Alecia said in her annoyingly perky voice.

"I know," Matt hissed. As if he didn't know his way around the residence where he'd spent his entire childhood.

Lucille hurried after him, whispering, "Matt! We don't know where she is. The throne room sounds like a good place to start."

"Sure, if you want to run straight into my mother."

Her whisper became more urgent. "Sam might be with her."

Matt shook his head. "Menuha said it was a trap. Melaney wants me to come to her."

As Rachel joined their little circle of conspirators, Lucille had a moment of thought. Then her eyes brightened. "Let's split up."

"Excuse me?"

"You really do have a death wish, don't you?" Rachel asked.

Lucille shook her head. "We need to find Samantha as soon as possible. So, you go that way, and I'll check the throne room. With Alecia."

Matt couldn't believe what he was hearing. "You can't trust her, Lucille. She's from the House of Envy."

"And she's a demon," Rachel pointed out.

Lucille just rolled her eyes. "What's she going to do? Be jealous of me?" She shook her head. "If she's a spy, she has every reason to be as inconspicuous as possible. Besides, I'm not some helpless damsel."

"Fine." Matt knew when it was pointless to argue with Lucille. "Summon me if you need help."

"I thought it wasn't possible to jump into one of the residences."

"It's possible inside of them. You just can't get in without alerting the guards."

Lucille nodded. "Okay. Stay safe." And with that, she ran after Alecia, who'd already started down the corridor.

Rachel snorted in disbelief. "You're just letting her go like that? With a hostile demon?"

While the House of Envy was no ally of the House of Lust—or anyone else's for that matter—Matt had no quarrel with Alecia. "Lucille can look after herself. And Samantha needs me more."

If Lucille wanted to take her chances with the House of Envy, it was her business. He had more important things to do than babysit the headstrong witch.

They were now in the Residence of Lust. Somewhere, in one of the rooms, Samantha was waiting for him. At least, he hoped so.

Balthasar

Balthasar was trying to enjoy some wineberries in his room, but his peace was disturbed by Caspar fidgeting endlessly in the chair in front of him.

"You seem a little... tense," he said, at last.

"Shut up!"

"Are we a bit moody?" Balthasar asked, amused by Caspar's blatant struggle.

Caspar raised an eyebrow. "We? I don't see you worrying."

"Please tell—why should I be worried?"

"Melaney," Caspar growled. "She claims she's choosing between the three of us, but she's already made her choice. And it's not one of us."

Undisturbed, Balthasar picked another berry from his bowl. "No archdemon decides who succeeds them."

"Right, and how are you going to stop Melchior? He's finally answered her call. Sightings of him in Lucin reached me hours ago."

In Balthasar's opinion, Caspar was putting far too much stock in Melchior's movements and intentions. Melaney may have been obsessed with the half-demon and was using him in her little ruse, but Balthasar cared little about that. Even if Melchior somehow managed to cut off her pretty head, Balthasar wouldn't be above a little fratricide to get what was rightfully his.

"If Melchior was seen in Lucin but not here, he's not on his way to Melaney's bed. He's looking for something."

"Samantha. I know."

Frowning, Balthasar sat up straight. "Samantha?"

"Melaney kidnapped her and locked her in one of her sex rooms. Apparently, she wants whoever succeeds to take her as their mate."

Balthasar snorted. "I'm definitely not going to choose a human for that position."

He hadn't really thought about choosing a mate yet. Back then, he'd deliberately turned down the role when Melaney had offered it to him. The last thing he'd wanted was to tie his life to his mother.

Caspar slumped in his chair and stared glumly at the table. "You're not going to be archdemon, anyway. She's for Melchior, of course. Remember, he's crazy about her."

Interesting. Caspar tried to disguise it in his usual clumsy way, but he seemed to care a little too much that Samantha had been kidnapped to sweeten the deal for Melchior. Balthasar still remembered their ill-fated ruse. He'd expected Caspar to kill or at least threaten Samantha when he'd brought her to him. Instead, the fearsome general hadn't just let her go, he'd returned to Ashuan to heal her. And he never healed *anyone.*

It was one of the little secrets Balthasar hadn't quite cracked yet. He'd always considered his brother to be simple minded, but this was a hidden depth he'd never expected.

He was about to open his mouth when Chay walked in. The Seer did a double take when he saw them sitting together in peace. "What is this? Another necessary alliance?"

Balthasar offered his bowl of fruit. "Berries?"

Chay shook his head while Caspar stood and glared at him. "Seer."

"General."

"Why aren't you with your favourite little mutt, holding his hand?"

Chay seemed completely unimpressed. "I don't need to. I already know his future."

Balthasar chuckled. He had no intention of intervening. Chay could easily stand up to Caspar, even if the latter lost his temper as he so often did.

"You know what I mean," Caspar snapped. "Did you see him become archdemon?"

"If that were the case, there'd be nothing you could do about it. Everything happens as it happens."

Caspar shook his head in frustration. "I won't let him get his hands on her." And with that he stormed out of the room.

"Her?" Chay asked.

Now that Caspar was gone, Balthasar put the fruit bowl down and stood up. "Obviously, Melchior isn't the only one interested in Samantha. I have no idea what Caspar sees in this human girl. Or Melchior, for that matter."

"You have to save her."

"Excuse me?"

Chay looked a little stressed, which told Balthasar that whatever he was up to this time had something to do with his grand plan. He wondered if it included the Six he so coveted.

"I've told you before," Chay said, meeting his gaze, "the way to Melaney is through Melchior. Only the Sword of Amain will separate her pretty head from her no-less tempting body."

Balthasar raised an eyebrow. "And the way to Melchior is through Samantha? So, I have to save her from the big bad lust demons?"

"If you want to be archdemon."

Balthasar groaned. He'd much rather do it the traditional way, but he trusted Chay to the core, and if the half-demon said only a stupid sword could kill Melaney, then he had to get the sword. A human girl for a powerful weapon. It wasn't the worst deal he'd ever made.

"You owe me for this."

Chay smiled mischievously. "No, no. You've got it wrong. You'll owe me."

Balthasar snorted, amused and fascinated at the same time. Chay was right. If he delivered what he'd promised, Balthasar would be his, for better or worse. That was the deal. Chay had promised to reveal everything he knew and make it worth his while.

All he had to do was save one stupid human witch.

Just moments ago, they'd been talking about Melchior being seen in Lucin. And now Balthasar heard him and someone else in the corridor in front of him.

"—he said you wouldn't succeed on your own."

It was one of Melchior's little friends. The dreamer.

Melchior frowned. "Strange. He didn't say anything to me about that."

Balthasar paid little mind to their conversation and approached them. As soon as they heard his footsteps, Matt drew his sword. The sword that would one day kill Melaney.

"Nice weapon."

"Want to find out if it's not just nice but sharp?"

Balthasar rolled his eyes. Everyone seemed on edge these days. "Who are you going to kill with it? Melaney?"

"Anyone who gets in my way," Melchior said, darkly.

Amused, Balthasar raised his hands. "I have no intention of attacking you. I assume you know how to use it?"

As he questioned his brother, Rachel watched them quietly. This one knew more than she let on. Too bad she was human. He could use a dreamer in his service.

"Chay taught me," Melchior said.

Of course he had. Chay had big plans for Melchior and probably saw a bit of himself in the young half-demon.

"If you're half as good as he is, that would be impressive." As far as Balthasar knew, there was no better swordsman than Chay. "He told me Melaney would die by this sword."

Melchior scoffed. "I'm not interested in becoming archdemon. I just want—"

"Sam, I know. Melaney took your toy away."

Predictably, Melchior's eyes narrowed. "Do you know where she is?"

"Not in the slightest, but I've heard Melaney plans to make her your mate." Balthasar shook his head. "It's a nice gesture, I suppose, but if you ask me, she's barely good enough for a little side piece."

"Keep talking like that and *you'll* die by my sword."

Balthasar eyed the tip of the sword, still pointed at him. He knew from experience Melchior didn't joke when it came to Samantha. "Is she really worth all this?" When Melchior frowned, he explained, "How long will she live, Melchior? Eighty years? Maybe even less?" At the rate Greenvalley was being attacked by monsters, less was very likely. "Don't you think you'll regret choosing her over power in a century?" He really didn't understand the fascination with short-lived races.

"Don't listen to him," Rachel hissed, glaring at Balthasar.

His brother, however, wasn't so human he couldn't easily grasp the problem. He may have been young, but he wasn't stupid. He must've known he'd live much longer than this human girl he was so fixated on.

Melchior took his time to answer, and when he did, he sounded quite subdued. "Even if I never gain any significant power... Even if..." He struggled to speak, but finally forced the words out. "Even if she's no longer around one day... she'll be worth it."

Balthasar shook his head in disappointment. "Humans. Oh well. Since you have no intention of becoming archdemon, may I borrow your sword?"

"Absolutely not! Why would you want it anyway?"

"To chop someone's head off, as I said."

"Get your own sword!" Melchior wrinkled his nose. "Now get out of my way before I make *you* a head shorter."

Balthasar snorted. "Melchior, Melchior. That tough guy act you try so hard to emulate? No one believes it. You're here because of Samantha and Samantha only. Love has robbed you of your sense and sensibility, otherwise you wouldn't be sneaking around here and would've simply chopped off the snake's head. The only thing of value to you is that sword."

"And it's mine," Melchior hissed. "Mine alone."

"Now you sound like my father. Whatever. Good luck in your quest. May it continue to keep you from my lust."

Obviously, it wasn't time to take the sword yet. It still eluded Balthasar why he needed to rescue Samantha when that idiot was already looking for her, but he bade Melchior goodbye and continued his own search. One thing was for sure, if he got to Samantha first, Matt would throw the sword at his feet to get her back. An annoying detour, but apparently a necessary one.

Caspar

"Tell him to mind his own business!" Caspar roared at Volac's hapless messenger. "I'm not his errand boy." He grabbed the messenger by the collar, his spittle covering the other's pale face. "Did you get that, cockroach?"

"Loud and clear, General."

Caspar snorted. "Don't try to belittle me just because you've been chosen by Volac to deliver a message. He'll probably rip your head off because I'm rejecting his summons, and he won't even pause to learn your name. I'm important to him. You're nothing. Get out of my sight. Now!" He shoved the messenger towards the exit and growled at him for good measure.

He didn't care what Volac wanted. Something that would pull him away from the Residence of Lust, that much was obvious.

The messenger left in a hurry and Menuha entered. Caspar turned away from her, but his sister didn't care and hugged him from behind.

Despite himself, he took a deep breath. "Did you find her?"

Menuha groaned softly. "Melaney's moved the room to her private area. Whoever wants to go there has to get past Melaney first."

Caspar snorted in disgust. There was no doubt about it, Melaney would ruin Samantha. She would take everything that was good about the little witch and twist it beyond recognition.

Menuha knew it, too. "Sam doesn't deserve this, Caspar. She's not like us. She doesn't belong here."

She wasn't telling him anything he didn't already know. Samantha belonged in Ashuan. With Melchior. But she was here... with him.

Annoyed, he pulled away from his sister's grasp and put some distance between them.

The disappointment on Menuha's face cut like a knife. "Why do you always have to want what's his?"

His breath caught in his throat. Was his sister suggesting what he thought she was suggesting? "This has nothing to do with Melchior. Samantha doesn't belong to him."

"She doesn't belong to you, either," Menuha said quietly.

Caspar bared his teeth. "Don't you think I know that?"

He'd already missed his chance in this cycle. Jeyne had been reborn and was beyond his reach. If only her soul wasn't so tantalisingly close.

"Why do you care so much about her all of a sudden?"

"I don't," was Caspar's first answer, but then he relented a little. "You wouldn't understand."

Menuha folded her arms and rolled her eyes. "You mean like I wouldn't understand what happened during those years you were stuck in a human world? Those years that changed you completely?"

Caspar looked away, avoiding her gaze. Ever since the memories had been triggered by Melchior's interference, the old pain had been his constant companion. Mostly it was a dull ache in the background, but every now and then it would flare up with the ferocity of a flesh wound. All it took was a single reminder.

He knew he couldn't go on like this. Being here with his memories of Jeyne as fresh as if it had happened yesterday and her reincarnation so close and yet so far beyond his reach was killing him. He needed to destroy something, to drown his soul in blood as he'd done the first time, but his hands were tied. There was no village of culprits to destroy. No master to take revenge on. Nothing to take away this pain.

"Samantha doesn't belong here," Menuha said quietly. "If she means anything to you, help me free her."

But did she? Samantha wasn't Jeyne, no matter how much he wished she was. She would never love him. Not with Melchior right there, who'd already won her heart, shattered it, then put it back together again.

But no matter how much he told himself they weren't the same person, that her soul had been washed clean of all the pain and heartbreak her short life had brought her, he couldn't stop longing. Couldn't stop feeling. And while part of him wanted to be selfish and claim her anyway, Caspar preferred her to be happy.

Though grumpy, he asked, "Do you have a plan?"

Menuha beamed. "You'll love it."

Menuha's plan was quite simple. She would go and rescue Samantha while Caspar distracted Melaney. If all went well, he wouldn't even see her before she was back in Ashuan, where he couldn't follow her. Nevertheless, he stood outside Melaney's main bedroom with Menuha, listening to her and Frennys.

While the two were tangled up as usual, Melaney's mind seemed to be elsewhere. "He's still not here."

"He's been seen in Lucin," Frennys replied, a slight edge to his voice.

"Lucin is big. Why is he hiding from me?"

She must've done something painful, because Frennys grunted, then moaned. "Who knows what the boy is thinking. He's half human. He'll come here sooner or later if he wants the girl."

"What if he doesn't like her as much as everyone says?"

"He's in Hescaryn, isn't he?"

There was a moment of silence and Caspar almost decided to enter, but then he heard a loud thud, as if something heavy had fallen to the ground.

"Nine hundred years, Melaney," Frennys said, his voice hard now. Apparently, he'd been unceremoniously pushed off the edge of the bed. "I trusted you with my life."

"And have I not rewarded you many times over?" Melaney asked, though she sounded bored.

"Countless times."

Melaney scoffed. "Go bring Melchior to me! And send me the demons responsible for Samantha's education. If he won't show himself, at least let me have some fun with his little girl."

"As you wish, my love."

As soon as Frennys was gone, Caspar and Menuha entered. Melaney was sitting in front of her mirror, brushing her hair, when her green eyes met Caspar's, cutting through him like a knife.

"Not this again, Caspar. I don't have time for your childish tantrums."

Anger rose in him, hot and hard. "Childish?" Did he really mean so little to his mother?

Menuha placed a hand on his shoulder, wordlessly reminding him of his task. An attack wouldn't distract his mother nearly long enough.

"I'm not here to kill you."

Melaney raised an eyebrow, still looking only in the mirror and not at him. "Then what did you come for?"

Caspar's mouth was full of bitter bile, but he forced the words out. "I'll miss you, Mother."

Delighted, she threw her head back and laughed. Then suddenly she was standing in front of him, one hand around his neck, pulling him forward. "Come here, my angry little boy."

Menuha stepped back, apparently to give them some privacy, but instead of leaving through the door they'd come through, she went into the tunnels behind the bedroom.

"Don't you get enough attention?" Melaney asked amused.

Caspar didn't even have to lie. "All your attention is focused on Melchior."

She laughed again. "You indulge yourself too much with envy, Caspar. I'd rather like to see your wrath."

Now she was speaking his language.

"As you wish, *Mother.*"

Samantha

When Samantha awoke, the curtains were not only open, they were gone. She had a terrible headache and struggled to remember what had happened just before she'd fallen asleep. Then she noticed the considerable lack of clothes she was wearing.

"No, no, no, no!"

In a panic, Samantha scrambled out of bed to look for her clothes, scattered on the floor. She hadn't had sex with anyone or so she thought, but whatever had happened, it'd been a close call.

She was losing it. Losing her control and her mind. Soon, she'd be a creature of lust, just like Melaney wanted.

The door opened and a pair of demons entered, siblings by the look of them. Since neither were topping up the potion or taking the food, they could only be here for one reason.

"Two?" Samantha asked, feeling massively overwhelmed.

The female demon scoffed at her. "Listen to her. And someone like her is supposed to be a playmate."

Her brother laughed sharply. "Wish I knew what the mistress was thinking. Humans are far too prudish to fall for the sins with heart and soul. What a waste of time trying to mould her."

Despite his words, he came over to Samantha and stroked her arm as he slowly walked around her. Samantha's brain told her to run, but her body refused to move, eager for his touch.

Instead of caressing her, the demon shoved her. She stumbled and fell at his sister's feet. Instinctively, she tried to weave, but the other woman stepped on her hand, applying just enough pressure to make her scream.

"Cute. She thinks she can cast a spell on us."

"The only magic that works in this room is what pleases Melaney, and you definitely don't *please* her," the male demon hissed.

His sister let go of Samantha and he grabbed her and pulled her back to her feet. As soon as she was standing, the woman slapped her.

Licking her lips, she said, "Let's have some fun with her."

Samantha's cheek burnt. "Fun?"

Suddenly, the man grabbed her throat and squeezed. Samantha's hands flew up in panic. At the same time, his sister knelt and spread her legs. Reacting instinctively, Samantha kicked and managed to hit her in the face.

Furious, she rose to her feet, her hand ready to shoot energy, when she was suddenly grabbed from behind and her neck broken by Menuha.

Her brother let go of Samantha. He retreated quickly as Samantha fell forward, coughing and sputtering. "We just wanted to refine her training."

"I'll refine your bowels if you don't clean up this mess and leave!" Menuha snapped.

The man bent immediately. "Of course." Grabbing his sister, he left.

Samantha was still on all fours, gasping for breath. As soon as Menuha's face appeared before her, she threw her arms around her neck and burst into tears. "I don't want to be like her. I don't want—"

"Shh, shh, you'll be fine." Menuha stroked her hair. "I'm here. Everything's going to be alright now."

Samantha sobbed with relief. The nightmare was over. Someone had come to save her. She was going home.

Jan

Go to Hell, they'd said. *It'll be fun*, they'd said.

Jan sighed as they reached the next junction in the Dûr Lôrac. Nothing about this journey was fun. Instead of Lucin, they were trapped in this cave system without a map or any sense of direction. They may have gotten out near the city, but after two hours of walking, they might as well have been in a completely different part of Hell. The only positive was they hadn't encountered too many demons. The few they'd come across had been small—though ferocious—and easily dispatched.

Worst of all, they had no idea if the others had made it. And even if they had, the thought of his little sister all alone among demons made Jan's stomach turn. He'd never forgive himself if anything happened to her.

"Why are we the only ones with swords and potions in our backpacks instead of rations?" Fabian asked, as he leaned against the wall to lighten the weight of the pack. They didn't dare take them off in case they had to make a quick escape.

"Because we're big, strong men," Jan said in a dry voice. "We don't need food."

Fabian huffed, slightly amused. "But we'll need water soon."

"Fabian." The other boy looked at Jan. "What are you?"

"I'm... Oh. But we'd still need bottles or cups or..." When Jan gave him another look, Fabian relented. "Fine, we can use our hands to drink."

"Seriously." Jan laughed softly, then pushed away from the wall to continue walking. "Honestly, I'm more worried that we're definitely not in the city. There's no one here."

Fabian groaned as he followed his example. "Be glad about that."

"Oh, I am." Since humour was the only thing keeping Jan sane, he joked, "You haven't said once how we're going to die down here."

Far less amused, Fabian snorted. "Do I really have to say it out loud?" He sighed. "We have to find a way out of here."

"Agreed. I kind of have this life waiting for me back home."

"Lucky."

Jan did a double take and stopped. "What do you mean, lucky?"

Fabian shook his head but said it anyway. "I'm just upset about my rejection letter. It's not fair."

Happy to talk about anything but their imminent death or where the others were, Jan decided to indulge him. "Have you applied anywhere else yet?"

"I don't want to move away. Not with my mum still struggling, and anyway, we belong in Greenvalley, don't we?"

"You mean because of the prophecy?" It was hard to believe they were chosen heroes when a little thing like travelling the rivers of magic could undo them. "Look, prophecy or not, don't let an old text dictate your life. The world is bigger than Greenvalley. Or should I say worlds? You'll find your way. And if you want to stay, you can apply again in the summer term or you can work here and there until things fall into place. It'll be fine."

Fabian smiled. "Thanks. You're actually the best example that it's possible to take a fall and still land on your feet."

"What do you mean?"

"When you left school, I thought it was a huge mistake but look at you now. Not only do you have a really cool career plan, you're top of the class."

Jan was glad for the darkness that hid his considerable blush. "Only in the practical part."

"Still, it's impressive." Fabian smiled again, then took a deep breath. "You're right. Not getting into university on the first try isn't the end of the world. I'll be fine."

"Only if we get out of here," Jan reminded him, jokingly.

Groaning, Fabian pushed him. Jan laughed and pushed back, starting a reckless—but probably necessary—little play-fight.

When they finally stopped for a water break, their spirits had dropped again. There was still no sign they were making progress, and Jan had forgotten why they'd thought this was a good idea in the first place. Lost in the Dûr Lôrac, they were of no use to anyone.

"How long do you think we'll be wandering around here until we get anywhere?" Fabian asked as he poured water into Jan's mouth.

Jan swallowed, then promptly said, "Exactly three hours and twenty minutes." The stream of water stopped. "I don't know, mate. But we'll get out of here eventually." There had to be a way out somewhere. Where it was and what might be waiting there for them was a bit up in the air, but the tunnels couldn't last forever.

Fabian didn't answer. He sat down and rubbed his face, looking far more exhausted than a few hours of walking should've left him.

"You're worried about Sam, aren't you?"

"How could I not be? She was *taken* by demons. Demons that have been trying to kill us all year." Fabian swallowed hard. "I just hope she's still alive."

Now Jan's throat tightened as well. "I'm sure she is," he forced out. "If they wanted to kill her, they wouldn't have kidnapped her. They want Matt, not Sam."

"Yeah, great." Fabian shook his head and took a deep breath, channelling hidden anger. "I hate Matt for this. He needs to get a grip on his stupid family."

"Hey, come on. You know you don't get to choose your family. Psychopath uncle, murderous brothers, sex-crazed mother—the boy was doomed from the start."

"But did he have to drag Sam into his mess? It's not her family."

The obvious answer would have been that Matt hadn't had anything to do with that, either. He hadn't chosen his feelings or done anything specific to endanger Samantha. Rationally, it wasn't Matt's fault, and Jan was convinced Fabian knew that as well. On an emotional level, however, he completely understood the issue. They'd known Matt for two years now—since they'd started hunting monsters together—and more than half their problems had been caused by Matt or his family. Even though it was unfair, it was hard not to resent him for it. Especially when the people they loved were in danger.

"I get it," Jan said with a sigh. "Because of this whole mess, my little sister is somewhere in Hell, and I can't do anything for her."

"Yeah, her and Ophelia." Suddenly Fabian got up from the floor and shouldered his backpack. "Let's go."

Jan struggled to follow as quickly. "Where?"

"Doesn't matter. But I can't just sit here and do nothing. So, let's move on."

Only half an hour later, the tunnel ahead of them lit up.

"Hey, there's a light." Fabian shouted, brightening for the first time since they'd arrived.

Tired, Jan joked, "You know what they say about lights at the end of a tunnel?"

"Jan, we're not dead."

The hairs on the back of Jan's neck stood up. "But we'll be dead soon. Run!"

A group of demons appeared behind them. Jan had no time to check how many there were or what they looked like. He just grabbed Fabian's arm and pulled him down the tunnel. No energy followed them, but that didn't stop Jan from running as fast as he could towards the light. Suddenly the corridor widened, and a shining city appeared as the ground disappeared.

Fabian slammed his arm into Jan's chest as he came to a halt. Jan clung to his shoulder, digging his fingers in until the momentum slowed and they remained safely on their own two feet.

The path had led them to some kind of terrace above what could only be Lucin. Breathing heavily, they took a step back.

"And now?" Fabian asked.

Jan glanced over his shoulder. Four demons in black armour were strolling towards them, cocky smiles on their faces. They knew exactly what they were and that they couldn't just jump or fly away, leaving the demons all the time in the world.

"We're going down."

Fabian looked at him questioningly, but Jan had already sat down and swung his legs over the edge of the platform. The rock was pretty rough with plenty of crevices for his fingers and toes to get stuck in. He quickly took off his backpack and dropped it on another platform below them. Then he climbed onto the cliff face.

From the sound of a second backpack hitting the ground, Jan could only assume Fabian was following. Soon Jan's fingers cramped and his muscles shook as he tried to descend as quickly as possible without losing his footing. Small stones were rolling down the cliff face—not a good sign if they lost their grip. He looked down to see how far it was to the ground and noticed two demons appear below him.

"Shit! Do you see another terrace?"

"There's only up or down," Fabian grunted.

So far, they'd only made it down three or four metres, with the ground still around eight metres away. "Go up. We're going to fight."

Fabian whimpered but pulled himself up again when a burst of energy hit the rock face beside him.

"Care—" Jan started to shout, but the rock crumbled under his fingers. "No, no, no, no, no!"

Screaming, Jan slid down the cliff face, a slab of crumbling rock beneath him. He tried to hold onto something, but everything under his fingers was in motion. Until it wasn't, and he slammed into the platform with his left foot, instantly toppling over in excruciating pain. Before he could even catch his breath, a small mound of rock had buried his leg.

The pain brought tears to Jan's eyes as he finally managed a shaky breath. He tried to move his leg but screamed instead.

"That was entertaining," one of the demons said, drawing Jan's attention to him. Two more demons joined him, standing in a rough semicircle around Jan.

Frantically, Jan looked up. Fabian had been unaffected by the rock slide and was climbing down faster than was safe for him, but he was still several metres above. Too high to be of any assistance.

When the demon who'd been talking raised his hand, all Jan could do was close his eyes and pray.

Lucille

Lucille had always wondered what kind of dwellings the demons lived in. It probably shouldn't have surprised her that in a world of caves, their homes would be massive caves as well. But these weren't the dark natural corridors of the Dûr Lôrac. The walls were polished obsidian with flickering lights that were somehow set inside the stone, giving it a translucent sheen. Lush plants with beautiful flowers were strategically placed along the walls, giving off the most sensual scent Lucille had ever smelled. She'd make a fortune if she could bottle it and sell it as perfume in Ashuan.

The floors were covered with a soft carpet that made her want to dig her bare toes in. Magic seemed to keep it clean—it looked immaculate. From time to time, she walked through silk-covered openings, the fabric caressing her shoulder like the touch of a lover. It was beautiful. The only thing she could've done without was the constant moaning from adjoining rooms. Lucille had never been to a brothel, but she imagined it'd be something like this.

From time to time, she snuck a peek at the envy demon they'd picked up. Alecia moved around the residence like a panther, confident and languorous. Her intricately braided hair was a similar honey tone to Chay's, while her skin was a warm bronze similar to Matt's, but her eyes... her eyes were unlike either of them, all jungle green, as if they were a reflection of her true home.

It made Lucille wonder. "What does a Devotee of Envy do?" With looks like that, Alecia certainly didn't have anything to be jealous of.

"I serve Pyke with my heart and soul." Her eyes twinkled as she glanced at Lucille. "Every archdemon has his highest-ranking servants. Melaney has her mate, Frennys. Hel has her admirers, Iyaga her treasurer, and Pyke has his devotees."

Lucille soaked up all the information about Hescaryn like a sponge. "I see, and what makes Pyke's First Devotee do such a lowly job as spying?" She would've thought a high-ranking servant would have better things to do.

Alecia grinned. "I was jealous of whoever got the job in the first place."

Lucille couldn't help but chuckle. There was something about Alecia or this residence that made her heart beat faster. It reminded her of the threesome she'd had with Philipp and his ex-girlfriend. *Melaney*, she decided. *It's Melaney's influence.*

"Pyke wants to know what Melaney is planning," Alecia explained, surprisingly open about her master. "He's afraid she's about to gain an unfair advantage."

"Oh." Lucille would've expected the other archdemons to be interested in what was going on in the Residence of Lust, but not for such base reasons. "It can't be easy with a master who's jealous of everyone and everything." If Pyke was anything like Melaney, he'd be a nightmare to work with. All archdemons would be.

Alecia shrugged. "Better than a mistress who keeps dragging you into her bed."

Lucille had never met a demon like Alecia, and it had taken her until now to figure out what made her so different: she'd never once tried to kill her. Lucille was sure Alecia could hold her own in a fight, but she didn't seem to have an aggressive nature. Perhaps envy demons were more tolerable—so long as they didn't get jealous.

She was about to laugh at her own thoughts when Alecia turned, pinned her against the plant-covered wall, and kissed her. Outraged, she was on the verge of pushing Alecia away, when she noticed a pair of guards hurrying down the corridor. Instead, Lucille closed her eyes and wrapped her arms around Alecia's neck, sinking into the kiss.

The scent of flowers hit her, making her head heavy and body hot. Her lips parted and Alecia's tongue slipped in without hesitation, eliciting a soft moan from Lucille. But as soon as she'd initiated it, Alecia broke it off. The guards were gone.

Still, she grinned at Lucille. "Not bad for a human."

"Not bad for a demon, either," Lucille countered, though in truth all her demon kisses had been absolutely spectacular. If only they were any good with relationships.

"Come on. The throne room is close."

But as they rounded the corner, Alecia pulled her back against the wall. Only this time, it wasn't to kiss her.

"What's wrong?" Lucille whispered.

"There are no guards outside the throne room." Alecia pointed ahead to a double door that was slightly ajar.

"That's good, isn't it?"

Alecia seemed reluctant to agree. "Let's find out."

Something wet was spreading under the doors. In the darkness, Lucille didn't recognise it until she was about to step into it. "Blood. That's blood."

Alecia was already at the door, peering in. "Someone's killing Melaney's people one by one. I think he's human." She swallowed, for the first time losing some of her cool. "A demon hunter."

Curious, Lucille pushed forward and peered into the room herself. One of the guards who'd passed them had just dropped to the floor, the wound in his stomach steaming. Five more bodies lay on the floor, all obviously dead.

In the middle of the room stood a familiar figure, though it took her a moment to recognise him, bloodied as he was. His left arm hung uselessly from his shoulder and his clothes were torn. In his right hand was a Torakh, like Samantha's, but he exchanged it for a pistol from his holster and aimed at Alecia.

"René?"

Matt's father's eyes widened as he recognised her. "Lucille? What the hell are you doing here?"

"We're here with Matt," she explained, moving slightly in front of Alecia to avoid further bloodshed. "He's worried about you."

"Please tell me he didn't come here."

Lucille frowned. "Of course he did. His mother kidnapped Samantha."

"That's terrible." For a moment, René seemed to come out of his daze, looking like the concerned father he was instead of a ruthless killer. But then his eyes glazed over again. "I'll take care of it when I find Melaney."

"Look, I don't mean to interrupt," Alecia said from behind her, "but we're about to have company. I reckon Melaney's entire guard is on its way here." She looked down at the blood at her feet. "Not surprising after this."

René sighed, looking tired. "I only have one bullet left." Still, he raised his arm again.

Alecia groaned softly, then grabbed Lucille's elbow and pulled her into the room. "I hope you can fight."

"I'm a witch."

"Good. Let's hope Melaney hasn't noticed your presence and blocked your magic."

Lucille inhaled sharply. Without her magic, she had nothing. She took a deep breath and cast her shield spell. To her great relief, it spread around her and the other two as they formed a small triangle with their backs together.

Alecia nodded appreciatively, then she watched the doors. There were two other exits from the room, but demons didn't need to use doors.

One by one, the guards appeared in the room. Alecia shot at the first, but the woman was prepared and raised her forearms. She was wearing dark leather armguards that seemed designed to block the demon energy. Instead, Alecia's shot hit the wall, splintering something.

The armguards didn't help when René shot her point-blank. He dropped the weapon and grabbed the Torakh again, twirling it once between his fingers. He looked like he was going to fight to the last breath—and fully expected to die.

Alecia was all lithe panther. As soon as two demons stepped forward, she leapt from the shield and onto the back of a much larger man. His neck snapped faster than Lucille could watch. She then used the body to shield herself from his partner's attack before returning fire.

Energy crackled across the shield, demanding Lucille's attention on the other side. "Globus Igneus!" She threw her trusty fireball into a demon's face, then followed it up with a second in his genitals. The man went down screaming.

They were doing surprisingly well.

Then seven more demons arrived.

Caspar

It was unclear to Caspar whether he was having sex with Melaney or fighting her. There were steamy kisses and painful bites, powerful punches and eager grunts, and so many scratches his entire skin felt as if it was on fire. He poured all his wrath into her, the anger he felt at being used by his old master, but also at the lack of action from the woman on top of him. All the pain of losing Jeyne.

Jeyne. He was doing this for her. He hadn't been able to save her all those centuries ago, but he could save her reincarnation, even if it meant letting her go.

The door on the right opened and Caspar hastily flipped Melaney over to block her view with his own body. Her nails raked across his chest, leaving bloody gashes, her eyes blazing with lust. Then suddenly her face fell. A second later, she shot energy through Caspar's shoulder and pushed him off the bed.

"Quick!" he heard his sister shout as he fell to the floor, writhing in pain.

The shot must've been aimed at her and Samantha, but it had shattered Caspar's shoulder on the way.

Panting, he looked up to see Samantha running for the door on the other side, but it slammed shut in front of her. She tried desperately to open it to no avail. As Melaney rose from the bed and made her way towards her, Menuha slipped in front of Samantha, ready to protect her with her life.

"A twin is rarely alone," Melaney said, her voice dangerously low. "I should've known you were planning something." She looked over her shoulder at Caspar and snorted at his bleeding shoulder. "Did you enjoy tricking me?"

Caspar ignored the pain and pulled on his pants. "Who's tricking who? A human as the new archdemon's mate?"

"She's not for you."

The words made Caspar grit his teeth harder than the wounded shoulder.

"I'm not for anyone," Samantha said shakily.

Melaney ignored Caspar and covered the rest of the distance between her and Menuha. Deceptively soft, she cupped Menuha's defiant face. "You and your exhausting passion for humans. When are you going to learn they're not worth it?"

"Please, Mother. Samantha doesn't belong here. She has nothing to do with us."

"Oh, but she likes it here. Isn't that true, my love?"

Samantha's eyes widened. She looked a mess. Her black curls were frizzy and knotted, a bruise darkened her right cheekbone, and a scabbed scratch ran from her chin to her collarbone. Dark shadows under her eyes suggested she hadn't gotten much sleep, let alone any real rest, despite having a bed at her disposal. But when Melaney looked at her, her cheeks flushed treacherously, and she lowered her eyes in shame.

Melaney smiled contentedly and turned her attention back to Menuha while Caspar nursed his shoulder wound, the healing process as painful as the injury itself. "Did Melchior put you up to this?"

"No, it was—"

"Me," Caspar said, not wanting Menuha to take all the blame.

Amused, Melaney turned to him. "You?"

It wasn't hard to lie. "Humans don't belong here. I would've killed her, but Menu... You know how she is."

Melaney raised an eyebrow. Before he could even blink, she'd jumped up behind Samantha, grabbed her hair, and dragged her screaming over to Caspar.

Menuha rushed forward in panic. "Mother, please."

Terrified, Caspar stared at Samantha as Melaney held her in front of him. His mother's nails must've been digging into her scalp. Her whole face contorted in pain, making Caspar's stomach turn.

"You want to kill her?" Melaney said, calling his bluff. "Go ahead, my dear. Do it!"

"Caspar, don't!" Menuha sounded frightened, knowing full well what he was capable of.

The look of desperation in Samantha's eyes almost destroyed him. She looked so much like Jeyne.

"Come on, darling, what are you waiting for? She's *human. Melchior's* beloved."

"Please," Samantha whispered, though Caspar couldn't tell whether she was begging him to have mercy or kill her.

Before he could make a decision, Melaney shoved her into Caspar's arms. "Kill her!"

He hesitated, then wrapped his arms around her protectively. Maybe he could just take her and escape.

"Please, Casp. Don't do it!" Menuha begged, tears streaming down her face. She was crying for a human, begging her twin, the *monster*, to reconsider.

Melaney snorted, disgust on her face. Then she turned away and Caspar almost sighed with relief. But Melaney wasn't done with them yet. Instead of retreating, she hauled Menuha to her and grabbed her throat, her long nails digging deep enough to draw blood.

"The human girl or your sister. It shouldn't be a hard choice, should it? Don't you love your sister?"

Menuha gasped in pain and Caspar stared at her helplessly. His grip on Samantha tightened, probably painfully, but the girl didn't make a sound. She probably thought she'd never leave this room alive. By all rights, Caspar should just kill her. She wasn't Jeyne, just some human girl he barely knew.

The moment Menuha's fear turned to confusion hurt Caspar physically. He loved his twin sister more than himself. She was his better half. His *much* better half. She was kind and curious. And she was smart, much smarter than anyone gave her credit for. He relied on her to guide him through this miserable life. He should've told her about Jeyne.

He was on the verge of a decision when Melaney made it for him. One minute, Menuha was alive. The next, blood splattered both Samantha's and Caspar's faces.

Caspar pushed Samantha aside to catch Menuha as she gargled, blood foaming around her mouth. "Why did you do that?" he cried in anguish, dropping to his knees.

Melaney looked down at him coldly. "She betrayed me."

"She…" He struggled to speak. "Menu."

His instincts kicked in. He lowered Menuha to the ground and held his hands over her throat, reaching into his healing powers. The pain was imminent. Menuha tried to speak, but only blood came from her lips. She raised her hand and weakly tried to push him away.

Caspar wouldn't let her. He would heal his sister even if it killed him. The wound beneath his fingers closed as his own throat opened. Somewhere behind him, Samantha screamed, but he didn't turn around. His whole focus was on his sister.

The wound in his neck widened and blood spilled onto his chest as he managed to close Menuha's. But when he looked into her face, her eyes were staring at the ceiling, her gaze broken. Her hand had fallen to the floor, and she was no longer moving.

Despite his pain, Caspar screamed his anger and agony into the world. Then he burst into tears.

Samantha

Samantha was dragged back to her room by her hair until she felt like her skin was being torn off. Melaney threw her on the floor next to the small table. Scared to death, Samantha crawled away from her.

"You sneaky little snake!" Melaney hissed, her voice so full of anger Samantha's entire body shook with fear. "My daughter is dead because of you."

"Because of me?" Samantha squealed in horror. "*You* killed her!"

The words caught in her throat as Melaney's face darkened and she quickly backed away until her back was against the wall.

"Is it not enough for you to corrupt one of my children?" Melaney asked, her eyes blazing. "Melchior wasn't enough for you. You had to turn my beloved twins against me as well."

Samantha was still in shock from what had happened. She'd been so afraid Caspar would kill her that it hadn't even occurred to her Menuha might be in danger. And then... Menuha's blood still covered her face and chest, mixing with the tears that wouldn't stop flowing. She doubted she'd ever forget those images.

"I didn't do anything," Samantha whimpered.

She let out a tiny sigh of relief when Melaney turned abruptly, but the archdemon just grabbed the pitcher of potion and made her way over to her. Samantha watched in horror, unable to move. Not that she could've run anywhere. Melaney grabbed her by the hair again and yanked her head backwards before pouring the potion down her throat.

No matter how much Samantha coughed or gargled, Melaney was unrelenting. The potion splashed all over her face, into her eyes, and down her shirt as much as it filled her mouth. Samantha tried to push it away but found herself drinking as much as she could at the same time.

Melaney didn't stop until the last drop was in her mouth. "You wanted to play with lust? Now play with it!" She let go of a sputtering Samantha and threw the jug against the wall, shattering it.

Samantha felt like she was on fire. It started in her face, ran down her throat, and spread from her stomach. Lust filled her against her will and her whole body shook as she gasped for breath.

"You turned his head," Melaney accused, a painstakingly beautiful goddess of vengeance.

"I didn't..." Samantha felt the urge to apologise, to say anything to ease the pressure of the archdemon's attention. "It wasn't planned."

She'd never pursued Matt. If anything, she'd pushed him away more than she'd drawn him in. She'd challenged him until he'd bent for her, but it hadn't been because she wanted his love. Love had simply blossomed between them. Not like a beautiful flower, but like a clinging weed that refused to die, no matter how hard she'd tried to pull it from the ground. It was undeniable. He was hers and she was his, but all that would change if Melaney got her way.

The archdemon wouldn't let them be together. She'd never intended Samantha to be more than a lure, a meaningless gift for her favoured son. She didn't care if she destroyed a human girl in the process. Caring wasn't something Melaney did. She only demanded, and when her demands weren't met, death waited in the wings of her passion.

"I never should've let him go to Ashuan," Melaney thought out loud. "He's too easily swayed. Too young to resist temptation." Her eyes narrowed. "You made him weak."

Samantha slowly calmed her breathing. The heat was still there, but the fear helped her keep her mind clear. "Having feelings is not a weakness."

It was the depth of his feelings, each painfully clawed from the indifference of demonkind, that Samantha loved so much about Matt. He'd fought for love. Not just hers, but his own capacity. He'd chosen to fall when he could've turned his back on her.

"He's my mate, not yours," Melaney hissed, as she grabbed Samantha's elbow and pulled her back to her feet.

Swallowing, Samantha tried to digest what Melaney had just said. "Your *mate?*" She quickly put together everything Melaney and Frennys had told her about the unique relationship between the Archdemon of Lust and her mate. "I thought you were planning to bestow your powers on him."

Melaney laughed, her eyes sparkling. "They all thought so. Who would do such a thing? Why would I give up all this?"

She showed off her body, looking glorious as always. It made Samantha hyper-conscious of the rat's nest of hair on her head and every smear of blood, tears, and potion on her face. Where the archdemon was tousled perfection, Samantha was—and looked—a mess.

"Did you think I'd let you have him after all you've put me through?" Melaney asked. "No, my love. You're not worthy of someone like him." She placed her hand on Samantha's cheek, making her tremble with pleasure against her will.

Melaney enjoyed watching her squirm. "He *will* come to me. You'll lead him to me. And then I'll take what's mine and get rid of you."

Matt

If he had to choose between fighting his mother or sleeping with her, Matt would go for the killing blow. It didn't matter that he'd made a promise to her. She'd broken the agreement when she'd taken Samantha and exposed her to every horror demons could possibly conceive of and more. Sex had never really been an option. Not since he'd set foot in Ashuan.

What he did today would define him for the rest of his life, but he didn't care if it broke him, so long as Samantha was safe again. Although he'd visited the residence regularly over the past two years, Matt felt uncharacteristically self-conscious. Rachel followed him in silence, never once commenting or judging, but Matt noticed it all for the first time. The depraved pictures, the statues that left nothing to one's imagination, the lush flowers of lust and their aphrodisiac scent. And the beds. So many beds. Not that his mother needed a bed to live out her sin.

When he remembered his own upbringing and the things he'd done within the shiny black walls, Matt felt as if it was a memory from a previous life. Back when he'd only indulged his demon side and ignored the needs of his human heart.

As they walked down the corridor leading to Melaney's most private rooms—the ones with highest security—Matt felt as if Rachel was silently judging him for everything he'd ever done. Only at Melaney's door did it occur to him that it was *him* who was doing the judging. He who didn't feel as comfortable with the sin of lust as he once had.

"This is it," Matt told Rachel, so she could brace herself. Then he pushed the door open. "I'm here."

But the room was empty—and quite messy. It wasn't unusual to see blood in the bedrooms, but rarely this much. "Melaney?"

He took a step into the room when suddenly Caspar jumped out of nowhere, grabbed him by the collar and slammed him into the door frame, causing Rachel to squeal and retreat.

"Bastard!" Caspar growled. As so often, he was covered in blood. From the looks of it, someone had tried to slit his throat and lost their life in the process.

"What are you doing in here?" Matt asked as he tried to free himself from his grip.

"I could ask you the same thing." Spittle hit Matt in the face. "Did you come to take what was thrown at your feet?"

Matt grunted, still trying to keep Caspar's fingers from wrapping around his throat. "I don't quite follow you."

"I'm older than you. More experienced. Stronger." Each sentence was punctuated by another slam against the door.

Finally, Matt managed to free himself and ducked into the room, drawing his sword. "Good, we cleared that up. I'm here for Sam, not you. Melaney took her."

Caspar sneered at him. "Oh, I know." He laughed, but it sounded all wrong, hollow and metallic. "She's a gift to you. Because you get everything. The power, the lust, and Jeyne."

Matt's eyes widened as he heard the name he'd never forget. The reason for Caspar's unquenchable hatred of humans. "Jeyne? Your Jeyne?"

"My Jeyne," Caspar repeated with a grimace. "Your Samantha."

"What?"

The pieces fell into place quickly. The time between death and rebirth was about five centuries. Caspar had lost the only woman he'd ever loved five hundred years ago. He'd healed Samantha without even so much as a question. He hadn't even tried to kill her when they'd been alone. Anne had said she'd thought he cared about her.

Jeyne. Samantha. Two girls. One soul.

"Who's Jeyne?" Rachel asked, but the brothers ignored her.

Caspar wouldn't quite meet his eyes. Matt had seen him angry before. He'd been on the receiving end of his brother's wrath and hatred and had always thought the older one was deranged. As it turned out, he'd never really known what deranged looked like.

"Melaney's drenching her in lust. Half the residence has already had the pleasure," Caspar hissed.

Matt's hand tightened around the hilt of his sword. Samantha had been in his mother's realm for two days and Melaney was turning her to lust. If Caspar was right... Heat filled his chest.

His brother nodded, a ghastly grin spreading across his face. "Don't you dare think I'll let you have her without a fight."

Even though he didn't want to hear the answer, Matt forced himself to ask. "Did you...?"

"Have sex with her?" Caspar laughed that false, gruelling laugh again. "Oh, yes. Many times."

"I'm going to kill you." Matt felt in his soul that he'd never spoken truer words.

Caspar gritted his teeth and growled at him. "No, I'm going to kill *you*. And when I'm done with you, I'm going to take her again, right down in—"

"Matt, don't!" Rachel cried from somewhere deeper in the room. "He—"

But Matt didn't care what either of them had to say. A fire roared in his soul, and he lunged at Caspar, swinging his sword. There would be no truce this time, no escape. He would kill his brother or die trying.

Fabian

Fabian swallowed hard. There was no time to fret, no time to worry. If he didn't move now, Jan would be dead. Holding onto the rock with one hand, he shot a thin but incredibly hard jet of water at the demon who'd raised his hand. The water hit him in the shoulder and pushed him over the edge.

Not waiting to see what happened next, Fabian scrambled down the cliff face, then dropped the last two metres, a decision that probably saved his life as energy hit the rock above him, causing more to slide down. A few pebbles hit Fabian's head, but he landed softly next to Jan, who groaned in pain, his leg still trapped under the rubble.

The two remaining demons hissed at him and Fabian growled back. "Did you think we'd just wait for you to slaughter us?"

Unfortunately, the last demon who was still on the top of the cliff chose that moment to jump onto Fabian's back, sending them crashing into the terrace. Pain shot up Fabian's arm, but he twisted just enough to grab the demon as they rolled to the edge of the cliff. For a brief moment, Fabian stared into the abyss, then he was on top of the demon, draining all the water from him, just as he'd done to the demon who'd ambushed him at the Magic Circle. When the demon was nothing but a dry husk of bone and papery skin, he threw him over the edge.

"Woah!" he heard Jan say, then, "Careful!"

Another demon lunged at him. Fabian shot water into his eyes, then a second hard stream into his stomach, sending him crashing into the wall, where he collapsed and coughed up bile. Mercilessly, he sent a third stream, knocking his head back. There was an ugly crack and no more coughing.

Fabian ducked under a burst of energy from the last remaining demon, almost threw himself down the cliff, and scrambled to his feet. His adrenaline peaked and he channelled all his anger, fear, and frustration into a vortex of water. Just then, the first demon reappeared, but the water caught him and sent him crashing into his companion. Relentlessly, the water spun them around and threw them into the depths, leaving them unable to escape.

Suddenly there was silence. Nothing moved except Fabian's heaving chest. No demons attacked. The adrenaline dropped and Fabian's knees buckled. He hit the ground hard, but managed to drag himself over to Jan, suddenly dizzy. Exhausted, he sat beside him and leaned against the wall.

In a minute, he'd help Jan out of his predicament, but for now he needed to breathe.

"That was amazing!" Jan gushed, so excited he'd forgotten all about his pain. "Honestly, you were—"

Something sharp hit Fabian in the chest. His gaze dropped abruptly. A thin sliver of energy flared where his heart was. Then he doubled over.

Rachel

No nightmare could've prepared Rachel for this sight. While Caspar had distracted Matt, Rachel had crept across the room to the opposite door. It was there that she'd stumbled upon Menuha. Blocked by Melaney's huge bed, Matt hadn't seen his dead sister, Caspar's twin. It had been immediately clear to Rachel that Caspar had been driven mad by grief, but before she could stop them, Matt, spurred on by Caspar's taunts, had lost his mind and thrown himself at his older brother.

Now, Rachel crouched low behind the bed as they fought, fearing for her life. Everyone's lives, really. She'd never seen Matt like this before. It was as if he'd been freed from the shackles that usually held him in check. He was untouchable as he leapt and spun, shooting energy and wielding his deadly sword. As Caspar roared and unleashed a barrage of black magic, Matt easily deflected the shots, sending them flying through the air.

Rachel ducked as one of the stray bolts flew over her head, taking out a bedside table. In a matter of minutes, the brothers had destroyed most of the furniture, and they weren't letting up.

The door Rachel had been about to go through opened and she saw Balthasar peering curiously into the room. A stray burst of energy made him retreat quickly.

Nervously, Rachel raised her head to see what was happening. Matt was being kicked in the gut, but he barely slowed as he continued his relentless attack on Caspar. Rachel swallowed, wondering if this was what he'd been like on his Blood Night, when his demon powers had been fully awakened. If so, it was absolutely terrifying.

On the other side, Caspar seemed to be losing his edge. Each move was a little slower than the one before. He was hit by energy and took a cut to his arm, but it was the other arm, his left, he seemed to be protecting. Despite the blood on his shoulder, Rachel hadn't seen him being attacked there.

A few more energy bolts hit too close for her liking, and she quickly dropped to the ground, covering her head with her hands and wishing she could wake up from this nightmare. She had a life to live. Adam was waiting back in Ashuan, and she'd be damned if she was going to die here before she could take a chance on him.

Suddenly, there was a pause in the constant bursts of energy and splintering furniture. All she could hear was heavy breathing and wet gurgling.

Fearing for Matt, Rachel's head shot up. But it wasn't her friend with blood dripping from his mouth. Matt's sword was buried to the hilt in Caspar's gut. The demon staggered. He tried to grab Matt's shoulder, whether to attack or hold onto him, Rachel couldn't tell. Meanwhile, Matt was frozen, as if he'd never realised that swinging a sword at people could kill them.

Only when he heard Caspar's death rattle did Matt break free. In a panic, he pulled the sword from his brother's body and threw it aside, as if he couldn't bear to touch it any longer.

Caspar grimaced and stumbled backwards. He hit the only remaining bedpost and clutched at the wood. Gaze on Matt, he fled, dragging himself towards Rachel. At first, she was startled, but then she realised it wasn't her he was after. Caspar dropped to his knees, blood dripping from his mouth. His eyes rolled, but he pulled himself up and staggered forward into the wall next to Menuha. He turned and slid down, leaving a wide trail of blood on the wall.

He was so pale Rachel wondered how he was holding on, but he kept going until his hand found Menuha's body. Only then did he relax, his head sinking back in relief.

A whimper escaped Rachel's lips and tears filled her eyes. This was horrible, so much worse than any nightmare she'd ever had.

"Caspar?" Matt had followed him, finally seeing what had been obscured by the bed and then by his fighting frenzy.

Despite the blood running from his mouth and the difficulty of breathing, Caspar managed to whisper. "I didn't... Sam..."

"You lied." Matt swallowed hard as Rachel gasped. "You son of a bitch!" Tears ran down his face, leaving bright streaks in the grime left by the battle.

Caspar, however, smiled. "She's yours... your Jeyne."

Then his eyes glazed over, and the smile faded, until only the grimace of pain remained. With a last sigh and his hand on Menuha's cheek, Caspar died.

Rachel didn't dare speak. She didn't know if she'd ever find words again. Caspar had meant nothing to her. He'd been a brute and would've killed her if he'd ever gotten his hands on her. But she felt for Matt, who looked crushed by guilt and heartbreak.

She had no idea what this Jeyne business was about, but it seemed to be something that bound the brothers together, a hidden secret that had bridged a lifetime of animosity. A secret linked to Samantha.

It occurred to Rachel now that Caspar had wanted to die. Either that or finally kill Matt, whom he'd blamed for all his misfortunes. He'd provoked this fight by saying exactly what Matt needed to hear to lose all reason and stop holding back. An all-out battle between the two that would leave only one.

And now the demon she'd feared most for his unpredictable and violent behaviour was dead. To Rachel's surprise, she felt sorry for him. There wasn't much to like about Caspar, but he'd been Menuha's twin, and from the looks of it, he hadn't been able to imagine a life without her.

She'd felt the same way when Nico had died. Suddenly it was him Rachel saw, and her stomach lurched. She bent over and threw up next to the dead demons. Her mind was spinning, mixing Menuha and Caspar with Nico and herself, and she felt way in over her head.

What were they thinking, picking a fight with demons? How could they ever think they'd make it out alive when not even demons could survive this hell?

A hand fell on her shoulder when she brought up nothing more than bile. Ashamed, Rachel wiped her mouth. With Matt's help, she stood. She still had no words and, from the looks of it, neither did he.

He searched her gaze just long enough to make sure she was with him, then he left and she followed.

Even when they left the room behind them, the dread didn't go away. Matt was deathly pale, putting one foot in front of the other, neither willing nor able to speak. Rachel dragged her feet beside him, feeling just as exhausted.

Time lost all meaning, and all the corridors looked the same. Here and there, a demon poked their head out of a room, but a glance at Matt made them reconsider quickly. No one stopped them as they trudged through the residence. Not until they came across Melaney and an unfamiliar man.

Panicking, Rachel took a step back. Melaney was the last person she'd wanted to see.

But Matt just lifted his head and looked at his mother like a lost puppy. To Rachel's surprise, Melaney's face softened. "Melchior."

"Don't..." Matt whispered.

He tried to back away, but Melaney quickly closed the distance and pulled him to her. As she stroked his head and back, Matt gave in and sank against her shoulder, sobbing.

Rachel was about to speak, not trusting the archdemon to be a caring mother who'd take good care of her grieving son, but just as she opened her mouth, Melaney's male companion stepped forward, covered her mouth and dragged her through the cold, slimy existence that was the abstract space.

Lucille

"Scutum Protecto."

The blue shield wrapped around Lucille once more. Five others had already been torn to shreds by the demons in the room. Instead of using Alecia and René for cover, Lucille retreated to the wall behind her, keeping an eye on the action.

Alecia was a fierce fighter, taking on two demons at once. She'd unfurled her bat-like wings, using them more as weapons than shields. Her speed and agility saved her time after time against the bigger, stronger demons.

On the other side, René seemed to be holding his own. He was stabbing a demon when a burst of energy hit his knee from behind. His leg buckled, which was a lifesaver as the demon he'd been fighting grabbed the thin air above him. As she reached for him again, he swung his arm and slashed her throat with the Torakh.

Meanwhile, Lucille was under constant attack, concentrating on replacing her shield as soon as it wavered. While it gave her some time to breathe, it prevented her from casting many other spells, and each time the shields lasted a little less. She couldn't rely on Alecia and René to take out the demons much longer.

There was one spell she'd always wanted to try. It was one her friends would've called "reckless", which meant it was perfect for this situation.

Grabbing her amulet for support, she read the incantation from her phone's list. "Vrelgi pestra isobrazsi se!"

The ground liquefied in front of her. One demon managed to jump out, but three others were trapped in the quicksand, sinking deeper and deeper. Lucille had no idea where they'd end up. Perhaps they'd become one with the stone at their feet forever or they'd end up in another dimension. For her sake, she hoped it was the latter, as horrible as it sounded.

The sinking was slow, and the demons multiplied their efforts to tear down her shield, hoping the spell would end if she died before them.

"Scutum Protecto!" she screamed, ducking for safety, nevertheless.

Just then, René stumbled onto the quicksand.

"Vrelgi pestra ustafi se!" The ground solidified instantly, making it impenetrable for the half-submerged demons and a tripping hazard for René, who crashed to the ground, at the end of his strength.

Lucille was breathing heavily. Some of the demons had been sucked in too deep to do any damage, but two were still shooting at her, even though the stone was crushing their insides. Once more, Lucille raised her shield. The last one couldn't have lasted more than a minute.

René was still on the ground, motionless, when another demon jumped on him.

"Sageat negru distrugere!" The arrow of black magic tore from her hands and slammed into the demon, gutting him instantly.

Someone appeared out of nowhere and grabbed her from behind, holding her in a chokehold as they shoved a hand into her back. Lucille screamed. The black arrow must've destroyed her shield prematurely. The new spell was on her lips, but she never got the words out in time.

Suddenly there was a loud snap, and the grip loosened. The demon sank to the ground, their neck broken by Alecia, who was sporting a freshly torn wing.

Lucille stared at her in surprise. They were allies only out of necessity, and yet the envy demon had come to her aid. At the cost of her own body.

"Thank you."

"Don't men—" Alecia's eyes widened as the opponent she'd left behind raised her hand and pointed at them.

The energy burst from her fingers and Alecia threw herself at Lucille, knocking them both down.

"Scutum..." Lucille struggled to breathe, pain flaring in her elbows and hips as she landed hard on the floor. "Scutum..."

"It's over," Alecia whispered in awe.

Surprised, Lucille looked to the side. The demon who'd attacked her was lying on her stomach, René on top of her. Although his hands were clasped around the steaming Torakh, he'd lost consciousness.

"René!" With no other demon besides Alecia still alive, Lucille scrambled to her feet and ran to Matt's father.

His eyelids fluttered and his breathing was shallow, but his lips kept forming one word like a prayer: "Melaney."

Jan

Jan was exhausted. He was leaning against the rock face, his broken leg stretched in front of him, looking as ghastly as it felt. He'd freed himself after Fabian had fallen, probably doing more damage to the limb in the process. Now, his friend's head lay on his lap where he'd dragged him, eyes closed and deathly pale.

There was nothing Jan could do but wait. He'd tried his best to heal Fabian, but the pain in his leg had been too much. The wound had missed the heart by a hair's breadth, but that didn't mean it hadn't done any damage.

A long time ago, Matt had told him never to try to heal fatal wounds and, as so often, Jan had ignored the advice. After pushing himself to the brink of collapse, he wouldn't have been able to go anywhere, even if his leg hadn't been broken. And as for Fabian... He looked at the small scar just below his heart. There was still no telling if Fabian would ever wake up from this.

Occasionally, Jan checked his pulse and dabbed at his forehead, but otherwise he waited. He was thirsty, his stomach was rumbling, and his leg wouldn't stop throbbing. If Fabian died here, so would he.

At least there were no demons. The demon who'd shot Fabian had done so on his last breath, while the other three lay somewhere far below, smashed to pieces. Jan had known his friend was powerful, but he'd never seen him fight like that. He didn't just control the water—he *was* the water.

In his mind, Jan replayed how Fabian had sucked the water out of the demon he'd been wrestling. Just like humans, demons were sixty per cent water, and that demon had been dead in seconds. And the vortex that had sent the other two plummeting to the bottom of the cave? Jan was still in awe. It would be a shame if it had all been for nothing.

His mind drifted in and out of sleep with vivid dreams of his friends' fate. Somewhere, Samantha was completely at Melaney's mercy. And somewhere else, Anne was lost in Hell, with nothing but her newfound faith to protect her. He didn't need a nightmare to tell him Anne had almost no chance of survival if she'd ended up alone in Lucin.

The red glow around him had faded slightly as Fabian's eyelids fluttered. When he finally opened his eyes, Jan began to laugh and cry at the same time. He was alive! Fabian was alive.

"Have a nice nap?"

"Nap?" Confused, Fabian blinked. "What... what happened?" He tried to raise his head but was immediately punished by the pain in his chest.

Jan put a soothing hand on his shoulder. "Take it easy. I could only do a quick and sloppy repair. I just couldn't stand the pain any longer. It was as if my own heart had been pierced."

"Heart?" Fabian's eyes widened. "You healed me. The demons..." He looked sideways in panic.

"They're all dead. Thanks to you. Unfortunately, one of them managed a last shot before he bit the gravel."

Fabian rubbed his chest just above the wound and grimaced. "Typical."

"Typical?" Jan laughed, feeling like he was going to lose it. "Man, you killed four demons all by yourself. You *destroyed* them!" He snorted. "All while I sat here, able to do nothing but watch."

A faint smile appeared on Fabian's face. "Looks like you've already returned the favour."

"Possibly. But honestly." Jan shook his head, still very much in awe. "Unfortunately, we're pretty screwed now. My leg's broken, and you need at least one more proper healing session before you can even think about getting up. This rescue mission was a total bust, if you ask me."

To his horror, Fabian rolled onto his side, grunting and groaning.

"Hey, what do you think you're doing?"

Unable to watch him struggle, Jan grabbed him by the shoulders and helped him into an upright position. The strain on his leg made him hiss, but the effort was nothing compared to what it must've cost Fabian. He leaned against the wall next to Jan, his head thrown back, breathing as if he'd just run a four hundred metre sprint.

Panting, Fabian whispered, "We've got to save Sam."

"Geez! I got it. You're not helping her by dying out here, so pace yourself, hero."

There was no reply from Fabian. When Jan looked at him, he was asleep again.

Snorting softly, he shifted until he was comfortable, with Fabian's head on his shoulder. He tried to keep his eyes open to look out for demons but found himself dozing off next to his friend.

Balthasar

Back in his rooms, Balthasar stared at the sword on his table. He'd never needed a weapon other than his own body and mind, so he was hardly an expert, but apart from the fact that it looked particularly fancy, he couldn't see what made this sword different from any other. It had a hilt and a blade, and a clear-looking sphere at the end of the hilt that looked fragile but was anything but. Runes covered both the silver blade and blue stone hilt. Stone, not metal. Perhaps that was its secret. Balthasar had never seen such material before. Certainly not on a sword.

Once again, he was no expert, and when Chay told him this was the sword that'd kill Melaney, he had to take his word for it.

In a surprising turn of events, he hadn't even had to trade Samantha for the weapon. Idiot that he was, Melchior had thrown it away after successfully doing what he should've done years ago. It didn't matter to Balthasar that two of his siblings had already died today. In Caspar's case, it was good riddance. The younger one had always been unpredictable, but lately he'd become unreliable, too. Balthasar had no use for a broken tool. As for Menuha, her loyalties had rarely aligned with his own.

Now Melchior, however, there was a formidable opponent. Not in terms of wit, but after seeing him fight without any reservations, Balthasar wasn't too sure he could handle him in a direct confrontation. Fortunately, he didn't have to. All Melchior wanted was his girl and to be left alone. Balthasar was confident they could come to an arrangement once he'd taken Melaney's power.

The door opened and a messenger from the Council entered. Bored, Balthasar turned to him.

"The Small Council requests your presence."

"What for?"

The messenger swallowed, barely able to hold his gaze. "There's been an outbreak of fighting. The Red Blade is attempting a coup."

The Red Blade, one of the larger factions in the Council, always attempted coups.

"Not interested."

"But you haven't shown your face for days!"

Balthasar rolled his eyes. He had no patience for idiots. "You seem a bit behind the times. Where am I?"

Confused, the messenger looked around. "The Residence of Lust?"

"Amazing," Balthasar said sarcastically. "What am I doing here?"

The messenger's eyes fell on the sword on the table, but he wisely stuck to a more general answer. "You're preparing to ascend to become the new Archdemon of Lust."

"Incredible! You're really clever, aren't you? Last question. Will I still have time for the Small Council once I'm Archdemon of Lust?"

It finally clicked for the messenger, and he lowered his gaze. "No, you'd be busy with the Council of Seven."

Balthasar was more going for "running the Council of Seven", but he took it. "See, that wasn't so hard, after all. The Small Council should look for someone else if they don't want the Red Blade to take over."

The messenger nodded, but idiot that he was, he didn't leave it at that. "What if you're unsuccessful?"

Balthasar gave him a well-rehearsed glare that made the young demon fidget, caught between wanting to retreat and fulfilling his mission.

"I suppose there's a bonus question: will I be successful?"

"Yes!"

The answer came so quickly it made Balthasar smile. "Good for you. Some brain activity at last. You're dismissed."

The messenger bowed deeply, then made a quick retreat. Balthasar turned back to his sword. He hated having to use such a crude weapon, especially after seeing the mess it had made of Caspar, but it wouldn't cut off Melaney's head just lying there. With a sigh, he picked it up and stepped out.

He was about to head for the throne room when he noticed the runes glowing in the corridor. Something had triggered a lockdown. Caspar's death, perhaps.

Annoyed, he went back to his rooms. Two or three centuries ago, he'd paid a couple of mages a lot of money to build a direct link from his rooms to Melaney's private realm, bypassing the security measures. He activated them in his bedroom and watched as the stone slid open.

The tunnel was short and ended at another wall. He listened with the help of one of the runes but couldn't hear anything in the corridor beyond. When the stone opened on this side, Balthasar had to move one of the flowers out of the way. He'd planted it himself to cover the single rune that would allow him to escape quickly. Anyone but him would be trapped in the wall, but it was a neat little shortcut.

Once in Melaney's private tunnels, he listened for his mother. Usually, he could hear her a mile away, but not this time. Instead, he came upon an unfamiliar door with a strange rune on it.

With growing suspicion, Balthasar opened the door and snorted. It was one of Melaney's many bedrooms—one of the gaudier ones. He preferred a more subdued atmosphere for his sexual adventures, but the pictures on the wall were certainly inspiring. He wasn't at all surprised to find a feral-looking Samantha fast asleep on the bed. Whatever had happened in this room hadn't been pretty.

As he entered, he noticed a table near the door with nothing on it but fruit and a pitcher of water. A sweet smell reached his nose. Not water, then. Balthasar leaned the sword against the wall, scooped up the jug and took a closer sniff. As soon as the unmistakable notes of the flowers outside reached his nose, he gagged. Nectar from the flowers of lust was like poison. It made anyone not just willing but *wanton* with lust.

He glanced over at Samantha, wondering how much she'd already ingested, then tipped the jug in the corner and set it down again. There wouldn't be any of that when he became archdemon.

Balthasar walked over to the bed and looked down at the girl. She was writhing and moaning in her sleep, caught up in dreams that were undoubtedly erotic in nature. But for all the lust coursing through her veins, she looked like shit. And that was a positive statement. Her hair was a mess and sticky with dried blood. Her body was covered in bruises and scratches, while her face was covered in even more blood and dirt. He suddenly wished for a huge basin of water to pour on her.

Instead, he leaned against the bedpost and said, "Hey."

Samantha almost immediately snapped out of her fitful sleep. She looked around wildly, then gasped as she recognised Balthasar. "You."

"Me."

"Are you here to... Are you...?"

"To do what?"

Ashamed, she lowered her eyes. "Teach me the art of lust?"

The thought amused Balthasar. Nothing about Samantha had ever inspired lust in him. Melaney was kidding herself if she thought Samantha would keep her entertained for long. Then again, she had both Melchior and Caspar lusting after her for some reason.

"Is that why she gave you the potion?"

"The potion!" Samantha jumped up and ran for the jug, only to find it empty. "Where is it?"

Balthasar watched her frantic movements from the bed. "I got rid of it."

"You can't."

"You'd be surprised what I can do when I set my mind to it," Balthasar replied amusedly.

Samantha paused, then cocked her head to look at him more closely. "If you're not here to further my education, then why are you here?"

"I'm bored." Far from it, but he was not about to discuss his plans with a potion-drunk human.

Something in her eyes was anything but human. "In that case, I know something to pass the time."

Balthasar's eyebrows crept up. "Seriously?"

She gave him a wicked smile, the kind Balthasar would never have believed her capable of. "You got something better to do?" Slowly, she walked back to him.

Even though she looked a mess, Balthasar felt a small twitch for the first time in her presence. "Is this what you really want?"

Samantha made it back to him. She didn't even hesitate before wrapping one arm around his neck and placing the other hand on his chest. Coyly, she batted her eyelashes at him. "Don't you?"

For a moment, Balthasar was tempted, but then he remembered why she was trying to seduce him. "No, thanks. I prefer my lovers willing."

"I'm very willing."

This was bad. Under other circumstances, Balthasar would've taken her up on her offer, just to see what all the fuss was about, but when she looked as if she'd not only been drugged but tortured, and with Melchior ready to put his money where his mouth was, butchering his way through the residence, there was no way he was going to touch her.

"You look like shit."

Her arm dropped, and for a moment, she looked as if she was about to cry, the real her peeking through.

Balthasar sighed. "Wait here."

It took him only a minute to find the nearest washroom and return with a basin of water. Not surprisingly, the first thing Samantha did was drink from it.

"You were supposed to wash."

Tentatively, Samantha took the sponge and instead of wringing it out over the basin, she squeezed it over her cleavage. "Like this?"

The water would have made the top transparent if it hadn't been soaked in blood. Still, the gesture had the desired effect.

"Give me that."

Impatiently, Balthasar snatched the sponge from her hands and almost slapped it in her face. Part of him wondered why he didn't just take advantage of her while she was throwing herself at him. But then Chay's face appeared before him, and he groaned. Half-demons and their stupid morals.

As Samantha squirmed beneath him, Balthasar washed her face, leaving her barely enough air to breathe. Slowly, her normal skin tone began to show through, leaving only the scratches and bruises that hadn't yet healed. The water was a brown-red by the time he was done.

Despite his manhandling, Samantha kept trying to touch him, until Balthasar had enough. He grabbed her thighs and threw her onto the bed. To death with Chay and his impractical morals.

With his full weight between her legs, he asked again. "Are you sure you want this?"

She wrapped her legs around him and dug her fingers into his shoulders.

Balthasar shuddered. "Your wish is my command." He kissed her neck and watched as she closed her eyes. "Let's find out if you're worth all the fuss Melchior's making about you."

Her eyes flew open. "Matt!" In an instant, her legs dropped, and she pushed him away.

Groaning, Balthasar retreated. "Really? All I had to do was say his name and... Oh, no."

The damn girl had started to cry. Humans were so annoying.

"I... I don't want this." She hiccupped, frantically wiping tears from her cheeks. "I don't want to be like you. I... I want to go home."

Frustrated, he made a sweeping gesture to the left. "Then go. The door is wide open."

Samantha stopped sobbing long enough to look at the gaping hole. "What if she finds me?" Suddenly she was clinging to his chest again. "You could take me home."

"And why on Hescaryn would I do that?" He wasn't in the business of saving pathetic little witches.

"Please."

Balthasar tore her hands from his tunic and dropped her back onto the bed. "If I'm going to fight my mother, it'll be on my terms."

"She's not looking for a successor."

The words made him stop. "What did you say?"

Samantha sat on the bed and swallowed hard. "Melaney is looking for a replacement for Frennys, not for herself."

Balthasar snorted. He'd known his mother wasn't really interested in stepping down. All his contacts in the other houses had told him their archdemons had no idea about this apparent decree. The only reason Balthasar hadn't made his move yet was that he hadn't quite figured out what her real plan was. Something to do with Melchior, he'd guessed. A ruse to get him home. But to take him as her mate?

"Oh, no. I'm not interested in that. I'm tired of lying under her. This time, I'll come out on top."

"She wants Matt," Samantha said, as if he cared.

"If that makes her happy. I'll claim the sin of Lust. Alone." He walked to the door, ready to finally do what had to be done.

Behind him, Samantha whimpered. "Balthasar, please! I know I'm only human and far beneath your attention, but I need your help. She killed Menuha."

So that was how Menuha had died. "Too bad. I liked her."

Samantha was shaken by sobs, a terrible sound at his back. Balthasar was about to leave when he remembered his conversation with Chay.

"The way to Melaney is through Melchior. Only the Sword of Amain will separate her pretty head from her no-less tempting body."

"And the way to Melchior is through Samantha? So, I have to save her from the big bad lust demons?"

"If you want to be archdemon."

He already had the sword, but Chay's prophecies never lied. It wasn't just the sword he needed but Samantha as well.

Sighing, Balthasar turned around. "Fine. But we have to get that potion out of your body or I'm not going anywhere with you."

Rachel

If Rachel hadn't been in panic mode when Melaney's companion had dragged her through the abstract space, she definitely was now as they stumbled into another bedroom. He let go of her and Rachel spun around in panic.

"Where are we...?" Her eyes fell on the painfully beautiful man in front of her. "Who the hell are you anyway?"

The man snorted. "Who the hell? You humans used to be more creative with your curses."

"I'll be prepared next time."

"There won't be a next time."

Rachel swallowed, suddenly aware of how little she'd be able to do if this demon decided to end her life.

But instead of attacking her, he spat on the floor. "Melaney gets what Melaney wants, and I will die."

She frowned. "Am I supposed to understand that?" He seemed a little lost, hurt, perhaps.

"No. You and I just need to get out of the way."

Out of the way of Melaney and Matt. The prospect didn't bode well for anyone's survival. Maybe if she could somehow use this guy's disappointment against Melaney.

"Does that mean you're not going to kill me?"

"I never said that, but first..." His hands flew to his belt. "Let me enjoy lust one last time. If I have to die, I want to do it inside of someone."

"Oh, no! You're not..."

But Frennys had grabbed her and thrown her onto the bed. He dropped his pants to his feet and pulled his tunic over his head.

Rachel froze as the naked demon advanced on her. A voice in her head told her to run, fight, or at least scream, but all she could do was sit there and wait for him to have his way with her.

Suddenly the demon staggered. He clutched at his chest, eyes wide with fear. He turned, but there was no one behind him. Rachel watched with bated breath as he stumbled towards the door, only to collapse on the way. He looked cold, shivering like a pile of jelly. Then the shivering stopped, and his limbs fell flat on the floor, his eyes staring blindly at the ceiling.

A moment later, a ghostly figure rose from his chest. Rachel laughed as she recognised Hugo.

"Miss Rachel," he said, worriedly. "Did that scoundrel touch you?"

She shook her head. "You came just in time."

Slowly the shock wore off as she realised just how close she'd come to a terrible fate. Anger replaced fear and she stood up to look at the demon's body. Hugo had stopped his heart just by stepping into him. He hadn't even known what had killed him so quickly.

"That was scary," she said to Hugo.

"I've never killed before," he confessed.

Rachel shrugged coldly. "Don't worry about that one. He was planning to die, anyway."

Though why, Rachel didn't know.

Matt

"You've finally come to honour your promise," Melaney purred in Matt's ear.

Matt barely heard what she'd said, let alone understood it. "I killed him."

Melaney sighed. "Who?" She didn't sound very interested.

"Caspar. He's dead."

"Oh, good. That saves me having to kill him later."

Melaney pulled him close, but Matt shook his head. "He wanted to die."

Hot, searing rage had made it impossible for Matt to see through Caspar's ruse until he'd buried his sword in his belly. The thought of Caspar—anyone—touching Samantha had made him lose his mind, and then it had been his Blood Night all over again. And just like then, it had ended in a catastrophic death.

Melaney shrugged. "Sounds like he got what he wanted, then."

Matt stared at his hands, still covered in his brother's blood. Red, just like his. "His blood is on my hands."

"Then wash them!"

He'd never liked Caspar. His worst memories were of his older brother, but lately... Seeing what had made Caspar a monster had changed Matt's whole perspective. Suddenly, he felt sorry for him, and it was almost as if they'd come to some kind of understanding, a common ground they could both stand on. Or maybe that was just Matt's half-demon desires.

Ever since he'd unearthed his memories and spent time in the Dark Cells, Caspar had changed. He hadn't been kind or anything, but if he had been a monster before, he'd been a lot more bark than bite after. Matt should've realised that, but his childhood experiences had made him unable to see through the anger until it was too late.

And now his brother, the only one who might have understood what it was like to be a demon in love—much to Matt's surprise—was dead.

A tear ran down Matt's cheek as he remembered Caspar's last words. How he had passed *his* Jeyne on to him. The love of his life to the brother he hated with all his heart. Fate was cruel to make Jeyne and Samantha the same person.

"Oh, come here." Melaney pulled him into her arms and rubbed his back. "You were always the most sensitive of my children."

He threw himself into his mother's arms and cried into her shoulder. Melaney continued to rub his back until her hands reached his sides. Slowly she unfastened the buckles of his leather breastplate one by one. As she pulled it over his head, along with the dark linen shirt underneath, Matt stumbled backwards in confusion. This wasn't comforting.

"What...?"

Melaney hooked her finger into his belt and pulled him close, only to send him flying onto the nearby bed. All Matt could think about was how he should have fallen onto his sword. But there was no edge pressing into his back, no hilt smashing into his head.

"Where's my sword?"

"In there." Melaney said, patting his crotch. "Let's draw it, shall we?"

Before Matt fully realised what she was doing, his pants were off and tossed away. Melaney pulled him back up and circled him, her fingers running along the lines of his biceps.

"Beautiful," she said, admiringly. "I've outdone myself with you." She pressed against his back, her fingers spreading over his chest muscles. "You remind me of your father. You're the same size."

As her fingers moved down his body, Matt finally snapped from his daze.

He jerked his mother's hands away from his stomach and gasped, "Stop it." Stumbling away from her, he spun around.

In one sweeping motion, Melaney stripped off her clothes. The silken fabric pooled at her feet as she took a step towards him, her intentions clear as day. "You took an oath."

The promise burned on Matt's skin. He'd promised to have sex with her if she'd leave Samantha alone. Instead, she'd kidnapped her. "You broke your end of the deal."

Her eyes blazed with anger. "You made me wait. I've waited enough, Melchior. You're mine. You'll always be *mine*." Then she grabbed his neck and pressed her lips to his.

As soon as her skin touched his, Matt felt his mind ignite with lust. Suddenly, he didn't care that Caspar was dead or that he was kissing his mother. He didn't care about anything but pleasing her.

"That's it. That's my boy," Melaney purred, slightly out of breath. "You're going to make a fine mate. Much better than Frennys."

Her words were like water on Matt's skin. They didn't penetrate his mind, didn't make him stop to think as she led him back to bed. He fell into the pillows, eager to surrender to her passion.

Melaney landed on top of him and was kissing his chest when she suddenly shivered. As her eyes widened, Matt's mind suddenly cleared. Horror filled him, washing away any remnants of lust. Quickly, he rolled out from under her and fumbled for his clothes.

What had she just said? Better than Frennys?

"You want me as your mate," he accused. "I thought you wanted me to kill you."

Melaney was still on the bed, breathing heavily, as if in pain. "I told you I was looking for a replacement. That whole thing about killing me was your own fabrication."

Matt managed to find his underpants and pulled them on, desperate for at least a modicum of modesty. A futile concept in the Residence of Lust. "You told us the Council accused you of infertility and demanded a replacement."

"They can demand a lot. Doesn't mean they'll get it." She laughed, though breathing was still a struggle. "There are dozens of outrageous demands every session."

"I don't understand."

Annoyed, Melaney clicked her tongue. "You're my youngest child and you're almost two decades old. Of course they're accusing me of infertility, never mind the fact I simply didn't want another one. Not when I already had the perfect offspring. Chay's little hero." She looked at him, daring him to deny her claims. "The Council doesn't care how big my brood is so long as I can satisfy everyone's sexual needs. And I'm far from spent." She caught her breath, still grimacing from pain.

"You lied," Matt said, incredulously.

He'd felt so sorry for his mother when he'd heard about the fake edict. For a year, the thought of her dying—at his brothers' hands or his own—had tormented him.

"Do you ever get tired of playing human?"

Matt swallowed hard. "I have no interest in being your mate." He picked up his pants and pulled them on. "You broke your promise. I don't owe you anything. We're done."

Melaney stood in one fluid motion and appeared directly in front of him. "You think you can resist me?"

"You can't force me to make the deal. It's voluntary." She could force him to do just about anything else, though.

"Frennys is *dead.*" She allowed herself to feel the pain for a moment, moaning sensually through it. "His place at my side is free."

"I don't want it!"

Matt realised what was happening. Frennys had died, and because of the deal they'd made, Melaney was in excruciating pain. It was the only reason her spell of lust over him had been broken before he went too far.

Melaney screamed, "What *do* you want, Melchior? What. Do. You. Want?"

The answer was on his lips without even thinking. "Sam."

That was it. He'd come for Sam before he'd been forced to fight his brother to the death and distracted by his mother. Suddenly, the thought of what he'd allowed his mother to do to him nearly ripped his heart out.

"You kidnapped her. I want her back."

"Done!" Melaney spat. Her fingers ran down his bare chest. "I'll make her your gift, in gratitude for your services. Is that voluntary enough for you? You'll appreciate what I've done with her."

Anger flared inside him. "Done with her?"

Seductively, Melaney smiled at him. "Your little Sam has enjoyed the many pleasures of lust and learnt a thing or two. She's probably having a good time with one of my servants right now."

Matt grabbed his mother's wrist and neck, but before he could squeeze, Melaney had turned the tables and slammed him against a wall. Her eyes blazed with anger as she pinned him down. "You belong to the House of Lust, Melchior. You're mine!"

At first, Matt tried his best to fight her off, but he was drowned in a wave of lust, robbing him of his senses. Suddenly, all he felt was an intense need to please the woman in front of him.

"That human witch turned your head. It's time to turn it back," Melaney hissed, every word etching itself into his mind. "You will know nothing but lust. You will breathe lust and feel it coursing through your veins. Every thought in your pretty head will belong to my lust. Understand?" She pushed him to his knees.

Matt looked up at her in total submission. "Yes, mistress." Anything to win her favour and find relief from the unbearable pressure inside.

Melaney patted his hand. A grim smile tugged at her lips as Matt grasped her thighs and slowly moved his hands up. Just as his fingertips touched the bottom of her ass, she yanked his hands away from her body.

"No, my love. I will decide when it's time for you to please me—or yourself. First, I'll take care of the human girl you worship so much. Time to brew her another potion."

There was no one else but Melaney. The world wasn't big enough for more than her. "You're the only woman I worship."

"Good. Let's make sure it stays that way. You have no permission to touch yourself."

And with that, she left him alone in the thrall of her lust, his body aching with unfulfilled desire.

Fabian

At last, the weapons and equipment in their backpacks had a purpose. Fabian held one of the two swords in its sheath against Jan's while he followed Jan's instructions to tie a rope around it, being careful not to touch the wound where the bone was showing.

"Tight enough?" he asked as he tied the last knot.

Jan moved the leg carefully. "Looks good. Now all I need is a crutch and off I limp."

"Right in front of you."

His friend groaned. "Fabian. You're barely strong enough to keep yourself upright."

Fabian scoffed at him. "Do you think I'm going to leave you here?"

"We won't get anywhere if you collapse again."

"I'm not going to collapse," Fabian promised, not caring if it was true or not. "We just have to go slowly."

Jan sighed. "Fine. Help me up then, Superman."

With a nod, Fabian leaned against the cliff face, hooked his hands under Jan's shoulders, and pulled him up. When Jan was finally standing, Fabian bent over and tried to catch his breath. His chest hurt and black spots danced in his vision.

But when Jan's hand fell on his shoulder, he straightened quickly. "I'm fine. Let's go."

"Fabian..."

"Stop whining and go." He really didn't have enough energy to waste arguing.

Luckily Jan had come to the same conclusion and put an arm around him. They left their backpacks behind, unable to carry much more than themselves. Fortunately, this terrace also led to the Dûr Lôrac. Fabian hated leaving Lucin behind, but there was no way they could climb down the cliff face in their state. Instead, they ducked back into the dark tunnels and tried to find a way down.

"This isn't working," Jan said, after less than ten minutes, hissing through the pain. "It hurts too much. And you look white as a sheet. You need rest."

Fabian didn't let him stop. "What we *need* to do is to find someone who can take care of your leg. We also need to find a way out and find Anne, Lia, Sam, and everyone else. Rest is very low on my list of priorities."

Jan snorted. "I didn't know you could be so stubborn."

"Decades of training with Sam." Something caught his attention. "I think this tunnel goes down."

The slope made it even harder to walk, but Fabian was too excited to care. Jan was leaning on him so heavily, he was practically carrying his friend. It was all worth it when the tunnel grew brighter, and he could feel a breeze.

"We're almost there."

It took them another ten minutes to finally reach the bottom. The exit was quite narrow, but this was definitely the lowest level of the huge cave that housed Lucin. It was so bright down here they struggled to make out much of the plain. When their eyes finally adjusted, dark figures appeared before them.

A demon in full armour sat on a monstrous-looking horse-like creature, chomping on its bit. Two other demons with gruesome artificial scars stood beside him, grinning.

"Here we go again," Fabian said wearily. He let go of Jan and pulled the sword from its sheath.

The demons laughed. Their commander nodded to the one on the right, who seemed delighted to have been chosen for this task. He also had a sword, though his looked more like a cleaver, the sharp edge glinting.

"You want to play a bit?"

"Fabian," Jan warned, but there was no other way. These demons spoke only one language: kill or be killed.

Fabian waited until the demon was almost close enough to attack before he raised his sword. Rather than attack, however, his left arm shot up and a jet of water hit the demon's eyes. Startled and blinded, the demon stumbled back. At that moment, Fabian lunged and drove the sword through the demon's guts, just as Matt had once shown him.

The demon fell to the ground, taking Fabian with him. Panting, Fabian caught himself on the hilt. With a mighty grunt, he pulled the sword out, and drove it through his throat for good measure.

His head was spinning, but he managed to look at the rider and grunt, "I'm in no mood to play fair."

Neither were the demons. The two remaining charged.

With great effort, Fabian managed to raise his sword and block the first attack, but the force behind the second ripped the weapon from his hand and threw him to the ground. Grunting, he pushed himself up on his elbows and reached for his water, but he was so exhausted, a meagre trickle was all he managed.

The horse rose, its heavy hooves directly over Fabian's head, when suddenly a winged demon crashed into both rider and horse. Shadows engulfed the second demon, dragging him away before slicing him to pieces. Vines sprouted from the ground near Fabian and wrapped around the horse's legs. It bit at one, easily tearing through the fleshy plant, but more shot up, quickly lashing it to the ground. The rider, however, had escaped the plants, if not the other demon, who looked vaguely familiar.

"Adrianes?"

Both demons ignored him as they rolled across the ground. One of Adrianes' wings snapped, the leather ripping from shoulder to tip, making Fabian flinch.

"Fabian!"

Before Fabian could react, someone threw themselves around his neck. Black hair filled his vision, and he heard a loud sob. "Lia?"

She pulled away just enough to cradle his face, searching it frantically. "Are you alright?"

"Almost died. What about you?"

"Thrown out on the streets."

He had so many questions, but Adrianes was still fighting the fearsome rider and taking a beating. Then a vine wrapped around the other demon's leg and pulled him off the second-class demon, who quickly rolled to the side.

"Adrian!" Jan called.

As Adrianes looked up, Jan threw him the sword Fabian had dropped. Adrianes caught it mid-air and turned just in time to plunge it into the rider's stomach. For good measure, he also shot energy into his face.

The rider collapsed in a bloody heap and Adrianes took a deep breath before turning to Jan. "Thank you."

"No, thank *you*! You..." Jan looked at Ophelia. "You two came at just the right time."

Ophelia helped Fabian to his feet, watching him with concern as he clutched at his chest. "We followed the Black Guard's movements. People said they saw a vortex of water smash two guards at once near here."

"Yeah, that was me."

She kissed his cheek. "I knew it." She looked at Adrianes, who was sitting on the ground, breathing heavily. "I told you it was Fabian."

He nodded and huffed, amused. "You did. Sorry about the Black Guard. They're a bit out of control, at the moment."

"Is their out-of-control behaviour any different from normal?" Fabian asked. He tried to get to his feet but struggled.

To his surprise, Adrianes nodded. "The Black Guard is usually more disciplined. Caspar has been neglecting them of late and now they're bored."

"Awesome!" Jan rolled his eyes and shook his head. His gaze found Ophelia. "Lia. It's good to see you. You wouldn't happen to know where my little sister is, would you?" He grimaced, preparing himself for the worst.

With Ophelia's help, Fabian finally got to his feet. "Jan..."

"We were separated," Ophelia said. "We arrived in Hell together, but we came across a Hanna temple. They immediately recognised her as one of their own and recruited her against her will. As for me, I'm not worthy of Hanna's attention. They threw me out."

"I'm sorry, Lia. We should've been with you. We should've..."

Suddenly the world tilted, and Fabian lost his footing. Ophelia screamed as the ground rushed to meet him, darkness closing in. The last thing he heard was something about a healer.

Lucille

Alecia guarded the doors while Lucille tended to René's wounds. She didn't have many healing spells—nothing compared to Jan's—but the wounds had stopped bleeding and he was regaining some colour. He wasn't going anywhere anytime soon, though. Nevertheless, he tried.

"You're hurt!" Lucille cried out.

"I have to go to her."

Lucille shook her head. "No, you don't."

Since the fighting had stopped, René had been obsessed with getting to Melaney. He wasn't his usual self, and Lucille figured he'd triggered some kind of defence mechanism when he'd slaughtered his way in.

Hurried footsteps came closer. Alecia raised her hand, but quickly lowered it when she realised who it was. Lucille remained tense until Rachel burst into the room, Hugo hovering ahead of her.

"There you are!" Rachel said in relief. "We have to hurry. Melaney has Matt."

"He promised not to sleep with her," René said, darkly.

"Not to... What?" Lucille turned to him. "Why would he do that? That's his mum!"

René's face darkened and he spat. "She wants him. He wants her."

"The only one Matt wants is Samantha," Rachel said, matter-of-factly.

Lucille nodded hastily. "Rachel's right. Matt's only here because of Samantha. You know that!" Whatever was wrong with René was driving her to despair.

"If he wasn't already possessed by lust, I'd say he's jealous," Alecia observed. "Just saying."

"Jealous of his own son?" Lucille repeated. And not only that, but willing to fight him over Matt's mother.

Alecia's eyes widened. "That's Melchior's father?" She seemed impressed. "It all makes sense now."

Somehow, René had managed to get to his feet. He swayed and stumbled, but he kept himself upright and shuffled slowly towards one of the doors. "I have to go to her."

Lucille hurried to steady him. "You're in no condition to go to anyone."

"Melaney's calling me," René said, with a look that was miles away.

Helpless, Lucille turned to Rachel and Hugo, but they both seemed as overwhelmed as she felt. Rachel just shrugged and Lucille groaned. She had to find a way to stop René or he wouldn't make it out of here alive. He might not care at the moment, but she was sure Matt would.

"We'll stop them." Lucille turned René towards her and looked him in the eyes. "We'll stop Matt from sleeping with your... woman. We'll do everything in our power to stop it. I swear." She patted his chest. "You stay here and wait for her while we go and take Matt away." For the moment, the throne room seemed as safe as anything.

She looked at Alecia and asked, "Where could we find her?"

"Since she's not here, she's probably in one of her bedrooms. Come with me!"

Lucille nodded to René and let go. As predicted, his knees buckled under him. He wasn't going anywhere without help.

Alecia hurried to the door opposite the one they'd come through and waved them in.

"You know we're too late," Rachel hissed as they followed Alecia through the tunnel. "If Melaney really..." She pulled a face. "You know what. She's had more than enough time to do it."

Lucille didn't even want to think about it. "I know, but René doesn't need to know that."

"What's with her?" Hugo asked on her other side. "Do we trust a demon?"

"She saved my life. I wouldn't exactly call it trust, but for now we seem to be on the same side."

Alecia must have heard her, because she looked over her shoulder and grinned wickedly. She slowed a little so Lucille could catch up, to ask, "Why is it so important that Melchior or Matt or whatever you call him, doesn't sleep with Melaney?"

"Are you kidding?"

Apparently not, because the demon just frowned.

"It's... She's his mother! It's disgusting, unnatural..."

"Says who?"

Lucille had no idea how to answer that. She guessed it didn't really mean much in demon terms, but the mere thought of it made her want to puke.

Fortunately, she was saved from the discourse when a familiar face appeared from a side corridor. "Chay!

He seemed as relieved to see her as she was him. "You're here. Perfect."

"Perfect?" Rachel asked.

Alecia pressed herself against the wall, apparently not too keen on attracting Chay's attention.

If he noticed her at all, he didn't show it. In fact, he seemed a bit on edge. "Hurry, we can't lose any more time. Matt needs your help."

"We know," Lucille snapped, her nerves frayed. "We're on our way to him right now."

"Then what are you waiting for? Follow me."

He strode off quickly while Rachel and Lucille exchanged a confused look. First, he'd insisted they save Samantha before Matt got to her, now he wanted them to save Matt. It was almost as if he was trying to keep them apart.

Lucille shook her head. What utter nonsense. Chay saw the future. He knew exactly who had to be where. Matt trusted him and so did Lucille.

She looked at the envy demon who Chay had completely ignored. Alecia just shrugged and let the half-demon lead them.

A few minutes later, they arrived in a majestic bedroom. Or at least it had used to be. Now, it was a pile of rubble and dust, fresh blood on the floor.

Next to her, Rachel sucked in a breath. "Don't look."

Lucille couldn't *not* look when she was told not to, but as soon as she saw why, she wished she'd taken Rachel's advice. "Menuha!"

Her favourite demon lay on the floor with a bloody neck, her head resting on Caspar's lap, who was as dead as she was.

Crying, Lucille ran over and dropped to her knees beside them, not even caring about all the blood on the floor. "No, no, no, please tell me this isn't true. Menu..."

"That's the General of Terror," Alecia said, in surprise.

"Matt killed him," Rachel said in a flat voice.

Alecia gasped softly. "Really?"

"It was meant to end like this." Chay sounded tired. "From the moment they met."

Lucille didn't care about Caspar. He'd probably attacked Matt again and gotten what he'd deserved, but Menuha... Sweet, curious Menuha didn't have to die. Especially not with her throat torn out by some kind of beast.

Still crying, she gently rubbed Menuha's arm as Chay urged her to leave. "We have to move on."

"Give her some time," Rachel snapped. "They were friends."

"Every minute wasted here is a minute closer to disaster."

Rachel crossed her arms and glared at him coldly. "And what disaster exactly are we talking about?"

Against her will, Lucille pulled herself to her feet. "Chay's right. We have to save Matt and Samantha."

He nodded sharply. "Right. We—"

"You're lying," Rachel accused him.

The half-demon frowned. "Excuse me?"

"You're planning something. You told us you didn't have time to go to Hescaryn yourself. And that we had to save Samantha because Matt would fail. But Matt's here. And you're here. So, what's really going on?"

Lucille held her breath. Rachel had said exactly what she'd been wondering. Only instead of trusting him despite it, her friend was accusing the Seer of lying.

With a sigh of despair and resignation, Chay slumped against the wall behind him. "It doesn't matter. We'll be too late anyway." He winced. "You'd think after over two hundred years I'd have learnt you can't change the future, even if you know exactly how it's going to turn out. It's a curse, not a blessing." He took another deep breath. "What happens today will cement Matt's fate. I had hoped to save him from it, but it's no use. I can't change it. Only she can."

Samantha

With fingers clenched around the bowl, Samantha puked her heart out. Balthasar patted her back, though it seemed more out of boredom than concern.

"Just keep going. It all has to go."

When the urge to throw up had finally subsided, Samantha felt a little more like herself. She wiped her mouth with her sleeve and looked at Balthasar. "I think I'm done. I feel a lot less crazy."

He tilted his head and grinned. "I can only reduce the level of insanity to its original amount."

Samantha rolled her eyes. "As if you weren't crazy too. You want to kill your own mother." She grabbed a glass of water and sipped, not quite trusting her stomach yet. When she put it down, she noticed the Sword of Amain leaning against the wall. "That's Matt's sword."

"I borrowed it."

"Really?"

Her heart fluttered at the thought of Matt being so close. Had he come to rescue her or had he been drawn into his mother's politics? What if Melaney was right and all he'd ever wanted was to get into her pants? Maybe he was perfectly happy with the arrangement she'd made for him.

Balthasar groaned in annoyance. "Don't worry. He'll get it back when I'm done with it. Eventually." He nodded at the Flowers from Freya's Gardens she'd taken from under the bed. "That's your Emblem of Power, isn't it?"

Samantha held onto them. "You definitely can't borrow them."

"That's okay. I'm not much for flowers. Swords are deadlier."

She wiped a strand of hair from her face, noticing how tangled it felt. In the right colour, the flowers were as deadly as Matt's sword, but Balthasar didn't need to know that. "Will you take me home now?"

His help so far had surprised her almost as much as his restraint. She hadn't expected a demon who'd hoped to become the next Archdemon of Lust to reject her embarrassing advances.

"Absolutely not." He stood and gave her a smile that promised death and chaos. "We're going to see my mother."

Samantha gasped. The very mention of Melaney made her want to curl up in a ball and die. "You said you'd save me."

"And I did. I saved you from the terrible, terrible lust. You owe me, so let's go." He pulled her up.

"She's going to kill me." She'd rip her throat out like she'd done to Menuha or something worse.

Balthasar snorted. "Not if I kill her first." He grabbed the sword and led her out of the room and down the same tunnel she'd taken with Menuha, stopping at another room. "Alright, show me what you've got, little witch. A protection spell, please."

"I..." Samantha looked down. "The demons said my magic doesn't please Melaney."

She still hadn't worked out how the residence worked. Her magic was sealed, but others seemed fine. The demons could jump short distances, but there was no constant coming and going. And Melaney could move whole rooms. It was almost as if she and the residence were one.

Annoyed, Balthasar grumbled, "One day, Chay will have to explain to me how your rescue will serve my goals." He drew the sword and opened the door.

Samantha hid behind him, not wanting to be seen by Melaney. "Melchior?"

As soon as she heard Matt's name, she came forward. "Matt?"

He was sitting on the bed in his demon form, wearing only pants, pants which left absolutely nothing to the imagination as to his state of arousal. His eyes were glazed over, and he didn't even seem to see her.

"Where's Melaney?" Balthasar entered the room and looked around, as if expecting his mother to jump out from behind the curtain.

"Not here," Matt said, between short breaths.

Balthasar snorted at him. "Has she finally got into your pants?"

Slowly, Matt rose from the bed and approached them. Ashamed of everything that had happened in the last few days, Samantha backed away until her body was against the wall. She was unable to look him in the eye.

"Samantha." He said her name in a raspy way that immediately rekindled the fire in her stomach that she thought she'd extinguished with Balthasar's anti-potion.

She raised her eyes. "Did you really sleep with her?"

Matt watched her as if he was already mentally undressing her. "She hasn't done me the honour yet."

Samantha swallowed hard. "The honour?"

"I'm afraid little Melchior here is under Melaney's spell," Balthasar explained helpfully.

It was small relief for Samantha to know Matt wouldn't do such a thing without magical compulsion. "A spell?"

Matt gave her a wicked smile that liquefied her insides. "She's chosen me as her mate. The lust is mine now."

"About that..." Balthasar began.

Whatever he was trying to say, Samantha couldn't hear it as Matt came over and pinned her against the wall with the bulk of his body. Samantha gasped as she felt his hardness digging into her hip, giving him access to her neck. He left a fiery trail of kisses on her skin, and a telltale little moan escaped her.

Startled, she placed her hands on his chest. "Matt."

She wanted to tell him to stop, but the word wouldn't come out. Not even when she knew it wasn't real, that it was Melaney's influence that made him act this way.

His nose was buried in her hair as his hot breath caressed her ear. "You smell like sex."

The reminder brought tears to Samantha's eyes. "I didn't want this. She poisoned me. She..." Samantha met his gaze, hoping to reach him. "Matt, she's doing the same thing to you. This isn't what you want."

"I know what I want." He took her hands and held them above her head.

"Matt."

He snorted softly. "Matt. Matt. I don't need that name anymore." Then he leaned forward and kissed her shoulder, then her collarbone.

For a moment, Samantha sank into the sensation of his searing lips against her skin, but soon her mind cleared, and she shook her head. "No! You're Matt. You're both Matt and Melchior. Demon and human. You grew up with lust, but you're not at its mercy."

"The only one at anyone's mercy is you."

Before she could say anything else, Matt kissed her. This was no feathery brush of the lips. He immediately forced his way into her mouth, filling it with unbridled desire.

Samantha tried to kick him, but her legs wrapped around his hips instead. Melchior let go of her arms to support her ass, then lifted her up without ever stopping to kiss her. As she buried her hands in his black hair, he carried her to the bed.

Her lips were swollen and aching for more as he released them to kiss her neck. His hands slid up her skirt. With eyes glazed with passion, he looked at her. "You want me."

The statement made Samantha's cheeks burn. She wanted him with the fire of a thousand suns. He made her feel everything when she was with him. His kisses made her lose her mind and she couldn't wait for him to set her body on fire. But not here. Not like this.

"Yes, Matt." She took his hand and pulled it out from under her skirt. "I want you," she admitted as she sat up and cupped his face, looking at those gorgeous lips and those chocolaty brown eyes, which had darkened with desire. "I want the kind of Matt to whom I mean the world. The kind of Matt who will go to Hell for me. Who will face his own demons, and I mean that literally and figuratively." Her eyes filled with tears. "I want my Matt, the one who's so much better than all this."

"This is what I am," he said, still in that low, raspy voice. "Melchior of the House of Lust."

Samantha shook her head. "No, Matt. You're so much more than that. You haven't just been Melchior of the House of Lust for a long time now." She stroked his hair, brushing her thumb across his forehead. "You changed, remember?"

He'd almost lost his humanity once, but he'd fought for it. For her. For them.

"For you," he whispered, his voice no longer quite as seductive.

Tears streamed down her face as she realised he was fighting now, too, and she smiled at him. "For me, yes. Change for me. And for yourself. It's a good thing. The best of things." She kissed his forehead and felt him shiver beneath her as he wrapped his arms around her body, holding on like a drowning man.

Something warm and beautiful washed over them, a colourful shimmer that seemed to wash away not only her exhaustion and despair, but Matt's as well. When he lifted his eyes, they were no longer glassy.

He looked at her with a mixture of horror, desire, and awe. "You want me?" It sounded hopeful and a little frightened.

Samantha laughed and kissed him on the nose. "Now and forever."

Still shivering, Matt put a hand in her hair and pulled her towards him. This time he waited, their lips just millimetres apart, their breath mingling. Samantha closed the distance, and he welcomed her with a sweet little sigh. Kissing him still filled her with heat, but it was no longer the searing desire of Melaney's lust, but a deep, fulfilling warmth.

When they pulled apart, Matt smiled in wonder. "You like me."

"I *love* you," Samantha corrected him, amused. "I really do."

He kissed her immediately. "I love you, too."

Behind them, Balthasar groaned, reminding them of his presence. "If you two are finally done with all this lovey-dovey crap, I'd suggest you leave. Melaney—"

As if he'd summoned her, Melaney appeared in the room. "She's gone—You!"

Startled, Samantha nearly fell off the bed. Matt's arm around her tightened, but his mother grabbed him by the neck and flung him against the opposite wall with inhuman strength.

Matt groaned in pain as he crashed into the stone, but quickly got to his feet. "If you touch her—"

"If?" Melaney shrieked. "*If* I touch her? Oh, my sweet, stupid boy. I'll rip the skin off that little witch."

Samantha was on the verge of fainting. Melchior jumped, but appeared halfway across the room, blocked by a silky shimmering wall that locked Samantha in with Melaney.

The archdemon smiled maniacally. "And you get to watch."

Panicked, Samantha tried to get up, but Melaney shoved her onto the bed and sat on her stomach, pinning her arms under her knees. Then she drove her nails into Samantha's face and she screamed.

Jan

Adrianes took them to the Temple of Hanna, which was like night and day to the Dûr Lôrac. They sat in a small garden with a sylver stream gurgling beside them. The priests had provided them with rich food and drink, and a healer was tending to Jan's leg, moving her hands skilfully around the bone.

Fabian was devouring the food. Apparently being an absolute hero and coming back from the brink of death had made him ravenous. Opposite, Adrianes sipped on a glass of wine while Ophelia paced the garden as if expecting to be attacked by the healers and priests.

While his leg was being repaired, Jan told Adrianes and Ophelia what had happened in the Dûr Lôrac. Occasionally, Fabian had interrupted him, but his mouth was so full he was of no use in telling their story.

"And that's when you arrived," Jan finished.

Adrianes looked at him in awe. "Impressive. I know of few demons, let alone humans, who can stand up to the Black Guard."

"It was incredible. You should've seen it. He took on four demons all by himself and completely annihilated them." To the healer, he quickly said, "No offence."

Ophelia paused long enough to say, "Of course he's incredible."

"Without so much as a scratch?" the healer asked, incredulously.

In a rare moment when his mouth was empty, Fabian said, "Of course not. I almost died, but Jan healed me. Now *that* was incredible."

The healer looked up at Jan. "You're a healer, too?"

"Well, I have healing powers, if that's what you mean. Nothing compared to yours, but I've only been doing this shit for about a year."

"And you brought him back from a mortal wound? Impressive. Who taught you?"

Jan shrugged uncomfortably. "The people at the hospital, I suppose. They don't know anything about my powers, of course, but they teach me all the other stuff, like how to do CPR and stop bleeding, which medicines to use in an emergency. Stuff like that." He'd wished he'd had some of the rescue equipment when Fabian had collapsed.

The healer shook her head. "I meant which healer is teaching you?"

"No one. I don't know anyone who can heal. Well, apart from Caspar, but he's not exactly the teaching type."

"No. No, he's not." The demon smiled. "You might be the perfect student for *him*."

"For whom?"

"An acquaintance of mine. Leandres. He's very knowledgeable, but he's fallen on hard times and could use a student. A new task, really."

Jan frowned, not liking the sound of that. "Is he a demon?"

"No, a human like you."

That made it much better. "I mean, if he wants to move to Greenvalley, because I'm not going anywhere."

The healer nodded quickly. "I think a change would be good for him." She bent his leg a few times. "Good as new."

"Thank you." Jan got up to see for himself and had no problems. There wasn't even a twinge of pain left. When the healer left, he looked at Ophelia. "So, about Anne..."

Ophelia stopped. "She's here, in this temple. But they won't let her go."

Jan's mood plummeted. "What did you say?"

"The priests here have decided to take her in as a novice. I don't know what that means, but they've put her in a green robe and gave her to an acolyte. I don't know any more than that because they sent me packing when Anne wasn't looking."

"I need to find my sister." Jan knew Anne was interested in becoming a priestess of Hanna but certainly not like this.

Adrianes stood up, looking dismayed. "If that's true then she's been initiated into the temple. Interfering might anger Hanna and the gods—"

"—can go where the sun doesn't shine. I won't let anyone take my sister away from me."

"You would have an entire temple against you," Adrianes warned. His own wounds from the fight with the Blood Rider hadn't fully healed yet.

Fabian stood. "Against me, too."

Ophelia came to his side immediately, crossing her arms. "Me three."

Jan almost burst with pride. He didn't care how many demons they had to fight, he wouldn't leave his sister in some nightmare temple.

Just then, the door to the gardens was thrown open and a novice in a pale green robe ran into the garden as if being chased. Jan recognised her at once, despite her strange clothes. "Anne!"

He rushed towards her, and she threw herself into his arms, sobbing. "Oh, Jan, it's really you! They were talking about two humans in the garden and... It's you."

Jan held her close and took one shaky breath after the other. "What's going on?"

When she raised her head, he almost lost his mind. Half her face was bruised, her left eye nearly swollen shut. "They made me a novice. Apparently, I'm supposed to learn Hanna's ways for twenty years." She sobbed again. "Lia and I found the temple, but now they want to keep me here and Lia..." Ophelia caught her gaze. "Lia!"

"Hey, Anne. I'm fine," Ophelia said, sounding immensely relieved.

"Oh, thank Hanna," Anne sighed. She looked at Jan and immediately started crying again. "I'm doing everything wrong and—"

"Anne!" Her name was spoken like the crack of a whip. A young demon woman in a darker green robe came towards them, sneering. "You are not to speak to the guests. I won't tolerate this kind of behaviour. Come here!"

She tried to grab Anne's hair, but Jan caught her wrist and glared at her. "Touch my sister and you'd better say your last prayer, priestess."

The demon looked at him coolly. "And who are you?"

"He is a healer of Hanna's grace," Adrianes said, before Jan had the chance.

There was an instant change in the demon's face. She backed away, then actually dropped to her knees in front of Jan and bowed her head. "Forgive me, Healer."

Flustered, Jan looked at Adrianes for a clue, but the gardener just shrugged. Jan decided he didn't have much to lose. "Whatever, just beat it." The demon looked at him in confusion. "Go!"

She nodded hastily and left. The look of relief on Anne's face told Jan more about what she'd been through than words ever could. He gently cupped her bruised face, healing it without asking what had caused the injury.

"How did you know she'd leave us alone if she knew I was a healer?" he asked Adrianes.

"They worship healers almost as much as their goddess. If you're going to kidnap one of their novices, the least you can do is be clever about it."

Jan grinned. "Thank you. We should probably get going then. How do we get out of here?"

"We have to find Samantha and the others," Fabian said, seemingly eager to get the shit beaten out of him again.

Adrianes looked back and forth between them as if they'd gone mad. "You want to go to the Residence of Lust?"

"Out of the fire and into the frying pan," Jan said grimly. "Yes."

They had Lia and Anne now, but they wouldn't leave without their friends.

The demon sighed. "I'll take you."

Matt

Samantha's screams echoed through the residence as Melaney scratched her face. Matt attacked the shield with energy, but it didn't even tremble under the impact. He tried to draw his sword and came up short. Then Samantha shrieked horribly, and Matt simply threw himself against the shield.

It was like a brick wall, if the brick wall had been covered with a layer of velvet. It stole something from him, leaving Matt gasping in irritation.

"You took my son!" Melaney roared at Samantha. "My masterpiece!"

Through her fingers he could see blood running down Samantha's face, and he threw himself against the wall again and again.

"Matt."

Suddenly there were people behind him. He barely recognised Rachel, Lucille, Chay, and Pyke's devotee, his attention fully focused on the impenetrable wall that kept him from the love of his life while his mother tore her to pieces.

"Step aside!"

Matt heeded Lucille's warning, and a moment later an arrow of black magic slammed into the shield. By all rights, it should've destroyed it, but all it left was a tiny hole, barely big enough to stick a finger through.

"It won't work," Chay said. "This is anti-magic material."

"My mother's about to kill the woman I love with every damn fibre of my being," Matt shouted at him. "I'm not going to watch that happen."

Another terrible scream made his head spin. Melaney had dug a hand into Samantha's hair and ripped her shoulder open with the other. His mother wasn't just killing her, she was doing it as slowly and as painfully as possible.

"She's going to be the death of you," Chay said in despair.

Matt shot him another glare. "Then I'll die happy."

That silenced his friend for good. Balthasar's hand fell on Chay's shoulder as he stepped forward and pointed a sword at the hole in the wall. "Then stop standing around and make the hole bigger. Leave the rest to me, *half*-blood."

Matt did a double take when he realised whose sword he was wielding, but he wasted no time in following the suggestion. Any second now, Melaney could end Samantha, and he knew in his heart it would be the end of him as well.

Without hesitation, he stuck his finger into the hole Lucille's arrow had left and tore it open. Much to his delight, it worked. Unfortunately, the anti-magic also worked, and he felt his powers drain away just as they had when Malcolm had blocked him from magic. His body was changing as the demon side of him was slowly drained. Matt had no idea if he would ever recover from this.

What had Chay said? That she would be the death of him?

He would gladly die if it meant saving Samantha. After all he had put her through, from Daniel to his crazy family, he owed her at least that much.

Even though his body was protesting and his efforts were getting weaker and weaker, Matt didn't give up until the hole was big enough for someone to duck through. Unfortunately, that was as far as he could go. His knees buckled under him, and he slumped against the wall. Samantha's screams were still ringing in his ears, but he couldn't even lift a finger to help her.

Instead, he had to watch as Balthasar stepped through the hole he'd made. A single touch of the anti-magic against his shoulder made his brother hiss.

Matt's eyelids dropped as someone pulled him away from the wall.

Chay cradled him in his arms, his heart pounding against Matt's chest. The distance from the anti-magic and Samantha's sudden gurgle kept Matt awake enough to see what was happening.

"Do it. It's your destiny," Chay said.

Balthasar didn't need to be asked twice. He swung the sword and chopped Melaney's head from her shoulders. Blood splattered across the room as the wall collapsed.

Samantha paused for a moment in shock, then let out a delayed scream that quickly turned into heartbreaking sobs. Lucille and Rachel ran to her and pulled her from under Melaney's headless body, before holding her as tightly as Matt wished he could.

"Melaney?" Suddenly René was in the doorway, looking like he'd been to the Land of the Dead and back again.

"She's dead," Chay said quietly, still holding Matt. "The sin of Lust belongs to Balthasar now. You're free."

René slumped against the door frame in relief, his spell of untamed desire gone.

"Well, now we've got a new archdemon, we should probably get going," said the envy demon, Alecia. "Unless anyone's in the mood for sex after all that."

Matt looked at Balthasar. His brother was still on the bed, panting like he'd just run a marathon. His eyes were glowing with desire and his lips were stretched into a manic smile. Matt had often heard of the moment when a new archdemon ascended. They were overcome by the sin with which they'd just become synonymous.

"Let's get out of here."

Fabian

By the time Fabian and the others arrived at Residence Square, it was all over.

Adrianes took one look at the dead guards and put his hand on the wall to announce: "It feels different. Melaney is dead. We have a new archdemon."

Several of the guards outside the other residences stirred when they heard that. Within minutes, all of Lucin would know.

"A new archdemon?" Jan asked. "Matt?"

"Never."

Fabian entered the residence, carefully stepping around the dead guards. He'd been angry at Matt before for dragging them all into his demon mess, but after two days in Hell, he had a vague idea of what Matt's life here must've been like. He really hadn't had much of a chance. Despite that, Fabian had also seen him at home, where he'd fought and laughed with them, and he'd seen him fall in love with Samantha. As much demon blood as Matt had in him, he was also half human, and that human side would have no interest in becoming an archdemon.

It wasn't long before they encountered another group led by Chay. Lucille and another woman he didn't know were supporting René. Behind them, Rachel helped Matt limp along, along with...

"Sam!"

Fabian ran to meet them and threw his arms around his best friend in a hug. He didn't care about the bloody lines on her face, the bruises around her neck, or the tangle of black curls on her head. All he cared about was that she was alive.

"Excuse me for saying this, but you all look like shit," Jan said.

Lucille snorted. "Speak for yourself."

"Melaney's dead," Rachel said, and Chay added to Adrianes, "Your father is the new archdemon."

"Of course he is. Anything else would've surprised me."

Jan joined Fabian and Samantha, quickly taking stock of the latter's injuries. "May I?"

"Please."

Fabian let go of her just long enough for Jan to put his hands on her face. Judging by Jan's hissing, the wounds were even more painful than they looked.

"What happened?" he asked quietly.

She regarded him exhaustedly and leaned against Matt, who looked as if he could do with two days' sleep. "So very much. But we're alright now."

Relieved, Fabian squeezed her hand. So much had happened to him, too. And to Anne and Lia. They'd need a few weeks to recover. Maybe months.

"Oh well," the unknown demon said, with a small bow to Lucille. "I have a lot to tell Pyke."

"Thanks for your help. We wouldn't be alive without you."

The blonde woman smiled. "Same. We'll meet again." She disappeared quickly.

"Who was that?" Fabian asked, confused.

Lucille shook her head, as if to clear her mind. "No one."

Fabian filed it under another "so much" event. Now that everyone was accounted for, he couldn't get out of Hell fast enough. "Can we go home, please?"

Samantha sighed. "Yes, let's go home."

As soon as they arrived at the Blackstone house, Neve surrounded them with a flurry of snow, most of it centred around Jan, who responded by laughing and dancing around the living room with her.

Rachel and Samantha helped Matt onto the couch and Samantha immediately took a seat at his side, fussing over him.

"Your demonic powers will recover one day. Until then... be careful," Chay said.

"So much for a quick jump to Fader to catch a lecture."

Chay chuckled. "You still have a gate right on your doorstep. And a little break would do you good. I'm sure you know what to do with your time." His gaze shifted to Samantha, and he flinched slightly. Then he nodded at them and disappeared.

Samantha frowned, shook her head and cleared her throat. "I want to thank you all for literally going to Hell for me. I... I don't know what to say."

"Please." Fabian snorted. "As if we would leave you with the demons. You would've done the same in a heartbeat."

"Is it over?" Ophelia asked, snuggling into Fabian's side, while he put an arm around her. "Will they leave us alone?"

Matt nodded. "I think so. My..." He licked his lips. "My mother is dead, and Balthasar has taken her place. He got what he wanted and I..." He looked at Samantha with a wistful smile. "I did, too."

Fabian figured the two had finally come to an understanding and accepted the undeniable love between them. Hopefully Matt was right, and they'd actually get some quiet time to explore these feelings.

He was about to ask if they should order pizza when the doorbell rang. Confused, Lucille opened the door.

To everyone's surprise, it was Robert. "I knew I had it right. You're back."

Jan tried to gaslight him by saying, "We were never away."

Despite everything that had happened, only two days had passed.

"Never away?" Robert repeated, in dismay. "The letter in the Magic Circle said otherwise."

"Woah, wait." Fabian let go of Ophelia and took two steps towards Robert. "How did you get my letter in the Magic Circle?" The letter had been for his parents and was very personal. It wasn't meant for their former classmate.

Robert didn't notice the charged atmosphere and continued, "I was passing by and saw you were closed. So, I looked for the spare key and checked it out."

Fabian ground his teeth so hard his jaw hurt.

"Your mother's still up north and you were gone, so I opened the shop so you wouldn't lose any more money or something."

"You... you..." Fabian was too angry to know what to say.

Ophelia took his arm and pulled him back. "It's alright. He only broke in to run the shop."

Jan huffed, looking just as angry. "Man, you're lucky I just broke my leg."

"You broke your leg? That's terrible." Robert was all over him. "Should I call an ambulance?"

"Anne," Jan called, "please be a dear and kill him for me."

His sister laughed before batting her eyelashes innocently at him. "I can't. I'm a priestess of life."

Robert frowned. "You're what?" Then he looked at them all, taking in the grime on their faces. He quickly lowered his gaze. "Anyway, I'm glad you're back. It would've been terrible if you'd all died before I could apologise."

"What do you have to apologise for?" Lucille asked in irritation. "You haven't done anything."

"Apart from breaking into the Magic Circle," Fabian muttered.

Robert nodded. "Yes, I did. You see, on the trip... I was avoiding you last week because of that esoteric stuff you guys are into."

It was news to Fabian that Robert had been avoiding them for any length of time at all. Too much had happened that week to pay him much attention. Especially when they were no longer at school.

"Occultism," Jan corrected him grumpily, "and you're welcome to avoid us a little longer."

"Occultism," Robert repeated, ignoring Jan. "Anyway, now you know you can count on me if you ever risk your life again or something."

"By breaking into my mum's shop. Wonderful." Fabian still couldn't believe it.

Lucille put on her cheesiest smile. "Thank you, Robert. Can we have the key?"

He handed it to her and placed a letter on top. "This came yesterday. Looked important."

"Okay." Lucille nodded, then turned to Anne. "I like you, but…"

Jan's sister understood immediately and put her arm around her boyfriend's waist. "I missed you. Let's go get some ice cream."

"Best sister in the world." Jan gave her a thumbs up as she led Robert out.

As soon as the door had closed behind them, Fabian let out the breath he'd been holding. "I don't even want to know what he's done to the shop."

Lucille laughed and handed him the key. "We'll have to find a better place to hide the spare key." She looked at the letter. "This is for you."

Fabian frowned, wondering who would send a letter to him at the Magic Circle. While the others got ready to order a pizza and quickly fell back into relaxation mode, he went out onto the veranda with Ophelia. Turning the letter between his hands, he noticed it was addressed to 'Fabian Frederick Bendtfeld' and sealed with an old-fashioned wax seal. The symbol was that of a fortress, with letters underneath he couldn't quite make out.

"Must be local." Though who would use his full name apart from his parents was beyond him.

Curious, Ophelia leaned over his arm. "Open it."

The whole letter was handwritten, but easy to read:

Dear Mr Bendtfeld,

I hope this letter finds you in good health. We would like to congratulate you on your recent graduation and are pleased to offer you a place at the Citadel of Magic, beginning on the 20th of October. You'll be joining our 'Elemental Magic' cohort…

Dumbfounded, Fabian looked at Ophelia. "Is this for real?"

"A magic school." Ophelia's eyes sparkled. "That's so cool. I'm sorry, but you have to go!"

And dedicate his whole life to magic? Fabian didn't think so. "It must be a joke." There was no magic school. Not in Ashuan.

"It would explain why you were rejected by GU so quickly."

"A *meddling* magic school. Now I want to go even less."

But in his mind, he suddenly remembered the glimpse he'd caught on his journey through the rivers of magic: a citadel in the snow. Just like the one on the seal.

Shivering, he stuffed the letter into his back pocket and put an arm around Ophelia. "Let's not worry about it. October is ages away. We'll have a whole summer to enjoy before then."

Balthasar

Balthasar had stood before the Council of Seven before, but never as one of their equals. He looked them all in the eye, one by one. There was Pyke with his shaved head, seething with jealousy, as if he weren't already an archdemon in his own right. As usual, Yash slumped in her chair, yawning through his introduction. She never did much of anything, but Balthasar wasn't stupid enough to count her out. Moloch barely fit into his seat, which was wider than any of the others, his gaze betraying an intellect to rival his own.

He met Iyaga's gaze, who watched him with undisguised interest and gave her an inviting smile. The new Archdemon of Greed was much prettier than his father and would be his first choice for an ally. It looked as if he was hers, too, the two new members of the Council.

At the head of the Council sat Hel, the most senior archdemon. Although she was seated, she looked down on him, and Balthasar knew he'd never make the cut for her. It didn't matter that he was nearly a thousand years old. Hel was much older and had been the Archdemon of Pride for almost as long.

Next to her, with only the empty black throne between them, sat Volac, Caspar's former master, glaring daggers at him as if it had been Balthasar who'd gutted his precious general.

Despite his anger, it was Volac who spoke. "The Council of Seven welcomes our newest member. Balthasar of the Houses of Lust and Greed will speak for Lust from now on. Take a seat."

Balthasar slid into his mother's old chair, which fit as if it had been made for him, while the other archdemons applauded without much enthusiasm. Yash had fallen asleep and Pyke was muttering about how he already had too many sins. Balthasar paid no attention to them. He was where he belonged and couldn't wait for the game to begin.

One of his first orders of business was to restructure the residence to suit his needs. Balthasar had hired demons to give it a good clean and remove all Melaney's broken furniture. There were a few pieces he'd keep, but most he would replace.

He could feel the power of the residence all around him. They were still getting to know each other. So far, it had responded beautifully to his touch, and he'd created a number of secret rooms where he could have private conversations, as well as larger ones for his amorous adventures. He'd also updated security measures, sealing off the entrance in the storeroom and two others he'd found.

But the best thing about the residence was the way it made him aware of the various people in it. It revealed their intentions to him. Most desired him, hoping to join his entourage, but there were a few who thought they could use him. And one who was determined to use him, and probably right about it.

"I wondered where you were hiding," he said to Chay before the half-demon had even entered the throne room. Allow me."

Balthasar led him into one of the new hermetically sealed private rooms. Inside was a comfortable seating arrangement and a small table with fresh wineberries. On a set of drawers in the back lay the sword that had cut off his mother's head, her blood still clinging to the blade. A spell was protecting it until he'd decided what to do with it.

"I helped bring the others home," Chay said as he sat down. His gaze immediately found the weapon, but he decided not to say anything. At least not now.

"How nice of you." Balthasar chuckled as he sat down. "What did you see?"

Chay sighed. "So much pain. But they're meant for each other, no matter how much pain it causes them."

"And that interests me, because...?"

Balthasar couldn't care less about his brother's relationship with a human. It had served him well in his quest to become archdemon, but now that he had what he wanted, love was the last thing on his mind.

"You want to survive the war of the worlds."

And there it was. Balthasar smiled and opened his arms. "Everything you said would happen has happened. I've become the Archdemon of Lust, and I've still managed to keep my grip on the Small Council."

The Council of Seven had been eager for him to keep his seat, hoping it would keep him from meddling too much in their affairs. Only Moloch and Pyke had complained that it was too much power in one person's hands. They were right, of course.

"You're not complaining about too much responsibility, are you?" Chay raised an eyebrow.

"More responsibility, more power."

"More power for you, more influence for me," Chay added.

Balthasar chuckled as he was reminded of the deal they'd made. "My services are yours... as promised."

Chay smiled. "The worlds will thank you."

"Let's drink to that." He rose to pour some wine, handing one of the glasses to his friend and partner. "To a fruitful collaboration."

"To the future."

They clinked glasses and drank. For the first time in a thousand years, Balthasar was excited. To the future, indeed.

Samantha

Later that night, when the others had gone home and Jan had retired to his bedroom, Samantha lay on her bed with Matt. They were both dressed and examining the Flowers from Freya's Gardens in her lap. The flowers weren't just brightly coloured anymore, they glowed. Samantha tested her magic, easily switching through the colours. It felt different now. Like a piece that had always been missing was now back in place. It felt like they could change anything. Even destiny itself.

"The first Emblem to awaken," Matt said in awe. He stroked her hair, still wet from the three-hour treatment she'd given it to untangle everything. "First in everything."

Samantha snorted softly. "It awoke when the power of change was strongest." She stroked his hand. "You changed for me."

Matt shook his head. "No, not for you. You simply changed me." He rolled onto his side to get a better look at her face. "Loving you changed me. Without you, I'd never have learnt what it meant to be human. I would never have learnt to love or that some things are worth fighting for, even if it means sacrificing my own needs. I only grew because you were by my side. Because you took a chance on me. Because you believed I could change."

He bent over her and kissed her softly. Samantha sighed happily and set the flowers aside. Wrapping her arms around him, she ran her hands down his back before sinking them into the softness of his hair. After all they'd been through, it was such a pleasure to be together like this.

"I love you more than anything in this world or the next," Matt said as he let go to catch his breath.

Samantha smiled at him. "I love you, too."

They kissed again. Samantha kept one hand in his hair while she ran the other down his side. Matt shivered slightly as her fingers brushed his midsection. A sensitive spot. Her hand slipped under his shirt and found it again without any fabric in the way.

Matt pulled away slightly and looked at her, an amused twinkle in his eyes.

Samantha bit her lip, a little embarrassed. "So, do you think you have really lost all your demonic... qualities?"

As expected, a grin appeared on his face. It was wicked in all the right ways. "Never." He kissed her chin until he reached her ear, his hot breath sending shivers down her spine to her very core. "The sin of Lust is still in me."

She laughed hoarsely and pulled his shirt over his head. Matt took it from her hands and threw it to the floor, as if he couldn't get rid of it quickly enough, before stealing her breath with a passionate kiss.

As the heat blossomed in Samantha's stomach, she thought they'd both changed for the better. He'd become more human, and she'd become a little more open-minded. With Matt by her side, she felt she could face anything: demons, monsters, even the end of the world.

As long as she had him, she would be okay.

What's next?

As the last three chapters heavily hinted, this is not the end. I'd say it's only the beginning. The characters are leaving high school behind and entering their college era. New challenges await, as well as new monsters.

With this sixth book, the series is making the shift from Young Adult to New Adult, so expect darker themes and more maturing for our young heroes. The next trilogy will be *Ashuan Envy*—you might've guessed from the inclusion of our little envy demon Alecia. She'll make a return, of course.

There will be more demon shenanigans, though the power balance has slightly tipped towards our heroes. How cool was Fabian when he took on the Black Guard? He's definitely come a long way, and with this mysterious letter, he'll go even further. *Ashuan Envy* was when I truly fell in love with Fabian, so get ready to switch allegiances!

As for Matt and Samantha, they've earned a bit of happiness, right? Let's just hope the monsters got the same memo.

Jan will continue his path to becoming a proper healer, both in the magical and real worlds. He's grown so much since the beginning of the series and will continue to do so. Same for Lucille and Rachel, who are ready for new relationships in their lives.

Our characters are all grown up now, but their adventures are only just beginning.

I'll leave you with a little sneak peek of *Ashuan Envy* (coming 2025).

Love, Janna

Alecia

Pyke's throne room was designed to impress. The walls were mirrored with shimmering golden columns, beckoning, and yet forever out of reach. A mosaic of broken glass covered the floor, each shard revealing unfulfilled desires and shattered dreams. It was bathed in an eerie green glow, casting every visitor in the most unflattering light. The throne itself was a mass of writhing obsidian serpents, each with an emerald for an eye.

The Archdemon of Envy was a plain man, forever cursed to desire more than he was. His head was shaved, his face unremarkable, his clothes simple. What he gained, he hid in his treasuries, always wanting more and despising anyone he thought superior.

As usual, Alecia stood to his right, dressed in an equally simple tunic. There was one rule among the devotees of Envy—never outshine your master—and Alecia was expert at it. She'd never given Pyke a reason to be jealous, instead making herself invaluable.

Her older brother, Xzar, may have served the House of Pride, but Alecia preferred the sweet pain of the unattainable, the constant striving for more than she had, without the need to cling to it like greed demons. It made her aware of exciting possibilities others might reject.

She was about to whisper her latest report into Pyke's ear—he'd be jealous if someone else heard it at the same time or, even worse, *before* him—when a cold draft swept through the residence.

Confused, Alecia straightened. The room had darkened, but she couldn't see anyone.

"He will step out of the shadows, as dark as the night."

The voice seemed to come from nowhere, echoing around the room, just out of reach. Shadows flowed down the walls and met in front of the throne, forming a vaguely humanoid figure. But where there should've been a face, there was only darkness.

Alecia stepped in front of Pyke to protect him, but he pushed her aside. A pang of annoyance crept into her envious heart.

"He'll serve envy, jealous of the light."

The shadow man knelt before Pyke and bowed his head. The archdemon held his hand over his head and closed his eyes in deep pleasure. He sensed the jealousy in this creature and was ready to heighten it. Alecia almost exploded with envy.

"His shadows will devour Ashuan, leaving nothing but blight."

The shadow rose and took his place at Pyke's left, a place of highest honour and one he hadn't earned.

Alecia leant over to Pyke and hissed, "Who's this?"

The archdemon smiled at her. "Someone whose jealousy you could never hope to match."

Alecia bit her lip hard. She'd worked hard for her position and wasn't going to let some shadow creature without a face take it away from her. Whatever the shadow desired, she would take it.

He wanted Ashuan? It would be hers.

Dramatis Personae

Family de Cerque

Lucille – 19, one of the Six, a witch and illusionist
    Bastien – Lucille's absentee father, a busy man
    Linda – Lucille's stepmother, a designer
    Pascal – 11, Lucille's adoptive brother, a telekinetic
    Cecille – dead, Lucille's witch grandmother, killed by the Archdemon of Wrath
    Alena – dead, Lucille's mother, died in a car crash
    Albert – the de Cerque butler, a mind reader
    Tobias – the de Cerque chauffeur

Family Kollmer

Samantha – 19, one of the Six, a witch and potionmaker
    Meg – 17, Samantha's little sister and Jan'sgirlfriend, best friend of Anne
    Ben – Samantha's father, runs a car workshop withJoachim Bendtfeld
    Juliane – Samantha's mother, an aspiring actor
    Elda – Samantha's grandmother, the Greenvalley Witch, lives in the forest
    Erich – dead, Samantha's grandfather, a demon hunter

Family Bendtfeld

Fabian – 19, one of the Six, a water elemental mage
  Joachim – Fabian's father, runs a car workshop with Ben Kollmer
  Caroline – Fabian's mother, runs the Magic Circle, a magic shop
  Merle – the family cat

Family Hadden

Rachel – 19, one of the Six, a dreamwalker
  Nico – dead, Rachel's twin brother, appears in her dreams
  Annette – Rachel's mother, a hair stylist with an alcohol problem
  Mick – Rachel's father, a Maths professor, lives in LA

Family Kerscher

Jan – 20, one of the Six, a healer, works at theyouth hostel
  Anne – 17, Jan's little sister
  Stefan – Jan's father, a coal miner
  Ida – Jan's mother, a nurse

Family Traidous and Matt's demon relatives

Matt/Melchior – 19, one of the Six, a half-demon of the House of Lust
  René– Matt's father, a former demon hunter and elementary school teacher
  Crumbs – the family dog

Melaney – Matt's mother, a demon, the Archdemon of Lust

Balthasar – Matt's oldest brother, a demon of the Houses of Lust and Greed, leader of the Small Council

Caspar – Matt's older brother, a demon of the Houses of Wrath and Lust, Menuha's twin brother, the general of the Black Guard

Menuha – Matt's older sister, a demon of the Houses of Wrath and Lust, Caspar's twin sister

School

Alan – 19, part of the Elite Clique, son of the local police chief

Ani – 19, part of the Elite Clique, Samantha's former friend

Björn – 19, part of the Elite Clique, Jennifer's boyfriend

Cheryl – 19, the Greenvalley High Queen Bee, leader of the Elite Clique

Cian – 19, part of the Elite Clique, in love with Samantha

Mr Herbert – teaches Physics, hates Fabian

Jennifer – 19, part of the Elite Clique, Björn's girlfriend

Ophelia de la Vega – 17, Fabian's girlfriend, can speak to snakes

Mrs Renner – the Greenvalley High headmaster

Robert – 19, a friendly guy who follows the Six around

Shayna – 19, part of the Elite Clique, parents own an inn

Mr Zobel – The Six's tutor teacher, teaches Politics and German

Demons

Adrianes – Matt's nephew, Balthasar's son, Chief Gardener of Hell's Gardens

Alecia – First Devotee of Pyke

Chay – "The Seer" a half-demon, Matt's best friend, can see the future

Frennys – Melaney's lover

Hel – the Archdemon of Pride

Iyaga – the new Archdemon of Greed

Malcolm – dead, Melaney's brother, the former Archdemon of Greed
Moloch – the Archdemon of Gluttony
Pyke – the Archdemon of Envy
Volac – the Archdemon of Wrath
Yash – the Archdemon Sloth

Others

Adam Black – 22, hospital technician
Andre – 20, paramedic trainee
Daniel – dead, Samantha's ex-boyfriend
Hugo von Hohenstetten – an old-fashioned ghost
Jeyne Winter – dead, Caspar's lost love and Samantha's ancestor
Jonathan Blackstone – dead, a writer, previous owner of the Blackstone House
Neve – a snow witch, occupies Blackstone House
Philipp Vendenberg – Lucille's boyfriend, a reporter for the Greenvalley View
Vivien – Philipp's ex-girlfriend, a journalist

The adventure continues in... Ashuan Envy

He'll step out of the shadows, as dark as the night.
He'll serve envy, jealous of the light.
His shadows will devour the earth, leaving nothing but blight.

.

Despite frequent monster attacks and trouble with demons, the Six have survived high school. Just as they're ready to spread their wings to embark on new adventures, a dark prophecy puts a spoke in their wheels. The Dark One, a mystical creature of shadows and envy, plans to cover the world in fire and ash.
The Six will have to find a way to stop him, or their studies—and lives—will be cut short.

.

The Element of Surprise is the seventh book of the action-packed *Ashuan* series, beginning the *Ashuan Envy* trilogy. If you like *Buffy's* wit and snarky one-liners, the magic of *Charmed,* and the supernatural drama of the *Vampire Diaries,* you'll love this monster-hunter urban fantasy series.

Other books by Janna Ruth

JANNA RUTH
A
FORCE
OF
NATURE
SPIRIT SEEKER BOOK 1

JANNA RUTH

GHOSTS OF THE CATACOMBS

PARISIAN GHOSTS 1